GOVERNOR

GOVERNOR

DAVID WEBER
RICHARD FOX

BAEN

A Baen Books Original

Baen Publishing Enterprises
P.O. Box 1403
Riverdale, NY 10471
www.baen.com

ISBN: 978-1-9821-2540-0

Cover art by David Mattingly

First printing, June 2021

Distributed by Simon & Schuster
1230 Avenue of the Americas
New York, NY 10020

Library of Congress Cataloging-in-Publication Data

Names: Weber, David, 1952– author. | Fox, Richard, 1978– author.
Title: Governor / David Weber and Richard Fox.
Description: Riverdale, NY : Baen, [2021] | Series: Ascent to empire ; vol. 1
Identifiers: LCCN 2021011110 | ISBN 9781982125400 (hardcover)
Subjects: GSAFD: Science fiction.
Classification: LCC PS3573.E217 G68 2021 | DDC 813/.54—dc23
LC record available at https://lccn.loc.gov/2021011110

Pages by Joy Freeman (www.pagesbyjoy.com)
Printed in the United States of America
10 9 8 7 6 5 4 3 2 1

To Professor Jennie Kiesling
Thank you for the introduction

And

To Alice Weber
You said I could

CHAPTER ONE

"TERRY, WE'RE GOING TO BE *LATE!*" SIMRON MURPHY SAID.

"Can't be," Commodore Terrence Murphy said with what could only be described as a smirk. "I'm the guest of honor. They can't start it without me, can they?"

"Terry!" Simron shook her head and glared at him, but it was a remarkably mild glare.

"What?" He looked at her innocently. "It's true, isn't it?"

"No, it is *not* true," she told him severely. "The limo is already waiting. And they can, and will, start precisely on schedule, whether you're there or not."

"Oh, give me a break!" He rolled his eyes. "This is your brother and my father-in-law you're talking about, Simmy! Have they *ever* started a social event 'precisely on schedule' in their lives?"

She glared up at him. Her father's genetic heritage was obvious in her sandalwood complexion and shining black hair, but her eyes were a startling blue, courtesy of her mother's side of the family. Well, that and a little discreet genetic tweaking a generation or so back. She was a small, compact, gracefully moving woman. Not a great beauty in any classic sense, perhaps—her features were too strong, too sharp for that, especially in an era when biosculpt could transform anyone into a god or goddess. Yet she was astonishingly attractive and stood out in any crowd, largely because she'd chosen to eschew any improvement on nature. That made her almost unique among the Five Hundred, the alliance of families which were the backbone of the Terran Federation's elite society, and uniqueness was always its own cachet. Of course, the fact that a razor-keen intellect and a lively sense of humor dominated those sharp features was another factor.

Alas, only someone with very poor vision would have called Terrence Murphy handsome. At just under two meters, he was almost thirty-eight centimeters taller than his wife, with sandy hair and gray eyes set in a strong-jawed face that seemed to be made out of randomly assembled bony planes. At the moment, those gray eyes sparkled with mischief as he gazed back down at his wife with the insufferable air of someone who knew he'd just scored a telling point.

"Maybe not," she acknowledged after a moment. "*But—*" she raised one hand, index finger extended as she made a point of her own "—Dad is in charge tonight. Rajenda loves this sort of thing but he's off-world on business. And Boyle will be there. *That* Boyle, and he won't too impressed if the guest of honor—one of the guests of honor—comes dragging in an hour late."

"We'll be there in plenty of time," Murphy assured her, turning back to the mirror and adjusting the set of his cuffs. Then he brushed at one of his lapels. The softly shimmering *sekyri* was a Rishathan import that had cost a small fortune, but it was also the latest fad. Anyone who aspired to the first rank of fashion had to have it. And he had to admit that his coat's dark, cobalt blue did go well with his coloring.

"Terry, we really are going to be late if we don't get a move on," she said in a rather more serious tone.

"Personally, I'd rather stay home and not go at all," he said, turning to consider his profile and smoothing the cravat, which had come back into fashion. "Politics." He shook his head with a sigh. "You do know how boring this is going to be, don't you?"

"Boring or not, it's important." She shook her head, her eyes darker. "This is a major step in your career, honey. You can't—we can't—afford to blow it."

Murphy made a noncommittal sound, and she grimaced. She knew her husband was more than smart enough to understand how important the endorsement of someone like Amadeo Boyle was. Boyle, the New Progress Alliance's party leader, stood at the very pinnacle of the Terran Federation's kingmakers. Although he occupied no office of his own, his NPA held almost a quarter of the Assembly's seats, and it was the NPA and its allies—especially the Future Cooperative Party and Jugoslav Darković's Conservative Coalition—who had put Prime Minister Verena Schleibaum into office. There might have been a half dozen people in all of the Sol System who could do as much for someone's political aspirations as Boyle, but there wasn't a single soul who could have done *more*.

"I know it's important," Murphy said now, "but I hate the entire political circuit. I've seen too many people get ulcers dealing with it. I'd really rather be—"

"Out on the bridge of a starship surveying new star systems somewhere," Simron interrupted, and smiled a bit crookedly when he looked at her. She patted his elbow. "Well, there's always time for that, too, but you said it yourself—you've got to have your ticket punched in more than one way to get where we both want you to get, and you have to get the order right. First you go to New Dublin and get that on the record, then you can go back to Survey. For a while at least. License some colony rights." She squeezed the elbow she'd patted. "I know you'd rather go back to Survey for good, sweetheart, but—"

She shrugged with an almost apologetic smile and it was Murphy's turn to grimace, but he also nodded. It might have been a bit grudging, that nod, but she decided to settle for it. Much as she loved her husband, there were times his...lack of involvement, for want of a better term, could drive her to distraction. Those were the times when he chose to take absolutely nothing seriously beside the far more important matter of how well his new waistcoat fitted or how the shade of his formal jacket's facings complemented his cravat.

What made it most infuriating was that he was one of the smartest men she'd ever met. He simply chose not to *use* that intelligence unless it was to get something he wanted, and, unfortunately, he seemed to want the political power that lay within his reach a lot less than he wanted to gallivant around the galaxy discovering new planets. In fact, she was fairly sure he saw the acquisition of that political power mainly as a way to push Survey's budget priorities, even if he didn't get to go play intrepid explorer himself. Yet for all his exquisite tailoring and general detachment, there was a sense of responsibility under that exterior. It was deeply hidden, almost as if he was embarrassed to admit its existence even to her, but it was there. Once he *had* political power, that responsibility would drive him to use it far better than all too many of the idiots who had it now.

She only wished he would enjoy it as much as the idiots did. He wouldn't, of course. But he would do his job *well*, and that was what really mattered.

Now he finished examining his appearance in the mirror, then turned and flashed her that wide, laughing smile that transformed his bony countenance as he offered her his arm. She shook her head again, eyes laughing back up at him, as she tucked a small hand into his elbow and they headed for the air car landing.

Kanada Thakore placed his palms against a darkly stained wooden rail. He brushed fingertips one way, savoring the feel of small scales against his skin, then moved them the other way and felt glass-like smoothness. Sharkskin wood was rare and scandalously expensive on Earth, imported from the Tesseract System, far beyond the blue line. He flashed a fake smile to a woman passing on the dance floor just below the raised platform he shared with a slightly shorter man. Amadeo Boyle wore a black suit run through with gold lustron threads and held a drink in his pudgy hand.

Music from a holo quartet carried perfectly over the low hum of conversation in the ballroom, speakers in the ceiling focusing just the right volume from the stringed instruments to Thakore's ears.

He swiped his thumb down a finger and tiny sensors in his skin lowered the music for him and him alone as he listened to the dozens and dozens of conversations from his guests. Scions of major corporations, established families, and Terra's intelligentsia were here. All the right people, and he was well aware of who hadn't sent their RSVP for the event.

Waiters—all actual humans—in archaic outfits complete with leggings and high-necked collars moved through the crowd carrying platinum inlaid trays with finger food or flutes of champagne. Robotic units could have done the job perfectly and cheaply, but paying the outrageous fee Authentic Limited charged to provide flesh-and-blood waiters to service the event was a flourish that would keep the newsies buzzing about the ball for days.

Everything was going smoothly. He flicked a nail against his middle finger and the time popped up on his synched contact lens.

Almost everything.

"Your boy's going to be late." Boyle swished thin black liquid in his glass and took a sip. "Not getting cold feet, is he?"

"Finish your singularity. His car's landing now." Thakore traced a tight circle over one eye.

"Your invitation said this was an un-linked event." Boyle held his nearly empty drink to one side and waggled it slightly. A waiter with a tray of a half dozen different potent potables seemed to appear out of nowhere and took the glass. Boyle dismissed him with a wag of his fingers.

"For the guests; I'm the host," Thakore said. "Don't think I haven't noticed you dipping into your link. What's her name?"

"Money." Boyle sniffed. "She never sleeps. Cruel mistress." He shrugged, and the gold threads in his suit morphed into a dragon and snapped its teeth at Thakore.

A set of double doors opened and a couple walked in, arm in arm. They stopped just over the threshold, and camera flashes sparked from the scrum of reporters behind a red silk rope.

Drones would have covered most events, but this wasn't "most events," and there were live reporters behind those flashes. Turn down an invitation from Kanada Thakore to rub elbows, however distantly, with the cream of the Five Hundred? Of course they'd come! And their glowing, firsthand reviews as they gushed over it on the social feeds tomorrow would be worth every penny he'd spent to get them here.

A potbellied doorman in a pure silver suit rapped a staff against the marble floor.

"The Honorable Rear Admiral-select Terrence Murphy and Mrs. Simron Murphy!" he announced, and the attendees broke into polite applause.

"Your boy and your lovely daughter are finally here," Boyle murmured as the new arrivals entered the ballroom and began shaking hands and speaking with guests. Both wore broad smiles that would make any politician proud. "I suppose that means the festivities can commence."

He removed a small box from his coat and golden lines of flame danced down his arm as the lustron flexed. He squeezed the side and the lid popped up, revealing a pair of twined starburst studs.

"How's this Navy nonsense supposed to go? I push the metal pin through his Rishathan silk shirt and beat my fist against it until it hits flesh?" Boyle asked.

"Don't be a pain in the ass, Amadeo," Kanada Thakore scolded. Aside from his coloring, he didn't look a great deal like his daughter. He was almost as tall as his son-in-law, with the broad shoulders and flat midsection of someone who kept himself fit on the microgravity handball court. His naturally dusky complexion was rather darker than Simron's because of the time he spent at the helm of the *Amphitrite*, his ninety-meter catamaran. "There's a representative from Bureau of Personnel in the crowd drinking my best alcohol. Soon as we're ready, he'll read some scripted business and then my daughter will hand him the rank. Then he's a real admiral."

"Murphy knows what to do after that? He still remember how to salute? It's been a while for him, yeah?" Boyle snapped the box shut.

"Whether or not he chooses to show it, Terrence is a very smart fellow. And don't forget the Murphy family name! He can be very useful to us, down the road."

Boyle grimaced.

"I know that—that he can be useful to us, at any rate. I'm not so sure about the 'smart fellow' bit, though. Oh," he waved one hand in a small throwing away gesture, "I know all about his aptitude testing and the Raymond Whoever Award and the rest of his towering scholastic reputation. But it doesn't matter how smart you are if you aren't willing to put that intelligence to work doing something *useful*. We have plenty of worker bees who can survey new star systems, Kanada!"

Thakore glanced at the shorter Boyle. There was something much too like disdain in the NPA party leader's expression, but there wasn't a great deal Thakore could do about that. For that matter, he wasn't positive the disdain was as unmerited as he'd like to think, and he hid a sigh as he looked back to watch his daughter and his son-in-law crossing the ballroom floor toward him.

They were a striking couple, Thakore admitted, and although he knew Murphy would have preferred to be almost anywhere else, no one could have guessed that from his pleasant smile, the way he paused to share pleasantries along the way as he worked through the crowd. One of the more maddening things about

Terrence Murphy was that he was just as effortlessly charismatic—in a very different way—as Simron yet seemed blissfully unaware of what a useful weapon that ability to charm people could have been. Indeed, at times Kanada was tempted to agree with Boyle, but he'd worked too long and too hard to put all of the pieces into position. He wasn't about to walk away from it all now!

And he is *a Murphy,* Thakore reminded himself. *It's been a while, but people remember his grandfather. That name recognition alone will be worth an extra five or six million votes when the time comes!*

Personally, a military career had never appealed to Thakore. Why risk his talents and all the good he could do for the Federation by dying in a deep space fight? There were colonists for that sort of thing, and he had too many other, more important things to do running Venus Futures.

There'd been suggestions, over the years, that Venus should be renamed, christened with some new and exciting title more relevant to humanity's expansion into the galaxy. Thakore had shot them all down, because some intangibles were more valuable than simple relevancy. As the very name suggested, Venus Futures predated the Terran Federation itself. For that matter, it predated even the internal development of the Sol System, far less humanity's sprawling outreach to the stars. And the originally modest little corporation whose highest ambition had been to place a habitat in Venus orbit all those centuries ago had become one of the dozen most powerful transstellar corporations in the galaxy. VF had led the way in penetrating the Rishathan Sphere's internal markets and continued to dominate the Federation's trade with the Sphere, and it showed in its hefty bottom line.

More than that, it was poised to grow more powerful still, thanks to its position as one of the Terran Federation Navy's primary suppliers. The endless, dragging war with the lunatics in the League was a terrible thing, no doubt, but there *was* that old proverb about ill winds blowing no one good, and there was no point pretending the war—and all those government contracts—hadn't done wonderful things for Venus Futures. Of course, other proverbs about war being good for business weren't lost on him. And when the Navy officially ordered the first of the *Cormoran*-class carriers...

Thakore rubbed his hands together.

That was one reason to put Terrence Murphy's face front and center during the appropriations process. Very few people were likely to forget that Terrence's grandfather, Admiral Henrik Murphy, had been directly responsible for the Navy's transformation from a batch of simple peacekeepers—little more than the "Coast Guard in space" old Henrik had called it in his more disparaging moments—into the genuine war-fighting force the Federation had needed so desperately when the League launched its war of aggression. Nor had they forgotten Commander Henrik Murphy's role in pushing the Federation's frontiers steadily outward before rising to such high command.

A few bribes paid to the right news organizations and the algorithms would link stories of the new *Cormorans* to Murphy, and his obvious need to have the best ships out there to fight the League. So what if the ships ran into cost overruns during production?

Terrence was a throwback to that earlier point in Henrik's career. Everyone knew his true interest lay in exploration and survey, just as Henrik's had, which had made the string pulling to get him his new command a bit more difficult than usual. He even looked quite a bit like the old man, and as was the Murphy family tradition, he'd graduated from the Academy and gone into naval service when it was his turn. And despite his personal preference for survey work, he'd actually done fairly well at the Battle of Steelman's Star. Better than his father had at the Brin Gap, at least. Probably best not to mention that part of his heritage and concentrate on Steelman's, instead. Oh, the odds had been nowhere near as unfavorable as Thakore's PR machine had suggested, but he hadn't done badly. And with his name, "not badly" was easily transformed into "brilliantly" in the public's mind.

That would be worth the odd hundred thousand votes, even though the war was scarcely a burning issue here in the Sol System or among the other Heart Worlds. It was too distant, and after over half a century, it had been going on too long for that. It had turned into little more than background noise for the *important* things in their lives. Still, there were those, even right here in the Sol System, who followed the war news. They might not be among the Five Hundred, but they did have votes, and the fact that Terrence had "distinguished himself in combat" wouldn't be lost on them.

And won't Madison eat her heart out when we land the primary contracts for the Cormorans, Thakore thought now. *Maybe she should have tried a little harder for Terrence when he was still on the market!*

Madison Dawson, the CEO of Astro Engineering, had a daughter about Simron's age, but she'd clearly failed to grasp the significance of a family connection to the Murphys in the midst of humanity's longest, bloodiest, and most destructive war. It was, perhaps, fortunate that twenty-five-year-old Simron hadn't realized just how assiduously her father had thrown her and then-Lieutenant Murphy together, of course. She was a stubborn young woman, his daughter, and if she'd realized how hard he was pushing, her auto response would have been to push back.

A valuable asset, my son-in-law, he thought. *I wish he gave a damn for anything besides his wardrobe and getting a ship's deck under his feet again, but still a valuable asset. He's a little too much like his grandfather in some ways, but it's probably just as well he doesn't have the old man's stubbornness.*

Managing the career of someone as smart as Murphy could get tricky, and there'd been a time or two—especially right after he'd come back from Steelman's Star—when he'd seemed a bit…restive. A bit prone to resist his father-in-law's advice and counsel. In fact, there'd been a time there when Thakore had been afraid he'd pushed too hard. He hadn't counted on how Terrence had taken his own war experience to heart or how that experience might shape his response to the sorts of opportunities which naturally came the way of a man with his pedigree and connections. He'd even been critical of Venus Futures' pursuit of the military contracts which were its corporate lifeblood, at least until Thakore sat him down and explained some cold, hard facts of life.

Someone had to build the Navy's ships, he'd pointed out, and it would be best for everyone if the "someone" in question had the resources, the engineering talent, and the proven ability to deliver that Venus Futures had demonstrated over the last several decades. And, inevitably, that meant Venus Futures—and thus Terrence's own family—would make a lot of money in the process. It wasn't *profiteering*, though! In fact, Thakore had been shocked—*shocked!*—that anyone would accuse him of that. But there was nothing wrong with making money, of being paid for delivering what the Navy needed when, where, and as it was needed. And it required a healthy cash flow to maintain the physical plant and human capital Venus Futures had amassed in the Federation's service.

Fortunately, Murphy had recognized the voice of reality when he heard it. He might be more focused on getting back into space—and on his wardrobe—than he was in driving Venus's opportunities, but Thakore could work with that. He'd been more than a little irritated, initially, by Murphy's insistence on adding another deployment to the pot, but he'd gotten over it, especially when the arguments Murphy advanced in favor of it had demonstrated that he understood—now, at least—the importance of political power.

He was the one who'd reminded his father-in-law that the Emergency War Powers Act had "temporarily" waived the constitutional requirement that federal system governors be civilian appointees approved by the local legislature and given the federal government the power to appoint them, instead. Olympia was still supposed to *consult* with the local government whenever possible, but the slowness of interstellar communications had clearly made that impractical in a wartime situation. And so, for the last fifty-odd years, the federal government had been routinely appointing those governors. And since the constitutional restrictions had been set aside, Olympia had taken to combining the office of governor with that of the system's military commander whenever possible. Especially in the systems closest to League space. So if he was on the list for deployment and Thakore could find one of *those* systems, preferably one that was a bit more important than the others, and get him appointed to it...

Thakore had to admit he hadn't thought of that possibility. He'd actually been focused on keeping Murphy *off* the active deployment list and right here in the Core Worlds. And he knew damned well that the political angle wasn't the only part of it—to Murphy, at least. Thakore was pretty sure he wouldn't want to surrender his upcoming task force command and come home again on schedule. But he'd do it, and however much the delay irritated Thakore, he'd been forced to admit Murphy had a point. It *would* look good on his résumé, especially with the added gravitas of a system governorship in his pocket. In fact, Thakore had been a bit chagrined to realize it had taken Murphy to point out to him that a survey mission punctuated by a battle was an insufficient influence-buyer, even for someone named Murphy. Tickets had to be punched and merit badges had to be earned, and successful command assignments were the currency that mattered to a military establishment whose members had been at war their entire adult lives.

Thinking back on it, Thakore was confident that for all his apparent disinterest in politics, Murphy had also grasped just how far someone with the Murphy name could hope to rise, especially when that name was backed by Amadeo Boyle's political blessing and Kanada Thakore's enormous wealth. And he'd been right. With a second deployment—this time, as a task force commander, not simply a squadron commander—on his list of qualifications, there was no limit on the political career waiting for him when he returned to Terra. The premiership itself would probably be within his reach, after five or ten years in the Assembly's trenches, and that had to be a dazzling prospect for anyone. Of course, even someone as smart as Murphy might not notice who was pulling the strings behind his premiership if it was done adroitly. And Kanada Thakore knew very few people more adroit than he was or—

"Good evening, Papa," Simron said, smiling affectionately as she and Terrence reached him and she laid her free hand on his arm. "Sorry we're late. *Someone* had to be sure his cravat was straight."

"Really?" Thakore cocked his head at his son-in-law. "Any idea who that might have been, Terry?"

"Haven't got a clue," Terrence Murphy replied, and smiled.

CHAPTER TWO

"DO WE *REALLY* HAVE TO DO THIS?" FLEET ADMIRAL ARKADIOS Fokaides growled. "The man's a damned *fop*, whatever the frigging newsies had to say about Steelman!"

The Terran Federation's Chief of Naval Operations was a man with exactly zero patience for fools at the best of times, and he was none too picky about who he assigned to the "fools" category. Although, in this case, Vice Admiral Yang Xiaolan reflected, he might have a better argument than usual. Yang had known Terrence Murphy for over thirty years, and he'd never impressed her as a suitable champion to uphold the Murphy family name. Not that he *couldn't* have been, just that he never had.

"The decision is up to you, Arkadios," she said now. "All I can say is that the arguments in favor of making Boyle happy are pretty convincing, and I think he's ready to go to the mat over this one."

"Probably because of how many credits Thakore's pouring into his goddamn party's slush fund. God, I hate politics!" Fokaides looked even less happy. But then he shrugged. "I don't suppose he can do *too* much damage."

The CNO had managed not to say "not even he," Yang noted. It had probably been hard for him.

"It's not as if he's going to have to defeat the entire *Rénzú Liánméng Hǎijūn* by himself," she pointed out, and Fokaides gave her a moderately dirty look. Unlike some, she had no problem pronouncing

13

the Terran League's Navy's proper name. The majority of the TFN's personnel, including one Arkadios Fokaides, simply referred to it as "the League Navy" or "the Leaguies" and got on with it.

"Of course he isn't," he growled back. "I just hate giving him the slot. It's not like he's *earned* it!"

Yang nodded. No one could really argue with *that* point, she reflected.

"I'm surprised Thakore didn't push for his son Rajenda to get the position," she said.

"Raw nepotism won't play for Thakore." Fokaides shook his head. "Besides, Rajenda has a combat command on the Beta Cygni front. We pull him out of that and it'll look like he's being politely fired."

"So they give Murphy the position at New Dublin with a significant force to command. It looks good in the faxes," she pointed out in return. "Boyle's publicity flaks are right about the way Public Information can play up the 'a Murphy goes to war' angle. Especially—and I know you're not going to want to hear this—after Steelman."

Fokaides glared at her, and it was her turn to shrug.

"I know the entire thing got blown out of all proportion, and if I had to guess, it was only O'Hanraghty that kept him from stepping on his sword. That's the way even Murphy's after-action report reads, if you read between the lines. But whatever the reasons, that's how the public sees him now. And however much it may grate, we're going to need all the political support we can get for next year's appropriations." Fokaides fixed her with icy green eyes, and she shrugged again. "I don't like it a whole lot more than you do, but if it helps us get the budget we need, I think it's worth the investment."

Fokaides leaned back in his chair and ran the fingers of his right hand through his hair. That hair was still thick and dark, thanks to antigerrone, but he was eighty years old, and he'd been Chief of Naval Operations for almost twenty years. He'd reach mandatory retirement in another five, at which point Yang would step into his shoes. She was seventeen years younger than he was, and she'd been named *Vice* Chief of Naval Operations two years ago expressly to give her the experience she'd need when it was her turn in the hot seat. He hadn't picked her at random as his successor, either. He'd chosen her because she was smart and capable and because the choice was too important to leave up to the civilians.

And she's right, dammit, he thought. *It just sticks in my craw. Wonder how much of it's because of how much I detested his old man?* Fokaides didn't like admitting, even to himself, that personal animosity could play a part in a decision like this, but there was no point pretending that he and Bartholomew Murphy hadn't despised one another cordially. And *Terrence* Murphy was the spitting image of his father. *Question is, is he as* inept *as his father was? Yang's right about the need to invest in political support, but Jesus I hate wasting even a light task force on a goddamn Murphy! Especially one who ran so scared before Steelman turned him into a "hero."*

That had been the true core of his initial refusal to sign off on the entire deployment, he told himself . . . and hoped he was being honest when he did. But Murphy had already ridden his family's name when he chose to go to Survey instead of following a Battle Fleet track. At a time when the Terran Federation was locked in a death grip with the League, he'd decided to keep his own precious ass out of the line of fire, just like he'd done with his older son. What if he chose to do that again? What if the "Hero of Steelman's Star" reverted to his true colors when the odds turned truly crappy?

Yet every time he asked himself that, he came back to Yang's point. Very few Heart Worlders understood just how bad things had become. It wasn't *completely* true that, as one of the more irritating newsies had put it, "the Fringe Worlds might be at war, but the Heart Worlds were at the mall." Yet the metaphor was reaching in the right direction. Fokaides knew the League couldn't sustain the current tempo of operations indefinitely. In the end, the Federation's larger population and far more massive industrial infrastructure had to win what had become an ugly war of attrition. But Arkadios Fokaides had been telling himself that for the last twenty years, and he suspected his predecessor had been telling *herself* that for at least twenty years before he'd become CNO. And somehow, half a century and more since the first shots were fired, the League stubbornly refused to lie down and die.

And it's been going on long enough that just convincing the Assembly to pay *for the war is getting harder and harder*, he thought grimly. *And that's because the voters—the precious, pampered,* useless *frigging voters—don't care. Why should they? We've managed to keep the fighting outside the Heart Worlds,* none of our critical star systems are at risk, *so the way they see it, they don't have any skin in the game.*

Unless their *kids are the ones getting assigned to combat duty, of course.*

"All right," he said finally. "You're right. We have to just swallow the pill and keep going, but I don't want him swanning around out there without someone to ride herd on him!"

"I think we're covered there, actually," Yang replied. Fokaides raised his eyebrows in silent question, and she snorted. "One of the reasons I'm convinced he's not a total idiot, really. He's requested O'Hanraghty for chief of staff."

"Has he?" The CNO let his chair come upright again. "That's encouraging. O'Hanraghty may be a dinosaur, but at least he knows his ass from his elbow when it comes to tactics."

Yang nodded in agreement. Harrison O'Hanraghty had graduated from the Academy only a couple of years after her, but he'd been only a commander when Terrence Murphy went off to Steelman's Star. He might not actually be the "dinosaur" Fokaides had called him, but he'd certainly managed to blot his copybook with enough senior officers to explain his career's glacial progress. His side trip through the Office of Naval Intelligence hadn't exactly helped him in that regard, either. Yang didn't know what he'd done to piss them off over at ONI, but she suspected he'd probably been poking his nose where it didn't belong. He'd done a lot of that in the last thirty or forty years. Which was a shame, because he truly did "know his ass from his elbow" operationally. If he'd just been able to stay out of trouble with his superiors and concentrate on that, he'd have had admiral's stars of his own by now.

At least he'd finally gotten captain's rank after keeping Murphy out of the crapper at Steelman's. And she'd made it quietly clear to him that if he could just go on keeping Murphy out of the crapper until they got Murphy's task force back intact, there was a commodore's star in it for him, as well.

"He does know his tactics," she said out loud. "And Murphy's already shown he's willing to listen to O'Hanraghty. I think the fact that he wants him as chief of staff shows he knows how much he needs to go on listening, too."

"I hope so." Fokaides sounded more than a little skeptical, but he also waved one hand in a brushing away gesture. "Either way, it's probably as close as we can come to disaster-proofing things. I guess we're just going to have to hope for the best."

CHAPTER THREE

THE STAIRS WERE NARROW, AND MURPHY STEADIED HIS WIFE BY
the elbow as Simron's heels and a few cocktails made the descent
more precarious than usual. The stairs delivered them to a garage
with a long line of waiting limos, and a young man in the same
uniform as the party servers opened a door to a vehicle with a
custom hood ornament and enough chrome highlights to make
it stand out even from the rest of the luxury.

"Dad doesn't do 'un-ostentatious' very well, does he?" Simron
said, shaking her head with a crooked smile as she slipped into
the back seat and kicked off her shoes. "He *would* have us in a
Ducati 11, wouldn't he?"

Terrence closed her door and went around the back with the
valet, and their muffled conversation lingered on the other side
of the limo.

A window between the passenger and driver compartments
lowered and the driver turned around and tipped his cap.

"Pleasure, Ma'am," he said. "Where can I take you?"

"Missing someone," Simron replied, and squinted at her arm
rest, searching for controls.

"I'll get it."

The driver hit a button. The window opposite Simron lowered
and she leaned toward it just as Murphy grasped the valet's upper
arm and shook his hand.

17

"You take care," the rear admiral said to him, then opened his own door and sat down.

"Home now," Simron said to the driver, then shook her head at her husband as the screen went up between the compartments.

"Now you're chatty?" she asked. "I have to twist your arm to say more than five words to Dad's chief finance officer and the new head of Stellara Lines—and I can't believe what she was wearing—but then you get buddy-buddy with the help?"

Murphy had a faraway look in his eyes as he glanced out the window.

The limo rose up over the car line on counter-grav emitters in the wheel wells.

"Terrence," Simron snapped, "care to explain?"

"What? Oh, he was aboard the *Carson*," Murphy said. "He wanted to . . . reminisce for a moment."

"You never served aboard any *Carson*." Simron narrowed her eyes slightly.

"It was one the ships we lost at Steelman," Murphy said. "We rescued some of her crew after the battle . . . He remembered me on the bay floor when we opened his pod. Said I was one of his litter bearers when he was taken to med bay."

"You remember him?"

"It was a long day, Simmy," Murphy said gently.

"I suppose his status got him hired on for the night." Simron flicked her hand twice and an emitter in a bracelet projected a screen showing her face. She adjusted the thin layer of the makeup liner with deft motions from her pinky nail. "He seemed all right."

The limo passed out of the garage and lifted up to crisscrossing levels of air traffic strung through the skyscrapers of Olympia. The Federation's capital was notorious for its crowded airspace, and Murphy tensed as the limo slipped into a gap in the air cars and sped up as it rose through faster and faster bands.

The human in the driver's seat was almost an affectation, he reminded himself. A networked AI handled their actual route.

"His arms are prosthetic below the elbow," Murphy said. "You didn't notice that the fingers on his left hand looked a bit arthritic? Low-quality replacements."

"This night wasn't supposed to be a Federation Service Veterans' lodge meeting." Simron sighed, and changed the projection to several media feeds. Pics of the two of them arriving at the

party and news articles scrolled up. "All positive coverage...
you're quite the war hero from these headlines."

"Your father 'adjusting' the algorithms again?" Murphy asked.

"You're a newly minted rear admiral. New command. Medals
from the Battle of Steelman's Star. Don't complain if we make your
star shine a bit brighter. Helps the family. And aren't you a hero?"

"No." Murphy looked away. "We were losing a fight and I
managed to turn it around. Any officer would've done the same."

"But it was you who did it and there's nothing wrong with
telling people that. Besides, wouldn't that valet back there think
you were a hero?"

"I'm just glad he made it out alive," Murphy said.

Simron pinched the bridge of her nose.

"Let's see if I've trained you right," she said. "Who was the
tech officer with the obnoxious cologne?"

"Lionel Fanx, Goodridge Shipping Conglomerate," Murphy
said. "He was with his assistant and not his wife for the evening."

"That wasn't his...he does like blondes. Anyway, he was going
on and on about the Beta Cygni Sector and how your post is in
New Dublin. What was he getting at?"

The limo's speed leveled out as they slipped past penthouses.
There was no traffic above them.

Murphy frowned. Travel in this high a band came with a
premium toll. A waste of money in his opinion.

"Don't even start about the cost." Simron raised a finger. "I
know you. Back to the guy that smelled like flour and vanilla."

"The bulk of the Federation Navy is fighting in the Beta
Cygni Sector. On the verge of a breakthrough—if you listen to
the news—the same breakthrough that's been promised for ten
years, since we lost at Mangalore. New Dublin is almost two
hundred light-years from Earth...in pretty nearly the opposite
direction from Beta Cygni," Murphy said.

"And?" Simron made a circular, wrap-it-up motion with her
hand, urging him forward.

"It was his way of implying I'm either not ready for a frontline
deployment...or afraid of one," Murphy huffed.

"Wait...you just let him get away with that?"

"Fanx was never in uniform. What do I care about someone
that got a deferment and skipped out of his mandatory service?"

"Because," Simron's finger shot up and the news feeds vanished,

"Fanx is from the Five Hundred and the heir to one of the more influential families in that group. His opinion *matters*, Terry. You can't brush people like that off just because they didn't go the same route you did. And you know who else hasn't been in the military?"

"Don't start," Murphy said.

"Vyom, our darling firstborn son." Her face darkened with anger.

"I'm well aware of who he is." Murphy sank slightly into his seat.

"The Federation is very clear that military service isn't needed from those with key positions in our economy," she said. "And Vyom is a rising star in father's company. He's already the head of the new destroyer concept team and—"

"I never said Vyom wasn't qualified for his position," Murphy said. "He's done very well for himself."

"But you were against his deferment. Don't deny it."

"Family tradition," Murphy said. "My grandfather and my father—"

"We've got Callum to follow in your footsteps," Simron said. "Vyom can take after his *other* grandfather. And I'm glad you're keeping such a close eye on Callum during your deployment. A deployment to a much quieter part of the war."

"Speaking of," Murphy slipped a matte black case from a pocket in his trousers.

"I told you to leave that at home," Simron said.

"You think a flag officer can just unplug from command? Even your father was still checking his updates during the party. Those lens implants are expensive, but he has a bad habit of drifting off when he's accessing information."

A small holo screen appeared over the case, the projection blurred from Simron's vantage point.

"You keep going on and on about how O'Hanraghty has everything under control," Simron said. "Maybe you should've hired someone from the short list that father put together."

"No disrespect to Kanada, but there's no one else like O'Hanraghty in the Federation Navy."

"Is that a good thing or a bad thing?" Simron raised an eyebrow.

"A good executive officer solves problems before they ever

reach the commander's attention," Murphy said. "But some will always be beyond his control."

The case buzzed in his hand.

"Just like—Here." He handed the case to her and she glanced at the screen, then rolled her eyes.

"Ugh," she said. "I'm not surprised. You get to deal with it. And you had better straighten this out while you're in New Dublin. His last name and the Peter Principle can only get him so far."

The limo landed gently at their building and Simron's door opened smoothly. She blew Murphy a kiss and went inside.

The screen between Murphy and the driver lowered.

"Sir?"

"Seems I've been invited to an after-party," Murphy said. "Take me to the Spring Mountain Gaming complex. Private entrance."

"Right away." The limo door snapped shut.

✧   ✧   ✧

Callum Murphy felt the world spinning as he lay on a cool tile floor. He knew he was perfectly still, but the flush of alcohol in his system made all of his perceptions a bit suspect. Drool seeped down one corner of his mouth and his feet kicked at the floor.

"He's...cheatin'! That dealer...had a card in 'is...fingers. Somethin'." His stomach heaved and he swallowed before its contents could go any farther than the base of his esophagus.

A pair of shiny black shoes stepped in front of him.

"Did jou...'rest him? Fer cheatin?" Callum tried to wag a finger and poked himself in the cheek.

"Yes, I'll authorize the dose," a voice said. "Go with a double."

"Oh...hi, Dad." Callum raised his head up then dropped it back down when the lights proved too bright. "Big...day 'morrow."

"Sir," a new voice said, "that much Teetotaler will—"

"You heard me."

Callum felt a bite of cold metal against his throat and heard a hiss.

"What're you—What?" Callum's brown eyes shot open as his heart rate soared. He sat up, panting as his vision went red, and his ears throbbed with pressure. A sheen of cold sweat slicked his face and he wiped his palms across his eyes several times. He tried protesting but only managed a high-pitched whine between gulps of air.

"Heart rate's at one-seventy and holding," the new voice said.

"So he can have more?" Terrence Murphy asked.

"Not recommended."

"Oh God." Callum crinkled his nose as he smelled his own alcohol-permeated clothing. "This won't ever come out. You know that, right?" He pinched the front of his soaked shirt and plucked it away from his body.

Murphy squatted down and looked him in the eyes.

"Son, I'm disappointed."

"What? What did I...?" Callum closed his eyes for a moment. "The Teetotaler will get the booze out of your system. Won't fix your memory, though," he said, opening them again.

"Then allow me to refresh it," Murphy said. "You created quite a scene on the gambling floor. I've got a bill here for a ruined roulette wheel and new felt on two different blackjack tables."

Callum brushed a hand across his lap.

"Funny, normally you get a hit of the drunk-no-more and your bladder..."

"The roulette wheel," his father said.

"Oh yeah..."

"You also proposed to several waitresses and a security guard, saying you were going to war tomorrow and wanted to—"

"Okay, that I remember." Callum put a hand to a temple. "Vyom will get all that honor, too. Can I get some water? Maybe something with electrolytes?"

"Get up." Murphy hooked his son by the armpits and hauled him to his feet. It took a little effort. Although Callum looked a lot like a masculine version of his mother, he was within eight centimeters of Murphy's own height. "The concierge gave me a courtesy call to deal with your situation before they called law enforcement. Do you understand what almost happened?"

"A quick trip to the courthouse for an annulment?" Callum smiled.

"No!" Murphy shouted.

The door to the room shut as the other man left.

"Callum...you were so drunk that you would've ended up in either a jail cell or a hospital before the night was over. That happens and you'd miss muster when our carrier group spaces out tomorrow. Do you understand what that would mean?"

"I'd...catch the next transport to New Dublin?" Callum tried to smile and got a shooting pain through his temples.

"You're a lieutenant in the Federation Navy and the flag lieutenant of an admiral who's deploying tomorrow," Murphy said, putting his hands on his hips.

"No, I'm actually in the merchant marine...or should be." Callum said. "But I'm on orders for active duty, yeah. Missing muster prior to a deployment is...pretty bad. Court-martial bad. But wouldn't you—"

"No, Callum. Not even I could get you out of a mess like that. The Federation's been at war for the next best thing to sixty years, and failure to report for duty when you've got orders to do so is not tolerated. Doesn't matter what your last name is."

Murphy took his son by the elbow and led him out of the room and into a hallway.

"War? Let's be real here, Dad." Callum stumbled a bit as he kept pace with his father. "We're going to New Dublin. I wouldn't even know where—Come to think of it, I still don't think I can find it on a star chart. It's a dead sector. Not even on any of the main trade lines. Just a bunch of colonists squatting on land and pumping out kids."

They exited onto an air car dock several dozen stories above street level. The giant projections of nearby casinos and nightclubs danced in the night. Lines of airborne traffic meandered through the colorful glow. Beyond them, the towering buildings of the Federation's capital rose into the night like titans, glittering with the gems of lighted windows and bathed in floodlights, like treasure heaped in some god's jewelry case.

"I guarantee they don't have anything like this out in the sticks," Callum said.

"Son," Murphy shook his head. "This is on me. This is my fault."

"Don't follow."

"You have...you have no idea of what it means to put on the uniform. You've lived in the Heart Worlds your entire life. The war means nothing more to you than what's in your news feed. That sound about right?"

Callum's arms flapped against his sides.

"Sorry? Was I supposed to go join the 'Public Marines' for summer break or something? I was in the reserve training corps in college like you asked, but I'm more interested in Fasset Drive construction and macroeconomics than shooting missiles.

Merchant Marine's a lot more attractive to me as a career than Survey Corps or the regular Navy. So I get the Navy hitch out of the way, then shift over to the Merchant Marine, like Grandpa wants. That a problem? After Vyom got a deferment I thought you didn't—"

Murphy's jaw tightened so hard Callum thought his father's teeth would crack.

"I'm on your staff," Callum said. "O'Hanraghty won't let me screw up too much, right? Two years sitting on our thumbs in New Dublin and then it's all over with," he shrugged. "I'll come back to captain a trader ship and you'll be...a senator or something."

"What did you mean earlier," Murphy tapped a screen on the car dock safety rail, "when you said Vyom was going to get 'the honor' before you?"

"Did I? Must've been the meds playing with my—"

Murphy gave him a glare that fathers had practiced long before humans adopted speech.

"Vyom's in Buenos Aries," Callum snapped in response. "It's a business trip...and just so happens to be where Ingrid's from."

"Ingrid. They've been dating for barely six months," Murphy frowned.

"Which is a record for Vyom," Callum said.

"No. Vyom can't..." Murphy ran a hand through his hair. "What exactly is he going to do? Propose?"

"It's just a suspicion," Callum raised his hands. "He gets stupider than usual when he starts talking about Ingrid."

"Does your mother know?"

"She practically set them up," Callum said. "Ingrid's the sole heir to another of the Five Hundred. Mom's probably got a list of focus-tested baby names picked out. I'll just point out that she's done precisely zero to hook me up with an heiress."

"You remember Jenny Schleibaum? When you were fourteen?"

"In my defense, snakes were still awesome back then. She didn't see it that way."

"Son—"

A beaten up taxi pulled up to the dock.

"You came in that thing?" Callum asked.

"We're leaving in this," Murphy said. "Keeps the paparazzi from knowing that a certain young officer came very close to embarrassing himself."

The door creaked open and the cylindrical head of the robot driver spun around.

"W-w-where to?" came from a microphone.

"Is that smell from the seat or from me?" Callum's nose wrinkled.

"Get in," Murphy pushed against Callum's shoulder, "and don't be surprised when your pay stub has a bunch of zeros in it for the next few months. Silence costs money."

"Eh. We'll be in transit anyway. You hungry, Dad? Last chance for a decent nosh. What do they eat out in New Dublin? Grubs and rats?"

CHAPTER FOUR

MURPHY SAT AT THE HELM AS THE SMALL SHUTTLE ROSE THROUGH clouds. In the copilot's seat, Harrison O'Hanraghty kept his green eyes glued to an altimeter. Light wavered across his close-cropped auburn hair until the shuttle cleared the thermosphere and they saw the thin blue line of the horizon.

O'Hanraghty snapped a small device into a data port and one corner of his mouth frowned. He drew a metal-cased pen from a slot on his uniform coveralls and jabbed the tip into one side of the control panel.

There was a hiss and a brief shower of sparks.

"One of the microphones was still on," O'Hanraghty said. "Completely by accident, I'm sure. But we can speak freely, at any rate."

"If someone was trying to listen in," Murphy said, "and that wasn't some innocent glitch, then you're kind of tipping your hand, no?"

"Letting them get away with it would be even worse, assuming they've got a gram of competence," O'Hanraghty said. "If i was a glitch, then I've given our techs something to do. If the think they can catch me on an open mic after four decades i uniform, much of that in the intelligence directorate, then it's a insult to *my* competence. They'd be a hell of a lot more surprise if I let them get away with it."

He shook his head.

"And how about our esteemed political lords and masters?" he asked, changing the subject.

"Everything's holding up," Murphy said.

"Yeah? How was your soiree with the rich and powerful? They anoint you with rose water and oil, or is that only after you become a patriarch in the Five Hundred?"

"Overpriced champagne and a lot of posturing," Murphy said. "I'm the son-in-law to a wealthy scion on his way to punch his career ticket. Social functions like that grease the wheels of the Heart Worlds."

"And here I thought it was the blood of spacers that turned the cogs," O'Hanraghty said. "You weren't invited into a smoke-filled room for a lecture on 'how things really are'?"

"This deployment is my audition." Murphy crossed his arms over his chest. "Just have to keep up appearances and then..."

"Then Thakore uses you like a sock puppet when he has to keep everything in line."

"Then I'm in a position to make some real change," Murphy said. "We're so close, Harrison. If the network can deliver, we can finally end this war."

"You mean 'win,' don't you?"

"Focus on the real threat, Harrison. Fifty-six years of killing League warships—and spacers—and the Federation's gained nine systems. More than a dozen habitable planets virtually depopulated—thank God no one's been stupid enough to bring out the world-burners...yet!—and six *billion* lives lost. So far. With the right push we can end it all. That's winning to me."

"Even after what the League did to your father?"

Murphy's jaw worked slightly.

"Eye-for-an-eye makes every man blind, old friend. We can punish the true monsters in the League and leave the rank and file alone."

"I remember the interim," O'Hanraghty said. "Six months of peace talks. Almost believed it would work, but then the League had a coup and hit Naha with enough k-strikes to send the planet into an ice age. No one's been real interested in peace since then. On either side."

"That coup...Sure was convenient, wasn't it?" Murphy observed. "All the senior members of the League government just so happened

to be on the same ship when the life-support systems had a sudden and total catastrophic failure. Then the hawks seized power, set up a coalition government, and declared themselves 'The Accord.' Just like that. Why, you'd almost think they'd seen it coming or something."

"Now now." O'Hanraghty wagged a finger. "Even the truest of true believers in the network won't go that far. It's the League. They're descended from a batch of holdouts who never even wanted to join the old Federated Government back on Earth! They don't have the sort of robust traditional of peaceful transitions of government *we* do."

"Certainly not." Murphy smirked and adopted a sarcastic tone. "The Federation is the direct heir or the longest tradition of self-rule in human history."

"And that's what we let the people believe." O'Hanraghty leaned forward slightly and tapped a code into a smart screen. "Coming up on the *Ishtar* now."

The stupendous *Marduk*-class FTL carrier's flanks gleamed with reflected sunlight. She wasn't the biggest FTLC in the Federation Navy's inventory—that distinction belonged to the appropriately named *Titans*, which were eighteen percent longer—but she was still enormous, stretching over four kilometers from the face of her bulbous Fasset drive fan to her autocannon-studded stern. The parasite racks standing out from her core hull like grooved flanges could have accommodated up to six sublight battleships and six cruisers, but they carried only two *Canada*-class battleships, two *Bastogne*-class heavy cruisers, and a quintet of *Culvern*-class destroyers. Unlike their mothership, the parasites were sublight vessels, with neither the drive fan nor the long, tapering hull extension which connected it to *Ishtar*'s core hull. Compared to the carrier, they seemed almost squat. Even the battleships were barely eight hundred meters long, but they were far more heavily armed than *Ishtar*. She was accompanied by her sisters, *Ereshkigal* and *Gilgamesh*, the rest of Task Force 1705's carrier group, but the other two ships carried only a single *Engineer*-class repair tender and a pair of *Dromedary*-class logistics ships. The rest of the task force's parasites awaited them at Jalal Station, one of the TFN's nodal bases in the Fringe.

"How's Callum?" O'Hanraghty asked.

"Why do you ask?"

"Sir, please. I'm your chief of staff. I exist to keep you out of trouble...and to do everything command related you don't want to do. I keep Callum out of trouble and that keeps you out of trouble."

"You know."

"The head of security at the Spring Mountain owed me a favor."

"This is my last chance with him." Murphy sighed. "He'll end this tour with his head on straight or on his way to being another kid connected to the Five Hundred who's too rich to fail...and won't ever succeed at a single thing."

"I'll let you know when he needs some fixing," O'Hanraghty said. "Did he mention the roulette wheel?"

"I heard."

"And the fish?"

"Fish?"

"Forget I said anything."

The two watched as they neared the carrier. The glowing void of an open hangar bay grew steadily before them, more than large enough to admit even one of the suborbital passenger transports that plied between continents, yet tiny against the FTLC's hull. Both of them were accustomed to the scale on which spacrcraft and orbital installations were built, but *Ishtar*'s sheer enormity dwarfed their shuttle into an insignificant mote.

"Quite the mission," O'Hanraghty said.

"It will end with total success or complete failure. There's no room in the middle. We keep our masks on until we can't keep up the charade, understood?"

"I've been mum for years, Sir. You're the one who has to keep up appearances."

"Appearances...yes." Murphy unstrapped as the shuttle slid into the cavernous landing bay. He drifted up out of his seat and used one polished bulkhead for a mirror as he adjusted his gig line to make it crooked and twisted a noncombat medal off kilter.

CHAPTER FIVE

CALLUM STUFFED A PAIR OF SCUFFED BOOTS INTO A BEIGE SPACE bag with the Harriman Academy emblem, then flung open a drawer and packed the rest of the bag full of socks and undergarments.

"Shirts! Dress shirts . . . utilities, I think I got those. Is it black shoes or brown on a carrier? What time is . . . ah hell." he opened a closet and lifted a full nonmilitary suitcase.

"At least you've got your head screwed on," a feminine voice said from behind.

Callum spun around and wiped sweat from his brow; his younger sister, Reagan, stood in the doorway to his room.

"You want to help or gloat?" Callum went back to ransacking his dresser.

"You know Uncle Harry sent you a packing list like a week ago?" Reagan asked.

"Was busy. Had to fit two years' worth of living into the time I had left. Do I need a pillow? The bunks on the ship should have pillows."

"And then Mom sent the list to the printers and had all new clothes and gear made up for you?"

"She what?" Callum dropped his bag.

Reagan went to a hallway closet and opened it with a swipe of her hand over a reader. Three vacuum-packed olive green bags were nestled next to racks of fluffy towels.

"She mentioned something about going to war in clean underwear." Reagan rolled her eyes.

"Why didn't you—I mean she—"

"Because you've got nineteen minutes before Mom gets here and the car takes us to Port Olympia," she said. "She's already planning to embarrass you with hugs and kisses before you cross the gates." Her eyes welled up and she turned away.

"Reagan . . . don't be like that," Callum said. "It's New Dublin! Two years holding down the orbital platforms and maybe light customs work." He put an arm around her shoulder. "And you know who's in charge? Our dad. The man doesn't go looking for trouble. He's a politician at heart, not a fighter."

Reagan sniffed hard and pulled away.

"It's just that my friend Susan lost her brother in Beta Cygni, and now you and Dad are leaving and I don't want you to—"

"Stop." Callum pulled her into a hug. "This isn't like that time Dad was out at Steelman's. That was a total fluke. This is a nothing deployment. Heck, you and Mom can even come visit us."

Reagan pushed him away.

"And spend weeks in a star liner listening to her complain about the food? I'll pass," she said.

"You can come by yourself. Crann Bethadh has skiing . . . and bears. Giant terrifying bears."

"What's Cran . . . Cranny . . . what you just said?" she asked suspiciously. "You're going to New Dublin."

"True," Callum said. "But the only inhabited planet's called Crann Bethadh." His tone was more than slightly smug, that of an older brother impressing a younger sister, and she rolled her eyes.

"What language is that?" she challenged.

"I don't know," he admitted after a moment in a somewhat less smug tone. "But it's something about a tree. And they do have skiing! I know how much you enjoy that."

"No promises from me. You just do what you can to stay away from farmers' daughters or getting all weird and deciding to live on the frontier selling organic candles or something," she said.

"I like girls with a bit of culture. I won't settle for anything less than a spoiled Heart World brat. So you just keep tabs on any of your friends from finishing school that—Ow! I need that foot."

"Get your stuff, spacer!" Reagan thrust a finger at the closet.

"And don't you dare make Mom cry when she sees you off, because then I'll start crying and—"

"New Dublin." Callum picked up a bag under each arm. "Get that one for me, please. And it's New Dublin! I might as well be posted to Centauri or Pluto for all the danger I'll be in. It'll be fine."

✧   ✧   ✧

The Murphy family limo stopped in an outer lane of the Port Olympia military terminal. Shuttle buses meandered along the curb to the main building, dropping off young men and women in midnight blue navy coveralls and digital pattern Marine uniforms.

Callum was the first out of the limo and he felt something in the early evening air, an almost palatable sense of dread. He slipped on a dark blue beret and adjusted it while looking in a window. The shape wouldn't hold no matter how hard he tugged, and the head gear looked more like an Italian chef's hat than the perfect slant and peak that his father sported. He gave up, comforting himself with the reflection that he only had to wear it through the lot and could remove it once inside the terminal.

A low chant carried on a breeze from one side of the fenced-in lot. Protesters in all black and with veils over their faces held up sticks with moving digital projections of antiwar slogans. One held a counter, displaying a number well over three billion and increasing by several dozen at irregular intervals.

"Ugh." Simron, dressed for a boardroom meeting, got out behind Callum and straightened out the top of her pants suit. She shook her head at the protesters. "How unpatriotic. Don't they know doing this gets them on hiring blacklists?"

"Maybe that's why they wear the veils." Callum went to the trunk and slapped it twice to signal the robot driver to pop it open.

"They think that will do them any good?" Simron sniffed as Callum hauled his space bags out of the limo. "Adorable. Callum, what are you doing? Don't they have someone to carry that for you?"

"No, Mom, that's not how the Navy works." Callum hefted one bag onto a shoulder. "Reagan? You coming out?" He bent over to look inside the passenger compartment. His sister had tucked herself against the far side, knees drawn up to her chest and hair covering her face.

"Reagan...come on."

"She did this when your father left, too." Simron gave Callum a quick hug. "Two years. Take care of your father. Don't go looking for trouble and don't come back with any medals. You understand? No medals."

"I think I get one just for showing up today. Federation Defense Service or something."

"Don't get the one your grandfather had. Purple Heart, I think it was. And none like your father has for being brave when he shouldn't have been."

"Valor, Mom. Those are for valor."

"Not a single one." She wagged a finger at him. "Now..." Her face held firm but Callum could see emotion building behind her eyes. "Now go on and muster or whatever it is you do in the Navy. Sorry Vyom couldn't be here, but he's at a critical design meeting on Luna and I'm due for a telecom at the office soon. I love you."

"Love you, too." Callum gave her another hug and lifted his other bag onto his back. He went to the window where Reagan was huddled and rapped on the glass. "I'm off. Can I have a hug?"

"No!" came her muffled reply.

"No boys while I'm gone. Vyom will back me up on this. Mom?" He looked up just as the opposite side door shut and the limo rolled away.

He watched it go for a moment, then inhaled deeply.

"Yeah...here goes," he muttered, and shifted the space-bag straps on his shoulders and started walking. He passed small knots of families as they said goodbye to sons and daughters. Most of those in uniform were in their early twenties, and wearing uniforms that looked fresh from the printers, with bare cloth where ribbons and unit crests would be.

He did a double take at a Marine with a worn patch on his right shoulder as the man spoke to four children, a pair of elderly grandparents behind them. Federation Marines wore the patch of a unit they'd been in combat with, which meant this man was clearly a veteran. What was he doing here at a muster station?

The feeling of dread grew as he joined a line outside the terminal leading to a barred revolving gate manned by armed military police. Those in the line were silent, eyes locked on the gate.

Callum fought the urge to look back for one last glance at his mother and sister, but that felt as weak as it was useless. They were gone. The line moved forward slowly as the MPs did a bio ident scan on each person before they went through the gate. He glanced at his watch and guessed he wouldn't be late.

Even the little time he'd spent in military training was enough to accustom him to hurry up and wait. Yet, for as much of his time the Navy wasted, they wouldn't tolerate him being late for anything.

"Lieutenant?" a woman asked from one side.

"Yes?" Callum craned his head over, careful not to bump the spacer behind him with the hump of his space bags.

A heavyset chief petty officer with graying hair beneath a maroon beret gave him a quick salute. Her name tape read HUGGINS.

"This isn't your line, Sir." She motioned to a door near the barred entrance.

"No issue. I can—"

"Not. Your line. Sir." A small but severe smile crossed her lips.

"Must have missed the memo," Callum said as he followed the petty officer. There was an awkward stiffness in her gait and she held a door open for him. Inside was a small office that smelled of old coffee. The spacer stepped around a combination scale-scanner and a tall desk, like she was going to check him into a flight.

"Bags to the scanner, if you please, Sir." She slipped off her beret and tucked it into a back pocket. "No offense meant, but regulations require me to offer you this opportunity to surrender any contraband with no legal repercussion or notations to your personnel file. Anything?"

"Some of my socks may be nonregulation," Callum said as he dropped the bags on the scanner platform.

"Must be your first muster," the petty officer said as she tapped on a keyboard. "Still have a sense of humor. ID, please." She tapped a small slate on the desktop and Callum laid his palm onto it.

"This fast-pass lane just for officers or . . . ?"

"The Navy decided long ago that its more senior members had better things to do with their time than go through a common muster. Most of the compulsories out there haven't declared for needs or preference, so they have more paperwork to go through. Hand off, thank you."

"Sorry, 'needs or preference'?"

Huggins stopped typing and gave him a funny look.

"You must not have gone to public school," Huggins said.

"No. Mostly tutors and the like. Then the Sorbonne."

"Must've been nice," she muttered under her breath. "Needs or preference, Sir, is the first and last choice the Federation military gives to those serving their compulsory enlistment. Those who choose to serve at the needs of the military have their specialty chosen by the military and they serve no more than three years. Usually. After that they're exempt from further compulsory service.

"Those that choose to serve at their preference pick their specialty—aptitude and service-need dependent. They'll serve three years plus twice the length of their training ... and are subject to recall for twenty years after their initial enlistment."

"That ... doesn't sound like a very enticing offer," Callum said.

"Let's see ... Murphy," she narrowed her eyes at him, "Callum T. Assigned to the *Ishtar*. New Dublin? That's not in the Beta Cygni sector." She scowled at him for a moment, then composed herself. "Scan complete. No contraband. I'll have your gear tagged and moved to your ship in just a moment."

She tapped her slate, then returned to their earlier topic. "Paying back training time with interest may not sound 'enticing,' Sir, but it has its advantages. For one thing, those that serve at the needs of the service are more likely to be assigned to the combat-oriented specialties."

"Which have higher casualty rates," Callum said.

"Exactly. And for another thing, those that choose preference can learn valuable skills for the job market at the taxpayers' expense." She shrugged. "This system's been in place since the first decade of the war. It's worked out well enough."

"Which was your choice?"

"Needs." She bent over and knocked knuckles on her pants leg and the metallic ring of a prosthetic limb came back. "Anyone under a hundred percent disability can refuse a medical discharge. I found a way to stay useful."

Huggins placed a deep blue pamphlet on the desktop.

"Your initial muster receipt. Orders assigning you to the *Ishtar* and alcohol chits. Don't lose those. Or sell them ... Murphy. The task force commander on the *Ishtar*'s named Murphy."

"The name's not that uncommon. Thanks, Chief." Callum slipped the pamphlet into a pocket. "So now I ..."

"Take this door, stay on the *orange* line and get to holding area thirty-seven and wait there. Transport will pick you up soon as it's available. By regulation I'm required to tell you that any attempt to leave this facility in anything but an authorized and assigned military vehicle will result in arrest and a mandatory sentencing for desertion."

"That's necessary?"

"Good luck, Sir." She touched an earpiece and went out the front door back to the parking lot. The lock snapped shut behind her. A panel opened in the wall and a robot wheeled out and collected his bags, then vanished into a dark tunnel.

"Am I in the military or a prison with strange rules?" he asked the air and went out the office's other door. It led to a narrow stairwell and up to a bar-lined walkway with four colored lines running down the middle.

The walkway extended over an open space where spacers and Marines waited inside painted squares, their bags piled in one corner. Drill sergeants in bright yellow berets barked orders as they prowled between the squares.

Callum felt self-conscious as he made his way down the walkway. He was an officer, yes, but being so high above the enlisted personnel made it seem like he was lording that over them. He passed over a square where a drill sergeant gave specific and high-volume instructions on the proper way to walk in a single file line. Callum stopped, noticing that several had their hands cuffed in front of them.

"Hey, one of our lords and masters is playing spacer!" a man in the line shouted up at him. "Don't worry, Sir, we'll be good little sheep!" He snatched up a water bottle and hurled it at the catwalk. It struck a bar and broke open, spraying Callum across the arms.

A drill sergeant tackled the protester to the floor and a dog pile of military police followed on.

The man let out a "Baaa," and the brays spread to more and more draftees. The drill sergeants promised dire consequences trying to shut down the chant, but the noise only spread and grew louder.

Callum shook water off his hands and increased his pace. The noise level behind him dropped as he went down another stairwell and found himself in a lounge that extended several hundred yards, with numbered gates on either side. Benches spread across it, filled with other officers and senior enlisted spacers and Marines who glanced at him, and then back to the walkway where the farm noises were settling down.

He passed a kiosk where a pair of elderly ladies offered

cookies and coffee and found his departure gate, halfway down the concourse.

The benches were nearly unoccupied at Gate 37. A single woman in dark green Marine fatigues with a corporal's stripe and medic's caduceus sat next to a pile of long gun cases. Uniform tops were draped over the bench beside her.

"This is...the *Ishtar*, yes?" he asked her.

She raised her gaze slowly. A row of tattoos like shark teeth stood out along her jaw, one eye was a pale green, and the other was a dark prosthetic orb. Her sleeves were rolled up above her elbows, and pale patches of replacement skin with dates inked to them stood out against her naturally olive complexion.

"Yeah. *Ishtar*, Sir."

"How long have you been waiting? Don't know if I have time to—"

"Nine hours." She stretched an arm over her head and leaned to one side. "Maybe we were waiting for you." She lowered that arm, raised the other one, and leaned to the other side. "Maybe we should check and see if the shuttle's here now."

"Nine? That's ridiculous."

Callum went to the gate and grasped the handle, but the door flew open and knocked him back before he could open it. He landed hard on his rear and winced in pain.

"Oops," a deep voice said. A massive man in a sweat-drenched undershirt and fatigue pants stood in the doorway. His craggy features and a nose left crooked by one too many breaks gave him an atavistic air. Another pair of Marines in a similar state stood behind him. "Best watch yourself, mate."

"He's a zero," the woman on the bench said.

"I mean...Sir," the big man said as he read Callum's name tag but made no effort to help him up. "Murphy but not Murphy. Not our principal."

"The secondary?" a whip-thin man with a tight beard asked from behind him.

"Suppose." The big man picked up a uniform top and wiped his face and neck.

"The secondary," the woman said. "Same ride."

Callum got up and brushed himself off.

"Any of you want to clue me in?" He glanced through the open door and saw an empty landing pad with three puddles of sweat on it.

"You're up." The big man slapped the woman on the shoulder and she stripped off her blouse, jogged outside, and began doing a round of calisthenics. "I'm Sergeant Major Logan," he said to Callum. "Chief of the Hoplon detachment assigned to Murphy, Terrence. One each."

"Hoplon? I thought you guys had the mech armor and all that," Callum said.

"We don't wear it all the time," a fair-haired man said as he plopped down next to Logan and looked over the weapon cases. "Steiner. Ugly there's Chavez." He tilted his head to the man with a goatee. "Faeran's out there, if she didn't say hi. She's like that."

"All that—" Callum gestured to his jawline. "That's a bit nonstandard. Right?"

"She's from the Fringe," Logan said. "Incorporation laws let her keep any religious markings. She was a shaman in training before she got drafted."

"Oh. Pleasant. Why are Hoplons assigned to the *Ishtar*? You guys are high-intensity combat ground troops."

"You mean why are we assigned to your father?" Logan leaned back.

"He is my father, yes," Callum said a bit stiffly, and Logan's mouth twitched into a brief sneer.

"We were with our cohort to deploy to Beta Cygni," Steiner said. "Then we got 'Hey you'ed to be a personal security detachment for some Five Hundred princeling—"

Logan grunted and Steiner went silent.

"Seems the brass are worried your daddy needs some extra muscle around him," the sergeant major said. "The Fringe Worlds have been a bit restive these past few years. We'll be along to keep the locals from doing a Gobelins."

"Gobelins. That's where the planetary government declared independence from the Federation a few years back," Callum said.

"And where the locals built a guillotine for all off-world officials." Logan nodded. "Got messy. Got messier when we got things back in line."

"You sure? The planet was brought back into the Federation through negotiations." Callum sat down on a bench facing Logan.

"That's what the news told you." Logan shrugged. "I've got scars that say otherwise, but don't you worry, Sir. We've got you." He smiled.

"Six months busting our chops training in Australia," Chavez said. "And two days before we're supposed to go break League skulls in Beta Cygni, we get this duty."

"Why's your old man so important?" Steiner asked.

"I doubt he requested your...services," Callum said. "More likely it was someone else's idea."

"Because?"

"Because he's a Murphy." Callum shrugged. "Maybe you've heard of Henrik Murphy? Father of the Federation Navy?"

"We only care about the Navy when they're taking us somewhere or providing orbital support," Chavez said.

"Okay. What about the hero of the Battle for Steelman's Star?"

"Lots of heroes out there," Logan said.

"My grandfather is Kanada Thakore," Callum offered.

"What's a Thakore?" Chavez asked.

"One of the Five Hundred," Logan said. "Big one, too. You got an uncle in command of a task force out in Beta Cygni?"

"Rajenda Thakore. That's the one."

"Makes sense now," Logan said. "But who'd we piss off to get a babysitting tour?"

"You know I'm his son," Callum said, his cheeks flushing with anger. "You figured that out on your own."

"What's he going to do?" Logan raised a palm. "Send us to war?"

"Terrence Murphy doesn't need 'babysitting,'" Callum said. "I doubt any Fringe World is that bad. Though I did just have a water bottle thrown at me."

"Ooooh, a water bottle!" Logan stifled a laugh. "You need a hug? Granny back there with the snicker-doodles might oblige you. Wouldn't ask Faeran. She bites."

"He's not kidding about that," Steiner said.

Callum got a whiff of the Marines' body odor and figured there weren't any cleaning facilities readily available.

"Two hours to the chow cart," Logan said to his men. "Clean weapons, then we can rack out." He slid a case from the pile, opened it and removed a heavy machine gun. He flipped the breach open and puffed air into the receiver.

"I'll just...wait here, then," Callum said.

No one replied. Nor did any of them speak to him while they worked.

CHAPTER SIX

THE YOUNG WOMAN HURRIED DOWN AN ALLEY, A SHAWL OVER her blond hair and a basket clutched in her hands. She passed a dumpster that reeked of rotting food and urine before she peeked around the corner into a street that was mostly empty in the early morning hours.

Inverness wasn't a bad world, so far as the Federation's Fringe went, but it wasn't known for its safety or friendliness. Or its warmth. Scotia, the system's red dwarf primary, had just crossed the horizon. It would take up nearly a third of the sky once it had fully risen, but even with it dominating the heavens, its weak light barely managed to keep the air frigid.

The young woman pulled her threadbare coat tighter and moved over a frost-covered sidewalk to a bakery window. The smell of fresh bread was a welcome improvement over the alley, and her mouth watered and her stomach rumbled as she waited, huddled next to a steam vent in the ground. A bit of warmth crept into her toes, and she wiggled them.

The window slid open, and a man with flour coating his hands and lower arms bent over.

"We don't open for another half hour, Eira," he said.

"But the fresh ones taste the best, Mr. Franco." Warmer air wafted over her from the window, and she smiled as her teeth chattered.

"Kills me to see you out here." He glanced back into the bakery. "Boss doesn't like you. You know that."

"He's not here yet," she said.

"No, he's . . . You want fresh, or day-olds? Hurry."

Eira placed a hand on the windowsill and had to pry its frozen fingers open with her other hand. Silver coins rattled onto the metal.

"Nine . . . twelve marks," Franco counted. "I can do four day-old or two fresh."

"I thought that was enough for five," she said.

"Governor raised the sales tax. Sorry. Four?"

"Four. Thank you."

The window shut, and Eira felt the last gust of warm air on her face. She turned away as a ground car rumbled past on the packed snow of the street. She bent over to stick her fingers into the steam grate and winced as the cold left her joints.

The window opened again and a white paper bag landed next to her. She snatched it to her chest and felt a hint of warmth within. Franco must have slipped her a bun fresh from the oven. She went back through the stinking alleyway, debating whether she should eat the warm one or keep going.

"But it'll be cold by the time I'm home." She put her back to the wall and took a bite from a golden-brown pastry. The taste of curried meat made her stomach rumble even harder, and she smiled as she watched steam rise from the half moon she'd taken out.

A flash of white struck her hands and exploded into slush. She gasped in shock as pain lanced through her left hand. The pastry lay on the ground, jumbled up with the remains of a snowball and a small rock.

"Hey, Leaguie!" a boy shouted. "You steal that?"

Another snowball burst against the wall next to her head, and Eira ducked down, clutching the white bag to her chest. Laughter rose from a bunch of teenagers as another snowball struck her thigh.

Eira reached down and snatched the rock out of the remains of her meal.

She whirled and flung it at a pack of boys too old for Inverness's schools and too young for military service. The rock struck one of them just above the knee, where his winter wear was thinnest.

He screamed in pain and went down. While his friends tried to help him up, Eira ducked into a park and ran as fast as she could over the icy ground.

She stopped next to a hedge, panting, her breath coming out in puffs of steam. She shook out her left hand. It hurt, but at least the cold numbed the pain of the scratches the rock had left on it.

"Little bastards."

She opened the rickety door of a crumbling building and went up the staircase two stairs at a time. She stepped over a drunk and went into her apartment. The place was a single room with a mattress in the corner, with a pile of blankets and a weak heater next to it.

"Eira, that you?" a man asked from the pile.

"Of course it is, Sam," she said. "Got some breakfast."

Sam sat up. He was a bit younger than she, with skin lesions on his neck and upper chest. A brand of cursive text had been seared onto his stomach.

"What did you...have to do for this?" he asked as she passed him a bun so cold the filling had ice flakes in it.

"I did laundry for some of the soldiers of the garrison," she said. "Shined boots. Straightened up their barracks. Got coin."

"That one still after you?" Sam wiped sauce from his mouth. "You know. Tried to hurt you."

"I think he's still in the hospital," Eira said. "The sergeant said no court-martial. So he comes back, and..."

"You don't have to feed me so much," Sam said. "It's not like I'm moving around a lot."

"Get healthy and then you can start working, too." She tore off a third of her bun and pressed it into Sam's hands. "Now shut up and finish eating. And then I need to look at that leg of yours again."

✧   ✧   ✧

"They're coming up on the Powell Limit, Sir."

Captain Yance Drebin nodded tautly and looked around TFNS *Burgoyne*'s bridge. The battleship, along with her sisters *MacMahon* and *Moltke* and their light cruiser escorts, rode the racks of TFNS *Ophion,* under strict emissions control, 39,286,000 kilometers from the planet Inverness and just under halfway between the M4 system primary and its 7.2-LM Powell Limit.

Drebin hadn't known what the incoming FTL footprint was

when it was first detected, but he'd been pretty sure what it *wasn't*, because Scotia wasn't exactly a crossroads of interstellar travel. None of the Level E star systems were, which was why they got pickets like his: just three battleships and half a dozen cruisers. No more than could be lifted by a single FTLC. In fact, the carrier which had delivered Drebin's command to Inverness had made the trip—minus the units under maintenance in New Dublin—with a third of her parasite racks running empty. And aside from the regularly scheduled, twice-a-year supply runs, he hadn't seen another Navy carrier in the entire three-plus years he'd been here.

The system was serviced by a single civilian FTL pod-carrier a bit more frequently than that—once every four months, not every six—to collect the products of the planet Inverness's orbital refineries. That was the only reason the system had ever been colonized in the first place. The system was metal-poor, but Kirkcudbright and Dunkeld, Scotia-II and III, were gas giants, almost as massive as their primary, and their atmospheres were a rich source of both hydrogen and much rarer gases.

The governorship of a system like Scotia was no great prize, or it wouldn't have been left for someone like Drebin, who lacked patronage or contacts. But it could still be lucrative, if it was squeezed the right way, and a few years as a system governor wouldn't hurt his résumé any.

That was how he *had* thought of the assignment, anyway. At the moment, he was having rather pointed second thoughts, because this incoming footprint had been neither his regular supply drop nor a scheduled tanker visit. That had meant it was almost certainly the Terran League Navy, and it was unlikely the RLH would have come calling without pretty damned good intelligence on Scotia's defenses.

And on what it would take to break them.

That was the bad news, and it was likely to be *very* bad. The good news had been that the reason he knew it wasn't his supply drop, which had in fact been scheduled to arrive today, was that the supply drop in question had arrived early. Even better, TFNS *Calcutta*, the trash hauler assigned to the Navy's Scotia cargo run, had blown a fan quadrant decelerating back to Jalal Station. Hardly surprising. *Calcutta* might have been a cutting-edge carrier once; now she was an ancient piece of junk working out her final days humping supplies on the ass-side of nowhere. But her misfortune—her most *recent* misfortune—was how TFNS *Ophion* had ended up pressed into service in her place. Not only that, *Ophion* had been ordered to pick up the current supply of refined gases while she was at it, which must have *really* pissed off Jefferson Locklin, her skipper. *Ophion* was a *Titan*-class FTLC, with sixteen-hundred-meter parasite racks. Her class was always in high demand for fleet movements, not for the ignominious task of hauling the trash.

Drebin's sensors had picked up the second incoming Fasset signature shortly after *Ophion* had mated with the cargo pods she'd come to collect. Its proximity to his supply shipment's *scheduled* arrival gave added point to his assumption that the League did indeed have excellent intel on Scotia. Intel good enough for them to schedule their attack when he should have been anticipating a friendly FTL visitation. He hadn't been about to let *Ophion* disappear again with that coming toward him, so he'd exercised his authority as a system governor—even if it was a piddling little system like Scotia—to hold the carrier "until the situation clarified."

Of course, a ship like *Ophion* was much too valuable a strategic resource to expose to unnecessary risk, so he'd ordered Locklin to this position, halfway to the Powell Limit, where the carrier would be safely out of the way. And he'd docked his parasites on *Ophion*'s racks so they'd be in a position to protect such a vital asset just in case the Leaguies—assuming that was who it was, of course—came in on an unexpected heading. From his current position, it would have taken him just over twenty-two hours to reach Inverness under fusion drive, with a nineteen-hour ballistic phase in the middle of it. But he wasn't too worried about that. After all, *Ophion* could return him to his station in little more than an hour, even this deep inside Scotia's Powell Limit.

Or not, depending on what the Leaguies did in the next ten or fifteen minutes.

The incoming ship had gone sublight 2,606,400,000 kilometers from Scotia—and 2,476,800,000 kilometers from the Powell Limit—just over four and a half hours earlier. Decelerating at a steady 1,800 gravities, its velocity was down to just under 2,000 KPS and it was about two light-minutes from the limit.

And during that time, Drebin's drone and the orbital sensor

platforms in Inverness orbit had had plenty of time to identify it: a *Sun Tzu*-class FTLC of the Terran League Navy, whose parasite racks could potentially carry up to twelve capital ships.

At the moment, it was also just over eight light-minutes from *Burgoyne*, which was precisely why Drebin's command was in its present position. If this was an attack, Inverness was the only logical target, and *Burgoyne* and her consorts were well outside any direct vector to the planet. In fact, the *Sun Tzu*'s vector had been almost exactly perpendicular to *Drebin*'s least-time vector to Inverness.

"Captain, they'll hit the limit in another two minutes," the tracking officer said. "After that—"

"Incoming transmission, Sir," the comm officer interrupted her.

"To us?" Drebin asked sharply. If the Leaguies had spotted them after all—

"No, Sir. To Inverness."

The comm officer tapped his screens, and the holo image of an arrogantly smiling woman appeared. Braided black hair was piled atop her head in a coronet that probably made problems inside a vac helmet, and her lip curled.

"People of Inverness, my name is Admiral Xing Xuefeng," she said coldly. "Remember it."

That was all she said. The display went blank once more and silence filled *Burgoyne*. Then the tracking officer inhaled.

"Sir, she's flushed her racks. It looks like four capital ships, probably *Hou Yi* battlecruisers, and three *Shui-Shen* heavy cruisers. Their vector is directly toward Inverness at one-eight-eight-two KPS. Range to the planet seven-point-two light-minutes. Time-of-flight at current velocity is eleven hours, nine minutes. Assuming a ten-gee deceleration burn for a zero-zero with Inverness, time-of-flight is thirteen-point-eight hours."

Drebin watched the master plot update. Commander Carson stirred beside him, and he turned to raise an eyebrow at her.

"Something on your mind, XO?"

"Sir," she waved at the master display, "these bastards are headed straight for Inverness, and there's only eight of them. We've got three battleships and the cruisers, and a *Conqueror*'s a lot tougher than a *Hou Yi* any day of the week."

"You're saying we should engage them." Drebin's distinctively nasal, gravelly voice was harder than usual.

"Well, Sir, if we fired up *Ophion*'s Fasset drive, we could be back to Inverness and drop the parasites in under seventy minutes."

"Are you out of your frigging mind?" Drebin stared at her. "Risk a *Titan* to cover a Level E planet?"

Lauren Carson's green eyes cored with something remarkably like contempt, and Drebin's stare hardened into a glare. He hadn't asked for Carson, and she hadn't asked for *Burgoyne*, but they were stuck with each other. It was just a pity she was such a pain in his ass. For such a physically attractive woman, the blond-haired, dark-skinned commander was remarkably cold. All he'd suggested was that they were going to be stuck in Scotia for at least a couple of years, and she'd hammered him in the teeth with the Articles of War's prohibition against physical relationships between officers and their direct subordinates. It had only been a *suggestion*, for God's sake—not a barroom proposition! But it had cast an undeniable pall over their relationship.

"Sir," she said now, "*Ophion* could drop us off in Inverness orbit and be well clear over twelve *hours* before they got there."

"And their carrier could do exactly the same thing for them!" Drebin pointed out.

"They'd have to redock all of them first, Sir, and that would burn a good two hours. Then they'd have to accelerate *and* decelerate, from a starting point thirty-six million kilometers farther out than we are. There's no way they could catch *Ophion*."

"Assuming this is their entire parasite force," Drebin shot back almost spitefully. "That's a *Sun Tzu* out there, Commander, and that's barely half a complete parasite loadout for a *Sun Tzu*! She could have four more goddamned *Hou Yis* on the racks!"

"Sir, why would they send in a force this light if they had that kind of backup?" Carson asked in a deliberately calm tone.

"How the hell do I know?" Drebin demanded. "But what I *do* know is that there's no way I'm taking *Ophion* into that kind of potential clusterfuck."

"Of course not, Sir. I see that now," she said, and the cold contempt had migrated from her eyes to her voice. She unhooked the tether that kept her stabilized in *Burgoyne*'s microgravity. "Excuse me, Captain, but I think they need me in Tactical."

She pushed off—hard—from the back of her command couch to glide gracefully and swiftly for the hatch, and he watched her go.

✧　　✧　　✧

"Better," Eira said as she finished checking the self-cleaning dressing on his left thigh. At least the medical treatment he'd gotten from the clinic had held up, she thought. One of the few perks of living in a nation at war for decades was that decent first-aid supplies managed to work their way down the economic ladder with ease.

"I think your leg's really making some progress," she told him. "How's it feel?"

"Better. I think I can put some weight on it today. Maybe we can go to the garage and see if Tommy will help me out. It's his fault I got hurt."

"I ran into his little cousin." Eira's lips pressed into a thin line.

"Ah . . . not again." Sam shook his head.

"They came after me. What was I supposed to do?"

"How bad did you mess him up?"

"A bruise. If I'm lucky. Not enough for him to go to the law about it, I don't think," she said.

"Fuck that Tommy," Sam said. "He hadn't dropped an engine block on me, and I'd be able to take care of my sister. He needs to pay up."

A door slammed elsewhere in the building, and Eira tensed.

"Baker said taxes went up," she said.

"What else is new? Governor needs a new wing to his mansion? He stops funding our orphanage. Girlfriend wants a dress made of Rishathan silk? Taxes go up. He's a dickhead. If he spent half as much time doing his job as he does on the public screens telling us how frigging *wonderful* he is—" Sam cut himself off with a grimace. "Oh, the hell with it! Let's go to the shop. We get there before Tommy starts drinking and he might be a bit more generous."

She helped him up and he stuck an aluminum crutch with an old towel wrapped around the top under his arm.

Eira bundled her brother up and helped him down the stairs. He managed to stump along at a surprisingly brisk pace, but their trip to the garage—a mile away in the industrial section of town—still took the better part of an hour.

"Almost there," Sam said as he stepped off the curb.

"Watch it!" Eira pulled him back just as a police car roared by, battering them with the icy wind of its passage.

"What the hell?" Sam thrust a gloved hand into the air in a

rude gesture. "Why was he going so damn fast without a siren on? Could've killed somebody!"

"That's odd." Eira looked up at a three-tiered light above the security camera overlooking an intersection. Each light was cold and dark. "Civil defense network is quiet."

"All the fighting's in Beta Cygni," Sam said impatiently. "Now let's talk to Tommy. Ramen will be on me."

A spattering of yellow light flashed across the sky, doubling their shadows against the snow.

A fireball expanded over the horizon, hanging in the sky but silent in the distance as a brief, bright star joined the red dwarf.

"Marauders?" Sam asked. "They found us—"

"It's not them. Look!" Eira's heart went cold as she pointed at the incandescent lines overhead. She'd never seen a kinetic energy weapon before—not with her own eyes—but that was all they could be: kinetic energy weapons. High-velocity, high-mass slugs that hit hard as nukes. They glared against the winter sky like curses, each tipped by a fiery nail, scarring its path across the sky, and she grabbed Sam by the wrist and pulled him toward a three-story building with broken windows.

"No, no." Sam refused to budge as he gaped skyward. "It's not fair! Why's this happening to us?"

A siren woke and wailed across the city in a hundred voices, echoes from megaphones joining into a single cry that sent Eira's heart racing.

"Come on! Bunker!" She jerked Sam's hand and he fell, his crutch clattering across the street. She tried to haul him up, then stopped as a falling nail dipped behind the tallest buildings at the heart of the city.

A burst of light seared her face and she went down, screaming.

Sam used his body to shield his sister as a blast wave of snow smashed into them. Eira's world went spinning as the explosion threw her sideways until she slammed against something hard. She stared up at a white sky, feeling hunks of ice land around her as they slid free of the roof of the building she'd hit.

She pulled herself out of the snowbank. Roofs had collapsed on the smaller buildings around her and people struggled out of them into the street.

"Sam!" she shouted. The name sounded muffled through her painfully abused ears. She looked around frantically and spotted a bit of his jacket sticking out of the snow. She threw herself toward it and called out to him again as she started digging.

The explosion of a more distant strike nudged her off balance, but she kept digging. She wiped snow from Sam's face and he blinked at her.

"Up, up!" Adrenaline lent her strength and she dragged him up by the arms and then into the building. Shattered glass was strewn across the bare concrete floor and she panted as she looked around the room frantically.

"Ow...Something got me," Sam said. He lay on one side, a hand patting around his torso.

"Where is it?" Eira demanded. "Where is it? I know it's— There!"

She ran to a pillar and found the metal hatch on the other side. She grabbed the handle and tried to lift it, but it resisted stubbornly. It took every straining muscle just to raise the edge a few centimeters.

White light flashed, and Eira fell to her knees a split second before the blast obliterated the last of the windows. She felt a tug against her face as the pressure wave rolled over her, then pushed herself up and went to her brother as the roar died away. Blood dripped onto his face when she leaned over to give him a shake. She blinked at it, then touched her cheek and felt a shard of glass. She pulled it out and tossed it away, then dug both hands into Sam's jacket and dragged him to the bunker entrance.

"Just...go," he said.

"No! We promised, *amaren*!" She grabbed the handle and lifted again, tears rolling down her face as her back and legs screamed with the effort. It was like lifting a planet, but somehow she got the lid high enough to wedge her shoulder under it and prop it there.

"Sam, I need you to crawl. Can you do that?" she gasped. The edge of the hatch bit through her clothes and her knees threatened to buckle.

Sam grabbed the edge of the entrance and pulled himself forward. He fell in and vanished into the dark. She heard him banging against the ladder and her heart froze. She had no idea how far he'd fallen.

"Ow..." came up out of the darkness.

Eira tried to push the heavy hatch higher, but she lacked

the strength. All she could do was thrust it up as hard as she could and hope she could drop into the hole before it hit her. She hurled herself into the opening but hit the ladder hard and failed to get a firm hold on the rungs. She plummeted, but then one leg jammed into the gap between a ladder rung and the wall and stopped her with a painful jerk on her knee and ankle.

The hatch slammed down and she hung, suspended in total darkness. Pain radiated from her face and ears, and it felt like a knife had been wedged into the joint of her trapped knee.

"Sam?" she panted, and tried to curl upward at the waist to grab the ladder.

A flashlight snapped on, and Sam shone it at her from only a meter or so below her.

"Found this on the bottom rung," he said. "Fall ain't so bad."

Eira managed to grip one of the ladder's uprights and twisted her ankle free. She landed in a heap next to her brother while the thunder of nearby strikes reverberated through the bunker. The roof creaked with each passing wall of overpressure, and she took the flashlight and looked around. The walls were lined with dusty boxes and folded-up cots.

"Where are we?" Sam asked.

"This was an old school," she said. "But before that, it was a militia training house. Some of the soldiers told me about it. Every military building has these shelters."

"And how come...no one took...this 'tuff?" Sam sounded as if his lips were getting fat.

"Hatch is always mag locked unless the civil defense alarms—" Eira began, then broke off with an impatient headshake and limped over to a stack of boxes. "Where are the first-aid kits?" She swiped her hand down a stack, sweeping away dust until she uncovered a red cross on the bottommost.

Another K-strike shook dust from the ceiling.

"So cold," Sam said.

"Is it?"

Eira managed to drag a box off the top of the stack and stopped to rest for a moment, then turned her head sharply as the flashlight Sam held fell from his grip. It rolled, sweeping the light around until it bounced off Sam's outstretched hand... and the weak beam reflected from the pool of blood under her brother's side.

"Sam? *Sam!*" Eira tried to run to him, but her twisted knee failed, and she fell hard. She crawled the rest of the way and rolled Sam onto his back. His breathing was quick and shallow, his eyes were glazed, and one side of his jacket was soaked through with blood, the tatters full of red chunks of ice.

"Hold on," she told him. "I'll get the med kit!"

Eira choked down a growing sense of panic and felt fury rise in its place as she limped back to the supplies. None of this was their fault. Their lives had been nothing but pain and desperation since they were children, and the only thing they'd ever had was each other. Now the League was destroying their home, and the Federation—which was supposed to be their salvation—had put the most important box of supplies at the bottom of the pile where they couldn't be used in an emergency.

She grunted with effort as she heaved the next box aside, then went to work on the next, dragging up strength her exhausted and emaciated body didn't have. The next box. And the next—

Barely a kilometer away, a K-strike obliterated the nearby barracks. The blast wave collapsed the training facility over the bunker and buried it in tons of debris.

The League attack ended minutes later, leaving Inverness's largest city a graveyard of smoke and ice.

CHAPTER SEVEN

"AND THAT'S ALL SHE WROTE," O'HANRAGHTY SAID AS THE TFN ships died inside the hologram. Another salvo of missiles ripped through the spreading wrecks, detonating at barely sixty kilometers and driving bomb-pumped lasers through their armor to rub salt deeper into the wound of defeat.

The *Ishtar*'s wardroom was largely empty. The long, real wooden table was made from Thraxix timber, with an almost digital pattern to the grain, and stewards cleaned out the remains of the dinner service while the task force's senior officers sat around a holo-station at the far end of the room. The station had two seats, opposite each other, with dueling projections.

O'Hanraghty reached back behind himself to the table to pick up a glass tumbler and took a sip of whiskey. Lieutenant Commander Tanaka Amari, Commander Eduard Ortiz, and Commander Raleigh Mirwani, each in shipboard utilities, sat nearby and watched in silence. Captain Joseph Lowe, *Ishtar*'s CO, glanced up from his tablet from time to time.

The light from the explosions played across Murphy's face as he leaned closer to the holo. He put one hand over his mouth, stroked his chin, and shook his head.

"You cheated," he announced.

"Cheated? Why I've never been so insulted!" The chief of staff chuckled. "Let's rewind."

He traced a circle several times on his controls, and Murphy's projection winked out, replaced by O'Hanraghty's view. Ships came back into existence and backtracked over the glowing lines of their maneuver vectors. The holo jittered as O'Hanraghty skipped around the play-through.

"Now you're just trying to cover up your malfeasance," Murphy said.

"Nonsense," O'Hanraghty said a bit absently. "I'm just looking for—aha! Here it is."

O'Hanraghty stopped searching and let the recording play forward at double speed, and his League ships made a sudden maneuver, altering heading by almost forty-five degrees in a matter of seconds and going to maximum acceleration in a blinding plume of ejecta from their fusion drives.

"I saw that," Murphy said. "The sim penalized you with onboard casualties for the acceleration spike. But you did it too early to catch me by surprise, so I—"

"So you changed your own attack vector…which put you back on a least-time intercept for the laser birds I fired during the course jink." O'Hanraghty leaned back and took another sip of his drink.

"What? No way!" Murphy's eyes narrowed. "I would've seen their Hauptman signatures!"

"Who said anything about Hauptman signatures?" O'Hanraghty inquired. "The missile drives were locked. Didn't you notice how long it took you to run into them? Or the fact that there was no terminal maneuvering at all?"

Murphy glared at him, but the commander had a point about the initial missile wave's time-of-flight.

"I burned through the entire maneuver stage when I launched. Between that and the launchers' mass drivers, they had all the velocity they needed, as long as you stayed on course to close to gun range." The chief of staff shrugged. "Given how much missile defense the *Su Wukongs* have, I figured you'd go for that instead of a missile duel if I gave you the opening. So I did. They still had their Hauptman coils in reserve—that was my fudge factor in case you weren't exactly where I expected you, but—" he smiled wickedly "—they didn't need them after all."

"I still should've seen the maneuver drives' plumes," Murphy said.

"I masked the launch with the jink," O'Hanraghty said, and smiled as Murphy took over the replay and zoomed into the moment a missile salvo left one of the League ships' launchers. "That many main engine burns make a pretty blinding flare and all your sensors were looking 'into the sun' at exactly the wrong moment. And once the missiles burned through their fuel and went dead, they gave you damn-all for radar targets."

"Then the sim is faulty," Murphy shot back.

"Sir, this is *Federation Commander*," O'Hanraghty pointed out.

"You sure it's not the civilian version?" Murphy demanded, as he pulled open the settings menu. "I still should've seen *something* if it isn't!"

"Nope. Flag edition, Sir." O'Hanraghty swished the ice cube around his glass with a certain undeniable complacency, and Murphy glared at him. The flag edition version was updated constantly by the Oval to reflect real-world conditions. Which was why it was loaded only to the Navy's FTLCs, not its sublight units, with access restricted only to commanding officers and flag staffs.

It was also why the FTLCs' skippers were required to slag the server if their ships were ever in danger of destruction or capture.

The civilian edition was wildly popular among Heart World adolescents, but that version offered only a general approximation of capabilities and all the tech had to be at least ten years out of date. It was also, unfortunately, *only* a game, divorced from the reality of the war, as far as most of them were concerned, Murphy thought.

On the other hand, none of those youngsters playing the game knew the Oval monitored the civilian leader boards. Those who showed aptitude got surprise appointments to Officer Candidate School, and the Admin side of the house saw that they were slotted into specialties suited to their talents and not necessarily their preference.

"Good thing it *wasn't* the civvie version," the admiral said sourly, sitting back from the holo in disgust. "I sure as hell wouldn't have been earmarked for tactical after *that* performance."

Ortiz looked quickly over his shoulder to be certain the stewards had left. O'Hanraghty chuckled, and Ortiz frowned at him.

"We're not supposed to talk about that," he said. As Task Force 1705's SO1, the commander was the staff officer charged with managing Murphy's personnel and administration. "Being able to do mandatory service with the appearance of a choice keeps the desertion rate lower," he added.

"You mean to say the Federation's government isn't entirely forthcoming to the people?" O'Hanraghty sneered. "I'm shocked. Shocked, I tell you!"

"It all serves to support the war effort." Tanaka straightened in her seat. "The greater good and victory is more important than anything else."

"Let's not dwell on the details of how the sausage is made," Murphy said. "And let's not discuss it with those that don't need to know." He gave O'Hanraghty a look, and the chief of staff shrugged.

At that moment, the wardroom hatch opened and Callum came in. His face was red from exertion, and sweat matted his hair to his forehead.

"Dad—I mean, Admiral." Callum held up a plastic tube the length of his forearm. "I got it!"

Murphy rolled his eyes.

"He has to learn," O'Hanraghty said from behind his glass.

Callum slapped the tube on the end of the table with obvious pride.

"Commander," he said to Tanaka, "this ship is critically short of grid squares!"

The logistics officer bit her lip.

"Are you—" She glanced at Murphy. "Are you sure, Lieutenant? Because I remember seeing them on the manifest before we broke orbit."

"I went to Damage Control, Fusion Two, Strike Ops Center—no one there, by the way—and several crew told me that I could get some at the particle flux monitoring station. But I think that's on the outside of the hull, and no one was willing to authorize going EVA in wormhole space," Callum said.

"I did find the lubricant to fix the desiccated fallopian tubing in Da—the Admiral's quarters, though," he went on, his face brightening. "This was the smallest unit I could find. For some reason, they keep all this all the way forward at Missile One. Good thing I got there in time. They had to do a resonance test on the mag driver clamps, and I had just the right mass to get it done."

"They...gave you the hammer?" Murphy asked.

"Sure did. Was tapping up and down the clamps. Made chalk marks where it sounded off," Callum assured him.

Mirwani pinched the bridge of his nose and bit his lips.

"Your first time aboard a warship?" Tanaka asked.

"How could you tell?" Callum gave the tube of lubricant a pat.

"Lucky guess," Tanaka mumbled.

"Thank you, Lieutenant," Murphy said. "You keep that handy. I may need it again later."

"Oh. But your desiccated—"

"I took care of it," Murphy assured him, then gestured at the holo. "Callum, you know how to operate *Federation Commander*?" he asked as he opened the menu and scrolled through preloaded scenarios.

"I had decent scores during college." Callum sat next to O'Hanraghty and pulled the chief of staff's interface over in front of him. "Never had the finesse that some have."

"Then let's make this a group session," his father said. "Historic engagement. Conflict at the Brin Gap."

O'Hanraghty glanced sideways at Callum, his eyes narrowed ever so slightly.

"The where?" Callum crossed his arms as League ships moved around a thick ring surrounding a gas giant and away from a larger Federation force.

"Callum, this is where—" O'Hanraghty began, then stopped as Murphy raised a hand.

"Okay, let's see here," Callum said. "Gravity wells known... composition of the rings are the usual ice and dust. Looks like our side caught them by surprise, though."

The League sublight commander's predicament was obvious. His force, labeled "BOGEY ALPHA," counted only three battlecruisers—the older *Fang Fengs*, not the new *Hou Yi*-class ships—and their escorts: three heavy cruisers IDed as early units of the *Shui-Shen* class, a pair of light cruisers, and a destroyer division. They were hopelessly outgunned by the Federation CO's forces: seven battleships, eight *Procyon*-class battlecruisers, eight *Bastogne*-class heavy cruisers, and two strikecarriers. Not only that, he'd been caught well separated from his own carriers. The initial range was just over 1,780,000 kilometers, but the TFN had a velocity advantage of 600,000 kilometers per second, thanks to the five FTLCs which had made a high-speed approach before dropping them into battle. Now, their jobs done, those carriers were decelerating away from the scene of the action hard. Ships like them had no business getting into shooting range of anything, and they obviously understood that.

The only good news from the League CO's viewpoint was that the attackers' position wasn't perfect, despite its advantages.

It looked like the TFN had been uncertain of the League defenders' exact positions, so the Federation FTLCs had dropped their sublight parasites in two separate task groups on approach vectors designed to converge on the gas giant, which meant they were currently out of mutual support range of one another and that even the closer of them would need almost fifty minutes of ballistic flight to cover the distance between it and his own command. Unfortunately for him, however, it *also* meant one of them would be on a heading to intercept him whichever way he ran, and he could never generate enough velocity to escape before one of them caught him. In fact, neither of the TFN forces carried enough fuel—or could pull a high enough deceleration—to generate anything except a passing engagement as they overflew him.

Four of the League's own FTLCs, labeled "BOGEY BETA," were visible at one edge of the holo display, but they were over 15,198,000 kilometers out-system of the gas giant, much too far away to swoop in and collect their outnumbered parasites even with the prodigious acceleration of a Fasset drive. Not without entering the attackers' range envelope, at least. They could have made rendezvous with ALPHA well before the TFN reached engagement range, but it took far longer—at least twenty or thirty minutes for a battlecruiser—to dock parasites to an FTLC's racks than it did to drop them. That meant they would still be trying to pick up ALPHA's units when the TFN drew close enough to take them under fire, and they were far too valuable to expose to that sort of risk.

"Why are the forces so unbalanced? The Federation's, I mean?" Callum asked with a frown. All the battleships and the strikecarriers were in one of the incoming forces, tagged "TG-1," whereas the second force, "TG-2," consisted only of the battlecruisers and the six *Bastognes*. "Our admiral could have put at least three battleships, four of the cruisers, and a strikecarrier into each force."

"Yes, he could have," Murphy acknowledged. His tone was oddly flat and he glanced at O'Hanraghty before he looked back at his son. "Although his intelligence wasn't conclusive—which is why he came in split in the first place—his staff's interpretation of the intel suggested that the League's FTL lift would be in the inner system, so he expected the parasite commander to break in-system to evade. So he weighted the task group on the in-system vector to make it his Sunday punch. The second task group was basically insurance, in case his interpretation was wrong and they broke out-system, instead."

"Um." Callum frowned as he considered that, then shrugged. "Sounds a little risky," he observed. "I mean, if he's right, he beats hell out of them. But it doesn't look like he guessed right after all."

"It happens." His father shrugged. "Want to watch the historic scenario play out before you try your hand as the Federation flag officer?"

"Why not?"

Callum punched the PLAY command, set the time compression to five, and leaned back on his side of the holo display. On the other side, O'Hanraghty handed Murphy a glass of whiskey as the assembled officers watched the tiny ships maneuver.

Orders went out from the TFN flagship to both task groups, and TG-1 began bending its vector toward out-system, but only TG-2 had a realistic chance to engage unless the hapless ALPHA was stupid enough to hang around for a suicidal engagement against them both.

Which, obviously, he was not.

Even though the RLH carriers couldn't rescue ALPHA before TG-2 caught up to them, they were still ALPHA's only ride home, and the League CO had gone to eight gravities on a heading toward them. That wasn't very high by FTLC standards, but it was about the maximum acceleration he could sustain for more than ten minutes or so, even with twenty-sixth-century medicine and life support, and he'd clearly decided his only hope, however faint it might be, was to run for his carriers. He'd have to survive a passing engagement with TG-2 first, but that was better than hanging around for a suicidal engagement against them both.

TG-2, on the other hand, was *decelerating* at 2.3 gravities while simultaneously bending its vector closer to ALPHA's. Its overtake velocity was so great that not only was there no way for its prey to escape interception, there would be precious little time to engage as their vectors intersected and then began diverging once more. Clearly, TG-2 was decelerating to extend the engagement window, whereas BOGEY ALPHA wanted to make it even narrower, if possible.

"Why aren't our guys decelerating harder?" Callum asked.

"Probably because there's not a lot of point to it," his father said, eyes watching the icons creep across the plot. "There's also the fact that they don't have unlimited fuel reserves, either. The carriers have only so much tankage for their parasites, and once it's expended, so is their ability to maneuver. But even if that weren't true, they're going to pass within gun range, Callum, assuming accelerations hold constant. With that many battle-cruisers and heavy cruisers against what the RLH is showing, even a high-velocity pass should be pretty damned decisive. In the meantime, there's no point beating his people up with an even higher deceleration rate. Two-point-three gees is punishing enough. ALPHA's CO's pounding hell out of his personnel with that kind of accel, and that's going to have an effect when they finally engage."

"Um." Callum's eyes had narrowed, and now he nodded slowly. "Good point," he conceded. "I should've thought about the fuel constraints, but the acceleration's physical effects wouldn't have occurred to me. Not something most of the guys I've played *Federation Commander* with would've thought of, either."

"No." Murphy took a sip of whiskey. "No, I've noticed that civilians generally don't think about that kind of thing. Or worry too much about casualties, as long as they win."

"Winning is winning, Dad," Callum said.

"For certain values of the word, at least," Murphy replied.

Minutes ticked away, numerals spinning past on the holo display's time-compressed internal chronometer, and the range between TG-2 and BOGEY ALPHA swept inexorably downward. Thirty minutes after the pursuit began, TG-2 was down to an overtake velocity of "only" 559 KPS. Its ships had traveled 1,043,460 kilometers in pursuit of BOGEY ALPHA, but the RLH ships had run 127,094 kilometers from their initial position, so the range had closed by only a bit under 1,355,000 kilometers and they were still over 1,600,000 kilometers apart. Effective missile range, given that geometry, was over 80,000 kilometers, however. It would drop slightly as the velocity differential at launch continued to decrease, but they'd still be in missile range within the next seventy minutes, and pass within effective gun range—no more than two or three thousand kilometers—11.7 minutes after that, at a crossing velocity of 114 KPS.

Callum yawned and stretched as he watched.

His father took another sip of whiskey and seemed to settle deeper into his chair. Another twenty minutes sped past in the holo. And then—

"What the *hell?*"

Callum jerked back upright as the four motionless icons of BOGEY BETA suddenly began to move. They were still over 17,900,000 kilometers from ALPHA, but they were also Fasset-drive ships, well outside the local star's Powell Limit, and they leapt almost instantly to an acceleration of 1,900 gravities, not the paltry 8 gees of their parasites. Callum stared at them, then looked at his father.

"What are those idiots doing now?" he demanded. "If they were going to try to pull ALPHA out, they should have done it a long time ago! This is stupid!"

"Really?" his father asked. Callum stared at him incredulously, and Murphy shrugged. "I guess we'll see," he said.

BOGEY BETA raced through space, building its vector with all the blinding speed of the Fasset drive. Five minutes ticked past in the sim. Then ten. Fifteen. Then—

"Jesus!"

Callum twitched as a horde of fresh red icons erupted from BOGEY BETA's quartet of FTLCs twenty-one minutes after they'd begun accelerating.

The sim updated, labeling the newcomers BOGEY GAMMA. A status bar for the new detachment spun up, and Callum's nostrils flared as it steadied and twenty-four fresh battlecruisers, escorted by an equal number of light cruisers, raced toward BOGEY ALPHA—and TG-2—at a combined closing velocity of almost 57,000 KPS.

"Son of a *bitch!*" he breathed. At their velocity on their current heading, the newcomers would cut across TG-2's position a full four minutes before TG-2's missiles could target BOGEY ALPHA even at maximum powered range.

The wardroom was deathly still as the lethal ambush played out before them. There was no way for TG-2 to avoid BOGEY

GAMMA. Indeed, the TFN task group was at a far greater maneuver disadvantage than BOGEY ALPHA had been when the Federation FTLCs arrived. Given their relative velocities, effective gun range would be enormously extended—the scarlet threat sphere delineating GAMMA's effective Kinetic Energy Weapon envelope had expanded from no more than 5,000 kilometers to almost 120,000. Of course, that same velocity meant they would cross entirely through even that engagement envelope in only about 2.2 seconds, so each unit would have time for no more than a single KEW broadside. On the other hand, that many League battlecruisers and light cruisers could put ninety-six of the super-dense slugs into space in a single launch, distributed between only eleven targets, and at well over 76,000 KPS, any hit would deliver almost five hundred and fifty megatons of kinetic energy to anything that got in its way. No armor was going to stop *that*.

TG-2 was doomed. There was no way to escape that oncoming sledgehammer, and Callum knew it. But then his eyes narrowed. TG-2 wasn't *trying* to evade. It had ceased its deceleration and gone to a full-power ten-gravity pursuit burn.

At that acceleration, it had to be under computer control, and its crews were almost certainly taking casualties, despite their acceleration bunks. But it also meant TG-2's closing velocity on BOGEY ALPHA had started to climb, instead of drop, and Callum's nostrils flared as the holo's vector projections began to shift.

The Federation units sustained that brutal acceleration for nine minutes. Then their acceleration cut off abruptly...and they turned to clear their broadsides and began belching missiles. The range was extreme. Indeed, even at their increased closing velocity their missiles' primary drives would burn out 70,000 kilometers short of their targets. But they emptied their magazines in the next forty seconds, and they staggered their missiles' Hauptman coil activation to bring all of them online together.

Eight hundred twenty of the big missiles screamed toward BOGEY ALPHA in a single coordinated salvo. It was the alpha strike of alpha strikes, completely stripping TG-2 of any sustained combat capability, and at such long range, individual hit probabilities were low, to say the least. But that many missiles were enough to thoroughly saturate BOGEY ALPHA's active defenses.

BOGEY ALPHA's counter-missiles raced to meet the incoming

fire, and they had time for multiple shots at each bird. Maximum velocity from rest for a TFN shipkiller was 1,760 KPS, and even after TG-2's massive burst of acceleration, closing velocity at launch increased that by only about ten percent. But the attack salvo was heavily seeded with EW platforms, and the penaids drove down interception probabilities inexorably.

Almost half the original launch broke past the counter-missiles to hurtle down upon its targets. A quarter of the incoming missiles were dedicated EW platforms, covering their more lethal sisters with decoys and jammers. But that left over two hundred and fifty shipkillers for only eleven targets, and if their Hauptman coils had burned out, they still had their own last-stage thrusters. Their fusion drives came on line sixteen seconds after their coils died. Their 250 gravities of acceleration were miniscule compared to the Hauptman drive's three thousand, but they lasted all the way in to their targets. Their fusion drives' ability to maneuver, even at that acceleration rate, was limited, but they'd tracked their targets all the way in, and the TFN's missile AIs were very good at their job.

Point defense lasers and autocannon fired frantically as the missiles came in on BOGEY ALPHA at 1,930 KPS, and dozens of missile signatures vanished from the plot. But the close-range point defense systems had time for only a single shot per target, and they simply didn't have enough lasers or cannon.

The Terran League Navy favored nuclear warheads that required direct hits or at least close proximity detonations while the Terran *Federation*'s navy preferred the laserhead, but neither navy relied solely on a single type, and a kaleidoscope of destruction ripped across BOGEY ALPHA.

The exchange was so quick, so savage, Callum couldn't tell how many nukes and how many laserheads were involved, but two of the League heavy cruisers and one of the battlecruisers simply disappeared, and every other unit of BOGEY ALPHA stopped accelerating as the Federation fire reduced them to tattered, mangled debris fields.

Callum stared at the wreckage for a moment, but then his eyes were snatched back to TG-2 as every one of its units suddenly blew apart. For a moment he didn't understand. They were still short, if barely, of GAMMA's engagement envelope and the incoming League parasites hadn't even fired yet, so what—?

Then he saw the spreading necklaces of life pods and under-standing struck. TG-2 had abandoned its ships and fired their scuttling charges rather than even try to survive the unsurvivable.

Three-point-five minutes later, BOGEY GAMMA slashed through the expanding sphere of life pods. Those pods were smaller than missiles, but they were also far slower, they weren't made of radar absorbent materials, and unlike missiles, they carried transponders. Beacons to lead rescuers to them in the enormous, trackless wilderness of space.

And now beacons to guide their executioners' aim.

Callum Murphy's jaw clenched as point defense lasers and cannon ripped out with deadly accuracy and wiped those pods from the face of the universe.

❖   ❖   ❖

Callum stared at the holo as the Federation's surviving task group headed for safety. None of the League parasites was posi-tioned to intercept TG-1 before it could recover to its FTLCs, but it didn't really matter. There wasn't much doubt about who'd won this one.

"They just... just *slaughtered* those escape pods," he said after a long, still moment. He raised his eyes to his father's face, and Murphy nodded. "But... but that's a *war crime!*" Callum protested.

"Yes, it was," Murphy agreed. "Like I said before, son, it happens."

"But—"

"The League's official position was that the TFN had already violated the rules of war by taking down the decoy group when TG-2 couldn't possibly survive," Mirwani said. Callum looked at him, and the commander—Murphy's SO3, in charge of operations and training, which also made him TF 1705's tactical officer—shrugged. "I didn't say it was a *good* position, Lieutenant. Just the official one.

"Of course it was," O'Hanraghty said. "All they did was execute a reprisal, wasn't it? And the injured party is authorized to do just that in *response* to a violation." Callum stared at him and he shrugged. "It's a strained reading of the understanding that fortifications at the bottom of a gravity well must surrender when summoned to do so because their position's ultimately hopeless and all their resistance can accomplish is to cause unnecessary casualties."

"But that's different!" Callum protested.

"Is it? You have to admit it does make a certain amount of sense. I happen to agree with you that it was an unjustified massacre, that it *was* a war crime. But this war's been going on for almost sixty years now, Callum. Nobody who might have been deterred from committing 'war crimes' by the possibility of retribution expects it to end anytime soon. Or to have to face the music even if it does."

"The boards and faxes don't mention anything like this," Callum said in an almost accusatory tone, but his father's chief of staff shook his head.

"They do if you bother to do the right searches. Of course, who's interested in looking for depressing stuff like that, right?"

Callum looked back and forth between O'Hanraghty and Murphy, then back down at the holo. He looked like someone looking for a way to disprove what he'd just seen, and he punched commands into the console. The holo lit with icons again, but this time moving backward from the battle's disastrous conclusion at an even higher rate of speed. The butchered escape pods sped backward into their motherships' icons, the shattered ships of BOGEY ALPHA reassembled themselves, GAMMA began its acceleration run, and—

Callum slapped the console, freezing the playback, and his eyes narrowed as he peered at GAMMA's status bar. Then he turned and looked back up.

"Are you sure this really happened?" he asked. O'Hanraghty started to reply, but Murphy shook his head at him.

"Why do you ask?" he asked in return, and Callum frowned.

"Because the sim's wrong," he said, and pointed at the status bar. "They couldn't have accelerated like that!"

"No? Not even redlining their Fasset drives? They didn't accelerate very long, Callum. And burning out a drive node or two wouldn't have been a disaster even if it happened."

"Doesn't matter," Callum said. "That—" his index finger jabbed at the status bar again "—isn't possible, if all of this really happened forty years ago. They couldn't have built that kind of drive mass. Hell, we had the third-gen Fasset nodes in general fleet deployment before they did, and *we* couldn't have done it—I don't care how much we overloaded the nodes—for a good, what? Eight *years*, I think, after this is supposed to have happened."

"All the sim data's correct," O'Hanraghty said. "I know. I was there. I watched it happen."

"Oh." Callum's eyes darkened. "That must've been awful."

"You were there?" Lieutenant Commander Tanaka asked O'Hanraghty. "I didn't know that."

"I was." O'Hanraghty twitched a shrug. "A lot of people were. Some of us even came home again."

"You're right that they had to have the third-generation nodes to pull it off," Murphy interposed, looking at Callum. "And, no, we didn't see it in general deployment from them for quite a while afterward. Why do you think it took them so long to fit them across their entire fleet? They certainly used the tech effectively here."

"Um." Callum frowned, then shrugged. "That's a good question, Dad. The manufacture wasn't too difficult once the engineers figured out the tweaks. We rolled it out pretty quickly, not that long after this battle. I just graduated from Harriman with a degree in propulsion systems, by the way," he told Tanaka as she raised an eyebrow at him.

Tanaka did not look overly impressed. Justin P. Harriman Academy was one of the most prestigious ship systems academies in the Federation. It was also purely civilian and sent its graduates almost entirely into safely deferred merchant marine billets.

"Top of your class?" she asked.

"In the fifth that made the upper four possible," Callum said quickly. "But back to your question, Dad, I don't know why they didn't get it into general service. You're right—it sure as hell worked for them here! Probably not a *decisive* factor in this one, really. Even with the older nodes, they'd have been able to pull off the ambush. But it would've given them a definite edge over us everywhere at the time. The only other navy with something like this was the Rish."

The wardroom went very still.

"Oh, no," Tanaka said into that stillness. "Not this nonsense."

"Nonsense?" Callum hit the PLAY command and the tiny carriers of BOGEY GAMMA raced across the holo. "That doesn't look like nonsense to me, Ma'am."

"There are some voices within the Federation—" Tanaka said "—discredited, shrill voices—that believe the Rish have been assisting the League since the very beginning of the war."

"That's dumb," Callum said. "We've got a nonlethal aid treaty with the Sphere."

"We do," Ortiz agreed. "No military equipment or technology that could be repurposed for the war effort will be sold or exchanged between the Rish and any human world. It was the Lizards' idea."

"And we're supposed to just take the Rish's word for it?" O'Hanraghty said. "The Rish have restricted our carrying trade to only a few of their systems ever since the war started in the name of 'neutrality.' Everything we send them has to be transshipped from the officially designated points of entry to its final destination in Rishathan hulls. So we're not really in a position to monitor even their internal trade, much less their trade with anyone else, now are we?"

"We're rapidly approaching tinfoil-hat territory," Tanaka said. "The Rish are a peaceful species. Oh," she waved one hand, "I'll grant that they weren't *always* peaceful among themselves, but they've obviously learned a thing or two since then. They probably had to, if a bunch as belligerent as they used to be was going to survive to get off their homeworld in the first place! All of the Federation's trade with them is in luxury goods and foodstuffs, so they're certainly not trading war materials with *us*, and they've never attacked a human world. Which shouldn't surprise anyone. They've been good-faith negotiators from First Contact. Everyone knows that."

"A clan mother did take the head off our first ambassador," O'Hanraghty pointed out.

"Cultural misunderstanding." Tanaka waved it off. "The Sphere was as upset as we were after it happened, and they accepted full responsibility and offered reparations."

"I think I've heard some of this before," Callum said. "Darknet weirdos are always going on about the Rish as puppet masters, and how the Quarn have these little sucker things they put on people's heads to control their minds. It's lunatic ramblings."

"If this isn't Rishathan tech," Murphy asked the room, "then why did it take the League so long to deploy the new-generation systems across their fleet?"

Tanaka opened her mouth to speak, but then closed it again.

"Callum?" O'Hanraghty asked.

"I don't know," the young officer said. "Maybe this was a

shakedown cruise and there was some flaw in the components, an engineering fault we don't know about? Maybe they had to go back to the drawing board?"

"Reasonable," Murphy said.

"Federation and League tech have been at near parity for most of the war," Ortiz said. "We're generally a little better than they are, but it seems like every time we inch ahead and they might be on the ropes—or headed that way—they always catch up just in the nick of time. Or even pull ahead a bit."

"And what are you implying?" Tanaka asked. "It's not like we can win a battle on the front line and be in orbit around Anyang dictating terms the next morning. It's months of travel from the disputed systems to the Core Worlds. Applies to us and them. No one's managed a strategic breakthrough since the war began, and even when one of us does score a lopsided victory, pushing on to the next major system means fighting through whatever defenses they have in place. They have time to react to our wins and bring new tech to the fight. We've got the same." She shrugged. "Both sides have a defense in depth."

"Then what're we fighting for, if we can't win?" Callum asked. "Even if the battles in the Beta Cygni Sector go our way, what'll change? What did *this*—" he waved one hand at the holo unit "—change? It's like it didn't even count!"

"Really?" O'Hanraghty looked at him. "None of this rang any bells?" It was his turn to gesture at the holo. "You don't know who died here?"

"Not off the top of my head, no," Callum said with an impatient shrug.

"Task Group Two's CO," Murphy said softly. "Your grandfather."

The wardroom was suddenly silent, and the rear admiral looked at his son.

"I was seven at the time. Studying this battle became very important to me," Murphy said.

"Oh." Callum looked away in shame.

"My father and six thousand six hundred and ninety-five other spacers died at the Brin Gap. And when the rest of the League's Ninth Fleet followed it up, we lost another fourteen thousand spacers and they blew past us into the Brin System—that's why we call this the Battle of the Brin Gap, by the way—and punched out the system fortifications. Then they hit the colony domes with a K-strike. Another six hundred thousand gone. That's why we keep fighting, Callum. Because the League are butchers. There is no live and let live with them. Not with their current regime."

"Not that our hands are clean," Ortiz said, looking at Murphy respectfully. "For shared totals of civilians killed, we're about even, aren't we, Sir?"

"Truth is only the first casualty of war," Murphy said. "Innocence is the second." He shook his head. "I've never had to deal with a population that's—What does the Oval call it, Harry?"

"'Out of compliance,'" O'Hanraghty supplied.

"Right." Murphy nodded. "I can't say I'm unhappy that I *haven't* had to deal with it, and at least I doubt that will be one of our issues during our time in New Dublin."

"The Oval has Standing Order 15," Tanaka said. "I don't care for it, but it's there."

"There are only *fourteen* standing orders," Callum said.

"Fifteen only applies to ships under combat orders," Murphy said. "Any human population over fifty thousand is to be . . . neutralized if it doesn't surrender as soon as it's summoned to do so. It was issued after the League's K-strikes on Aggamar killed two million people. Again, I doubt it will be a factor for us."

"But—"

"We're three days out from Jalal, Callum," O'Hanraghty interrupted. "Have you finished that intake assignment I gave you?"

"No," Callum said. "I was running around the ship and—"

"And that's your excuse?" O'Hanraghty's eyebrows rose. "It's due before midnight, I believe."

Callum looked at him for a moment, then nodded curtly and stood.

"Excuse me, Sir," he said to Murphy, and hurried out of the wardroom without another glance at the chief of staff.

Mirwani, Ortiz, and Tanaka left a few minutes later. Lowe followed them, with a courteous nod to Murphy, and O'Hanraghty settled back into the chair Callum had left with a refreshed glass.

"Tanaka's not with us," he said. "She wasn't my choice to be on the staff."

"Nor mine." Murphy stretched. "She's a Yang loyalist, and that's who she'll report to. But she's logistics. Not a pivotal part of the plan."

"Callum's going to take some time." The chief of staff finished his drink, then popped a Teetotaler pill to kill the alcohol's effects in a few minutes. "But he's smart enough to see reason."

"Just make sure there's no video of him tapping the launcher mounts." Murphy shook his head. "Then give him a gentle talking to about delivering me the lube."

"I can't believe he fell for that old trick, either." O'Hanraghty picked up the tube and juggled it like a pen as he made for the board room door.

"I'm sorry I accused you of cheating," Murphy said. "Have to keep up appearances."

"You know I didn't cheat," O'Hanraghty said, "and I know you didn't let me win. Better luck next time, Sir."

He stepped through the door, and Murphy smiled after him.

CHAPTER EIGHT

IT WAS A WARM DAY FOR A CRANN BETHADH WINTER.

Cormag Dewar stood on the Tara City sidewalk, outside the row of concrete bollards that surrounded the New Dublin System's capitol building. The top of the capitol's dome was lost to the surrounding fog. Even the blinking beacon at its top to ward off aircraft in the bad weather was little more than a dim, pulsing glow from ground level.

He brushed beads of moisture off his uniform's long coat. Its pale green melded into the surrounding fog, but the golden stars of his rank marked him out from the bodyguards around him.

The tap of a cane sounded behind him, and he turned around as a slightly stooped elderly man emerged from the gray and raised the tip of the cane in his right hand in greeting. Alan Tolmach's long, thin hair hung limply down past his chin, and the monocle of an inexpensive, external prosthesis over one eye was attached to the side of his head by a wire.

"So, are the rumors true?" Dewar asked, joining Tolmach as the older man started down the sidewalk, away from the capitol. The uniformed bodyguards formed a loose perimeter around them, while more of Dewar's security in civilian garb walked ahead, invisible in the fog.

"You know damn well they are," Tolmach replied. "Why even ask?"

"Because I want to know if Governor Babikov finally admitted it to you."

"He did, I'll have you know."

The older man stopped and shook moisture from his monocle, and Dewar suppressed a familiar surge of affectionate exasperation. Tolmach was the System President, for God's sake, and the New Dublin System would have replaced the crappy prosthesis in a heartbeat...if he'd let it. But he wouldn't. Not until every war vet could have equally good medical care, anyway, and that wasn't going to—

"We have a new federally appointed leader on the way," Tolmach resumed, interrupting the general's well-worn thought as he plugged the monocle back in. "Babikov's tenure ends as soon as the new guy arrives. Should be just a few weeks."

"The standard is at least three months' notice," Dewar pointed out. "And they're *supposed* to bring in a new military commander with local consent, not by federal decree."

"And since when has the Federation cared about the finer points of its own laws, eh?" Tolmach reset the monocle and shuffled forward. "We protest the replacement, and Old Terra and the Oval will just tell us that the state of emergency supersedes the finer points of the Constitution, etc., etc. Why are you being so salty on such a fine morning as this?"

"Who is it? What Heart World ninny do Olympia and the Oval plan to install to lord over us this time?" Dewar asked.

"Spoiled." Tolmach gave the other man's shin a gentle whack with his cane. "You're spoiled. You're worried the new boss won't give you the same freedom Babikov did as chief of the Civil Defense Force."

"No. Well...maybe a little. I'm more irked that I don't know who the fop is. None of my people in Babikov's staff could get me a name."

"Spying on the governor?" The older man said shook his head. "Tsk, tsk."

"Hypocrite."

"The name is Murphy," Tolmach said. "Terrence Murphy."

Dewar came to a sudden stop. Tolmach kept walking.

"Wait. What? Who's Terrence Murphy?" Dewar touched an ear and repeated the name to an agent at the other end of the line.

"Just because I'm old enough to actually remember Henrik

Murphy and you're not doesn't give you an excuse to not know the Father of the Federation Navy's last name," Tolmach said over his shoulder. "That line of Murphys. This one was in Survey, though."

"Oh, no." Dewar caught up with him, rubbing a temple with his fingers.

"And fought with distinction at a somewhat noticeable fight at Steelman's Star," Tolmach continued. "No, he wasn't in command when the shooting started, but he did take over when his CO was killed, and he managed to win a fight the League had in the bag. So it's not all bad. And...he's bringing a task force with him."

"What? The fighting's in Beta Cygni. What do we need with a task—" Dewar broke off, his mind racing, and his eyes narrowed. "Is this an occupation force?"

"Settle down, boy." Tolmach shook his head. "Regular redistribution of force. We get into a good scrum with the butchers, and they're liable to try to find a soft underbelly to kick. And," he conceded, "the upgrades to the yards might make us a mite more attractive as the belly in question. I doubt it's any more than that. The Oval's changed up where we keep the reserves before, you know, and they'll keep doing it. Don't you remember when you caught them at Far Star?"

"I'd forget that day if I could." Dewar grimaced. "This means more ships in orbit. Spacers on shore leave. There's a pain in the ass I don't want. They'll be after our girls and—"

He broke off and touched his unobtrusive earbud again.

"Got the file on Murphy," he announced. "Married into the Thakores...but they've got a son to take over that business. Murphy's just out here to punch his ticket, isn't he?"

"That was Babikov's MO, wasn't it? Although our current governor did extend his stay for many more years than usual." Tolmach gripped his right forearm with his left hand.

"He stayed on because of his pool of secretaries, not because he loved Crann Bethadh," Dewar said, eyeing the other man's hand. "You all right? Moira will tan my hide if I let you stay out in the *draich* too long."

"You tell my daughter I'm just fine," Tolmach said, pressing his left thumb into his sleeve. "It's just the nerve shunt acting up again. Have to reset it a couple of times a day or—Ah, shit."

His right hand popped off his arm and splatted into a puddle, the cane twisting in its grip.

"I'll get it." Dewar thrust a foot under the wood and flicked it up to catch. Then he pressed the jack on the hand's wrist into the housing on Tolmach's arm and locked it in with a twist.

"Showing off your unearned youth, are ye?" Tolmach rapped the cane tip against the ground.

"Age happens to the best of us and to the rest of us," Dewar said. "And leaving parts of yourself on Isonzo wasn't your idea, is my guess."

Of course, refusing to use your position to replace them with parts that actually work just because none of the other wounded vets can do the same is your idea, isn't it? The general's expression gave no sign of his thoughts. He knew exactly how Tolmach would have reacted if he'd said it out loud.

"Now you're bragging about three tours and not a scratch, you bastard." Tolmach crossed the street to a rock-and-iron fence. A few rows of gravestones were visible in the morning fog beyond it.

"Murphy's a fop." Dewar joined Tolmach as they watched the graveyard grow more and more visible as the fog burned away. "Another Heart Worlder here to make sure we pay the blood tithe and our taxes. He'll leave with a chest full of medals he didn't earn and go home to play the game with the Five Hundred and pretend he's some sort of conquering hero. Same as it ever was."

"Same as it ever was," Tolmach agreed. "But you keep your eye on him. He'll be an empty suit to leave us to our own devices or I, as New Dublin's President, and you, as her system militia commander, will make his time as unpleasant as possible. And if that doesn't work...accidents do happen."

"They do, indeed."

Dewar crossed himself as golden sunlight broke through and spilled across the graves.

CHAPTER NINE

"SUBLIGHT IN FIVE MINUTES," THE ASTROGATOR WARNED, AND Murphy nodded.

The admiral sat in his command chair on *Ishtar*'s flag bridge, watching Captain Lowe and his bridge crew on the main display as they went about the transition from wormhole space back into normal space. Faster than light carriers like *Ishtar* had plenty of internal volume, and some of that space was used to provide both a well-appointed combat information center and a comfortable flag bridge. Captain Lowe had invited Murphy to watch the current maneuver from *Ishtar*'s command deck, instead, and Murphy had appreciated the courtesy. Lowe was under no obligation to issue the invitation—he was *Ishtar*'s commanding officer, not Terrence Murphy—but Murphy had no desire to step on his flag captain's toes, and so he had declined the offer.

In some ways, the flag bridge was an even better vantage point, anyway, because its displays were configured in tactical mode, watching a three hundred sixty-degree sphere around the ship. Not that there was an enormous amount to *see* at the moment.

Ishtar and her sisters had flipped and begun decelerating just over fifteen minutes ago. At the moment, their velocity—or, rather, their *apparent* velocity, by the standards of the rest of the universe—was a tad under six hundred times the speed of light and dropping rapidly as they decelerated at approximately twelve hundred gravities, but no one would have guessed it from the quiet efficiency of the FTLC's bridge.

It was one of the ironies of naval service that the sublight parasites which did all the fighting were fuel-limited, had a maximum sustainable acceleration of only twenty gravities—0.19 KPS^2—and that anything over a couple of gees was punished by the crushing grip of acceleration, whereas the enormous FTL carriers, accelerating or decelerating at eight hundred times that rate, required no reaction mass and actually needed spin sections to provide their personnel with a sense of gravity.

The Fasset drive, the key to interstellar travel, functioned by creating a modest-sized black hole...and falling into it. The exact mechanism was just a tad more complicated than that, but the analogy worked for a practical spacer. What actually happened was that the black hole was generated at the far end of a rigid but immaterial line of force—known as a Zadroga conduit after Lena Zadroga, Cesar Fasset's research partner—projected from the drive fan at the very front of the ship's hull. As long as that was all it did, nothing much happened. But if the Zadroga conduit collapsed, the ship was suddenly subject to the enormous gravitational field of its own black hole. It fell into it, accelerating at a very high rate, until it hit the *second*, permanent, and much shorter Zadroga conduit, which halted its fall. At which point the primary conduit reestablished itself, distancing the ship from the black hole once again, and the entire process repeated.

It all happened very, very quickly, and no one liked to think about what might happen if the second conduit failed. Fortunately, that never happened. Or, at least, no one it *had* happened to had come back to report on it.

A starship's maximum acceleration rate was dependent upon both the mass of its black hole, which governed the maximum possible acceleration, and the repetition rate and length of its Zadroga conduits, which governed the time it actually spent accelerating. But the entire time that it was under acceleration, it was effectively in a state of freefall into the Fasset drive's massive gravity well and its hull—and any parasites riding its racks—were in zero-gravity. Thus the need for crew quarters' spin sections far larger than an FTLC's organic crew might require. Most parasite personnel preferred to bunk aboard their own ships in the comfort of free fall, but they spent as much time as they could aboard their FTL motherships where they could function under the comfortable 9.8 meters-per-second gravity in which they had evolved.

It was fortunate that a *Marduk*-class FTLC's 4.3-kilometer length and 286-meter beam provided ample length and diameter for very *large* spin sections.

As the ancient scientist Einstein had postulated, it was impossible for any object in normal space to exceed the speed of light. What Einstein hadn't allowed for was a ship which could accelerate to *ninety-nine percent* of the speed of light very, very quickly with the equivalent of a small star stuck onto its nose to distort the space ahead of it.

The approach to the light barrier was spectacular as aberration and the Doppler effect took charge. The ever-contracting starbow drew farther and farther ahead, vanishing into the blind spot created by the Fasset drive, while a ship sped onward through the abyss. Until the transition to superlight chopped off even that like an ax. Then there was only wormhole space—no longer black, neither light nor dark, no stars, no moons, but simply nothing at all. An *absence* which no one cared to look at, and which actually sent some unfortunates into uncontrollable hysteria if they gazed upon it too long. And once it crossed that crucial threshold, a ship broke through into a subcontinuum where the rules of physics acquired some very strange subclauses.

For starters, the effective speed of light in wormhole space was far greater than in normal space, yet the maximum attainable velocity was limited by the balance between the relativistic mass of the starship and the rest—*not* the relativistic—mass of its Fasset drive's black hole. The astrophysicists still hadn't figured out precisely why that was, but they'd provided the math to describe it and the engineers had built the hardware to make it possible.

One consequence of the relationship between the starship's and its black hole's mass was that continuous acceleration eventually stopped increasing velocity and simply held it constant. Another was that reducing acceleration was the equivalent of *decelerating* on an ever steeper gradient. It was impossible to break back out of wormhole space and into normal space without actually decelerating; at some point, reduced acceleration simply equalized at a lower apparent supralight velocity. But if a ship actively decelerated, its velocity eventually dropped below the critical threshold once more and it erupted back into normal space at just under 0.99 *c*.

Wormholing was like crawling into a hole and pulling the hole in after you. Almost, at least.

For all intents and purposes a starship which had entered wormhole space was in its own private, vest-pocket universe. No one not in phase with it could interact with it in any way. But that didn't mean someone else couldn't crawl into the hole with it, because wormhole space was less a dimension than a frequency. If another ship could match relativistic velocity within fifteen or twenty percent, its wormhole space and yours were in phase. If the other fellow was a friend, that was fine. If he was an enemy, he could go right on trying to kill you. Fortunately, matching velocities that closely was extremely difficult unless the ships involved—like *Ishtar* and her consorts—actively cooperated.

Wormhole space was a handy way to cross the light-years, but it had a few military shortcomings. For one thing, any ship traveling faster than light ran blind. Gravitic detectors in normal space could detect the mammoth gravitational anomaly of a supralight ship at varying ranges—up to four or five light-months, for a really fast mover—but no one could see *out* of wormhole space into normal space. That was why it was advisable to make damned sure of course and turnover time before you went in, because you couldn't make any astrogation sightings for course corrections in transit.

Of course, a starship didn't have to accelerate into wormhole space. The Fasset drive operated just fine in normal space, too, and Terrence Murphy, like every professional naval officer, longed for the ability to incorporate it into a genuine warship. Unfortunately, it was entirely too big and the engineering constraints of the Zadroga conduits required too much hull length. Which meant they cost too much and represented too big a chunk of industrial output and military infrastructure to be wasted as warships. That same length was what allowed them to mount parasite racks, however, and each of *Ishtar*'s was capable of carrying a single ship up to thirteen hundred meters in length. No one actually built sublight warships that large, however, so the racks were normally configured to carry multiple, smaller ships.

In addition to their parasites, ships like *Ishtar* generally carried hefty missile armaments, but the majority of their magazine space was filled with counter-missiles. They were also well-equipped with point defense, while their drone racks carried heavy loads of missile-defense platforms. And if they found themselves under fire with parasites on the racks and weren't able to deploy them—because they were withdrawing under fire, for instance—at least some of the parasites' weapons could be brought to bear, as well, although that could be an iffy proposition under the wrong circumstances.

Although, now that Murphy thought about it, it was hard to imagine an instance in which letting the parasites engage from the rack could happen under the *right* circumstances.

"And sublight . . . now," the astrogator announced, and the FTLCs blinked abruptly into existence 2.3 billion kilometers from the Jalal System's primary.

Their astrogation had been spot on, Murphy noted with a certain satisfaction. They were precisely where they were supposed to be on exactly the right heading. At a shade under 297,000 KPS, it would take them over four and a half hours to decelerate to rest relative to Jalal Station, their destination in orbit around the system's sole more or less habitable planet. At the moment, thanks to relativity, *Ishtar*'s onboard time was moving eighty-six percent slower than that of the universe around them. That was another of the interesting little quirks of interstellar travel. By the clocks of the universe in general, TF 1705 had spent eight weeks travelling the 138 LY to Jalal; by *Ishtar*'s clock, the trip had taken only a bit over one. But in another twenty-five minutes the FTLC would be down to 120,000 KPS, a mere forty percent of light-speed, and the time differential would have dropped to a negligible eight percent.

He touched the comm key.

"Bridge," Lowe's voice responded.

"My compliments to Commander Creuzburg, Captain. That was a well-executed piece of astrogation."

"Thank you, Admiral," Lowe said. "I'll pass that on to him."

"Murphy, clear," Murphy said. He released the key and sat back, gazing at the distant pinprick of the system primary. They were almost as far from it as Neptune was from Sol, so there wasn't very much to see. But the rest of his task force was waiting for him in orbit around that tiny speck of a star, and he felt his mind reaching out toward the challenge.

✧　　✧　　✧

O'Hanraghty frowned and tapped a query into one of the touchscreens.

Ishtar was still 17.3 LM—and more than ninety minutes—short of Jalal Station, with her velocity down to "only" 98,850 KPS. That was still much too far for any convenient two-way conversation, but the station's nav beacons and general "notice to spacers" messages were on auto-repeat, and the flagship's comm section had been relaying them to the flag bridge for several minutes now.

O'Hanraghty's frown deepened, and Murphy raised an eyebrow at the chief of staff.

"A problem, Harry?"

"Just…an anomaly, Sir."

O'Hanraghty tapped the screen again and a schematic of Jalal Station's central spindle and triple surrounding rings appeared on the main display, surrounded by a spangle of ship icons. As he swiped a cursor over the icons, each of them obediently displayed its transponder code.

"We've got the rest of our assigned parasites right here," O'Hanraghty said, highlighting the icons of three battleships, two strikecarriers, three heavy cruisers, and one lowly destroyer.

Added to the ships already on the FTLCs' racks, it made an impressive force, Murphy thought. Certainly adequate to garrison New Dublin. But then O'Hanraghty flipped the cursor across another small group on the display sidebar and the admiral's eyes narrowed.

"*Burgoyne*?" he said. "Isn't *Burgoyne* assigned to BatRon Seven-Oh-Two out at Scotia?"

"Yes, Sir," Commander Mirwani replied. As Murphy's ops officer, he'd been checking the same lists. "As a matter of fact, there are a couple of other ships from the Seven-Oh-Two."

Murphy exchanged a glance with O'Hanraghty, then looked at Tanaka.

"I hope they're not going to slow us down in the logistics queue," he said. "The station's only got so much capacity, and we have a timetable to keep."

"I'm sure we'll be okay, Sir," Tanaka replied.

"You're probably right, but go ahead and check now," Murphy said. "Best foot forward and all that, yes?"

"Aye, aye, Sir," Tanaka said with a slightly annoyed expression and turned to her comm.

"Something wrong, Admiral?" Callum asked quietly.

"Nothing," Murphy said, tapping his fingertips against his armrest. "I'm sure it's nothing."

✧ ✧ ✧

The door alarm woke him.

It wasn't the normal melodious chime. It was the raucous "wake-you-from-the-dead" override alarm, and someone was obviously leaning on it hard.

Captain Yance Drebin sat up, his head swimming from what was either the beginning of a hangover or the tail end of his night bar-hopping on Jalal Station.

"What the hell?" he mumbled.

The ear-splitting racket continued, and he dragged himself off the couch and threw on a uniform jacket. He crossed his small suite's vestibule and pressed the panel beside the door. It slid open, and white light from the passageway outside his quarters stung his eyes.

"What the—" he began to repeat in an irate tone, then stopped.

A very tall man he'd never seen before took his thumb from the door alarm button. He wore a dress uniform, and the twin stars of a rear admiral glittered in the light. A pair of bruisers and a mousy-looking commander stood behind him.

"Good evening!"

The admiral's tone was entirely too cheerful, and he stepped forward. Drebin found himself involuntarily stepping back from the bigger man's presence. Somehow, the admiral and his escort were inside his quarters, and the door closed behind them. One of his uninvited visitors hit the light switch, and Drebin blinked. At least it wasn't as bright as the light in the passage.

"Captain Drebin?" the admiral continued. "From Scotia? Do hope I have the right quarters."

"Who are you? And what're you doing in my quarters...Sir? Rank and all, but there's still protocol."

Drebin turned around to reach for the glass he'd left on the counter with a half finger of gin, but the admiral poked it and sent it skidding out of his reach.

"You weren't answering your comms," the intruder said. He picked up an earpiece from beside the glass and wiggled it. "I didn't want to ask the station master to do an emergency override on your doorlock, though. Seemed a bit unnecessary."

"For *what*, exactly? And I already asked who you are. Sir."

Drebin smacked his lips over fuzzy teeth, not caring what his breath smelled like to the interloper.

"Murphy," the admiral said. "Terrence Murphy. And I read your initial report on the League attack on Inverness. I have a few questions about it."

"Now just a goddamn minute." Drebin raised a finger. "Who the hell do you think you are that you can—"

One of the bruisers, a hulking sergeant major with a crooked nose who was a centimeter or so taller than even the admiral, put one hand on Drebin's shoulder and forced him into a chair.

"A force of warships entered the system you were assigned to as governor general," Admiral Murphy continued, as if Drebin had never spoken. "You ordered a strategic withdrawal, and then—"

"The Leaguies were too strong," Drebin interrupted with what might have been an edge of fear. "Scotia is a Level E system. If faced with an overwhelming force, then the Fokaides Directive applies. Give ground and retain combat power."

"Give ground? Give...ground." Murphy said the words as if they stung his tongue, the corner of his mouth twitched. "But of course. Level E. So then you and your ships—"

"We pulled back and monitored the League's attack. Waited until they wormholed out on a vector to their territory," Drebin said. "Then withdrew here for further instructions. It's not like I had any kind of choice. If we'd stayed and fought, the League would've destroyed my entire command and still fragged the colony. This way, the Seven-Oh-Two lives to fight another day. I did what I had to do. What my orders *required* me to do."

"Destroyed your entire command. With four battle cruisers and three heavy cruisers." Murphy gazed at him for a moment, then shrugged. "You are adept at following your orders, Drebin. No question of that. But what about survivors?"

"Survivors?"

Murphy held out a hand, and the mousy commander, whose name plate said "ORTIZ," handed him a sheet of paper. It was a printed, computer-generated map of both hemispheres of Inverness, Drebin realized. The locations of K-strikes and population centers had been mapped out with bright icons. Now where the hell had they gotten—?

Carson. His exec's—his good old, reliable, *dependable* exec's— name flashed through his brain. She was the one who'd deployed the recon drones before *Ophion* pulled them out. Who else had she given—?

"The main city took a beating, but the outlying towns were spared direct hits," Murphy interrupted that thought. "The League did scratch every power station, bridge, port, and other major infrastructure target. Including the orbital refineries." He grimaced. "Doubt there were any survivors from that. But there had to be others, Captain. So, what about them?"

"We . . . we couldn't go back," Drebin said. "The Leaguies have been known to leave mines after a raid. And I had *Ophion* to worry about. Had to get her out of there before they figured out they'd missed her and came back to clean up. Besides, I had to get here and warn—"

"It's winter for most of the survivors, isn't it?" Murphy asked. "I imagine they're waiting for help."

"I'm sure they are," Drebin said, watching Murphy warily. "But *Ophion* was under priority orders to pick up a parasite group in Trevor. She'd already been delayed by what happened in Scotia, so the station expedited her departure. And with her gone, there's not a Fasset drive-capable ship that could get a rescue effort there in time to do any good. It's pointless."

"Ah, that's where you're wrong," Murphy said. "The *Ishtar*'s here, along with *Ereshkigal* and *Gilgamesh*. We can make it back to Scotia just as quickly as you—I mean *Ophion*—made the run here. And *Calcutta*'s repairs will be completed very shortly, so she'll be available in the next few days, as well."

"Don't let me keep you waiting." Drebin shrugged.

"Well, there's the thing," Murphy said. "With your extensive knowledge of the system, we'll need you to come with us. You and your squadron."

"What? No way. The Seven-Oh-Two falls under Third Fleet out of—"

"Actually, Captain," Commander Ortiz interrupted and tossed a small packet into Drebin's lap. "As a flag grade officer, Admiral Murphy can requisition functional and ready naval vessels to respond to humanitarian crises as he sees fit. Now that you've confirmed that Scotia is indeed in a state of crisis . . ."

It was Ortiz's turn to shrug, and Drebin stared at him in shock until Murphy's crisp voice jerked his eyes back to the admiral.

"Recall your crews from shore leave and be prepared to dock with my transport group in the next six hours."

"But—" Drebin paged through the orders. "But we just arrived, and—"

"Have I introduced Sergeant Major Logan?" Murphy gave the massively muscled man a pat on the arm. "He's part of my Hoplon detachment. Should I leave him here to make sure you're locked into a carrier rack within the next six hours?"

Logan leaned over slightly and spat tobacco juice at a wastebasket. Most of it missed.

"I only ask because you have your lawful orders in hand and you've received instructions," Murphy continued. "No risk of your missing movement, correct? Out here in this declared conflict system."

That sobered Drebin up immediately. Missing movement orders in a declared conflict system—in the face of the enemy—was a capital offense.

"My squadron will be ready. Sir," he said.

"Wonderful." Murphy smiled. "We'll get this all settled as soon as we can. Welcome aboard!"

The Sanctuary Saloon on Jalal Station pulsed with music and noise as Callum Murphy stepped inside. A large circular bar with robot tenders on rails served spacers and Marines, mostly male and mostly out of uniform regulations with their collars open and one corner of their tunic fronts unsealed.

Holo projections of a band dressed up as Old Earth prospectors and playing instruments with colored lights for strings and rainbow hues rising from the notes gave the place an almost psychedelic air. Several levels of rooms formed a cylinder over the bar, and laughter and shouts from the upper levels promised more entertainment.

The place smelled of body odor and spilled alcohol, and Callum hesitated before moving up to the bar. He wondered if there was another establishment nearby more to his liking, but a robo-tender mixing a drink for an already drunk spacer convinced him he might as well not be parched while he went looking for another spot.

"A starlight," he said, rapping his knuckles on an order pad. He got a sad-faced symbol in return.

"No genever," a robot squawked as it rolled past him. "We have gin."

"I'd be insulted, but you aren't to blame for your programming," Callum muttered. He frowned and tapped in another drink…and got the same error message.

"Don't waste your money," a woman said into his ear from behind him. She smelled of cheap perfume with a hint of antiseptic. "It's all watered down, and the only thing you'll get is a mean hangover."

She wore a dermal layer that gave her a look of all gold with blue highlights. Sea green hair hung almost to her shoulder on one side of her head; on the other side, a patch of tattoos depicting intimate acts stretched around her shaved scalp from her temple to behind her ear.

"Better spent on an experience, anyway." She smiled. "And the memory. You just arrived?"

Callum glanced down at her skimpy attire, counterintelligence warnings from the pre-shore leave briefing fresh in his mind.

"Off the *Ishtar* group, is my guess." She waggled her fingertips at the uniform patch on his left shoulder. "All the boys from the Seven-Oh-Two and the *Orcas* have been here for a bit, and you look positively fresh."

"Whiskey sour?" Callum asked as a robot came back around. It froze, then spun around to the bottle rack and prepared the drink.

"I'm Cherry," she said, "and I'm thirsty, too."

"Beat it." Corporal Faeran materialized out of the crowd like a tattooed genie and wedged herself between the two of them. "He's just about to leave."

"He's got more rank than you," Cherry sneered, "and you don't look like his type."

"A broken nose will cut into your night's take," Faeran said. "Now piss off before I stop asking you nicely."

"Bitch." Cherry snatched her clutch from the bar and made for the stairs.

"Corporal, I wasn't going to—" Callum took a quick sip from his drink.

"No, things like that are too base for a highborn like you," the Hoplon said. "Recall's in effect, though. Captain O'Hanraghty sent me to get you."

"Recall?" Callum glanced at the smart screen built into his sleeve. "I don't see an alert."

"Verbal condition. Admiral's order." She shrugged and swiped a hand at an abandoned glass. It went over the edge of the bar, but a robo-tender zipped over and caught it before it could break.

"A standard, tin can!" she snapped.

The robot placed a can with an off-white label in front of her. She cracked it open with one hand, watching the crowded saloon with alert yet disinterested eyes.

"Is this some sort of a joke?" Callum rolled his eyes. "Shore leave for all of...thirty-seven minutes? The Admiral worried his crews will get into trouble that fast?"

"Don't know." Faeran put the can to her lips, tilted her head back, and chugged the entire drink before slamming the empty back down. "Don't care."

"And you're not leaving without me." Callum took a longer slip, then held the drink up to a light over the bar. "She was right—it is watered down. Shame."

"Come on." Faeran jerked a thumb toward the door. "It's about to get rough in here."

Callum paid for both their drinks with a swipe of his palm and they made for the door. Cherry blew him a kiss as they left.

Ding ding.

Callum heard the alert chime from inside the saloon and glanced down at his forearm screen. Still nothing, but a roar of anger and expletives rose behind them and there was a sudden rush to the bar as patrons shouted last-minute orders at the robo-tenders.

"Guess they *are* recalling everyone," he said. "We under attack?"

"Leaguies would need most of their fleet to take Jalal," Faeran said. "Nah. But the boss got a burr in his boot about something. So now we get to jump through our ass. Same as it ever was."

"Not going to be a popular decision, is it?"

"Which is why I had to get you out of there before some drunk decided to take out his frustration on a zero like you." She shrugged. "Least I got a beer out of it."

"Much appreciated." Callum climbed a metal staircase to the tube station that would deliver them back to *Ishtar*. "Can't say I get why this is happening. The Admiral's always been a bit more...happy-go-lucky, shall we say. In my experience."

"Probably the chief of staff," the medic said. "O'Hanraghty's a right bastard. Got us drilling aboard ship when we could be sleeping. At least my team'll be sharp after this tour."

Glass shattered as a stool went through one of the saloon's windows.

"Damn, shore leave is a bit more serious than I'd imagined," Callum said, looking down from the platform as they waited for a tube to slow down for them. Faeran leaned back against the railing, elbows propped up beside her, and shrugged.

"You spend a tour in the red zone," she said, "and make it out alive and uninjured. Then you come to a pleasure stop like Jalal with a full bank account and zero alcohol tolerance. Steam needs to get blown off. Now we get to carry all that with us to New Dublin . . . or wherever."

"Thank you," Callum said.

She raised an eyebrow at him, and he shook his head as a table sailed through another window to join the stool in the street in front of the saloon.

"For getting me out of there," he amplified, and she grimaced.

"Easier to do it before the news hits than drag your bloody carcass out after." She shrugged again.

A tube slowed to a stop and the doors slid open.

"Where's the shore patrol?" Callum asked, pausing half in and half out, still looking back at the brewing riot.

"They don't care." Faeran pushed him into a seat. "Property damage gets docked against pay. So long as no one assaults anybody, or starts a fire, it don't matter."

CHAPTER TEN

"SHE'S NOT GOING TO MAKE US WAIT."

Third Admiral Than Qiang glanced at his chief of staff, Su Zhihao. The younger man's long goatee showed strands of gray, at odds with his fit physique and the relatively light rack of medals on his dress uniform.

And speaking of medals...

Than rolled his left shoulder to move a fastener caught on his undershirt and tugged at the back of his jacket. The weight of so many awards tended to sag after too long. The two men stood alone in the control room overlooking a shuttle bay open to vacuum. Shanhaiguan, a fortress world on the edge of League space, hung in the distance.

Than didn't like to wear his entire dress uniform unless it was necessary, but when the future president of the Terran League wanted ceremony... the whole panoply *became* necessary.

"No, she won't keep us waiting," he said, and leaned forward to look down at the assemblage of politicians, news crews, and a full brass band. The band was flanked by ensigns holding red banners bearing the name of Fourth Admiral Xing in gold thread. "One does not keep inner Accord reps in suspense. Doesn't matter what you've done."

"Member Liu's put a good deal of effort into this little... announcement," Su said.

"The feeds need good news," Than replied. "The fight in Beta Cygni's a holding action and won't get any better. A victory... a new 'hero.'" He shrugged ever so slightly. "The people will embrace it."

"And vote for Liu's Eternal Forward faction over the moderates." Su fiddled with the tip of his goatee.

"My, my. You think the Accord would cater to such a low common denominator?" Than rubbed a growing headache from his temple and looked at his reflection off the glass. His crow's feet were getting longer, he noted.

"What's the butcher's bill from Xing's raid on Inverness? Eight hundred thousand?" the chief of staff asked.

"Less, from the K-strikes." Than leaned forward as the shuttle appeared outside the shuttle bay. Test notes from the band carried into the control room. "But she did it on a shoestring and without the loss of a single League spacer. You have to admit, she's got gall. Talent."

"Sure she does," Su said sourly. "You know that whole 'Operation Han Xin' of hers was just a stunt to get herself back in the limelight. The post she was in was a bit too quiet for someone like her."

"As I said, the newsfeeds need *good* news. She knows that." Than's tone was more serene than Su's. "I happen to agree with you that she came up with the entire idea primarily as a way to enhance her own career, but that doesn't make it pointless. Certainly not from a political perspective. She knows the game."

"She barely scratched a nothing colony that doesn't matter to the Heart Worlders." Su spat on the deck.

"Not 'barely.'" Than scratched his jawline. "She destroyed the orbital refineries—which actually had at least some genuine military value—and wrecked every power plant, dam, and critical infrastructure target on the planet. And the public doesn't need to be told it was a 'nothing colony.' In fact, I'm certain it won't be."

"I'll grant the refineries had *some* military value, Sir. But enough to justify risking a carrier strike group to take them out?"

"It's not just Scotia, and it's not just the physical destruction," Than said. "The Feds are going to have to worry that we'll hit additional lightly defended systems in the region, and that may suck some of their reinforcements away from Beta Cygni."

"And that's a *good* thing, Sir?"

"It is as far as anyone else—including her—knows," Than replied just a bit repressively. "And the fact that most of the colonists survived actually creates a bigger drain on their resources, because it means they have to mount a humanitarian response. Same theory as using a smaller landmine in ground combat. Kill a soldier with a big explosion, and that's the end of him. But blow off his foot, then two or three men will go out of the fight with him to get him back to a field hospital. He won't come back to the battle any more than he would have if you'd killed him, but this way he'll be a drain on their logistics. They'll have to treat him, move him back to safety, rehabilitate him.... Then he'll limp around as a civilian once he's discharged, casting a pall over the entire war effort."

"There's a reason Stalin sent his battle wounded to the gulags," Su said. "Old lesson, if you're not up on your historical tyrants."

"I know of him," Than said. "But the feeds will play up Xing's mercy in letting the Fed civilians live, when what she did was actually the cruelest thing possible."

"I don't follow," Su said.

"It's the dead of winter for the inhabited hemisphere on Inverness." Than clasped his hands behind his back, his expression bleak. "She's doomed them to a slow, cold death. The Federation will—probably—scramble to help, and they'll show up to a world that tore itself apart trying to survive. Kinder to K-Strike the entire place. Put them out of their misery in one go."

"Mercy killings? That doesn't sound like you, Sir. It's been almost twenty years since you won the Battle of Callao, but you've never led a raid on the Feds' civilians."

"The butcher's bill gets higher every day. Maybe I've been staring so long at the number I've started to become cynical. But bombing cities isn't much of a challenge," Than said. "Smashing the orbital installations was all Xing had to do to get her victory and her pat on the back from the Accord. What she did was cruelty for the sake of cruelty. I'll stay in the ship-to-ship fight...if the Accord will ever let me back to the front."

"Maybe Eternal Forward has a new darling," Su said. "They can make Xing the face of the war effort and we can get back to a proper fleet command." Than glanced at him, and he shrugged. "What, Sir? She's a good deal easier on the eyes than you are. No offense."

"That's a low bar to clear." Than sighed as the shuttle's forward ramp lowered and Fourth Admiral Xing came down it into the blare of horns and the opening bars of the League anthem.

He had to admit Su had a point about looks, he thought. Xing was tall, with bold eyebrows, dark eyes, raven's-wing hair done in a braid around her head, and a pistol hung low on one hip, like a gunfighter of legend. A troop of armored Marines followed her as she marched down to Liu and gave him a crisp salute.

"She's playing the part already," Su said. He shook his head as Xing and Liu shook hands. They were careful to do it slowly while the camera drones circled around them, recording the moment from several angles.

Than glanced at the clock and grimaced. It was time.

"She's no fool, Zhihao," he said, turning toward the door. "We can't forget that."

"Will the Accord give her the Combination?"

"That's what I'm afraid of." Than reached for the door switch. "The elections are later this year. Beta Cygni is still holding— barely—and the Accord's going to have to talk to the voters about something. It's turning into a perfect storm for her and Liu, and they're not ones to waste the opportunity. Come on. We can be late for Xing's reception...but not too late."

"And then the Fed commander turned tail without firing a shot!"

Xing's laugh filled the small compartment and Than pretended to laugh with the others. He'd heard the other admiral recount the "fight" over Inverness several times. She'd made minor changes to her narrative each time she regaled a different Accord member, testing parts for better reactions.

Liu laughed just as hard with each punch line. His small clique of Accord functionaries remained silent just behind him.

Liu, a dapper man of mixed heritage with a well-manicured coif of hair, clapped his hands twice, signaling the end of the reception. Military officers and politicians set down drinks and plates of finger food and meandered toward the exit.

"Not you, Than," Liu said. "We have something to discuss with our guest of honor."

Than nodded, keeping his face expressionless even as bile rose in his throat, and glanced at Su.

"Have the *Cai Shen* prep for departure, Zhihao. Use my codes to get the shipboard supplies topped off."

"Yes, Sir." Su gave Liu a polite smile as he hurried out.

One of Liu's hangers-on removed a silver case from inside her jacket and twisted the top. A low, teeth-grating whine filled the room.

"Forgive the pitch." Liu touched an ear. "I had the room scanned for bugs before we arrived, but we can't be too careful."

"What's there to discuss that warrants so much secrecy?" Xing moved a strand of sable hair from her face.

"The Accord is very pleased with your track record," Liu told her. "Successful commands from corvettes up to battleships. Victorious in every engagement with the Feds. And no family attachments to anyone in Capitol Dome."

"My parents are factory workers." Xing shrugged. "Sometimes the apple falls from the tree and just keeps rolling."

"The Accord has authorized a new assignment for you," Liu said. "One that we expect you to do great things with."

"But can I get to Beta Cygni in time to turn the tide?" she asked, eyes flashing.

"Not the Liberation Fleet, or even Vanguard Command," Liu said.

"It isn't ready, Minister," Than said. "There have been construction setbacks, and we haven't even—"

"Thank you, Third Admiral," Liu said. "But it's been decided."

"You're not going to pull me off the line to oversee the shipyards around Hwando," Xing said. "That's a retirement command. Waste of my talents."

"She has no idea." Liu's eyebrows peaked. "I'm surprised."

"The project only works if the secrecy holds and—" Than stopped and shook his head. "I don't want to say it even here."

"Don't. The Combination's rules apply even to us when we're outside the system," Liu said, and turned back to the other admiral. "Xing, the League has been engaged in a long-term effort, one hidden away from the public's knowledge. We simply couldn't risk the Feds learning about it. We've built a force—a fleet not seen since even before the Battle of Callao. One that can bring the Federation to its knees and end the war."

Xing put her hands on her hips, her expression skeptical.

"And how is it I've never heard a single thing about this?"

"Security's been paramount. Some of the support structure is...drawn from outside the League." Liu swallowed hard. "And all personnel assigned to it came from planets devastated by the Federation. It will all make sense once you arrive at Bastion."

Xing's lips pressed into a thin line.

"I'm loyal to the Accord," she said. "I've done nothing but deliver you one victory after another, but you're going to...shunt me aside, aren't you?"

That was more than a bit of an exaggeration of her track record, Than thought. Not that he was surprised by the protest, especially after the way Liu had burnished her accomplishments for the feeds.

"This is no trick," he said aloud. "Not some gilded command post on the fringe. This has been in the works for decades, Xing. You'll be part of the final effort to win the war."

"Not just part of it," Liu piped up. "In command."

"She's what?" Surprise startled the question out of Than and his brow furrowed in confusion.

"*Second* Admiral Xing will command the entire effort." Liu reached to one of his minders and received a small, velvet-lined box. "Officially, she'll maintain her current rank and be on patrol against Fed incursions." He popped the box open and removed a rank insignia—a deep red star with an obsidian border. "And she'll stay there until such time as the new command, which we've designated Dragon Fleet, is ready to leave Bastion."

"I'm honored." She took the rank badge and ran a thumb over it. "But where is Bastion, exactly?"

"Than will take you there. He's to be your second-in-command." Liu smiled and both admirals turned to stare at him. "His experience, your tenacity—a match made in heaven."

"Sir," Than's jaw tightened for a moment, "the Bastion force—Dragon Fleet...We don't even have crews for the ships. How are we—"

"We have an ample pool of discharged veterans scattered across the League's worlds," Liu said. "The next draft lottery will be a bit larger than usual, to provide the recruits you need, and veteran spacers will be put back in uniform to provide more experienced personnel. One last push to win it all. We've been seeding the feeds with stories of noble sacrifice and eternal duty for months. Internal projections for disharmony are quite low."

"Was it going to be your command?" Xing asked Than.

"I'd . . . assumed," the older man said.

"There was quite a debate over this within the Accord." Liu adjusted his cuffs. "It was decided that defeating the Fed navy in battle wouldn't be enough to force an armistice. Not even a battle as decisive as your victory at Callao managed that, and it's unlikely another one like it would do so now. The Five Hundred who control their government don't care about the loss of blood. They care about the loss of treasure."

"You still mean to spill blood," Than pointed out.

"Semantics." Liu shrugged. "You will introduce Second Admiral Xing to the key individuals once you arrive at Bastion. She's to have the entire Combination. This is clear?"

"Clear . . . Sir," Than said.

"Then I'll return to Capitol Dome and arrange for the necessary manning. We expect the Dragon Fleet to be at full readiness in eight months."

"Or less," Xing said. "I'm sure I can find some lost efficiencies once I take full command."

"Or less," Liu acknowledged. "I'll leave you to it." He gave Than a pat on the shoulder and left.

"I'm honored." Xing gave the older officer a crocodile's smile. "I'll transfer my flag to *Cai Shen* and *Chen Qingzhi* can accompany your carriers with my squadron. How long to depart? Twelve hours?"

"If I may, Ma'am, your squadron's fusion drives got worked pretty hard during the raid on Scotia. Let the Shanhaiguan yards make sure of their tolerances before we ship out. It'll take another . . . eighteen hours. At most."

"Why dawdle? Just transfer the yard workers to *Chen Qingzhi* and they can make the repairs underway."

"Because any personnel below the rank of commander that set foot in Bastion are never allowed to leave. At least until Dragon Fleet is ready. If we take the trained crews from Shanhaiguan and they don't return, it will raise a number of questions we don't want asked . . . or answered."

"That serious." Xing nibbled the inside of her bottom lip for a moment. "A few more hours, then."

"Let's assume we're being watched by the Feds," Than said. "Act as normally as possible. It keeps them from snooping around."

"The Federation *should* be looking for me after what I did

to Inverness. But a bit of time out of the limelight will do well. Let my name circulate through the Heart Worlds. They'll know me by the time Dragon and I are ready. This fleet is truly as formidable as Liu suggested?"

"Ma'am, you have no idea."

Than stepped out of the elevator onto the 195th floor of the Todaeima Arcology.

He glanced up at the ceiling, covered by a holo filter that was meant to emulate blue skies, pleasant weather, and just at the right illumination to match the time of day. He could barely tell that he lived twenty levels down from the penthouse and beneath a dome nestled into an ancient impact crater on Shanhaiguan's outer moon.

Until one of the panels washed out with static before snapping back into normal function, that was.

He frowned up at it and made a mental note to comm the arcology's manager in person as the elevator door closed behind him. A diplomatic ass kicking about poor maintenance by a third admiral tended to get results. He should have done that sooner—*would* have done it sooner, if he'd realized it needed doing. But his visits to his family had been far too rare over the last couple of years. That was what happened when the Accord assigned an officer to a top secret project in a star system weeks of travel from everyone he loved, although he was far luckier than most personnel assigned to Astra. At least he did get to come home…occasionally.

He shook his head at the thought, then he checked his uniform—changed to less spectacular but far more comfortable tan shipboard utilities—and pressed his palm to a reader.

The opening door caught for a split second before it retracted all the way into the frame.

"Dad?" The question came from inside, along with the smell of fresh cooking.

"Better be me," Than said as he hung his cap on a hook. He toed off his boots and tightened a Velcro strap around each ankle. A boy in his early teens slid around a corner on his socks, and Than gave him a hug.

"Oof! I swear, Idrak, you've gotten taller since I saw you a few days ago," the third admiral said.

"Qiang? Set the table!" his wife called from the kitchen.

"Why didn't you volunteer for that?" Than ruffled Idrak's hair as the teen pulled away.

"Studying for exams."

The boy turned to leave, but Than grabbed him by the elbow as he spotted the green and red armband around his bicep. The look in his eyes was not one of approval.

"What?" Idrak said. "The Forward Party came to my school. I liked the presentation."

"What did I tell you—?" Than began, then stopped. "Let's just eat first," he said, and let the boy go as he stepped into the dining room, where an elderly man with an eyepatch sat reading a data slate.

"Uncle Rao." Than opened a china closet and pulled out plates and sets of chopsticks. He set a plate in front of the older man. "Uncle Rao?"

"Huh? Than! Didn't hear you." Rao removed an earpiece and fiddled with tiny dials. "Thought you were in space again."

Than kept setting the table until Rao put the earpiece back on. The older man tapped the side of his head, then the table, then gave a thumbs-up.

"Delayed to take on a new strike element," Than said then. "Where's your eye?"

"Damned thing itches. My real one works just fine." Rao tried to get up, struggling with a lame leg and arm. Than touched his shoulder and pushed him back into his seat.

"If you don't use the prosthetics, the nerve shunts decay," he said. "Makes it even harder to use the device when you need it." He set out small dishes and little ceramic stands to keep the chopstick tips off the table.

"And I'll still have to go all the way down to the center for recalibration every month. You know what a pain that is?" Rao slipped his data slate into a pocket.

"You can't sit here reading all day." Than looked over the setting and turned a dish so that the decoration lined up with the others.

"I'm halfway through the Tingle archives," Rao said. "You'd do well to appreciate the classics."

"'Classics.'" Than mimed air quotes.

"Who wants golden rice?" Than's wife, Cayha, walked in with

a steaming bowl of white rice and several small dishes of cooked and cubed meat swimming in sauce. She set the tray on the table and wiped her hands on an apron.

Than gave her a quick kiss. She leaned into it, then looked at him for a moment with a growing frown.

"What?" he asked.

"Nice of you to drop in, but a little more warning might have been nice. I'd have more than just the supplement ready for you."

"Because I'm not...here," he said. "I cut out a gap in my schedule and dumped everything on Su. Not that he minds. He enjoys the practice."

"Oh, so nothing's wrong?" She looked skeptical. "Because the last time you dropped by unannounced you were about to leave to spend nine months, fighting the Feds in the Apricum Sector."

Than felt Rao watching him.

"Nothing's wrong," he said, and gave her a thin smile. "Just decided to skip class a little before I head back out to Training Command."

Cayha's narrowed eyes told him she didn't buy it. But—

"You need to have a talk with your son," she said, then looked over her shoulder. "Boy! Kristina! Come eat."

"My sister's here?" Than sat at the head of the table, his mouth watering at the smell.

"Transit barracks were full again...according to her," his wife said, moving to the foot of the table.

Idrak sat down next to Rao and rubbed his palms together.

"Nutritionally fortified rice product, vat-grown protein cubes, and curry sauce from powder," he said. "Again. And it's still yummy."

"Spend a couple of months in the trenches—" Rao began.

"—and you'll never taste anything as delicious as golden rice," Than finished. "How is it all we have is the standard supplement? What happened to our ration coupons for the admiralty market?"

"Mom...she sort of—" Idrak took a bite, then tugged off the armband.

"She traded them to some Forward flunky to get your boy into an indoctrination center," someone else said, and Than raised an eyebrow as a woman with long, messy brunette hair sat opposite Idrak. She was in her late thirties, Caucasian, and wore a threadbare sweatsuit.

"Kristina." Than handed her a plate, which she accepted with a hand clasped beneath her chin and a slight bow of her head. "Do you want to explain further, or should Idrak?"

"Snitch," the boy said to his aunt, then turned back to his father. "It's the spring season work camps, Father. I get to work for the people of Shanhaiguan and meet a lot of other kids my age—"

"Girls," Kristina interjected.

"Will you stop?" Idrak said. "It's great networking," he went on, "and I can get in with the Party before the next round of elections, and then—"

"What have I told you about the Eternals? Or any party?" Than set a plate aside for his wife and sat down. He steepled his fingers in front of his chin and stared at Idrak.

"That party affiliation is not meant for anyone in the military," Idrak replied. "That officers dabbling too much in politics is what almost lost us the war before the Battle of Callao."

"So why are you so interested in a work camp? Your grades are high enough to get into the Academy on Freehold."

"You mean my family name's good enough," Idrak mumbled.

"He's being modest," Rao said. "He's top two percent of his class. I tutor him in the evenings."

"So your grades are high enough," Than said. "Names and Party won't get you into Freehold."

"Yes, they will," Kristina said. "Last two classes taken in were all related to Forward members, or to someone with flag rank. Would've been quite a scandal, if the feeds had been willing to carry it."

"Two years? How come I never heard of this?"

"What? You didn't get my messages?" Kristina raised an eyebrow. "I'm shocked. Shocked, I tell you." She shook her head, but her expression was serious. "The Party's grabbing more power, Qiang, and the more power they grab, the worse they get."

"I'll look into this," Than said. "The Admiralty isn't as . . . compromised."

"The Party's one strong election away from an outright majority in the Accord," Kristina said. "They get that, and we'll be as bad as the Fed Heart Worlds in less than a generation."

"Always so much fun to have you over, Auntie," Idrak said.

"So that's why they put her in—" Than cut himself off in

midsentence and refocused on his son. "But back to you, Idrak. Those public-service camps look like fun and exercise in the commercials, but they're indoctrination centers. You show up, and they'll be all over you like—"

He picked up his chopsticks and poked them into his white rice.

"I can think for myself." Idrak raised his arms. "I mean, you're around Party types all the time, and you're still independent. Just because I go to the camp doesn't mean I'll come out a zombie that hates his family and only cares about the League's unassailable right to forward progress and—"

"Just stop," Kristina said. "You're going for the girls."

"Just because it's coed doesn't mean—"

"No," Than said. "I won't allow it. You're smart, hardworking, and talented. You don't need the Party to get into Freehold. If you do go and you don't leave singing the Eternal Forward anthem and with a membership card in your pocket, they'll . . . take offense. Young men like you can get into trouble in that sort of environment, especially with a little help. I wouldn't put it past the Party to see you find some trouble that they'll hang over my head. Or yours, once it's time to send off your application."

"This isn't fair!" Idrak shot to his feet.

"No, it's not," Than agreed. "It won't ever be fair, son. That's war, and that's life. Don't forget what happened to everyone who was part of New Democracy after we lost at New Derba. The military purged them from public life, and Eternal Progress will head down that same road if they're not careful. I'm saying 'no' to protect you. That's my only reason."

Idrak rushed out of the room. Than half-rose from his chair, then settled back down.

"You handled that better than Dad ever did," Kristina said. "And a damned good thing, too. Eternal knows what happened to New Democracy. I doubt they'll make the same mistake."

"He'll get over it," Rao said. "If it's a girl, they're like buses. You miss one and there'll be another a few minutes later."

"This is why he has four ex-wives." Kristina jerked a thumb at him without looking away from Than. "We'll soften the landing for Idrak, Qiang."

"Being in command is easier," Than said. "I just tell my officers and people to do something, and it happens. Try the same thing with my son, and he'll resent it until he's old enough to understand for himself." He shook his head and changed the subject. "And why are you here, exactly, Kristina?"

"I got fired from my feed," she said. "Posted too many stories about Forward's corruption. The feeds stopped pushing my work to subscribers, and then my identity docs kept getting deleted from the system. I'm not the first reporter to get deplatformed. Won't be the last."

"What kind of corruption?"

"The League's been in a total war economy for decades. Most workers are taxed at nearly ninety percent of their income level, but the amount of income the central government takes in and its expenditures don't add up," she said.

"Deficit spending isn't exactly something new for a government," Than pointed out.

"There are deficits and then there are deficits, Qiang. The last war-bond drive was supposed to fund six new carriers... but where are they? No keels have been laid at satellite yards like Shanhaiguan, Keralta, or Xiaopei, and damn few at Dongguan and Urumchi. I did some digging and found one hell of a black budget."

Than took a bite of his dinner, hesitant to give anything away, even to his sister.

"It makes sense not to let the Federation know our shipbuilding timelines," he said. "If they know what we're spending, they can overmatch us."

"The Feds' economy is nearly three times the size of ours," she replied. "They could outbuild us anytime, if they really wanted to, but the Five Hundred would rather bleed their sheep with taxes than go to full-on war production and cut into their profit margins. You know they still have a luxury market? The League's been getting by on the standard ration for so long we—Did you know there are kids who have never eaten chocolate? Never worn clothes other than the recycled fabric that comes out of the printers? I've read the draft bills to lower the conscription age to—"

"We're a bit better off than most," Than said.

"There's a black hole in the League's treasury, and meanwhile Accord members are living in their own arcologies and don't have to worry about rationing, or knockoff nerve shunts, or—"

"Is the Accord so big that this 'black hole' in the budget can cover those expenses?"

"No, it's much deeper than that," she said. "We're talking about enough to finance fiefdoms out past the Fringe. Pirates and barbarians still take League dollars. Maybe the higher-ups think the Beta Cygni front will collapse and those that can are prepping an exit strategy."

"Careful." Than leveled his chopsticks at her. "That's dangerously close to treason."

"If all the money that's vanished had actually gone to new ships, we might not be hanging on by our fingertips in Beta Cygni."

"Who told you it's that bad?"

"Is the news good? Because my former coworkers who still play the game say the next big story is this Admiral Xing Xuefeng and her 'humanitarian' victory on some Fed trash world. Where's the big win in Beta Cygni? When do we retake Tantor III?"

"Beta Cygni is holding." Than went back to his meal. "The Feds won't get past the Green Line."

"Not exactly a winning message, is it? Meanwhile, Party boss Liu's got a mistress on every region capital world. He's got an appetite for needy widows."

"I think I'll just go and get the dessert," Cayha said, getting up from the table, and Than shook his head at her with a smile before he looked back at his sister.

"Now that's just yellow journalism," he said. "You published that story, didn't you? *That's* why you had your license yanked."

"I probably should've led with the black budget, but my editor thought it was too much of a conspiracy theory. So I went with the tabloid piece first, and—" Kristina motioned to him and the apartment. "I wonder if that snake tipped off the Powers That Be about my other byline, because he threw me out in the cold without much of a fight. Maybe if I looked more like the war hero Admiral Than, Forward would know who they were messing with. God knows I'm too much of a *gwáipò* for anyone to figure out we're related! Probably should've taken Than as my surname after the adoption instead of hyphenating. Wish I'd done that for Mom and Dad, now."

"Such is life," Than said, then sniffed at the air just as Kristina covered her nose and mouth. He turned and beamed as Cayha returned to the dining room with a fruit in the crook of one arm. She'd cut a slice out of the spiky skin and a spoon stuck out of its yellow flesh.

"Durian!" Than smiled even more broadly, took the fruit from her, and set it on the table.

"Oh, God, please no." Kristina waved a hand in front of her covered mouth.

"What? This stuff is the best!" Than pried out a hunk and took a bite. He gave his wife a loving glance, and she stroked the back of his head.

"It smells like someone on a rotten egg diet just farted." Kristina pushed her plate away.

"If you'd come into the Than family a little earlier, you'd love it, too." Than kept eating.

"It smells like turpentine and hatred." His sister wrapped her arms over her face.

"I wish you'd been here to give Idrak that talking to earlier," Cayha said. She clasped her hands over her waist. "He was much more insistent with me. And I'm not getting those ration coupons back."

"I can't." Kristina gagged and fled.

"What is her problem?" Rao stuck a fork into the fruit and pried out a knob of its stringy, off-yellow flesh. He dipped it into his curry sauce before taking a bite. "It's almost fresh."

"I'll get another ration book delivered," Than told his wife. "Idrak deserves a decent cake for his birthday. I'll probably miss it. Again."

"How long will you be gone?" she asked.

"That's hard to say. This tour will be a bit different. But if things work out, it will be the last one for a long time."

"You mean you'll finally retire?" Cayha asked.

"Retire? I've only been in uniform for forty years. But we'll see. We'll see. I should be home more. For Idrak, and for you."

CHAPTER ELEVEN

"THIS IS BULLSHIT!"

The Federation Navy commander kicked the trash bin built into the side of the turbo shaft car. He couldn't put much power into it in the microgravity without breaking his other foot's maglock to the car's floor, but he seemed to get at least some satisfaction from it.

The shaft ran down the outer skin of TFNS *Ishtar*'s core hull, along the base of one of the six massive, flangelike ribs which carried the FTLC's sublight parasites, and at the moment its only passengers were him and four other commanders of CruRon 1102. Their heavy cruisers were distributed between *Ereshkigal* and *Gilgamesh*, and this summons to the carrier division's flagship was the first time they'd all seen each other since they'd been hauled back off Jalal Station.

"By all means, Stanley. Take it out on that poor, poor can," one of his companions said, and the others chuckled.

"Piss off, Gao. You and *Saint Elmo* got into the fight later than my *Changsha*." Commander Joseph Stanley anchored both boots to the deck one more as he crossed his arms so he could glower more ferociously. "I promised my spacers a proper shore leave once we cycled out. Jalal was a shitpot, but at least it wasn't some kinetic'd wasteland on the way to a dust-choked ice age."

"So they got pulled before they could go broke," Abraham

Whitten said. He was a burly man, blond hair stranded with early gray. "They worried all the booze and whores of the galaxy will be gone the next time they touch civilization? My boys and girls on the *Austerlitz* can drink, but not that much."

"With the amount of alcohol my chief of the boat's confiscated, that seems to be what my people were afraid of," Elaina Iglesias, TFNS *Maplplaquet*'s CO, said. "Anyone else having that problem?"

"I'd be disappointed in my spacers if they didn't try and smuggle anything," Stanley replied. "We have a reputation to maintain. Fight hard, play hard."

"So morale took a hit." Vincent Gao shrugged. "It happens, and it'll be worse when we get to Scotia. Won't be any 'rescue mission.' It'll be mass graves and PTSD cases for everyone who has to set down. Anyone ever been to a world hit by K-strikes?"

"I was on Nuevo Paso," Whitten said. "I can still smell it before I fall asleep. Sometimes."

"Who does Murphy think he is?" Stanley demanded. "I hope Captain Penski's given him the 'this is how things run in the real Navy' spiel by now. Yanking spacers out of shore leave... That just isn't done."

"Murphy probably doesn't know that," Gao said. "He was Survey, after all." The others snorted derisively, but Gao shrugged. "He does have a combat command under his belt, though. Took the bridge at some minor engagement after the rebels got the drop on his ship. Managed to pull out a win when he should've ended up as a statistic."

"And he's related to *that* Murphy," Whitten said. "Which makes me worried that he thinks competence is hereditary. It's not. In case anyone's wondering." He snorted again, more harshly. "As his own father demonstrated."

"Murphy's not the problem." Iglesias yawned and stretched. "It's his chief of staff, O'Hanraghty. Guy was an up-and-comer before he got on too many people's bad side. Some intelligence operation that went to shit. Details aren't exactly available."

"So O'Hanraghty gloms onto Murphy to keep his career afloat, and Murphy's just an empty suit." Stanley raised a hand and looked around for agreement. "If that's the case, then at least we know who we have to keep happy."

"I doubt it's that cut and dried," Gao said. "Why'd Murphy

volunteer for command out on the Fringe? Guy's connected to all the right people back in the Heart. He could be eating grapes and having his feet rubbed by nubile women at any other assignment."

"Ambitious? That's all we need. Somebody playing war to up their profile in a board room." Stanley shook his head. "Or is O'Hanraghty vying for something outside a Survey officer's shadow? Guy should just resign his commission and reenlist under a fake name. He'd have better luck."

"Murphy's got his kid in tow," Iglesias said. "Callum. He's so new he squeaks."

"Doubt some Heart World schmuck's going to put his flesh and blood on the line for the pat on the back a tour out in New Dublin will amount to," Stanley observed. "So we just salute and execute until the clock runs out. Fine. Better than going back to the meatgrinder in Beta Cygni."

"Sounds like a plan," Whitten said. "We can get shore leave on Crann Bethadh."

"Place is Fringe," Gao said. "Internal Affairs rates it high on the insurrection scale, too. It's not exactly quality leave if you have to go down armed and in groups."

"Exactly!" Stanley retorted. "Especially when we could still—"

He paused and looked up as a light panel flashed and a tone chimed.

"Warning," a melodious recorded voice said. "Warning. Approaching spin section interface."

The other passengers joined Stanley, with both feet maglocked to the car's floor as it car began to slow. It stopped completely for a moment, then bumped hard as it locked to the face of the rotating personnel section and gravity abruptly reasserted itself.

"Especially when we could still be on Jalal," Stanley resumed. "I had two doses of Teetotaler and a liver out of practice ready to go, damn it."

"Boo-goddamn-hoo." Gao straightened and moved to the door. "Game faces. We keep the brass happy, and it'll be decent end-of-tour evaluations and a shot at a training command to finish out our service obligation."

"Yup," Iglesias said. "That's why I went to the officer corps—to do the bare minimum and get out with my skin intact."

"What?" Stanley elbowed her in the side. "You, too?"

"Stow it." Whitten pointed down the passageway as the doors

opened and they saw CruRon 1102's CO and Commander Tsimmerman, his flag captain aboard *La Cateau*, waiting for them. "There's Captain Penski. He's a true believer."

✧   ✧   ✧

Stanley sat in a ready room chair, drumming his fingers as a holo-globe of Inverness spun slowly beside a lectern on a slightly elevated stage. *Ishtar*'s briefing area's walls were lined with pictures of ships she'd carried through her quarter-century of continuous service. Several bore black "lost in action" ribbons across the upper left corners of their frames.

He looked over his shoulder to a small group of officers in the rows behind him, all in tight conversation.

"They're taking this a bit seriously," he said quietly to Gao.

"Maybe they know something we don't," his fellow CO said. "You think the League's still in the system?"

"Hell, no. It was just another of their raids. Besides, they know how close Scotia is to our nodal base here at Jalal. They hang around and they're just asking for it."

"They cleaned our clock at Callao when they suckered Fourth Fleet into thinking just that," Gao pointed out. "Which is why we generally won't retake a system after the Leaguies hit it."

"Somebody better tell Murphy or O'Hanraghty about that," Stanley said. "I'd hate for my family to get a death notice saying 'Oops, we fell for it again.'"

"You're just a real ray of sunshine, Stanley—you know that?" Iglesias hissed. "Game face. There's enlisted around and we have reputations to maintain."

Stanley's countenance became deadly serious and she rolled her eyes.

"It's like I'm back in grade school. With the class dummies," she muttered.

The door at the back of the stage opened before Stanley could reply and Rear Admiral Murphy, Captain O'Hanraghty, and Captain Drebin—who walked with slightly hunched shoulders—came through it.

"Task Force commander," Captain Lowe announced, and the assembled officers came to their feet.

Stanley's eyes hardened as they focused on Murphy, noting his single combat ribbon, unscuffed shoes, and a uniform tunic that looked like it had come off the printers just yesterday. That he shared the green command line down the side of Stanley's own trousers made him almost physically ill.

"Be seated." The words came from O'Hanraghty, not Murphy, who moved to one side of the stage with Drebin.

"We're underway, so this information can be shared," O'Hanraghty said. "We reserved this for ship's captains as the news is... distressing. Approximately nineteen days ago, at 06:43 Inverness Zulu time, a League attack group numbering some seven vessels struck the planet's capital. Over the next eighteen minutes, kinetic energy weapons destroyed key infrastructure targets across the inhabited northern hemisphere. Unlike previous League raids on our colonies, the population centers were largely untouched."

Small expanding sets of rings peppered the holo planet.

"We believe this was done to elicit a humanitarian response," the chief of staff continued, "which this group is providing. It's possible that the atypical League attack profile was designed to draw in a humanitarian response in order to ambush it on arrival, but the probability of that is low, in our estimation."

"Pardon, Sir," Gao stood up, "but how did you come to that estimation? Respectfully."

"First, because they would have to anticipate that any response would come from Jalal and, therefore, would presumably come in force. But secondly, and more to the point, because Captain Drebin observed the League sublight units recover to their carrier and accelerate to supralight before he... effected his own withdrawal."

Silence fell as Stanley and the other captains' eyes swiveled to Drebin. If he'd seen the League exit the system, why hadn't he gone back to help?

"We've used Captain Drebin's knowledge of the planet to put together a preliminary plan to evacuate survivors," O'Hanraghty said. "We're not a merchant fleet with lots of extra parasite racks or a dedicated relief effort, but we have our Hoplon contingents and landing craft. Our goal is to evacuate those most at risk to New Dublin, then provide adequate shelter for those we cannot remove until such time as a proper relief force can arrive."

"Oh boy," Whitten muttered, rubbing his face as his mind moved ahead of the briefing. "This'll be a mess."

"I'll turn the lectern over to Commander Mirwani to brief the relief effort."

O'Hanraghty stepped away and Stanley turned his eyes back to Murphy while the ops officer moved to take his place. The admiral was smiling slightly. He seemed almost uninterested.

Something's off, Stanley thought. *This move is entirely too ballsy for some Heart World fop. What's he really playing at?*

Murphy's smile returned no answer, and the commander removed a data slate from his pocket as Mirwani transmitted orders to the room.

CHAPTER TWELVE

SIMRON ADJUSTED THE EMERGENCY AIR HOOD SLUNG OVER HER shoulder, careful to keep it from creasing the exotic silk of her sarong or tug at her hoop earrings. Her father carried his hood strapped to a thigh, and his empty cigar-holding hand twitched as they floated down a long catwalk toward an observation dome.

Below—so far below Simron was afraid to look—a stupendous new FTLC, the largest faster-than-light carrier ever built for the Federation's navy, nestled in a vac dock, but even its mammoth bulk was dwarfed by distance. The monstrous Thakore Yard was one of the largest structures ever built by mankind, outmassing the Great Wall of China and the Egyptian pyramids combined. A significant percentage of the TFN was commissioned here, but that percentage could always be higher.

Down, past the carrier, she glimpsed Saturn's rings.

"How do you keep doing this?" she asked Thakore. "Is this why your secretaries keep quitting? Because you terrify them with this little jaunt?"

"I cut my teeth on vac walks and high-risk hull repairs," he said. "Microgravity's fun, Simmy! Back in the days of steel construction in America, it was 'American Indians' that did the high-elevation work. Same thing holds true today. Just different Indians."

"I did not inherit your gift." She let her hand slide along

a railing to stabilize herself and kept her eyes focused straight ahead on a small group of people waiting on the observation deck. "Seems to have skipped a generation."

"You hold your own in the board room. That's Thakore enough for me." He rapped a thick platinum ring against the railing to alert the people waiting for them of their approach.

"Mr. Thakore!" A secretary pushed off hurriedly to meet him. "We've got camera drones set along the initial projection course and media affiliates prepared with their talking points."

"That's the easy part." Thakore floated on into the observation dome and put a hand on Vyom Murphy's shoulder. The younger man, who looked a great deal like a merely mortal-sized version of his father, wore an engineer's vac suit with a helmet attached to the small of his back. "The media does whatever we pay them to do. Can't do that with the laws of physics and the finer points of ship design, can we?"

"Everything's checked out on the new Fasset drive," Vyom said. "But I'm a junior lead on the project. We should've had Dr. Gerald here to—"

"He's old. Sickly," Thakore huffed. "He can watch this from home. This is your win...unless something goes wrong, at which point Gerald will get all the attention." He glanced at his secretary.

"That contingency is prepared, Mr. Thakore."

"Win-win for you, my boy," Thakore told his grandson. "But it's not just the better drive we're testing, yes? So let's hear it."

"The next-generation field attenuators are projected to increase Fasset drive acceleration by up to six percent," Vyom said. "Though the initial costs run beyond the current budget ranges of the Federation, we anticipate—"

"Don't worry about the budget," Simron said. "That's for me and your grandfather to work out with the government."

"They'll pay." Thakore's cigar hand kept twitching. "They always pay. Remarkable how people at war will do that."

"I'll defer to you two on that," Vyom said. He cleared his throat and resumed his rehearsal. "We're also testing a new drone swarm control technology," he said. "Predictive software with a higher computational density to offset the time lag from both transmission ranges and the differential of relativistic sublight velocities. The new AIs are—"

"Boring," Simron said. "Not for me, son. But for the layman.

What's your line for the budget committee when you brief them on this?"

"We've upgraded the drone AI systems to handle complex maneuvers just before—or just after—a Fasset drive translation, and the same upgrade will improve drone deployment and maneuvers at extended range," Vyom replied. "The system potentials haven't been fully tested yet—"

"No." Simron shook her head.

"I mean...the system potentials are unlimited," Vyom said.

"There you go!" Thakore beamed. "We can have him on the board in no time. I doubt I'll ever get Rajenda out of the Navy before it's too late. He'll be too much a military man to grasp the nuances of business."

"Rajenda's...a special case," Simron said.

The secretary touched an earbud.

"*Cormoran*'s bridge crew are ready to shove off in two minutes," he said.

"Places, everyone," Thakore replied, and moved to the edge of the dock. "Where's my script?"

Camera drones moved around him, and he checked to be sure there was nothing in his teeth, then smacked his lips.

"Two dozen damask dinner napkins," he said. "Larry sent the latter a letter later."

Simron pulled her son to one side.

"What's Grandfather doing?" Vyom asked. "And what's this about the board?"

"He's rehearsing," she said. "He does that before any public statement. It's good practice. And the family needs you on the board. The budget committee's going to decide on the next battleship class to go into production sometime soon, and we can't lose the bid to Astro Engineering like we did with the *Hornet* interceptors. That one still bugs me."

"I have my first win with this ship, and then I'm done with being an engineer? Doesn't that seem fast to you?"

"Hardly. For one thing, *Cormoran*'s hardly just any old ship. And for another, look how far your father took one victory over the League." Simron paused and shook her head. "Bad example. He could be the one taking a seat on the board, but he insists on playing spacer again out on the frontier. At least he's there to keep an eye on your brother."

"You're not worried about them?"

"I learned to not worry a long time ago." Simron swallowed hard and hoped Vyom wouldn't pick up on her anxiety.

"Ingrid will be happy that I'll be based on Earth," Vyom said. "She doesn't care for the trips all the way out here. Oh—I wanted to show you this."

He reached into a pocket and removed a small velvet box.

"Vyom, you hardly know my tastes, and it's not the time to—Wait. What?" Simron snatched the box from her son and cracked the lid. "No. I'm not ready for this. Ingrid, really?"

"Yes, really. She's incredible. When I'm not working on engines all I want to do is be with her, and even when I'm working, I—"

"You haven't asked yet. I'm holding the ring. So when? Have you cleared this with her family's media rep?"

"I haven't even asked her *father* yet," Vyom said, looking at his mother as if she'd grown a new head.

"You're part of the Five Hundred, son. We have obligations to maximize the event. I am...so happy for you. When are you going to pop the question, and does your father know?"

"I meant to tell him before he left, but *Ishtar* broke orbit early. There's a secure message in transit for him. We won't have the ceremony without him there, so there's plenty of time to prepare."

"He should be back on leave in the Fall, so maybe an island wedding? This is so exciting. So much planning to do!"

"I've unleashed the kraken, haven't I?"

"Every mother is like this, Vyom. I kept a pin file of ideas for this event since you started shaving. We get *Cormoran*'s acceptance trials behind us, announce the new contract, and then your wedding will raise our profile to the top. Marvelous. Marvelous!"

Applause burst out from the group behind them as the enormous carrier detached the final umbilicals and maneuvering thrusters pushed it slowly, majestically away from the dock.

Kanada Thakore raised his arms triumphantly and his secretary passed him a lit cigar.

"I wish Dad and Callum could've been here to see this," Vyom said. "It's a great moment for the family."

"Your father thinks the family is just Murphy," Simron said, "but we're equally Thakore, no matter how much he may not like it. Sitting in a starship over some Fringe planet isn't the future, son. This is. He'll figure that out when he comes home. I hope."

CHAPTER THIRTEEN

"STILL NOTHING FROM INVERNESS, ADMIRAL," LIEUTENANT MAS-
troianni, *Ishtar*'s communications officer, said respectfully as
Ishtar and her consorts decelerated toward the star named Scotia
at twelve hundred gravities.

Murphy's flagship and her consorts had dropped sublight
3.6 billion kilometers from the star, approximately the same as
Pluto's distance from Sol. After almost five hours of deceleration,
their velocity was down to 86,700 KPS and the range to Scotia
was "only" 1.85 billion kilometers. That was still over 102 light-
minutes, a bit more than twenty percent greater than Saturn's
distance from Sol, but *Ishtar* had been hailing the planet ever
since her arrival.

And no one had said a single word back.

"Won't be any good news when we get there," O'Hanraghty
said from his station at the control holo.

"Less bad may be more good, in a way," Callum said from a
bank of displays behind the chief of staff. He had no duties in
his flag lieutenant's capacity at the moment, so he'd been assigned
to back up the chief of staff at Tactical as a learning assignment.

"If that makes any sense," he added now. "Which it doesn't.
At first."

O'Hanraghty muttered something under his breath as Murphy
walked around the holo tank, a cup of coffee in one hand. The

display showed the system's five inner rocky planets close to the red dwarf primary. TF 1705 was a blinking blue arrow following a dashed course toward Inverness, the lone colony world.

Holo projections of Commodore Pokhla Sherzai, Captain Lowe, and Yance Drebin were already visible around the control ring. Sherzai commanded BatRon 809, Murphy's battleship squadron. That made her his senior parasite commander, and she appeared focused on controls not visible in her holo. All three of them wore their combat utility vac suits, although Drebin's collar was unsealed and his helmet wasn't on his thigh like Sherzai's and Lowe's. A moment later, images of Captain Marnix Jurgens, *Ereshkigal*'s captain, and Captain Tahlia Sacks of *Gilgamesh*, joined them, and Murphy stopped pacing and turned to face the display.

"As Captain Lowe already knows," he said without preamble, "we're still picking up nothing from Inverness, not even the nav buoys."

None of them looked very surprised by the buoys' silence. Their continuous transmissions should have been picked up the moment *Ishtar* dropped sublight, but no League commander would have left them intact after hitting the system. The lack of response from an inhabited colony world was more than simply ominous, however.

"What do the visuals show, Harry?" the admiral asked, turning his head to look at O'Hanraghty. "No League invasion fleet, I assume."

The chief of staff swiped a hand through the holo and refocused it on Inverness.

"No Leaguies, Sir. And not a lot of detail on Inverness from this range, either. But the atmosphere is showing heavy particulate density, which is consistent with K-strikes. Less than I'd expect after a normal League bombardment, though."

"Fits with the initial account," Murphy said. "The League delivered a mortal blow to the colony. We're just trying to stop the bleeding."

"This could still be a trap," Sherzai said. "Plenty of spots for the bastards to be hiding in close orbit of the other planets or on the far side of the star."

"Then a full deployment is warranted?" Murphy sipped coffee thoughtfully. "We wouldn't want our parasites on the racks if the League *is* here."

"Sir," Lowe pointed out, "if we deploy all the parasites, it'll take over four hours to recover them, and that will put us that much further behind on our arrival in New Dublin. We're already cutting that pretty close, and—"

"How many survivors are we going to evacuate?" O'Hanraghty asked the flag captain. "If there are more than a handful, just *finding* them is going to take a hell of a lot longer than four hours. And how much risk do you want to take if the League is still here?"

"They're not," Drebin said from *Burgoyne*'s command deck. He put his hands on his hips. "This was a raid, like I said. Smash and run. I doubt we'll find enough left over to fill the cargo hold of a fleet tender. And—"

"Admiral, I think I've got something," Callum interrupted with a raised hand.

"What?" his father—and every other eye—turned to him.

"I'm picking up something on one of the weaker AM bands," he replied. "Not something Lieutenant Mastroianni would be monitoring—we pulled it in on the tac sensors—but it's strong enough to break through atmosphere."

"What is it?" O'Hanraghty asked.

"Dot-dot-dot." Callum cupped a hand over his earbud and looked at his father. "Dash-dash-dash, then dot-dot—"

"SOS," Murphy said. "Help."

Drebin looked away.

"No satellites in orbit," O'Hanraghty said, continuing to study the visual imagery. "We are picking up a few heat plumes, though. Fires or emergency generators, I'd guess."

"Who knows what we'll find down there?" Murphy set his cup onto the control ring. "Captain Lowe, the task force will proceed to Inverness, standard orbital insertion but deploy the recon drones to sweep ahead of us. Commodore Sherzai, we'll launch parasites once the carriers have decelerated to twenty KPS—I want them covering us when we enter orbit—but be prepared for a crash launch if we detect any League presence on our way in. Captain Sacks, for the moment, I'm designating *Gilgamesh* as our primary receiving ship. Please alert your sick bay accordingly."

Murmured acknowledgments came back, and Murphy nodded, then looked at Drebin's holo window.

"And I'll need you on the ground to help coordinate the rescue effort, Captain Drebin," he said.

"But... Admiral," Drebin looked to the other officers, "I highly doubt any of that will be necessary. There can't be much to—"

"You were stationed here for years." Murphy's tone was pleasant but his eyes were hard. "You're our subject matter expert. Any issue?"

"No. No, of course not, Sir," Drebin said. "I'll see to it that I take a full staff down with me."

Images of Inverness continued to come in as the FTLCs neared the planet.

O'Hanraghty had tasked two of *Ishtar*'s Heimdallar drones for a close recon flyby. Equipped with a lower-powered, more durable version of the Hauptman coil drive which powered the Federation Navy's missiles, the Heimdallars were capable of eight hundred gravities' acceleration for up to twelve hours before their onboard power was exhausted. Given that their maximum deceleration rate was lower than *Ishtar*'s, they'd drawn well ahead of the FTLC and their imagery showed a lot more detail.

Now pictures of the wrecked capital city came up in the holo tank: buildings flattened by blast waves, blocks blackened by fires, frost- and snow-covered cars and roads. Murphy touched one picture and shifted the view to the side. The next one in his queue came up, and a park appeared. The letters "SOS" were written across it in what looked like blackened dashes, and Murphy's eyes narrowed.

"Ops, how long are the segments in those letters?"

"They vary between about one-point-five and two meters, Admiral," Commander Mirwani replied quietly. "Average is approximately a hundred and fifty-seven centimeters."

"Did they use... bodies?" Callum asked.

"It wouldn't be the first time we've seen that," O'Hanraghty told him, and the younger man swallowed.

Murphy looked at the holo for another moment, then turned and walked over to Callum's station. His face was impassive, but his expression couldn't hide the emotions churning behind it.

Not from his son.

"It... I'm sure it's not that bad," Callum said. He couldn't have said whether he was trying to reassure his father or himself.

"I want you down with the rescue effort," Murphy said. "You'll be the Operations liaison. Stay close to Drebin."

Callum's eyes widened, and Murphy keyed his personal comm.

"Yes, Sir?" Sergeant Major Logan's voice said in his earbud.

"I'll be sending Lieutenant Murphy planetside as operations liaison, Sergeant Major," Murphy said, never looking away from Callum. "I want your people with him. Full kit."

"Full kit? Roger, Sir. Though I doubt the young sir will get into any trouble."

"I hope not. On the other hand, I believe the presence of Hoplons will nip any trouble that does arise in the bud, and you'll be available to assist the rescue effort."

"Power supply might be an issue, but it's not like we'll be under fire during a hot swap if we have to change cans," Logan observed.

"We enter orbit in forty-seven minutes," Murphy told him.

"I'll be ready, Admiral. Logan clear."

"I'm going?" Callum's face went a bit pale. "Down there?"

"You'll be my eyes," his father replied.

Callum started to say something, then closed his mouth, and Murphy put a hand on his shoulder.

"You were wrong, Son," he said very quietly. "It *is* going to be bad. Worse than anything you ever imagined. But I need you down there."

"But what if—I mean..." Callum swallowed. "What do I do if...?"

"You drive on," Murphy said, squeezing his shoulder. "You drive on. Those people down there need us."

Callum stepped out of the command tent and shivered as the icy winter air hit him.

He looked up to gray skies. The entire task force hung in orbit overhead, the parasite warships deployed in a protective hemisphere around the mammoth FTLCs, and an intermittent stream of shuttles came and went through the cloud layer above the broken city. Drones swept a methodical search pattern overhead, spreading out, broadcasting a message on repeat that promised medical treatment and evacuation here at what remained of the capital's largest sports stadium.

The evacuation center had sprouted with near magical speed, he thought, lowering his gaze to the field hospital, triage center, and mess halls on the ruined playing field. The "magic" of six decades of experience dealing with situations just like this one, he thought grimly.

It was just a pity they'd had so few survivors to use all that expertise on yet.

It was fifteen below zero in the open—six degrees on the old Fahrenheit scale—and all of those facilities were in tents, but those tents' smart fabric was a far, far better insulator than any pre-space material might have been. Their interior temperature was forty degrees warmer than the air outside them, and he adjusted his field jacket's fur-lined collar in an attempt to block out the cold.

It was useless.

He shivered again, pulled out his personal comm, and punched a combination.

"O'Hanraghty," a voice said after a moment. "Dare I ask why you're using your personal comm and not the net?"

"Dad said he wanted me to stay close to Drebin," Callum replied.

"And?"

"And Drebin has just 'suggested' I'd be more useful leading one of the SAR teams. I don't think he wants me looking over his shoulder. Or it might be Chavez and Steiner." Callum's lips twitched. "I think he finds their presence, um . . . threatening. Although he did point out the suits would be useful clearing wreckage if I took them out on search and rescue."

"I see," the chief of staff said. "Hold one."

The comm went silent for several lengthy seconds, and Callum watched his breath drift away from him in white clouds while he waited.

"Okay," O'Hanraghty said finally. "Take the team out. Drebin's right about how useful the suits could be, and we'll get another set of eyes on him. Someone too senior for him to send off on an errand."

"Are you sure?" Callum asked. Enough reports had already come in for him to dread what he might encounter out in the ruins.

"Yes," O'Hanraghty said crisply. Then his voice softened just a bit. "It won't be fun out there, Callum. I know that. I've been there, and I wish I hadn't. But Drebin's got the authority to send you, unless your dad overrules him, and that'd be . . .

counterproductive. And you can do some good out there, Callum. You really can."

"If you say so," Callum said dubiously. "Clear."

He tucked the comm back into his pocket and drew a deep, icy breath. Then he went looking for "his" Hoplons.

Even through the cold, the smell was everywhere.

Callum longed for the forgotten warmth of the HQ tent as the cold ate deeper into his bones despite his cold-weather gear. He and his team had been out in the shattered city for over three hours, and he'd already seen enough ruin—and death—to last him a lifetime. What he *hadn't* seen was a single living survivor, although many of the other SAR teams had. He'd come to the conclusion that Drebin had deliberately assigned him a sector where there wouldn't be any for him to find. It would have been petty, but then, Drebin was a petty man, wasn't he?

"Nothing in here, Sir," Corporal Steiner's voice said in his earbud. "Wasn't much of a shelter to start with. Looks like it caved when the back wall came down."

"Check." Callum made a note on his handheld control slate. "Come on back out. Map shows a sidewalk shelter down the block."

"On my way."

At least they were on the last leg and headed back in, Callum thought. Check the sidewalk shelter, then that "visual anomaly" SAR command wanted him to check out, and then maybe he could at least get warm again. Maybe grab a late lunch before Drebin found some other way to get him out from underfoot.

A shadow fell across the packed and dirty snow around him as a war suit stepped through the broken glass of a storefront to join him. The Hoplon stood about 2.3 meters in height, with wide, blocky shoulders and a domed, turretlike helmet that made Steiner look more like a robot than a Marine in powered armor. The suit's hands ended in oversized fingers, and the whine of servos within the metal housing carried on the wind along with that godawful smell.

Chavez stood just behind Callum in the same armor. One of the Hoplons was always at his back, and at the moment Chavez had what Callum thought of as the babysitter's job. The private carried a "carbine" Callum was sure he couldn't have lifted if his life depended on it, but the weapon was mag-locked to his armor's torso at the moment and he'd extended what looked like a half-meter sword from his suit's right forearm. It moved, extending and retracting like a cat flexing its claws. Light wavered oddly around it and Callum heard a faint crackle each time the wind caressed it.

"Cut your blade." Steiner's voice came through the speaker at the base of his helmet. "You're just bleeding charge."

"I don't like dead places," Chavez said. "Just don't."

"Wasn't that you with me at the Siege of Gettys? That place was dead as hell." Steiner reached down and thrust angled fingertips beneath the snow to pry up a metal hatch. He flipped it open and looked down a dark stairwell.

"That place was *dying*." Chavez rotated his force blade, energy snapping as snowflakes hit it. "Big difference."

"One second," Callum said. He pointed a data rod at the stairwell, then shook his head. "Two pings off personal transponders. Both ... inactive."

"At least we got here before the implants faded," Steiner said. "You imagine having to clear these places manually? To hell with that. Just write off anyone that doesn't make it to the evac shuttles and have bots bulldoze the place. Recolonize a few years later, after the dust settles."

"That's barbaric," Callum said.

"It's been done before," Chavez said. "I heard the colony ticket costs less after every cycle. Bet you could get a homestead on Rabita for like ... a month's salary. Before tax."

"Who's got Rabita right now? It changes hands so often I can't keep track," Steiner said.

"My point exactly." Chavez's helmet rotated from side to side. "Big boss is en route."

"What?" Callum looked up as shuttle lights descended in the distance. "The Admiral's on the way?"

"On the shuttle." Chavez gestured at an incoming shuttle with the force blade. "That's Sergeant Major Logan, Sir. His beacon popped on our tracker. Wouldn't be here if your father wasn't."

"We're almost done with this sector." Callum stamped his boots into the road to get his blood going. "Drones are almost done with their sweeps. We check that 'anomaly' and we can head in."

"Suits me, Sir. Could use a battery change, anyway."

"This way, then." Callum pointed down a side street, where a path the width of a ground car was open but covered in a few inches of fresh snow. "Come on."

"Stay behind," Chavez said. He moved ahead of Callum, force blade deactivated and carbine at the ready.

"You guys are paranoid," Callum said, but he followed along obediently behind the towering war suit.

They'd covered another half block or so when his control slate tingled with the vibration that indicated fresh data had arrived. He looked down, then frowned.

"That's got to be an error," he muttered.

"What kind of error?" Steiner asked, and Callum reminded himself that Hoplons had excellent audio systems.

"Probably nothing," he said. "One of our peripheral drones is getting a garbled return a couple of blocks beyond our sector. Coming from what the map says was a schoolhouse." He shrugged. "If I get close enough, the signal will clear up."

Steiner grunted in acknowledgment and Callum concentrated on his footing as they slogged through the snow. The icy wind grew stronger as they neared the end of the current block, and Callum winced as an even worse smell of decay hit him.

"Ugh. What is that? Busted sewer line?"

"What's what?" Steiner asked from behind him.

"Yeah, you guys can't smell in there, can you? At least you're warm," Callum said.

"These things can get pretty funky after a couple of days buttoned up," Steiner replied. "'Course, by then you're so full of amps and stingers that the smell really ain't a problem."

"You ever see the elves?" Chavez cut a tight corner and signaled Callum forward. "The mechanical elves? I saw them on Gettys."

"Everyone sees the elves," Steiner said.

"You guys hallucinate in those suits? Isn't that a bit dangerous?"

"We don't shoot the elves," Chavez said. "It's bad luck. And they don't look anything like Leaguie ground pounders, either."

"Plus the squad leader will hit anyone that sees them with a sedative," Steiner put in. "Which gives you the worst damned jitters a few hours later."

"Civilian sector doesn't let workers operate heavy machinery when they're amped up, or on downers," Callum said, then stopped walking as he heard Steiner's laugh over the speaker.

"Something funny?" he asked.

"Nothing, Sir. Longshoremen and ship's crew are always stone cold sober, I'm sure," the Hoplon said.

"Well—" Callum began.

"Fuck me running," Chavez interrupted. He'd stopped, his armor facing around a corner, and the force blade had extended from his wrist again.

"What?" Callum stepped closer to a wall, his boots sinking into deeper snow. "What is it?"

"Guess . . . guess you'd better come see."

Chavez's force blade fizzled out and the stink of ozone washed over Callum as he stumbled awkwardly out of the snowbank and rounded the corner.

His data slate slipped from his hands and bounced off his boot.

They'd found the "anomaly."

The mound of corpses was taller than the Hoplon. Snowfall had partially buried it, but not enough to hide the horror. Most of the dead were in black body bags. Others were wrapped in plastic and tape, and still more wore the clothes they'd died in, lying in a fan around the larger pile.

Column's eyes darted from one nightmare to the next. Men, women . . . children. Deep red birds, the size of crows, picking at exposed flesh. Eyes frozen open. Blue lips, sprinkled with fresh snowflakes.

"Can't bury 'em when the ground's frozen." Steiner's voice seemed obscenely calm. "First batch were taken care of right. Newer dumps were just thrown at the pile. Pretty standard pattern when things go bad. Hope's the last thing to run out."

"Fuckin' Leaguies." Chavez's arms fell to his sides. "Would've been kinder to just glass the planet. My biohazard's picking up a cholera variant, on top of everything else."

"Navy fuckers should've stayed in-system." Steiner's voice was still calm; his expression was not. "Could've sent *Ophion* for help. They could've done everything *we're* doing. Hell, they could've dropped a power plant, got the utilities back up."

"Navy always runs when it gets tough," Chavez said. "Smaj got abandoned back when he was green. Said his ride got scared off after a drop, then him and his platoon lasted six months in some jungle before a Survey ship swung through."

"He told me it was four—Hey. The zero okay?" Steiner nudged

Callum on the shoulder with a war suit knuckle that sent him half a step forward.

"They . . . they—" Callum waved at the bodies. "They're all—"

"Uh-oh. Pull your collar down, Sir," Steiner said.

"I . . . I . . . *urrrk.*" Callum pitched forward and vomited. He braced on his hands and knees, then heaved a plentiful breakfast onto the road.

"Love to help you, Sir," Steiner said. "But mission parameters mean I have to stay buttoned up. So sorry."

"This your first time seeing something like this?" Chavez asked.

Callum threw up again, his shoulders trembling.

"That's what I thought. Just be glad this isn't a vacuum reclamation. I had to do one of those. Some cruiser got scratched out past the snow line like two decades ago. Had to do wrecker for engineers to get to the power plant. Whole crew was flash frozen. All looking the same as the moment they died all those years ago."

"You don't think he's got enough nightmare fuel?" Steiner asked. "Sir? Sir, how about you do a close sweep with your drones so we can catalog the transponders and get the hell out of here. Beacons are good through twenty feet of packed earth."

Callum reached for his slate and swiped two fingertips across the screen. The air filled with the buzz of drones as they crisscrossed over the mound, and Callum wiped his sleeve across his mouth.

"We should . . . um." He choked back bile.

"Head back, yeah," Chavez said. "Don't feel bad, Sir. Us Hoplons have to make it through an infantry tour before we can apply to be metalheads. They don't want us losing our lunch inside the suits."

"That's not why—"

"Shut up, Steiner. I'm trying to make the kid feel better," Chavez said. "What? My speaker's on? Shit."

"I've got them all." Callum thrust his slate into a pocket. "The sector's clear. Let's get the hell back." He looked at the bodies again, then shook his head. "Soon as we have eighty percent of the population accounted for, we can leave the system. That's federal law."

He turned on his heel and marched back the way he'd come, not waiting for his escort.

✧   ✧   ✧

Terrence Murphy stood to one side of the shuttle ramp as Inverness's survivors shuffled past him. They were dirty, haggard. Most didn't seem to care that he was there. They only clutched foil ration packets and shambled into the warmth of the cargo bay, where long rows of seats had been installed to get personnel off the planet as quickly as possible.

Not all of them, though.

An old woman spat at Murphy's boots and flashed him a hand gesture with three fingers.

"The evil eye," Drebin said from just behind him. The captain wore a full-face weather mask and had no ship insignia on his uniform. "Local superstitions. Bunch of ingrate Fringers."

"At least she's alive to be rude," Murphy said. Logan's and Faeran's armored presence had kept the colonists from threatening the admiral or other staff outright at the evacuation point. Some of the rescue efforts in outlying settlements had been met with anger, even some violence, but no serious injuries to Murphy's people.

The admiral glanced at Drebin.

"What's their burial custom?" he asked.

"Doesn't matter, Sir. This planet's Category Epsilon. No viable way to sustain Federation presence. Regs are to incinerate anything and everything—leave nothing for the League if they try to seize the system after we pull out."

"So the enemy expects us to finish the job," Murphy said. "Such a waste."

"This is the Fringe." Drebin shrugged. "Inverness has been in range of a League raid for years. They could've relocated farther from the frontier with a federal tax credit." He shrugged again. "They knew the risks."

"And they also had you and your squadron in-system." Murphy walked away from the shuttle as the last colonist stepped onto the ramp. "There was a promise."

He walked through pallets of emergency supplies and battery packs with Drebin and his Hoplons at his heels. He paused for a quick conversation with a surgeon outside a field hospital, then waved to Callum as his son came through the outer perimeter of the evacuation center.

"Admiral." Callum tapped his slate against Murphy's to transfer its data. "Bravo-Twelve's clear. I...resolved that anomaly the drones picked up."

Murphy's eyes lingered on some lime green stains on Callum's jacket, then gave him a curt nod.

"Looks like we've got ninety percent of the colonists accounted for," the admiral said. "The League commander didn't make much of an effort to target the population centers, just the utility networks. Hitting those was a fatal wound to life support." He swiped his screen to a map of the city.

"It's still a crime against humanity, what's happened here," Callum said. "Who was the commander? The League might listen to reason and hand him over, like they did with the Butcher of Baiknor."

Drebin laughed.

"What's so funny?" Callum asked, his face dark.

"Baiknor was during the first five years of the war," Drebin said. "Scratching civilians with K-strikes wasn't new even then, and it stayed the same after Baiknor. The reason the Leaguies gave the Butcher up was because he scratched a League planet that was in open revolt, and they didn't want to deal with his trial. And the League commander here was a she, some new hothead named Xing."

"Xing?" Murphy repeated sharply. "How do you know her name?"

"She ... sent a transmission to Inverness. Before she K-struck it," Drebin said uncomfortably.

"And you didn't mention that in your report? Or in any of our earlier conversations?"

"It ... didn't seem important," Drebin said.

"Not important. I see." Murphy looked at him very levelly for a moment, then glanced down at his slate.

"Callum, did you sweep the schoolhouse bunker on Noborn Street?" he asked.

"Bunker?" Callum leaned over to glance at his father's slate and grimaced. Murphy was looking at the map data Callum had just transferred to him, and the garbled drone signal blinked on it. "That's outside my sector."

"It was only a couple of blocks outside your sector. You didn't send your drones in for a closer look?"

"I didn't ... No, was I supposed to?"

"The other lieutenant assigned to it didn't get very close, either ..." Murphy stood looking at the slate, then shoved it into his pocket. "Let's go for a walk, yes?"

The admiral adjusted his kit and took off at a brisk pace. Drebin didn't move for a moment. Then he started back toward the landing pads.

Murphy stopped and looked back.

"Do come along...Governor," he said. He motioned to one side and Logan's helmet spun to Drebin. The captain looked back and forth between the admiral and the Hoplon, then turned and began slogging sullenly through the snow behind Murphy.

Callum caught up to his father.

They walked in silence through the stench and the ruin, and Callum thought about the look in his father's eyes when he'd asked about the garbled return. It wasn't fair, he thought. The schoolhouse *was* outside his sector, not his responsibility. And he'd *meant* to check it, anyway, if he hadn't been...distracted by that horrible pile of death. But that look in his dad's eyes...

"This is...Is it always like this out in the Fringe?" he asked at last.

"It's not how the feeds show it, but are you actually surprised by that? Fifty-six years of war and the Heart Worlds know the statistics, but that's all they are—statistics. They know the economic cost from the chunk wartime taxes take from their wealth, and maybe they know a few who have served. The Fringe gets hit like this every so often, but it barely makes the feeds anymore, especially when the cost in lives is only a few hundreds of thousands. This wasn't a forward deployment world, and the total population was under a million. Nobody back home knows about it, and frankly, son, nobody really cares. It's not *their* war anymore."

"But we had the mustering station at Olympia."

"Veteran hiring quotas." Murphy shook his head. "And who did you see in it? Anybody *you* knew? Did you know there are some Heart Worlds with no mustering stations at all? A few of the Five Hundred don't care for their workforce to be subject to the draft or recall. Cuts into 'vital' economic output, you know."

"What? I thought compulsory service was...not optional if your number comes up," Callum said.

"It's not hard to get a deferment, and when the Five Hundred wall off a significant portion of their economic empires for the sake of the wartime economy, or when others of the Five Hundred get *their* sons and daughters into safe billets close to home, like the Army, what do you think happens? The obligation for military service falls on those that aren't as critical to the economy, that's what. It falls on the Fringe. Those outside the Heart Worlds. Did you know the casualty rates are fifteen times higher per capita for those outside the Heart? Not even factoring in strikes like this."

"No, I didn't."

"The *Fringe* knows it. The feeds have a way of keeping such news out of the public's eye back home. Not so much out here, son." He stopped, looked around, and pointed. "There. That pile of rubble looks like the schoolhouse. Your drones, Callum?"

Callum stepped to one side and tapped his screen to send a small swarm of drones over what remained of the three-story building.

"Admiral," Drebin looked furtively from building to building, "I trust your report back to the Oval will be transparent."

"Oh, I'll put in every detail," Murphy said. "No doubts as to the sequence of events from the League's initial attack to the moment you exercised your commander's discretion to preserve combat power in the face of an overwhelming enemy force."

"We would have lost my entire squadron. Then none of the colonists would have survived if I hadn't made it back to Jalal."

"I am curious about one point." Murphy clasped his hands behind his back and turned to face Drebin. "As I looked through some of the records recovered from an emergency data core, why did the civil alert alarms go off so close to the time of the first K-strike?"

"That—" Drebin's shoulders hunched slightly. "You'd have to take that up with the ground emergency coordinator. He was in a bunker that's a smoking hole a couple of kilometers from here."

"Hmmm...And the core aboard your ship has a number of gaps around the same time," Murphy said thoughtfully.

"What are you suggesting?"

"I'm not suggesting anything. I'm simply gathering information to assure a complete and thorough report to the Oval."

"I've told you everything." Drebin straightened. "Don't bother with what the Fringers have to tell you. They're likely still in shock from the tragedy."

"Got something." Callum raised his slate and the drones formed an orbit overhead. "Looks like it's just a ghost image or two."

"Are we done out here?" Drebin asked.

"What's the sensor rating on that bunker?" Murphy asked him. "Because if it was built to spec, it's meant to block League detection."

"To spec? In the Fringe?" Drebin sniffed.

"Logan."

Murphy pointed at the collapsed building, and the four Hoplons waded into the debris. Steiner thrust his hands beneath a segment of broken wall and flipped it up and over across the street, bouncing a shower of loose masonry off Faeran's back. She didn't seem to notice as she kicked a steel beam to one side.

"Not the most subtle approach," Callum observed.

"The bunker held," Murphy said, studying the data from the drone's ground penetrating sensors. "Drebin, signal all ground teams to do a close sweep of every such facility in the city."

"Sir, the sweep is over," Drebin said.

Murphy looked at him. For a moment, Drebin tried to meet those gray eyes, then he turned away to speak into a microphone on his wrist.

"Hatch," Chavez announced, raising one arm. Logan waded over to him and tugged at the metal handle, but it didn't lift.

"Bolt locked," the sergeant major said to Murphy, and a cutting torch popped out of his forearm.

"No," Murphy called out. "If there's anyone alive inside, you could injure them."

"Fair enough." Logan extinguished the torch. He gripped the hatch in both massive hands, instead, and servos whined as his armor pulled against the handle. For a moment, nothing happened. Then the hatch came off with an explosive, metallic crack.

Callum put the back of his sleeve against his nose.

"I don't smell anything," Murphy said.

Callum's cheeks bulged and he swallowed whatever had come up.

"I'll handle this one." Murphy gave his son a pat on the shoulder and went into the rubble. He leaned over the open hatch.

"Federation forces," he called.

There was no answer, and he removed a flashlight from his belt and started down the ladder.

"Sir, let me unbutton and go with you," Logan said as the admiral descended into the darkness.

"How about some light, instead?" Murphy replied.

Logan bent forward at the waist, across the ladder, and an armored disk popped off his breastplate to expose a floodlight that came to brilliant life.

The white light was a pool around Murphy's feet, shining off the ladder rungs as he got to the bottom. The bunker was in total darkness, but for the halo around the ladder. He sniffed hard, smelling body odor and a thin scent of rot.

He raised his flashlight and stepped away from the ladder. His light passed over a jumble of ransacked boxes, then to a cot. A thin man lay there, his torso wrapped in bloody bandages. Both arms hung off the side of the cot, and his face was covered. Next to the cot was a pile of blankets and empty food cartons.

"Federation forces," Murphy repeated. He moved closer, his light lingering on the pile. Then he knelt next to it and tugged at a blanket. A patch of blond hair appeared, and he pulled away another blanket. A pale face looked up at him. The girl's lips were badly chapped, her pale blue eyes hollow-looking, her cheeks sunken.

She stared at him, lips quivering.

Murphy moved his light to one side.

"Can you hear me? My name is Terrence. Terrence Murphy." He flipped the base of his flashlight to the ground and pressed down. The handle rose, transforming into a lantern, and he took a canteen from his belt and pressed it to her lips. Clear water flowed around her mouth, and she coughed.

"There we go." He let go when skeletal hands emerged from the blankets to grip the canteen. "Drink all you can. This is all over, okay? I'll get you out of here. Both of you."

He reached for the blanket covering the man's face, but those skeletal fingers closed on his wrist with iron strength.

"My brother's eyes are gone," she said. "I don't...I don't know when it happened. Are you taking us to heaven?"

"I'm no angel," Murphy said. "No demon, either. Just a man. I know you've been down here for a while, but there's still a world up there. It's a bad one. One you can't stay on, but I can take you someplace better. How's that sound?"

She began to cry, and he put an arm around her shoulders and pulled her in gently for a hug.

"I got here as fast as I could," he said softly. "I'm sorry it wasn't fast enough."

"I prayed for him," she said. "For so long—"

"Dad?" Callum called from the ladder where he'd followed his father down. "What have you—She's alive? Hey, Logan! Call in an ambulance!"

"Let's get you out of here," Murphy said. He scooped her up in his arms and gave Callum a stern look as she covered her face with her arms and clutched at his jacket.

"This is why we're thorough," Murphy said. "You understand, son?"

"It wasn't my—"

Callum stopped when Murphy shook his head.

"I'll escort her to medical," Callum said, holding out his own arms. "Make sure she gets straight to the docs. The other one..."

Murphy looked at him a moment, then passed the slight, trembling body to him. He pointed his son at the ladder and went to the man's body. He lifted the stiff arms back onto the cot. The corner of a piece of cardboard fell out from beneath the blanket and onto the floor, and he picked it up. He held it to the light, reading the poorly written, badly spelled words, then went to his knees beside the cot and recited the old prayer from memory.

"May brooks and trees and singing hills, join in the chorus, too, and every gentle wind that blows, send happiness to you."

✧   ✧   ✧

"More?"

The young lieutenant held a spoonful of ice chips to Eira's lips.

She lay on a gurney inside a white hospital tent. She and the lieutenant were the only ones inside a facility with room for nearly a dozen more. With blankets up to her armpits and in a simple smock, her pale skin and blond hair almost blended into the sterile environment.

She studied an IV line stuck into the back of one hand, then brushed hair down to cover the mark above her eye.

"Why?" she asked.

"Because you're dehydrated," he said. "This is packed with salt and glycogen, great after a night out on the town." He pressed the spoon to her lips as if she were a recalcitrant child.

"Why do you even—no." She spat out the ice and pushed his hand away. "Why are you bothering with me? You have the Admiral's look. You have his name." She glanced down at his name tape. "You're a Heart."

"Well," he rested his hands on his lap. "I—What's your name?" he asked. "You already know mine, the last one at least."

"Eira," she said. "My name's Eira."

"Well, Eira," he said, "I should have found you sooner. My dad—I mean the Admiral—he's an engineer by training. That's how we realized that bunker was intact. Me, I'm a Fasset drive engineer. Okay with vac equipment and such, not so much with dirt side and atmosphere. But I'm good enough with drones. Except that I sort of... walked past you. Twice."

"What will you do with me now?" She held out a trembling hand and he passed her the bowl of ice chips and spoon.

"I don't think anyone can live on Inverness for a while." He shrugged. "My guess is that we'll evac you all to Jalal, or take you on to New Dublin. You ever been there?"

Eira shook her head and took a little bite of ice.

"Any family elsewhere in the Federation?"

Eira paused, then shook her head again, quickly.

"Well, the Colonial Board has a lot of practice at this," he said. "You'll be up and around in no time."

"The Federation left us without firing a shot," she said. "I had... some time to think. The civil alarms went off so close to the first strike. We should have had at least an hour's warning. That was the drill. And we didn't get *any*. How could the League get so close without anyone knowing?"

"That's a very good question, Eira," he said. "One more people should be asking."

His gaze lingered on the scar tissue on the right side of her face, and she turned her good side to him.

"Sorry, sorry," he said. "That looks treatable, why—"

"Come closer." Eira motioned and he leaned over. She pressed fingertips around his face gently. "You're so perfect. I heard the Five Hundred can spend money and wipe away any marks, but in the Fringe, we're worth only what we can give."

"No work done. Mom didn't approve." He took her by the wrist and gave her hand a squeeze. "Although, come to think of it, everyone I ever went to school with did have great skin and amazing hair. Huh. Never thought about it."

✧   ✧   ✧

Callum sat there, holding the waif's hand, looking into that thin, three-quarters-starved face. He couldn't imagine what she'd endured, and he knew it. But he was pretty damn sure he couldn't have survived it as well as this skinny, forty-kilo ragamuffin. In fact—

"Just get me out of this shit hole." The voice from outside the tent interrupted his thoughts as the silhouette of two men showed dimly through the walls. Callum recognized Drebin's high-pitched voice. "Murphy expects me to be the last shuttle up. Does he think the frigging lights need to be turned off? Just get my ship. Now."

The girl's head snapped up, her eyes suddenly wide. Then the bowl crashed to the floor as she flung her blankets aside. She exploded from the gurney and bolted out the door flaps, pulling her IV stand down with a clatter before the needle ripped out of her hand.

Callum sat dumbstruck. Then a crash and screams from outside snapped him into action. He slapped the door aside and found the girl straddled on top of Drebin in a patch of muddy slush. Another man lay in a heap of tumbled boxes, struggling to get up.

The girl screamed as she beat at Drebin in a wild fury. The governor had one arm up, trying to block, but Callum heard the meaty smack of knuckles against his face again and again. She landed a hammer blow to his mouth and a bloody tooth went flying.

Callum froze, uncertain. He'd never witnessed anything so savage in his entire life.

"Eira? Stop. Stop!" He bent to grab her from behind and caught an elbow to the bridge of his nose. There was a sharp crack, light exploded across his vision, and he fell back on his haunches, blood choking his sinuses and pouring down the back of his throat.

Eira's banshee wail cut off as her head lunged forward. Her teeth snapped shut on Drebin's ear, and he screamed as she jerked back again. His ear came with her, and he panicked and grabbed her by the front of her hospital smock. He jerked her to one side and she landed on a tie-down rope for the hospital tent.

Callum touched his face, and his fingers came back covered in blood.

Eira spat out the severed ear contemptuously and gripped the stake at the end of the line. She yanked it out of the ground, flung the rope aside, and gripped the metal spike like a knife.

Drebin rolled onto his stomach and tried to crawl away.

"No, don't!" Callum lunged forward and caught Eira by the ankle before she could finish Drebin off.

She looked back at him, her face a mask of rage and her eyes on fire. She kicked him away and snapped back toward Drebin, and Callum saw Logan—in fatigues—running down the duckboard walkway, pistol in hand. The pistol barked, and Eira jerked as something hit her in the sternum. She looked down at the purple lump of goo. Then her eyes rolled up and she tipped over to one side into a mound of dirty snow.

Drebin kept screaming as he ran.

Logan was there a moment later, weapon still trained on Eira.

"You hurt?" he asked Callum.

"Ah. Owndly by doze." Callum pressed between his eyes and down the bridge of his nose, wincing in pain.

"That's not hurt." Logan kicked the fallen stake back under the tent. "This is the Chief," he said into his duty comm. "Got one in custody. Secondary has minor injuries. Alert primary that the natives are getting restless and he needs to prioritize evac."

"What did you do to her?" Callum pulled Eira out of the snow and brushed icy chunks off of her.

"Nonlethal munition. Low powered, subsonic." Logan shrugged. "Massive sedative. Comes with one hell of a hangover. What happened?"

"She just...heard Drebin and went berserk." Callum held a handful of snow against his bleeding nose. "Ugh. When does this stop?"

"That was Drebin? Didn't recognize him with all the bruises." Logan looked over one shoulder, then waved at Faeran as she and the rest of the Hoplons appeared. "Too bad he tripped."

"Tripped?" Callum repeated.

"Yeah. You didn't see him trip?"

"What? I was inside and then—"

"Didn't see him trip." Logan sniffed hard, then bent over, picked up Drebin's ear, and shoved it in a cargo pocket. "Got to be careful out here, young Sir. Fringe is dangerous."

He slapped a plastic band around Eira's wrists and it bent into cuffs. He tossed her over his shoulder and walked away.

CHAPTER FOURTEEN

"I WANT THAT PIECE OF TRASH'S HEAD ON A PLATE, YOU HEAR me?" Yance Drebin slammed a fist onto the oak desk in Murphy's shipboard office. His newly reattached ear was lined with pink flesh where a stem cell binding had reknitted the body part to his skull.

"Of course I hear you," Murphy said as he leaned back in his chair. "You're screaming."

Callum knew his own cheeks were flushed, but he couldn't decide if that was an aftereffect of his time with the surgical robot that had repaired his nose or from the growing tension in the compartment. He stood to his father's left against the office's rear bulkhead, and Lieutenant Prajita Tripathi, Task Force 1705's JAG stood to the admiral's right. Sergeant Major Logan and O'Hanraghty stood to one side.

"Assault on a system governor is tantamount to treason." Drebin drew a deep breath and tugged at the bottom of his tunic. "Given the circumstances, I'm willing to settle for a more merciful execution and have her shot before she's ejected from the airlock."

"There are details we should clarify," Murphy said. "Lieutenant Tripathi, am I correct that Captain Drebin's—"

"*Governor* Drebin, in this case," Drebin interrupted.

Murphy glanced at him, then turned back to the JAG.

"That *Captain* Drebin's decision to preserve combat power activated Section Nineteen of his appointment writ?"

Drebin's head jerked back as if he'd just been punched.

"You are indeed correct, Sir." Despite her name, Tripathi had straw-colored hair and a ruddy complexion. "His decision to transfer his command back to *Burgoyne* in his role as squadron commander and then withdraw his forces from the system made a Ms. Genovese the acting system governor. Unfortunately, Ms. Genovese was subsequently lost in the League attack. Along with the rest of the designated survivor list."

"Most tragic," Murphy said.

"Why are we wasting time with all this legalese?" Drebin demanded. "I'm back in Scotia. I'm the governor."

Murphy pursed his lips thoughtfully, then waved one finger at the JAG, who cleared her throat gently. Drebin's eyes swiveled to her.

"I'm sure you're aware of Section Thirty-Two of the Colonial Settlement Act, Captain," she said. "In the event of the loss of all designated survivors, executive authority falls to the highest ranked military officer in-system until such time as the federal government can appoint a new governor. Which, ah, would be *Admiral* Murphy at this moment."

"Now, wait just a minute—"

"You don't want to stay here, do you?" Murphy asked. "I understand this is just late fall, not even true winter. It was rather chilly down there. And I'm afraid you'd be a bit lonely."

"Now, don't be ridiculous. The first thing I want is justice for the assault I suffered—the *unprovoked* assault!—at the hands of that Fringe garbage," Drebin said. "You've got the witnesses here. What are we waiting for?"

"Yes, about that." Murphy tapped a stack of data slates on his desk. "The witness statements I have are . . . a bit contradictory."

"*Contradictory?* How?" Drebin turned his reattached ear toward Murphy. "Wasn't this put on right? I can't believe what I'm hearing!"

"But let's not beat about the bush." Murphy leaned to one side to look at an antique wooden clock with golden hands. "*Ishtar* and her squadron are about to break orbit for New Dublin. That's a problem, since my duty as task force commander is to safeguard the survivors, and obviously New Dublin is almost as exposed as Scotia was. And, of course, it's not a designated refugee center, either." He shook his head. "Fortunately, *Calcutta* has just dropped sublight, and she has the four emergency personnel pods I requested from Jalal on the racks. She'll reach Inverness orbit in about twelve hours, which gives me additional options. I've decided to transfer the survivors from Scotia to San Gabriel, which *is* a designated refugee center and happens to be much closer to the Heart Worlds and thus a far safer destination for people who have already been through so much. Unfortunately, *Calcutta* has no parasite group, so I'm detaching your *Burgoyne* and two of your light cruisers—*Indus* and *Tsangpo*—to provide her with a security element during her voyage."

"I'm lost." Drebin flopped his arms against his sides. "Was I the only one to receive a massive head trauma down there?"

"Well, clearly I have to meet multiple requirements out of limited resources," Murphy told him pleasantly. "I'd prefer to send more of your squadron along for security, but *Calcutta*'s racks have too little capacity for the rest of your squadron and the personnel modules. And it would be grossly unfair of me to not send you personally with her, since I've finished my report on the League attack here." The admiral took a small golden rod from his desk and rolled it toward Drebin. "I'm sure you'll want to get this into the proper hands as quickly as possible. I've cypherlocked the original, level two." He smiled pleasantly; a level two cypher could be opened—or altered—only by flag grade officers. "I'm sure you can find someone on San Gabriel to forward it to the Oval. I'll have draft copies sent to you, of course."

"I don't . . . I don't understand." Drebin picked up the rod and studied it.

"I'm sorry; I thought it was clear. You'll dock *Burgoyne*, *Indus*, and *Tsangpo* to *Calcutta* as soon as she makes orbit and supervise the transfer of all the Inverness survivors to her personnel modules. And then you'll take that report to San Gabriel and make certain that it goes straight to the Oval. I can't trust anyone else with something so important, now can I?"

He smiled thinly, and Drebin swallowed.

"*All* the survivors?" he asked.

"All of them." Murphy nodded slowly. "*Calcutta*'s onboard life support is limited and her spin sections are designed for much smaller crew numbers, I'm afraid, but the personnel modules are largely self-contained. A bit crowded, and spending such an extended period in microgravity is less than desirable, but it may actually be for the best, considering how physically traumatized some of them are. And I'm sure *Calcutta*'s captain can arrange exercise time for them under gravity aboard his ship in shifts. Of course, she's a little long in the tooth, not as fast as a newer ship. Anticipate some time in wormhole space."

"You're going to leave that animal on the same ship as me?" Drebin's eyes went wide. "Then execute her now! You can't risk my safety by—!" He swallowed again harder, his face pale. "I'm... I'm at risk with *any* of them!" he blurted. "You can't do this!"

"Actually," Lieutenant Tripathi raised a finger, "the Federation Code of Military Justice is clear in that—"

"Your assailant won't be aboard *Calcutta*, you'll always have your quarters aboard *Burgoyne*, and *Burgoyne*'s zero-gee gym facilities will be available to you," Murphy said. "No worries there. Now, I know you'll have a lot of details to work out, given this sudden change of plans, so I'm sure you need to get started on that. Rest assured that I'll deal with the assault issue here and that you'll be informed as to its final resolution. Sergeant Major? Would you please escort Captain Drebin to the shuttle bay and be sure he gets off to *Burgoyne* safely?"

"Pleasure." Logan grabbed Drebin by the arm and hauled the spluttering man out of the compartment. The door closed behind them, and Murphy sighed and looked at the JAG.

"Paperwork calls, Sir," Tripathi said. "Loss claims, final survey information. If there's nothing else? I think Logan's got enough of a head start I won't have to share a tube car with that...person."

"Thank you, Lieutenant," Murphy said.

"If I may, Sir, this time it was my distinct pleasure." She came briefly to attention, then followed Logan and Drebin out the door.

Murphy unsnapped his collar as she left. Then he tapped on a slate and a holo of a brig cell appeared over his desk. Eira sat on a cot, her knees pulled up to her chest.

"This one's interesting," O'Hanraghty said. "For one thing, she's League."

"Come again?" Callum asked, his brow furrowed in confusion.

"Genomic data has her as born on Athenaea, an outlying League world that borders Rishathan space," the chief of staff said. "According to Inverness records, she and her brother were captured during a slave raid some years back. The slave ship decided to skirt Fringe space—even they're not stupid enough to cross into Rish territory—on the way to a feral planet beyond the blue line. One with no League or Federation presence. She was marked for the pleasure pits of some despot—that's the brand on her face. And her ovaries were surgically removed. Not that uncommon for the slave trade."

"The Federation *allows* this?" Callum demanded.

"We do not," his father replied. "But many of the feral worlds do, and with the war against the League, we don't have the resources to send task forces months or years away on humanitarian missions. That means anyone beyond the blue line is beyond our help or concern for the duration, and they've had almost sixty years for things to get even worse, Callum. That's just the way it is. Doesn't make it right."

"But the slave ship carrying Eira and a few hundred others fell afoul of a Federation patrol," O'Hanraghty said. "The farther out into the Fringe you get, the more likely you are to find... local arrangements, let's say, with smugglers and pirates, Callum. Like your father says, that doesn't make it right, but the people who live out there have to *live* out there, which means they've got to make some accommodations with the other people in the vicinity. In this case, the slavers were doing a little smuggling on the side, and they had a consignment for someone in one of our Fringe World systems. Unfortunately for them, there were regular Navy units in-system for a change."

Callum stared at him, processing a lot of new information, and the chief of staff shrugged.

"Quick trial and execution for the slavers. The...cargo was turned over to Colonial, and they resettled her and her brother to Inverness. The only name on record is Eira. Seems single names were the custom back on her home world. She worked menial jobs to scrape out a living." He shrugged again, eyes on the holo. "Nothing else of note in her file."

Logan returned to the room and gave Murphy a quick nod. The admiral glanced at him, then turned back to O'Hanraghty.

"So what do we do with her?" he asked. "The allegations against her *are* rather severe."

Logan's heavy jaw worked from side to side, and Murphy looked at his son.

"Callum, what do you want to happen? And how's your nose, by the way?"

"It was nothing, Sir. An accident." Callum shook his head. "I don't...*can't* blame her. She was in that bunker for how long? Trying to keep her brother alive, then the lights go out, she's trapped in there with the body..."

"Circumstances of the 'accident'?" Murphy tapped a finger on his desk, still looking at Callum.

"The walkway was pretty slippery, Sir," Logan put in.

"Slippery?" Murphy's eyebrows arched. "You agree with that, Callum? Slippery."

"Oh, definitely." Callum nodded quickly. "Those duck boards must be from the lowest bidder. And I'm not used to snow and ice. For sure."

"I daresay. I almost lost my own footing a few times." Murphy frowned. "Is she a threat, or can she be an asset? I'm not inclined to do anything for Drebin's sake, but she's been through trauma that would break battle-hardened spacers. Or Marines."

"You put her on the *Calcutta* for weeks or a couple of months and she'll spiral out of control with no goal," O'Hanraghty said. "We've seen this before. Being in a tiny box in one of those personnel modules with her own thoughts is not what she needs. She's had plenty of that already."

"How old is she?" Callum asked. "Old enough to sign a contract?"

"What are you getting at?" Murphy asked.

"Let's not just throw her away," his son said. "If she's of age she can opt into service. And we'll be in New Dublin for a while, so..."

✧　　✧　　✧

Eira rocked gently on the brig cot. She'd spent so long in darkness that she'd expected light—any light—would be a blessing. But the incessant illumination in her cell was just as oppressive in its own different way as the black of the bunker.

Her mind drifted to Sam in their last hours together as the final glow lamp faded. In the darkness...

Something clanked. Then the bars rolled to one side and Murphy—the younger Murphy...Callum—was there, smiling at her.

She buried her face against her knees.

"Eira—just Eira, right?" he said. "You okay in here? Eat

something?" He sat at the far end of the cot. "I have some good news and some bad news. Which do you want first?"

"If they're going to space me for assaulting a Heart, then there isn't any good news, is there?"

"Stole my thunder," he said, and she raised her head. "No charges."

"No charges?" she repeated as if the words were in a foreign language.

"Nope."

She looked at him, studying his nose. It looked no worse for wear, other than some slight bruising.

"I broke your perfect face," she said.

"That was my fault. I should have known Logan was right around the corner and he was going to . . . take care of things. No harm, no foul, right? Although, I've gotta ask—how did you know it was him?"

"You've heard his voice?" she asked, and shrugged when he nodded. "Well, he really likes hearing it himself. He was all over the boards. Being God." She waved that aside, and her eyes narrowed. "And he's letting this go?"

The disbelief in her voice was palpable, and Callum shook his head.

"No, there won't be any charges relating to the incident. Not at this end, for sure, and the Admiral's fairly certain Drebin—well, we'll let the admirals back home worry about him. And even if *they* can overlook everything that happened, he's done. My family knows everyone in the Five Hundred, and he really, really pissed my dad off. He'll be lucky if he can find work programming sanitation bots on a garbage scow."

"He deserves worse," she said. "Lots worse."

"He does, but it's not on us to give it to him. And that brings us to the bad news. The Admiral doesn't want you to go back with the rest of the survivors, but *Ishtar* can't transport civilian traffic to any place other than the nearest refugee station. Some weird wartime reg. So . . . I'm here to ask you to enlist in the Federation Armed Forces."

"Do what?" She rubbed an eye and stared at him. "I wasn't even born a Fed!"

"Yeah, about that. First, don't call anyone a 'Fed.' It tends to make some folks angsty. Second, you can enlist, since you were a legal resident via resettlement without petition. I read up on all of this on the tube over, and I gotta say, immigration laws are ridiculous. But what it boils down to is that it's either the *Ishtar* in uniform, or *Calcutta* in civilian clothes. Which would you prefer?"

"What would I do? In uniform?" She turned to one side and put her feet on the deck.

"Now, this is the best part, in my opinion. You'd be a 620W-X, which is Navy-speak for 'needs of the service.' And our needs for you would be as my assistant. The Admiral thinks I could use a subordinate. And other duties would include tasks from the Hoplon detachment. Sergeant Major Logan was very impressed with you. Something about being an ingot he could hammer into shape. Or something. Sure hope you like calisthenics."

"I can stay with you? With Admiral Murphy?"

"That's the idea. Unless you have some other special skills where you could be more value-added. Any engineering background? Programming? Drone wrangling?"

Eira shook her head.

"Hydroponics or protein resynthesis?"

Another shake.

"Read and write?"

Eira raised a hand and moved it in a so-so gesture.

"Then we know where to start. Come on. There's some paperwork for you and—"

"Just let me stay with you," she said. "Please. Murphy and Murphy. Just let me stay. As your servant. Your companion... anything."

"No worries," he told her. "No worries there... although I can already feel my mother giving me one of *those* looks. But same as it ever was during the war, right? We're just building up a bit of a cadre as we go along. Now let's get you to the adjutant for the contract. You can sign your name, at least?"

Eira nodded and traced an X in the air. Callum winced, ever so slightly.

"Lots of work," he sighed. "But we've got some transit time to deal with it."

✧   ✧   ✧

The sound of bodies slamming against mats and the slap of leather against bags drew Eira down the dimly lit shipboard passage toward an open, outsized blast door. She reached it and paused, then tugged at the edge of her new uniform, drew a deep breath, swiped at her hair to cover the brand around her eye, and stepped through the opening into a cavernous bay.

Ishtar boasted three well-equipped gymnasiums for her eight-hundred-strong crew, but certain of her current passengers weren't prepared to wait their turns to use them. That was why this cargo bay had been repurposed into a dojo, with practice mats and racks of dull training weapons. Almost four dozen Hoplons in workout gear sparred, drilled with weapons, or did rounds of burpees and pull-ups at a row of bars.

Three men sat on metal bleachers, watching the training with the perpetually dissatisfied "I'm not *quite* pissed" scowls of professional noncoms.

Eira swallowed hard and turned toward them.

"Whoa, there!" Faeran, who'd had her back to the bulkhead beside the door, watching the activity with a medic's eye, saw her and waved her over. "You must be the Greenie. Wolf Mother, do you know what you look like?"

"The petty man said to find a s-major," Eira said.

"The *petty officer* told you to report to the *Sergeant Major*." Faeran shook her head. "And he let you do it looking like a soup sandwich. Bet he thought it was going to be funny when you walked into that chain saw."

"Sandwich?"

"Come here."

Faeran folded Eira's collar down, buttoned all her pockets, and sighed at her unpolished boots.

"What have we got here?" She moved the hair away from Eira's scars, and Eira slapped her hand away.

"*Now* I know who you are. Is it religious?" Faeran brushed the side of her fingers against the tattoos on her own face.

"Slave brand." Eira's tone was tight, and Faeran nodded slowly.

"Okay, you get one because you're a Greenie. But you strike anyone off the mats, and it'll go bad for you quick. The zero's aide or not."

"Sorry, Mistress. This is strange to me."

"It's corporal." Faeran tapped the rank sewn onto her uniform. "Come on. Let's get this massacre started. Stay strong. That's the only advice you need with the Sergeant Major."

The medic led her over to the three seated men. Logan spat tobacco juice into a plastic bottle as they came and gave Eira the once-over.

"Holy shit, Faeran," one of the other men said. "Better get your aid bag."

Eira stamped her foot against the deck and brought her left hand, palm out, up to her eye.

Logan spat again as the other men chuckled.

"You saw the puffies do that on Inverness?" Logan asked. "Put your damn hand down, Greenie. You're not even using the right one."

"This must be the new 'personal secretary,'" one of Logan's trio said.

"Master Sergeant Bridger, why don't you and Sergeant Falco go roll around and then do push-ups until I get tired?" Logan asked. Bridger slapped the other noncom on the shoulder, and both of them stripped off their blouses and trotted over to an open spot on a mat.

Logan worked his dip from one side of his mouth to the other.

"How old are you?"

Eira looked down at her feet.

"Your ears work?" he asked.

"I don't know," she said. "No one ever told me my birthday. The doctor measured my bones and said I was close to nineteen, standard."

"Okay, at least you're old enough to be here."

"You shot me." Eira touched her chest, and Logan chuckled.

"You're welcome," he said. "If I hadn't hit you with a non-lethal I know you would have killed that Heart piece of shit, and corpses get real hard to explain. Especially ones with lots of rank and titles. You got a bruise instead of the airlock or a noose. So you're welcome."

"Medic!" came from the mats.

"It's always him," Faeran snarled. "Such a bleeder."

Faeran ran back to a pack by the door, and Logan stood.

"Steiner! What did I tell you about throwing elbows with no pads on?"

"Sorry, Smaj," Steiner called back.

"Cortez! What did I tell you about getting *hit* by elbows?" There was no answer, and Logan scowled. "Ah, I bet he's knocked out."

Logan shook his head and sat back down.

"Back to you, Greenie. The zero wants you around him, and that's his call. Not unusual for an officer to pick up someone like you during a long deployment away from home and significant others."

"I'm no whore."

"Never said you were. But I saw you tear that Heart apart, Greenie. I know what you've got inside you. That's why I'm taking an interest in your well-being instead of ignoring you to the best of my ability, you follow?"

"Not really."

"We'll get to you properly addressing me later." Logan shifted in his seat. "For now, take no offense to this, as none's meant: you're a pretty young thing. Even with that brand. You're going to be a supernumerary to the zero and the principal. The perception from the colonists, from Leaguie spies—from anyone wishing harm on the principal—is that you *are* the staff whore, and you're not a threat. Which is where they're wrong, Greenie. You're a fighter, aren't you?"

"I can fight. I've done it before."

"And you've got a killer instinct. That's not something that can be trained; it has to be discovered. But fury and adrenaline alone get you only so far in a fight. Training will get you farther—a *lot* farther. So what we're going to do is train you to be a bodyguard for the zero and the principal. You'll be my secret weapon to keep them safe. Sound like a plan?"

"It sounds good. Very good. But the only thing I really know how to do now is the wash," she said.

"Armies have had a lot of practice taking someone like you and getting them somewhat competent for the battlefield in a few months. We'll get you up to standard."

"Will I get a metal suit?"

"No."

"But you said—"

"Hoplon armor takes years of training and it's meant for shipboard actions and direct action against key targets. You learn to shine your boots before you worry about putting on the iron. Now...that brand. It has to go."

"It's a scar," she said. "Scars are forever."

"The zero can authorize the ship's doctor to do a proto-skin graft. Expensive, but he'll do it if you ask. And you're no slave, Eira. Never again—you understand that?"

"Murphy was . . . I saw him talking to the medic and touching this part of his face." Eira motioned to her brand.

"The zero was already on it. Huh."

"Is Callum the zero? Because it was the Admiral with the medic," Eira said.

"The Admiral." Logan pursed his lips. "And here I thought the zero wanted his staff looking pretty, but it was the Admiral. Interesting. Heart Worlders aren't against debt slavery, but that's not here nor there, is it? Rest of this cruise to New Dublin, you're assigned to the Hoplon detachment. It's only the four of us with the principal, but I consolidate the rest of the task force's complement here for training and to keep us civilized. Go grab a pair of strike gloves and report to that ugly mug over there by the bags. He'll walk you through boxing drills to get you started."

"Thank you, s-major."

"Sergeant. Major. Two words."

"Sergeant Major."

"Better. We'll see if you thank me in the morning. Now that we understand each other, this will be our final friendly conversation. Now move out. Draw fire."

CHAPTER FIFTEEN

"HE DID WHAT?"

Fleet Admiral Fokaides set down a glass of clear alcohol and turned away from the beach outside the villa. Admiral Yang, in a dress uniform at odds with the fleet admiral's more relaxed linen clothes and the civilian trappings of the glass-walled den, waggled a slate in one hand.

"Spaced out from Jalal Station almost immediately on his arrival and took his entire command on a rescue mission to Scotia," Yang replied. The crash of a wave rumbled through the villa. "He also took the fleet detachment assigned to Scotia—and the governor—with him. All of which was at Murphy's command discretion."

"That...does not sound like Terrence Murphy."

Fokaides sat down and a corgi hopped into his lap. He scratched its head, frowning out at the beach.

"Do we—" Yang glanced at a closed door "—want to involve your host in this discussion?"

A woman's laughter carried through the door.

"Mr. Boyle is a bit preoccupied," Fokaides observed. "Now why...why in the hell would Murphy haul his entire command, and a force he—I don't want to say 'stole'—"

"Dynamically retasked?"

"Dynamically retasked to go back to some third-rate Fringe

planet that barely had the population density to man a cruiser? His orders are to be in New Dublin by the end of this month. We don't have time to shift deployments around to cover the gap. Thakore is going to throw a fit when I have to relieve his son-in-law for cause."

The closed door opened.

"Don't be so dramatic." Amedeo Boyle came out of his bedroom in a bathrobe, pajamas, and slippers. "Murphy will make it to New Dublin on time. Says so in the timetable he sent back before he left Jalal."

Yang frowned at the slate in her hand, then looked back at Boyle.

"How do you know that? I just got this three hours ago. I came down from the Oval as soon as I got the word," she said.

"A little birdie told me." Boyle winked at her. "But that timetable holds, yes? They were due for a stopover in Jalal with time for fleet maneuvers to integrate the task force. Murphy just decided to spend that time digging Fringers out of rubble, instead."

He crossed to a comfortable chair and sank into it.

"Give me that." Fokaides swiped the slate out of Yang's hand and began reading.

"This is not what we expected from Murphy," Yang said. "We gave him the easiest command the Federation has so close to the frontier. All we need him to do is sit on New Dublin and not lose the keys to his carrier division. I don't like this."

"This doesn't really sound like O'Hanraghty," Fokaides announced, tossing the slate on the coffee table.

"You can tell? How are you even aware of Murphy's batman?" Boyle asked.

He clapped his hands at the dog and patted his lap. The corgi didn't move.

"O'Hanraghty's a special case," Fokaides replied. "He's been involved with a number of wrong-think groups in the past. Helps to keep people like that under watch."

"Oh . . . one of those Rish conspiracy nuts?" Boyle rolled his eyes.

"It's a common enough suspicion among Fringe-born officers and enlisted," Yang said. "We haven't gone so far as to cashier everyone that seems warm to believing the Rish are somehow pulling the League's strings. Not that we haven't been tempted. But if we take any action, it looks like their theories are legitimate. Then it snowballs from there."

"Public ridicule and stymied careers are enough to keep ambitious officers from joining that cult," Fokaides said. "And Murphy's too smart to fall for anything like that. But now he's yanking on the leash."

"It *was* within his prerogative," Yang pointed out.

"Prerogative, maybe, but I don't like commanders with too much initiative." Fokaides waved a finger at Yang. "They think they're smarter than you, and then they'll go off and make a decision that throws off planning done at higher levels. The only thing worse than an intelligent and energetic officer is a *stupid* and energetic officer. And we didn't give Murphy this command because of his stellar track record."

The fleet admiral glanced at Boyle, and the other man shrugged.

"The business side prefers intelligent and lazy executives as well," he said. "But how is the rescue mission to Scotia a bad thing? Lives saved. Good news story for the nets instead of a text line at the bottom of the broadcast listing the casualty numbers. Thakore will be thrilled when he hears about this."

"It may play well in terms of public perception," Yang said, "but the Admiralty is not amused. One event isn't a trend, but I still don't like this. Murphy needs to get back on the program."

"We need the League's focus on Beta Cygni," Fokaides amplified for Boyle's benefit. "Murphy's task force is stronger than most of the system pickets we've been forced to divert to the Fringe, but there are a lot of them. More than most people realize. Frankly, even prioritizing to protect just the most significant of our assets around the periphery, we're spread way too thin to stop a committed assault anywhere besides Beta Cygni. If Murphy decides to play cowboy out there, the League may think we're readying a push in his command area. Especially if they notice how we've upgraded the maintenance facilities in New Dublin. It may not be much compared to a Heart World, but the system's in a good spot to serve as a logistics nexus for the Concordia Sector in general. That's why we've invested in the improvements there— as a support point for the local defense forces, not an offensive springboard. But if they add those improvements to any loose warhead tendencies on Murphy's part, they may decide two plus two equals five and think we *are* beefing up the sector to prep for more offensive action on our part. And if they think that, they may just decide to beef up their own forces in response."

"How is that bad?" Boyle asked. "The less League in Beta Cygni, the easier our fight."

"Because we don't have the ships or the logistics to push into League space from New Dublin," Yang said. "Inhabited systems are few and far between out that way, but that area is even more Fringe for the League than it is for us. There's a reason neither side's authorized fleet actions in that sector for years. Raids like this business at Scotia, yes. They happen from time to time, although we haven't seen one as ugly as this appears to have been for quite a while. But *we* don't push anything like that, because we have more settled systems and more populations in the sector. More to lose if the League attacks. If Murphy makes noise, the League will investigate . . . and realize just how thin we are out there. In which case, they may decide on something a bit more ambitious than just K-striking an epsilon-tier world in the middle of nowhere."

"But his show of force at Scotia sends the opposite message, doesn't it?" Fokaides said thoughtfully. "Shows we're there and ready to respond if the League pushes things. That's one way to look at it, anyway." He laced his hands behind his head. "Even a blind squirrel can find a nut now and then. So maybe his initiative deserves a sudden promotion back to the Oval?"

"Two birds with one stone?" Yang murmured.

"No," Boyle said firmly. "Murphy stays in command. We need him to come back as planned."

"Sir," Yang became flustered for a moment, "political considerations aren't—"

"A moment, Xiaolan," Fokaides interrupted. He glanced fleetingly at Boyle as he crossed a leg, careful not to disturb the resting dog, and bounced a foot. "One event is not a trend. So let's make sure a trend doesn't develop. Let's get someone we trust in-system to keep a close watch on him."

"A minder," Yang said slowly.

"A reminder that he's under scrutiny," the fleet admiral said. "This way, everything goes the way my Oval wants it to go, and other parties are also satisfied. Yes?" He directed the question at Boyle.

"Fine." Boyle waved a hand. "Send him a plant to be something on his staff. Perhaps with additional instructions to keep O'Hanraghty from being too much of a negative influence?"

"Or one less pain in my ass?" Fokaides huffed. "That can be arranged. Xiaolan, I hope you brought the latest stats from Beta Cygni? Boyle has a real chef in the kitchen, and he's got fresh octopus for xtapodi. Stay for dinner."

"I do have the preliminary report with me," she said.

"Then take your coat off and stay a while." Boyle waved at the bar. "The war's not going anywhere."

CHAPTER SIXTEEN

CORMAG DEWAR PULLED ON HIS FORMAL UNIFORM JACKET AND buttoned the front. It was a bit tight around the waistline, he noticed.

"Just a touch of winter weight," he told himself, looking out the window. A snowstorm had turned the morning sky to a gray abyss, and flakes whipped around the panes and built up near the base. "Ach. Should have prayed for better weather."

Someone knocked at his office door, and he turned as Patrick MacDowell, his aide, opened it.

"Sir, he's here!"

Young MacDowell had tawny hair, blue eyes, a pale complexion, and a deceptively weak-looking chin. Dewar knew better than most just how deceptive that chin was, but the young man was paler than usual.

"The President's here this early?" the general asked, eyebrows raised. "He and I were supposed to meet at the spaceport in—" he double-checked the time "—two hours."

"No, I mean *him* him. Governor Murphy." MacDowell shook his head. "He just showed up and—"

A massively built Marine sergeant major with a Hoplon patch pushed past MacDowell into the office. He was bareheaded and wore only a light fatigue jacket, despite the bits of ice clinging to his eyebrows, and his hard eyes circled the office once, like a tactical sensor drone. Then he sniffed and stepped to one side.

The admiral who entered was taller than Dewar had antici-pated. Bit uglier, too. He wore a black greatcoat and beret, both dusted with melting snow, and he stripped off his right glove to extend that hand to the general.

"Governor." Dewar gripped the offered hand. "Your task force only just arrived and we weren't expecting you groundside for hours. There's a fife and drum corps at the spaceport that's been rehearsing for—"

"And all your hospitality won't go to waste, I promise," Murphy said as a red-haired Navy captain followed him into an office which was becoming distinctly crowded. "This is O'Hanraghty, my chief of staff," the admiral said, waving at the still-shivering captain. "You're aware of what happened to Inverness?"

"Where's the bloody heater?" O'Hanraghty muttered, clapping his gloved hands together. He looked around, spotted the heating vent beneath the window, and made a beeline toward it.

"Tea, Patrick," Dewar said. "Tea!"

MacDowell disappeared, and the general pointed Murphy at the desk and angled one of his office chairs to sit in himself.

Murphy shrugged off his coat and hung it on a rack near the door, then sat . . . in the chair, not behind the desk.

"This is your office, General Dewar," he said. "I've got my own big chair in the governor's mansion, correct?"

"You . . . should," Dewar said, sinking back into the chair behind his desk. "Though I believe your predecessor packed up a fair amount of the furniture when he left."

"Governor Babikov is gone?" Murphy raised an eyebrow.

"Two days ago. Something about a family obligation and he was sure you'd understand. That's not quite how I understood it, but let's not waste time on rumor." He jammed a thumb onto the comm key on his desk. "Patrick! Tea!"

"If the previous governor had a reputation, I'd like to know," Murphy said. "He was here for many years. I'm fairly sure his . . . performance has created a certain expectation of the *new* gover-nor. For good or for ill."

Dewar's interest piqued. Maybe this man wasn't here just to mark time after all.

"Babikov had several local hire . . . secretaries. He decided he'd leave the system with one." Dewar shrugged. "The others took offense at their exclusion and complained to their clans. I believe a number of their male relatives were planning a visit."

"He didn't have a security detail?" the sergeant major asked.

"He did," Dewar said dryly. "Some of them were the male relatives. Governor Babikov was, ah...not known for his judgment. But what was that you were saying about Inverness?" His eyes narrowed. "Scotia's only a few weeks away by merchantman, but there's not much traffic with it. So in answer to your earlier question, Governor, no, I'm not aware of anything that's happened there."

"It wasn't pretty, I'm afraid." Murphy had an excellent poker face, Dewar thought, but his gray eyes were bleak. "A few weeks ago..." he began, and the general sat back to listen as the admiral laid out the League attack and the rescue effort.

Dewar sat silent until the new governor finished, then shook his head.

"And the system picket didn't even fire a shot?"

"They did not," Murphy said. "That decision wasn't popular with the crews of BatRon Seven-Oh-Two, either, I'm afraid. And such a...passive response isn't exactly likely to discourage future raids. Which brings me to why I came to you first. The League force that smashed Inverness likely based out of Shanhaiguan, and they've had enough time to return to base and receive new orders. I don't know what those orders will be, but if they're to launch another attack, New Dublin is the next most likely target and the attack's likely to be heavier rather than lighter. How prepared is the system to defend against the same force? Or a heavier one, for that matter?"

There was a knock on the door and MacDowell came back in with a silver tea service. He set out cups and saucers and poured.

"Finally, something warm!" O'Hanraghty took his and drank it as fast as he could, then picked up the pot and poured another cup.

"President Tolmach has been calling, Sir," MacDowell said, looking at Dewar.

"I promise I'll make my scheduled appearance at the spaceport." Murphy sipped from his own cup. "Please pass on my apologies for jostling protocol."

"Right away, Governor."

MacDowell turned to hurry out, but a meaty palm in the center of his chest stopped him.

"We're not here," the sergeant major rumbled.

"Who's not here?" MacDowell blinked guileless blue eyes, and the Marine grinned.

"You get it," he said, and slapped the young man on the shoulder as he let him pass.

"New Dublin was attacked nigh ten years ago," Dewar said. He swiped a finger across a reader and a holo of the system came up.

The system primary was an F7v star, considerably hotter than that of the Sol System, but Crann Bethadh—the third of its eight planets—had an orbital radius of seventeen light-minutes, more than twice that of Old Earth. So despite its toasty warm star, it was a decidedly chilly planet, as the weather outside Dewar's office window demonstrated. Its next nearest neighbor in, Goibniu, on the other hand, was only about 34,000,000 kilometers farther from the primary than Old Earth from Sol...and hotter than the hinges of hell, so far as habitability went. Despite which, almost a quarter million New Dubliners lived there.

The system possessed an asteroid belt, about 250,000,000 kilometers farther out than Crann Bethadh, followed by a super-Jovian gas giant, Dagda, which fell just short of brown star status, with an orbital radius of 59 LM, and slightly smaller gas giants—Brigit and Cailleach—at 115 and 227 LM, respectively. Bodach and Donn, a useless pair of frozen balls of ice, completed the stellar family at 445 and 869 LM.

"As you can see, we're a bit more exposed than some, out here at the outer edge of the Goldilocks zone, especially for a star as hot as New Dublin." Dewar shrugged. "They didn't drive in too hard, and thank God they didn't, because we didn't have a lot on hand to stop them. What we did have was mainly about ten percent of the missiles we really needed, and we only had those because we had half a battle squadron in for its sixty-month maintenance cycle. We sort of...borrowed the missiles they'd off-loaded."

"Borrowed?" Murphy arched an eyebrow, and Dewar shrugged.

"Stole, really. And Olympia sent us a bill for them, afterward." His tone was flat and he met Murphy's eyes levelly. Then he shrugged again. "Choice between seeing your home slagged and pissing off the federal government, and decisions get real simple."

"I imagine so," Murphy murmured with a nod. "But if the ships were down for overhaul, how did you launch them?"

"Borrowed our main cargo station's drone cells," Dewar said. "The resource availability here in New Dublin helped push the decision to upgrade our yard facilities, and Goibniu—" he gestured at New Dublin's second planet "—is lousy with metals. One of the reasons we're a category delta system. It's cheaper and easier to use mag drivers to launch cargo drones than to use manned ships, and loads of ore don't mind the acceleration. So Goibniu kicks them off, they use their onboard drives to kill acceleration at the other end, and then they dock. We send them back the same way, except they insert themselves into orbit until the mines dirt-side need them. And it just happens that the mag drives we were able to get hold of were old surplussed Mark 37 drone launchers. So—"

"So," Murphy said, eyes gleaming suddenly as he glanced at O'Hanraghty, "you used your cargo launchers to fire off all those missiles you 'borrowed'?"

"Exactly." Dewar nodded. "And President Tolmach authorized us to use them all in a single launch. So we did, and we seem to have taken 'em by surprise. Don't think they saw them at all until the fusion drives lit off on final. 'Course, we didn't have Navy fire control, so they were inaccurate as hell, but we did score a couple of hits. No kills, but I think it scared them, and they didn't know how many more we might have. Probably scary as hell if they never figured out where they came from. Anyway, they turned and ran for it."

"Excellent move," Murphy congratulated him. "I've seen something like it used in a combat simulation, and it completely blindsided the other commander."

"May've gotten them to break off," Dewar said, "but the bastards launched an alpha strike of their own before they vectored out of the system. And maybe it would have been better if they had figured out where they'd come from, because they targeted our largest space station, instead. Four thousand, six hundred and twenty souls lost that day."

"Alpha strikes are hard to defeat, even with a long time of flight," Murphy said quietly.

"I know. And, like I said, our orbit makes us more vulnerable than some. But, coupled with the mines on Goibniu and the smelting stations in orbit around Crann Bethadh, it also makes us a logical place for ship repair. Our yards have seen a lot of use repairing Navy ships and merchantmen for a long time—more traffic than Jalal, some years, especially with the upgrades. That's why we've usually got at least one FTLC and its parasite group in-system for local defense."

"I'm aware." Murphy nodded.

New Dublin's population was the next best thing to a hundred million. That was tiny for any Heart World—there were single megaurbs that had populations of well over fifty million—but it was enormous for a system this far out in the Fringe. And, as Dewar had just pointed out, that made it a valuable industrial node, well situated to support the Navy in the Concordia Sector.

It also made what had happened in Scotia even more ominous, and he leaned forward to examine the system holo.

"If the League were to hit New Dublin again, with a force, say, twice as strong as the one that hit Inverness, what would you people have to back up my task force?"

"Governor, I...I haven't even shown you around the capital and you're already measuring the system's drapes. But then there's Inverness and...I wanted orbital launchers and actual fire control put in years ago." Dewar narrowed his eyes slightly. "Never had the budget or the trained manpower to make that happen, though, and Olympia—Well, keeping the yards up and running has been the main federal priority."

His eyes met Murphy's for a moment, and the admiral nodded ever so slightly. The federal government didn't much like the notion of allowing Fringe systems the firepower to stand off a League raid. The same weapons might find themselves used against the Federation by a star system far enough "out of compliance." No wonder they'd been...less than cooperative about building up New Dublin's defenses.

"Our local defense budget's always been tight," Dewar continued, "and after we 'stole' the Navy's missiles, it took us years just to pay for them instead of buying new. I've got a few in-system ships to patrol the inner system, and the standing militia as a garrison."

"How do you manage a 'standing militia'?" O'Hanraghty asked. "Permanent ground forces are restricted to the federal government. That means the Federation Army."

"And when was the last time you saw the Army out in the Fringe, Captain?" Dewar asked dryly.

"About the Tenth of Never," O'Hanraghty conceded with a tight grin. "But how did you sneak a *permanent* force past the Oval?"

"Didn't tell them we had one. For that matter, we don't... technically. We discharge them every three hundred sixty-four days Standard. Then we reenlist the lot two mornings later. I'd advise you not to allow shore leave during that interval. Crann Bethadh gets a bit rowdy."

"Neatly done," O'Hanraghty congratulated him with a rather broader grin. "But what are your in-system craft armed with?"

"Basically they're old *Saber*-class destroyers we picked up cheap when the Navy decommissioned the last of them," Dewar said, and O'Hanraghty nodded.

The *Sabers* had been effective ships—for light combatants, at least—in their day, but that day had ended the better part of two decades ago. They were heavier metal than most Fringe Systems could command, but that didn't mean they'd count for much against modern designs.

"I'll need the repair timetables for every warship in your docks," Murphy said.

"Well, we've got most of CruRon Four-Sixty-Nine in for their yearly overhaul, and CruRon Twenty-Six just completed theirs," Dewar said thoughtfully. "And I suppose you already knew about *Patton* and *Foch*?" TFNS *Patton* and *Foch* were the other two units of Yance Drebin's BatRon 702, detached to New Dublin for their regularly scheduled sixty month deep-maintenance overhaul. "They're due to complete sometime in the next thirty days," Dewar said. "Don't imagine there's much point sending them back to Scotia when they have, though."

"No, there isn't," Murphy agreed grimly.

"We've been alerted to expect another task group, en route to Zaragoza. Don't have an exact movement schedule on them, though. Just an alert that they're coming through to pick up CruRon Twenty-Six and that we're to stand by to provide any maintenance they may need."

Murphy nodded. Given how long messages took to travel across interstellar distances, it wasn't unusual for ship movement information to be incomplete. Sometimes it was even flatly wrong.

"Aside from that," Dewar continued, "we do have BatRon Nine-Twelve and BatCruRon Eighty-Four in-system at the moment."

"We noticed *Ninhursag*'s and *Tiamat*'s transponders on our way in," O'Hanraghty said with a nod. "What's the story with that?"

"*Tiamat* kicked up a harmonic in her drive fan. A pretty bad one. Commodore Granger decided to stop off here on her way back to the Heart and see if we couldn't put it straight. Been working on it for about a week now, and the yards think they've found the problem, but we're having to fabricate some of the components, so they'll be here a while."

"Interesting," O'Hanraghty murmured, darting a quick look at Murphy.

"Governor," Dewar said, "I know you said you just came from Scotia. But are you aware of an actual imminent threat to New Dublin? Because if there is one, we can mobilize more personnel. An awful lot of the able-bodied—and once able-bodied—adults here on Crann Bethadh. All veterans."

"I don't have any actionable intelligence about an imminent threat." Murphy slapped his palms against his knees. "But we just left a system the League decimated and left to die. Consider me a bit more motivated than usual. Harry, have Ops organize a recon from Drebin's group. I want a fresh gravity well survey done on every object bigger than Io."

"Aye, aye. They won't be happy about it."

"They need the practice." Murphy turned back to Dewar. "So we need to beef up Crann Bethadh's missile power. I have a few thoughts about that. What else do we need?"

The general locked eyes with him again for a moment.

"Governor...perhaps you'd like to unpack your things before we get too far down in the weeds. Then there's the matter of your welcome ceremony."

"I appreciate the effort, but every moment we're not working on the system's defenses is time given to the League to better prepare for their attack," Murphy said.

O'Hanraghty cleared his throat, and Murphy glanced at him, then back at the New Dubliner.

"We can talk on the walk back to the spaceport," he said.

"That's a far piece to walk," Dewar replied.

"Exactly what I'm thinking. It will give us time. And besides, Captain O'Hanraghty needs the exercise."

"Dragging me back out into the cold already," O'Hanraghty said, rebuttoning the coat he'd never actually taken off. "Thanks, Sir."

"Fresh, planetside air is good for you, Harry! Especially after all the time we spent breathing that anemic, recycled shipboard stuff."

O'Hanraghty rolled his eyes, and Dewar chuckled.

"We've time to finish tea first, though, Captain," he told O'Hanraghty, pouring the other man a fresh cup. He topped up his own and then raised an eyebrow at Murphy.

"Yes, please," the admiral said. "It's remarkable. Local variety?"

"Came by way of a League supplier." Dewar chuckled again, louder, at Murphy's expression. "Smuggler had the wrong excise tax stamps on his crates. Forfeited the goods instead of seeing the magistrate. We'll see some illegal trade come through on the way to feral worlds beyond the blue line. Couldn't sell it. Shame to see it go to waste."

"Shame, indeed." Murphy sipped. "Talk to me about your militia's loadout."

CHAPTER SEVENTEEN

SECOND ADMIRAL XING STOOD FACING A SEALED SHUTTLE HATCH, her hands clasped behind her back. Her staff sat in rows along the bulkheads, all still strapped in. She felt the slight vibration of the shuttle's maneuvering thrusters through the soles of her feet and unclasped her hands to key her wrist comm.

"Than...what is taking so goddamned long?" she snapped.

"One moment, Ma'am," a voice replied in her earbud. "Your shuttle's coming in on remote."

"You locked me in your ship for the entire voyage. Didn't tell me where the hell we were going or how long it would take to get there. Now we've arrived, and my staff and I can't even look out of a porthole? How, exactly, do you justify treating your commanding officer like this?"

"The First Admiral established this protocol, Ma'am. It will all make more sense very soon. Also, your staff isn't allowed off the shuttle until we have final approval."

"Approval? Approval from *whom*?!" Xing's face contorted with anger, then snapped back to neutral. "But you said 'soon.' *How* soon?"

The shuttle's rumble as its landing gear hit a deck answered her question. Her staff began unbuckling, but she shook her head.

"Wait here, Yong-Gi. Than's found one more hoop for me to jump through." Zhang cracked her knuckles. "We'll be done with him before too long."

"As you wish, Second Admiral," her chief of staff said.

The hatch slid open and the shuttle ramp lowered to the floor of what was obviously a shipboard hangar, empty of any other craft. Only Than was there to meet her. She strode down the ramp and jumped off the end before the edge could set down.

"Welcome to Diyu, Ma'am," Than said.

"Really?" She shook her head and rolled her eyes. "A system named 'Hell'?"

"It used to be call Yuxi," Than said.

"Never heard of it."

"Not surprising. We renamed it for all official correspondence as another security measure," Than told her. "It's an absolutely useless star in the middle of nowhere. That's one of the things that made it perfect for Project Astra. But the new name's appropriate enough in a lot of ways, including the fact that there's no going home until Project Astra's completed. If you'll come this way?"

"My staff has a bet going that this is all an elaborate joke," she said as he led the way toward a set of double doors. "Are they right?"

Than touched a remote on his wrist and the shuttle ramp lifted as the hatch sealed behind them.

"How did you bet?" he asked.

"They didn't include me in the pool, but I still know about it."

"It's not a joke," Than assured her. "But our partner in this project has a number of security protocols. We've found it best to cooperate—it removes a good deal of the friction." They reached the doors, and he tapped a long code into a panel. "Only a few dozen people in the League know the full extent of Project Astra."

"I'm a bit perturbed that *I've* never heard so much as a whisper about it," she said.

"Then our partner's security protocols have worked," Than said.

A hatch opened on the wall and a metal globe floated out over their heads. It turned to direct a built-in lens at them and its surface changed through a myriad of colors and reflections.

"One word of advice," he added. "Remain calm."

"That's . . . different," Xing said. "What happens if I don't 'remain calm'?"

"There was one incident. A face bitten off. Something of a diplomatic flap, but it was just the one case," Than said, then clapped his hands together twice and bowed to the floating globe.

"The Terran League Navy presents its choice for final command. May we have an audience with the War Mother."

"Wait. What?"

Xing looked back and forth between the globe, Than, and the doors. Then there was a hiss, and musty air washed over them as those doors opened into a spherical room. A large holo screen on the bulkhead showed endless shipyards, teeming with activity as robotic construction units swarmed around scores of warships. Dozens of completed ships floated in parking orbits with them, stretching around a barren planet with a red dwarf in the distance. A gray-scaled, saurian alien, with enormous shoulders covered by a spiked, articulated carapace, fully erect scarlet cranial frills, and a short, clubbed tail stood at a control panel on a raised dais at the chamber's center. It was at least three meters in height, naked but for the diaphanous streamers falling from its carapace to hang about it in a shimmer of vivid, eye-battering colors. It had the powerful, fanged jaws of a carnivore but startlingly beautiful golden eyes looked out of that hideous, scaled face.

Smaller saurians, no more than half its height and without carapaces, clustered around it.

"High War Mother Naytash," Than said with another bow. The hovering globe translated his words into a high-pitched, squeaky snarl. "I greet you. May your clan increase."

"And may you birth many daughters." The globe translated the Rish's words as it had Than's. "Although you and your mate are past such times, are you not?"

"We have many children. Raising more is out of the question." Than touched fingertips to his face, just below his eyes, then spread his arms to the side.

"War Mother Naytash, I present Second Fleet Mother Xing," he said.

"Come." The Rish extended a hand toward the humans, then curled its four fingers one digit at a time, clicking its claws together. "Come and show me this new one, Than. I have heard so much."

Even the redoubtable Xing stood motionless for a moment, and Than put a hand into the small of her back and gave her a gentle push forward.

"Security has held, War Mother," he said. "Fleet Mother Xing as yet knows...very little about Project Astra."

"The new fleet mother can speak, can she not?" Naytash's lips curled, revealing serrated teeth, and she snapped her jaws with a loud click.

"Interrogative gesture, non-hostile," Than said to Xing.

The second admiral glanced at him, then her nostrils flared and she turned back to the Rish.

"What place is this?" she demanded.

"It is my ship, an extension of my clan hearth," Naytash replied. "It's name...you would call it 'Dagger,' I believe. It is close enough." She tossed her head in what might have been a shrug. "It is a weapon in my clan's hand, ready to aid those we call friend."

Xing looked at her for a moment, then turned and pointed to the holo.

"How many ships are there? Those are *Fúxī*-class carriers. How many? Battleships? Cruisers? Crews? How is all this possible?"

"Good...good!" Naytash turned to the control panel and her clawed fingers tapped across a circle of unlabeled buttons. "The answer is that there are fifty-three of your *Fúxī* FTLCs, each designed to lift six of your *Huang Di* battleships and six *Hou Yi* battlecruisers or *Haneul-nim* strikecarriers. At present, a fifth part of the FTLCs are operational, or nearly so, although only eight of them have completed trials. We await a last shipment to bring the other FTLCs' drives online and sharpen the rest of your sword, War Mother. Ninety percent of the parasites have been completed through the engineering stage and passed propulsion trials, but very few of them are yet armed and even fewer are adequately crewed as yet."

Xing's eyes narrowed as a text holo came up, detailing the entire fleet under construction.

"This is impossible," she said. "How did this stay hidden for so long?"

"Because the Rishathan Sphere has an interest," Naytash said. "We supplied the critical components, most built to your specifications, although we also improved some systems where your designs were flawed." The clubbed tail flicked in what clearly *was* the Rishathan equivalent of a human shrug. "The League but built the shipyards and provided the technicians to build the hulls and assemble those components."

"Why? The costs...This represents several years of the League's entire naval budget," Xing said.

"The Federation...is greedy," Naytash replied. "Truth requires truth, Fleet Mother, and we do not do this out of mere generosity. Both the Federation and the League have encroached upon the greater Sphere of the Rish, but as you know, the Federation is closer to us than you are. They are the greater, more immediate threat to our territory, and the Sphere must remain whole. The greater Sphere which shields it must likewise remain whole. The League guarantees our integrity. We do not trust the same promise from the Federation."

"The Rish have provided us with key drive systems and components for years," Than said. "Along with intelligence. Their assistance has turned the tide in several battles. We owe the Sphere much."

"And now they've built us a fleet." Xing put her hands on her hips. "Are the crews...Rishathan?"

Naytash sucked air through her teeth.

"Laughter," Than murmured in Xing's ear.

"Our influence must remain hidden," Naytash told her. "Some of your crews are already on board, readying for...shakedown?" Naytash looked past Xing to Than, who nodded, then looked back at Xing. "As I have said, only a small percentage of all these ships are operational, but I have been told that the additional war daughters required to crew all of them will be made available shortly."

"That is correct, War Mother," Than said. "We're reactivating retirees and others from outlying planets who have completed their service terms."

"My spacers are old crocks and dischargers?" Xing frowned.

"Experience is invaluable." Frustration edged Than's voice. "They'll be able to grasp Project Astra's purpose, even if they don't have a target right in front of them. And a lot of them have been drawn from planets the Federation's raided. There may be some initial unhappiness at being recalled, but once they realize they're the ones who're finally going to win this war, they'll be ready."

"Win the war?" Xing's eyes glowed. "Damned right it will! When I bring this—" she waved at the endless display of ship icons "—out of wormhole space on the Beta Cygni front, the Feds will shit their vac suits!"

"It's not going to Beta Cygni," Than said, and she scowled.

"What the hell are you talking about?" she demanded.

"We realized some years ago that we've been fighting this war all wrong," Than said.

In fact, although he wasn't about to tell Xing that, he was the one who'd first pointed that out to the Admiralty. Which was why he'd been chosen—initially, at least—to command Dragon Fleet when the time came.

"When the war first began," he continued, "fighting for frontier systems made strategic sense. Our carriers were slower in wormhole space than they are now, and there were enough... reliability issues with military-grade Fasset drives to limit practical operational radii to about fifty or sixty light-years. So both we and the Feds built up a glacis of frontier systems and nodal bases to support that sort of operational 'bubble.' But the technology's changed—improved—over the last twenty or thirty years, and it's time we took cognizance of that. We have the capability now to launch 'deep strikes,' hundreds of light-years behind the front. We don't know whether or not the Feds have figured that out, but *we* have. The problem's been that we haven't been able to withdraw the forces for it from where they're already tied down. If we pull out units to concentrate for an attack like that, the Feds will probably notice. Not only that, if our forces aren't in a position to keep theirs tied down, there's no reason they can't respond with 'deep strikes' of their own. But now—"

"But now we have an entire fleet they don't even know *exists!*" Xing interrupted.

"Exactly." Than nodded. "The Admiralty's unwilling to commit entirely to a completely new strategic paradigm, however."

Which, now that he thought about it, might be one reason the Admiralty had been willing to go along with Liu's decision to put Xing into the command which should have been his. The First Admiral was one of the senior officers who'd been most worried by his own "possibly excessive enthusiasm" for the new concept.

"What does *that* mean?" Xing asked.

"They're not ready to commit to a strike directly into the Heart," Than explained. "They're too worried about task forces from the Feds' nodal bases getting into the rear of our own attack force." He shrugged ever so slightly. "Based on earlier war experience, it's not an entirely unreasonable position." Not *entirely*... just mostly. "So they're prepared to sanction a strike deep into the Federation, but they want a corridor of cleared bases in its rear. Which is why Dragon Fleet's been built here."

"Here?" Xing pounced. "Here where? Where *are* we?"

Naytash tapped another panel and a schematic of the local star system appeared. Its primary was a dim M5v, barely out of the brown dwarf category. It had a single asteroid belt, and none of its planets were remotely habitable, although icons showed both the shipyards and extensive mining habitats in orbit around its second planet, labeled Songdi. Although Songdi was barely two light-minutes from the star, it was considerably colder than the Sol System's Mars.

"We chose Diyu because no one could have any possible reason to come anywhere near it," Than said. "Unless—"

He paused as Naytash touched a button and a map of the local galaxy appeared beside and beneath the system schematic.

"Oh, my!" Xing's eyes lit up. "We're nowhere near Beta Cygni. That's the Concordia Sector." She pointed. "New Dublin, Jalal, Mannerheim . . . it's the Acera Corridor straight into the Heart Worlds!"

"And that's exactly why the First Admiral has kept the Beta Cygni front so active," Than said in a grimmer tone. "The Dragon Fleet equals a third of the fleet strength we have deployed around Beta Cygni—more like half, given the power of its individual units—and the fighting there has sucked in the Federation's strength, as well. They don't have anything that could possibly stop you short of the Heart Worlds themselves, and they can't even try to redeploy from Beta Cygni when you attack without opening a gaping hole in the front there." He looked Xing squarely in the eye. "We've lost a lot of lives to create this opportunity."

"And what will you do with this gift, Fleet Mother Xing?" Naytash asked. "If I agree to give you command. What would a war mother like you do?"

"I have no sea to march to," Xing replied. "With a fleet this size, I would tear a wound through the Federation and let the Heart Worlds bleed to death. I killed Inverness—dealt a mortal blow to the Feds there and left them to die. With this Dragon Fleet . . . With Dragon, I could reach Old Earth itself. I wouldn't even need to fire a shot when I got there. The trail of dead behind me would deliver an ultimatum even the fat sows in the Five Hundred will understand."

"We don't need to inflict that many civilian casualties," Than said. "Destruction of all their key bases would—"

"This is why the First Admiral gave *me* the command," Xing snapped. "Because I have the strength to do what must be done.

For decades we've been content to bleed against the Federation while their Heart Worlds feel no pain. Enough! I'll teach them what this war's *really* like!"

"She is accepted," Naytash said. "Rishathan males are meek and have limited uses. I am glad that a human female can live up to our expectations."

"Excellent." Xing rubbed her palms together. "When will the fleet be ready?"

"As I have said, we await a final shipment before we can complete the FTLCs' Fasset drives. Once it arrives, we will require perhaps two of your months for installation and engineering trials. Once that is accomplished, it depends on crews."

"The next round of call-ups is underway," Than said. "Reinforcements for Beta Cygni—that's the official version."

"Which is my flagship?" Xing asked. "I want fleet exercises with the ready ships starting tomorrow morning. Your carriers will be our Fed stand-ins."

"Ma'am . . ." Than hesitated. "The operational FTLCs have almost full complements, but that's because the Admiralty's given them priority. Most of the parasites are only partially crewed. I doubt more than a handful of them have sufficient personnel onboard for exercises."

"Unacceptable," Xing said flatly, and Naytash sucked in air with another of those hissing laughs and touched yet another button. A manning graph replaced the display of ship names and types, and Xing frowned as she studied it for a handful of seconds.

"We have enough personnel to fully man the parasites for at least six of the carriers," she said. "It's just a matter of distributing them properly."

"The First Admiral wants skeleton cadres aboard as many ships as possible," Than said tonelessly. "His intention is to slot reactivated personnel into existing crew matrices."

"Then, presumably, the personnel already assigned are of exceptional quality," Xing retorted. "It won't hurt them a bit to spend some time polishing their skills while we await the next personnel draft. They can always return to their original ships as additional personnel become available."

"The First Admiral—"

"Isn't here," Xing interrupted. "And he didn't select me to not make my own decisions. See to it."

"Ma'am—"

"See. To. It." She glared at him for a moment, then snorted as he locked his jaw on further remonstrance. She looked back at Naytash.

"Now, which is the flagship?"

"The *Nüwa*," the Rish replied. She gazed at Xing for a moment, then clicked her claws. "Than ... let me speak with the Fleet Mother."

"Of course."

Than bowed slightly and went to the doors. The smaller Rishathan males hissed at him as he left.

CHAPTER EIGHTEEN

"NO MORE STAIRS... AND WAY TOO MUCH STUFF."

Callum stamped snow off his shoes and dumped a space bag in a hallway. Its walls were lined with holo prints of Crann Bethadh's seacoasts and mountains that displayed new angles of the places every ten or twenty seconds. There was a single static picture as well, and he did a double take as it caught his eye. It showed the outside of a barracks, separated from rows and rows of young men and women in civilian clothes by white ropes decorated with red poppies. The captured moment took his mind back to Olympia, when he'd first reported for duty, and a bit of dread built in his chest. He wasn't sure if it was from the memory or something about the photo.

Eira came around the corner. She wore simple fatigues, with a space bag over each shoulder, and her legs and back quivered under the weight.

"Eira, I can carry my own crap." Callum grabbed a bag off her and she shrugged out from under the other. She bent forward, resting her hands on her knees, and breathed deeply.

"What did Logan do to you? It's like you enjoy the hurt."

"Pain... pain is weakness leaving the body," she said.

"Okay, that's carrying physical fitness a bit too far." Callum checked a room number and opened a door. Inside was a single-occupancy apartment with plastic-wrapped furniture. "Not bad."

He dropped the bag and kicked it to one side, then went into the living room, spread his arms out, and spun slowly. "Ah—space!"

"I'll unpack your things," Eira said. She picked one of his bags back up and carried it into the room. "You have a reception dinner in ninety-six minutes. The Admiral specified the following uniform: berets, medals—"

"I saw the message, and I can handle it myself. Why don't you get yourself situated? Maybe unwind a bit from all that Hoplon brainwashing."

Callum opened the closet and the Crann Bethadh equivalent of a moth flew out.

"The troop barracks are on the other side of the governor's palace." She set down the bag she'd been carrying and started for the door. "I can be back in twenty minutes."

"What?" Callum said. "Your quarters are across the hall. One more run down to the lorry, and we're done. Although I think Logan wants you with him during the meet and greet."

"I have a room?" She turned around, confused.

"Of course you do. No more being packed together like mackerel on *Ishtar*. One of the biggest ships in space, and you'd think they could've been a bit more generous with the crew compartments. Trust me, merchant ships are! 'Course, they have a lot smaller crews...and the crews can *quit* if they decide to, now that I think about it."

He walked into the small kitchen.

"Did they stock the fridge? They did not. Not that I cook. Eira, how long until—Eira?"

He leaned into the hallway and saw her apartment door open. She was inside, running one hand down the bedcover.

"It's not bad," Callum said, following her into the apartment. "Is it me, or do they keep the thermostats just above freezing on this planet?"

"Sam and I used to...we'd joke about what we'd do if we could ever get a bed," Eira said. "All we had was a mattress I scrounged out of a dumpster. When he was on that cot in the bunker...He was so happy he didn't have to sleep on the ground anymore."

The skin around Callum's eyes tightened for a moment as he stood behind her, but then he tossed his head.

"And now you're the aide to the aide to the Admiral-slash-Governor's...aide," he said. "I think I got that right." He thought about it. "Yeah." He nodded, then frowned. "Do you...have any civilian clothes? No, of course you wouldn't. We'll make a trip to town later." He gave her a gentle pat on the shoulder. "And then we'll take you to a plastic surgeon. Get that brand off of you."

"How much? Faeran talked to me about the costs while we were in transit. I understand that I'm paid twice a month, but with the taxes and withholdings to pay for my uniforms...the math works out to—"

"It's nothing," Callum said. "So far, Logan and his knuckle-draggers have taught you how to kill a man with a spoon and assemble a carbine while blindfolded and floating upside down in micrograv. I, on the other hand, will teach you the glories of an expense account. Lot fewer bruises involved, so long as you keep all the receipts." He brandished a finger. "Always keep the receipts! And never lie to your accountant; they know everything. I'll take you in the morning, and then we'll figure out our routine for the next two-ish years."

Eira nodded, and he patted her shoulder again and left. After he'd gone, she went to the sink and stared at the faucet, looking for knobs. She reached for the spigot, and water poured out of it as the sensor caught her hand's motion. She jerked the hand back, then touched the sink gingerly. Red and blue boxes lit up beneath the marble façade. She tapped the red one, turning the water as hot as it would go, and flicked her fingers through the stream as steam rose.

"Ian Markel, ND Extractions," O'Hanraghty whispered to Murphy as a heavyset man walked toward them and extended a hand.

The cocktail party was in full swing, with several long rows of food and a robot-staffed bar in the governor's mansion's ball-room. The room had real wood furnishings, more reminiscent of pre-spaceflight Earth's England than the more modern trappings back in Olympia. The guests' conversations struck Murphy as subdued, and he wondered if that was the local custom or because the news of Inverness had spread since his arrival. Senior officers from the task force had taken up roost closer to the alcohol.

"Governor, so good to finally meet you," Markel said. "I under-stand you're in the Thakore family back in the Heart Worlds."

"I see my wife's charms beat me here," Murphy said.

"Did you know that Goibniu has double-surveyed deposits of platinum group ores? Including very high concentrations of both rhodium and osmium? Demand's due to pick up in the next few years, given the depletion of the Leucippus System's deposits. Now, there's a sunk cost to the mining, just from the gravity well, but my crews are—"

"Ian, is it? Ian, I'm not here on family business, and Venus Futures is primarily invested in shipbuilding, not mining."

"But they could put one of their micro-gravity smelting platforms in Goibniu orbit. Frankly, the processing platforms here at Crann Bethadh are...well, 'long in the tooth' is putting it mildly. Their efficiency curves are pathetic. With one of your smelting platforms orbiting Goibniu, we could at least double, probably triple, profit margins. And Goibniu has more than just the platinum group, you know."

"Astro Engineering makes those, not Venus Futures," Murphy said with a smile.

"What's the difference?" Markel's tone sharpened. "The Five Hundred is just a name for one big economic conglomerate. The Thakores don't know the Astro Engineering people?"

"My wife...did go to school with the CEO's daughter." Murphy's smile grew wider, and he tapped his right toe to signal to O'Hanraghty that the conversation needed to end soon.

"Don't pester the Governor with your platinum-plated dreams." President Tolmach had walked up behind Markel. Now he rapped his cane against the floor, then whacked Markel's calf. "He tried for years to get the old governor to send someone from Survey Corps to confirm his suspicions about what's hiding on Goibniu, Admiral. Though my guess is that the cost of the permits will be higher than whatever you can dig out."

"It's *been* surveyed," Markel said looking at Murphy. "He's seen the reports. I think he just forgets."

"Keep on making ageist jokes." Tolmach nudged the other man with the prosthetic hand holding his cane. "They'll come back to you. Age happens to the best of us and to the rest of us. Now go make your third pass at the food line. They have more of those pink things with the shells."

Murphy looked at the President. The old man wore his own awards, and the admiral's eyes lingered briefly on an exquisitely wrought, stylized silver leaf over Tolmach's breast pocket. It was accompanied by a five-pointed star with black points. Three smaller black stars formed a column next to the larger device.

"I was in Survey," he said, turning back to Markel. "Have your scans sent to my office."

"Shrimp," Markel said, nodding quickly. "They're called shrimp."

"Don't have those in our seas." Tolmach turned his good eye to Murphy as the mining executive headed off obediently. "Too cold, I suppose. We do have oil squid—taste awful, although our whales love eating them. 'Course, our 'whales' probably aren't much like the ones you're used too, either."

"Nice to see you again, Mr. President," Murphy said. "The reception at the spaceport was exceptional."

"You're my fifth governor since I took office. Likely my last, if you extend your stay like the last one. Sorry General Dewar couldn't be here. You've already got him running around with his hair on fire."

"Seems prudent, given what happened to Inverness," Murphy said.

"The League hasn't launched a raid like that in our sector in over five years. I wonder what changed?"

Tolmach reached back to a younger man holding a plate of shrimp with red sauce. He sniffed at the food, then dropped it back on the plate.

"Beta Cygni, probably," Murphy said. "The front there's been fairly static for a long time, but cracks are showing in the League's defenses. My guess is that their Assembly authorized the strike for a propaganda win."

"What's the bill?" Tolmach asked. "Seven hundred thousand dead?"

"Seven hundred and fifty." Murphy's mouth tightened for a moment, his eyes bleak. "Of course, that's just our estimate, based on the survivors we found. We don't know how much the population had grown since the last census."

"Leave it to the Leaguies to spill innocent blood for a few headlines. What will the Heart Worlds do? A reprisal? You've got a task force in orbit. You could visit one of their outposts and be back before the Oval can say no."

"Better to ask for forgiveness than permission?" Murphy asked.

"Always." One side of Tolmach's face tugged to the side. "There'll never be peace with the League, Governor. Too much blood between us. Although I don't think you have to be convinced of that."

"The safety of New Dublin is my primary concern," Murphy said. "We can partner on that, yes?"

"I joined the first levy off Crann Bethadh to defend the Federation," Tolmach said. "Came back, and then sent three more generations of boys and girls off to the fight. Working to keep the Leaguies from destroying our home isn't much of an ask, lad."

"Once I have a fuller picture of the system's defenses, we can work out a plan together."

"Why just this system?" Tolmach chuckled. "New Dublin's the regional capital for the Concordia Sector, and our regular Sector Conference is coming up shortly. I expect all the other chief executives to be here in about two months—travel times are a little iffy out this way. And Scotia won't make it, this year. Is it true you put Drebin in the same ship with all the survivors?"

"Needs must." Murphy took a sip of his drink.

"And it was a...slow ship?"

"Only one I could spare, I'm afraid."

"Not bad. Not bad at all," Tolmach said with a grin.

"I'm not certain what you're getting at, Mr. President," Murphy said innocently.

"Of course not." Tolmach shook his head. Then his expression sobered. "We've got our annual Remembrance Day coming up. You'll join us for the ceremony? Good chance for the people to see your face."

"I'll be there. I have no intention of being a stranger out here."

"Heh. They all say that. Then they go outside during the winter and decide to hibernate. Did your ships bring anything but those awful shelled creatures?"

"Nothing on a par with Dewar's tea, I'm afraid."

"Bah. Hope you enjoy potatoes, Governor. Crann Bethadh makes the best of them this side of the blue line. And now, begging your pardon..."

Tolmach thumped his aide on the knee to get him out of the way and made for the restroom.

"Did that go well?" Murphy asked O'Hanraghty, watching the New Dubliners go.

"Not entirely sure, Sir. There's been a low level of hostility ever since we arrived. Can't tell if the locals are like this to every off-worlder, or if it's local custom. Almost like I'm back home on New York. And what happened to the persona?"

"Murphy the merry bumbler had to die on Inverness," the admiral said. "Lives aren't worth keeping the Five Hundred blissfully unaware that I do have a clue. If I keep up the act here and now, then what? Tolmach would pigeonhole me as a Heart World empty suit out here to get my ticket punched, and then nothing would change with the system's defenses."

"Inverness did move up our timetable," O'Hanraghty agreed, pursing his lips slightly. "Still no word on how Fokaides and the Oval reacted to our efforts there."

"What were those awards?" Murphy brushed a hand over his breast pocket. "I've seen others with the black-tipped stars, but not the leaf."

"That's a *duilleog airgid*—means 'silver leaf,' as nearly as I can translate it—and it's an actual leaf, not something some metalsmith whipped up. And it's from a very specific tree. The locals regard the giant silver trees scattered around the planet as sacred. There are maybe a dozen species of the smaller ones, but there aren't many of the giants, and they're about the size of an old earth sequoia—maybe even bigger. Pretty spectacular, I understand. No one's allowed to collect the leaves or cut a branch from one of the giants ... unless the Congress awards you the Order of Craeb Uisnig. I think I pronounced that pretty close to right; it's a reference to a sacred tree back on Earth." O'Hanraghty turned his head to look Murphy in the eye. "To date, only President Tolmach has that honor."

"Hmmm ... the rest?"

"The black-pointed star's for being combat wounded. The all-black stars are for loss of a family member." O'Hanraghty took a pull at his drink. "Three sons."

"*One* child's too many for a father to lose," Murphy said softly, gazing after the vanished President. Then he inhaled deeply.

"At any rate, our handling of Drebin seems to have gone over well out here. Back in the Heart Worlds? At least they'll blame you as a bad influence." His lips quirked a brief smile at the chief of staff. "Drebin, on the other hand, will be the same insufferable ass when he reaches the Heart. My report and what data we could pull out of the rubble should be enough to give the Admiralty a nice fat public target to keep attention off of us."

"You really think they'll crucify him?"

"He deserves a hell of a lot worse than that, but he's got some connections to the Five Hundred. Probably remote, but how else do you think he got that assignment? His family might disappear him into an arcology, and then he'll crawl out of that hole a few years later with a new face and a new name."

"Meanwhile, everyone he abandoned on Inverness will still be dead," O'Hanraghty said. "Hardly fair. Logan should've let that wild child have him."

"Decisions were made, and we can't unmake them. All we can do is make the best of the consequences. Does explain some of how the locals see us, though, doesn't it? The Heart Worlds come to the Fringe to demand taxes and warm bodies for the wartime grinder, and then Drebin won't risk his precious ass to even try to protect them."

"If the League wasn't such a bunch of murdering bastards, the Fringe would've gone into open revolt years ago, Sir. You've seen the studies. We've got a hell of a job in front of us. One that might get tougher once our contact arrives."

"And when'll that be?"

"He doesn't like to give specifics. Says details like that can get him killed."

"You think there's a threat to him on Crann Bethadh?"

"It's not paranoia if they really are after you, Sir. More shrimp? Doubt we'll get another shipment for a time. I'll just go and see about getting some more while the getting's good. Oh, and here comes Ms. Abigail Shoonhowser. She has a daughter Callum's age. Be careful."

"You're abandoning me now? Some chief of staff *you* are!" Murphy muttered through gritted teeth, then smiled as he welcomed his next guest.

"He's a problem," Tolmach said as he accepted a whiskey. He and Dewar sat in a book-lined study, and a woman in her early fifties handed a second drink to the general.

"No, he's not." Dewar lifted his glass to the woman. "What do you think, Moira?"

"He's been here less than three days. Every new governor shows up full of piss and vinegar. Then they get it out of their systems." She shook her head. "Just wait."

"Which means he's not a problem," Dewar said. "You should trust your daughter, Alan."

"How can I trust her when she waters down my drink like this? The ice cubes are floating, deary." Tolmach gave his glass a little shake.

"You're not that thirsty, Pa." She gave him a kiss on the cheek and her husband's shoulder a pat before she left.

"She takes good care of me," Dewar said as the door closed. "And speaking of taking care of annoying old codgers, you know she does it because she loves you."

"Defiling proper Glenn's with vile H_2O is a crime. Water. You know what fish do in it?"

"Back to Murphy not being a problem." Dewar leaned back and the leather upholstery creaked. "He and O'Hanraghty actually care about the system's defenses. What they've got in mind for Goibniu is...aggressive."

"You really think the Heart is going to sign off on a Fringe system acquiring 'aggressive' defenses?" Tolmach asked sardonically.

"They'll be under Murphy's—federal—control, not ours. For now, at least."

"And who's going to pay for all this, unless you've found a *leipreachán* or two in your pocket?" Tolmach grumbled. "We don't have the funds, and if we ask the Heart for the material—*and* they agree to let us have it, which is iffy as hell—it'll still take years for the back and forth, the committee meetings, the votes... then the money will evaporate for 'handling' as it changes hands. It's an idea Murphy can't deliver on."

"He says he can do it with what he's got on hand." Dewar raised an eyebrow. "He's already authorized a draft on federal funds to pay for the heavy lifting, so we're covered on that end. May have to arm wrestle some Heart bean counters over it, but his signature's on the order. Seems like a pretty strong indication he's serious about this. And he wants to get it done in the next couple of weeks."

"Why so soon? He drops millions' worth of munitions and guess who gets to spend the money to maintain all of it?"

"I imagine because of Inverness," Dewar said dryly. "Goibniu's coming up on inferior conjunction, and the way he and O'Hanraghty are thinking, that means it's going to be in just about exactly the right position for the next four or five months.

Be better if we were in opposition to Goibniu rather than the other way around, but Dagda's too far out and there's not enough mining activity in the asteroid belt to use it for cover. Let me show you."

Dewar took a handful of walnuts from a glass jar.

"Stow it." Tolmach squeezed his one eye shut. "I was a ground pounder. You try and math at me, and I'll doze off. That'll show you. But I know planets move around their orbits. What if the League attacks when Goibniu's in the wrong spot?"

"Murphy's dealing with an immediate threat, and this is designed to cover us in the short term. If the Leaguies don't turn up in the next six months, he can use that time to make other preparations. He's already looking at our unused yard capacity and what he could do with it. And don't worry so much about maintenance! Markel's going to be covering a lot of that, whether he knows it or not. And Murphy can always reclaim his munitions after Goibniu moves out of position. But as your top general, I'm all for this project."

"Which is going to pull in a fair amount of our vacuum manpower, which means other projects won't be worked on. Which means time lost and money lost. So I get the flak from the reps and the general public. Thanks for that."

Tolmach rubbed a knuckle against his dead eye.

"It's for the common defense." Dewar raised a palm.

"It *smells* like a boondoggle. A 'look at me' for the Heart Worlders to give Murphy a pat on the back when he cycles back home. Spend money. Give the appearance of competence. Go home. That's why he's a problem."

"You'd rather he self-medicate through his assignment and do nothing to defend New Dublin? You heard he was on the way, and you were worried he'd be like the last waste of oxygen. Now you're whinging him because he's doing too much. Come on, old man. Pick one."

"Even the Devil needs an advocate, son. Say I join your little cheerleader section—then what? We charge ahead into everything with Murphy and we look weak. Like the Fringe peasants his kind think we are. The Heart Worlds led us into the war with the League. They're the ones put us where we are. You really want to trust them to change spots now? Just because Murphy says they will?"

"*This* Heart just came from a smashed colony. Still has the smell of death on him. And he's got the pedigree, at least," Dewar retorted.

"I trust men, not their names, and this Murphy's still too new for me." Tolmach swished his drink around. "Too much damn ice. But what happened to Inverness is another problem. One I'll speak to the other system executives about."

"The problem that the system governor ran without firing a shot? Or that the League killed it?"

"Both. Oh, I doubt Murphy will pull the same thing, but not every system's got a full task force in orbit. Panic's coming." Tolmach sighed. "The vote still might happen."

"Secession? They can't be serious..."

"We pull out of the war and maintain neutrality. We'll never side with the League; the Hearts know we hate them too much," Tolmach said. "The Leaguies have their hands full fighting the Federation. The Rish leave everyone well enough alone. We just need a bit of a navy to keep the Heart from coming back and to warn off pirates."

Tolmach glanced up at the ceiling.

"So you're shaking Murphy's hand while planning to stab him in the back?" Dewar set his glass down hard.

"Murphy may yet prove to be a good man, my boy. It's the Heart we have to break from. Too many years we've been fed into the grinder to fight their war. They've got no plans to win it, and no plans to end it, and it's our blood and treasure that's spent, not theirs. I sent three sons to fight. None came back. Another draft's coming up, and I'm tired of seeing New Dublin's future wasted."

"So you think Murphy's a problem because he's got a bit of a spine and a plan." Dewar's eyes narrowed. "You're worried *this* Heart Worlder will be popular with the man on the street, and when it's time to break away...we'll have a civil war on our hands. Anyone that wants to stay in the Federation will just point at Murphy as a tangible reason to remain."

"What a problem to have." Tolmach chuckled. "If he's good at his job, he might save us from the Leaguies, and then we stay on as cannon fodder. If he's a useless toff, we can break away and be a minnow between two whales fighting. Not good problems to have."

"The solution will be somewhere in the messy middle." Dewar picked his glass back up and sipped. "So then, what are we to do?"

"The Sector Conference's coming here, and nothing's set in stone until then. So let's see if Murphy's got the brains to deliver what he's promising. We can always secede *after* the next League attack."

"I'll work with him, then." Dewar shrugged.

"And I'll remain a curmudgeonly bastard that puts up just enough trouble to keep him honest. Won't be a stretch for my acting skills."

"No, you've got curmudgeon down pat."

"Sod off." Tolmach poked Dewar's shin with his cane. "My Moira hears you talking like that, and *I* won't have to beat respect into you. Now pour me a proper drink."

"I'll have worse things to worry about than you if I have to get you home when you're right pissed. How about a game of chess?"

"You know you can only beat me after I've had a few."

CHAPTER NINETEEN

CALLUM RUBBED SLEEP OUT OF HIS EYES AND KNOCKED ON EIRA'S door again. He checked his watch, then knocked a third time.

"Did Logan drag her away for more PT?"

He took an override key fob from his pocket and pressed it to the lock reader. Magnets snapped off, and he opened the door a few centimeters without looking inside.

"Hello? Eira?" He pushed the door farther open and saw a perfectly made bed and a set of civilian clothes laid out on a dresser. "Eira, you know we're off today? I'm coming in. Don't jump out of a corner and stab me."

He glanced at the shower stall and noted that it was bone dry. He leaned around the partition separating the kitchen from the bedroom and finally found Eira. She lay on the floor, clutching a thin blanket. Her eyes were shut and her lips trembled.

"Eira?" He leaned over and gave her ankle a shake.

"Ah!" Her eyes snapped open. She lunged to her feet and banged into the nightstand.

"Ah!" Callum backpedaled into the wall. "Good Lord, Eira! Who scared who more just now?"

She looked around, confused, and scrunched the blanket against her chest, exposing bare legs and shorts.

"I'm sorry, Sir. My alarm...I'm sorry."

"No, it's okay." Callum shook his head quickly. "Don't even need coffee now."

"I need to find—no, I don't. I don't need to find anyone."

She reached under the bed and drew out a compact pistol still in a holster.

"Nightmares?" Callum asked.

Eira only pressed her palm to the grip and holographic sights lit up.

"I've had them, too," he said. "Since Inverness. And you've got better reason to have them than I do. There's plenty of medical types to talk to. Dad says this sort of thing's normal and it'll fade with time."

"I'm fine."

She stuffed the blanket into the corner next to the nightstand, picked up the civilian clothing, and went into her bathroom.

"Eira...there something wrong with your bed?" Callum pressed on the top sheet and noted how firmly it had been tightened.

"Too soft, Sir," she called from the bathroom. "Can't sleep."

"But the floor?" He shook his head. "Maybe I do need some coffee."

He opened her pantry and found a single glass and plate along with several fortified bread wafers from the *Ishtar*. There were two water bottles in the refrigerator.

"I'm glad we can finally get out and about today," he said. "You need to shop."

Eira emerged from the bathroom, clothes changed. She'd already donned the padded jacket Crann Bethadh's winter climate made de rigueur for outerwear, and her hair hung down the right side of her face to cover the slave brand.

"Didn't you go in there with a gun?"

She touched her waist through the jacket.

"Where's yours, Sir?"

"In the armory. Wait. Why are you even carrying that?"

"To protect you, Sir."

"I don't—This is Crann Bethadh, Eira. Who'd want to hurt us?"

"As your personal security detail, it's my duty to always be ready. All times and all places. Crime along our itinerary is low, but still—"

She shrugged, and Callum shook his head.

"I swear, you're getting as bad as Dad and O'Hanraghty. Do they ever sleep? No, it's updates and building projections and virtual drills with the battleship captains. This is the first day with a couple of hours of white space on the calendar. Let's go make the best of it before they remember a report that needs to be filed."

"They can still call us if we're needed," Eira said.

"Only if we answer the comm."

Callum winked and her eyes widened.

"I'm kidding. Kidding! Probably. Now let's go see what passes for a good time in Tara City."

Callum turned into an alley as a gust of wind sent snowflakes past his face and dispersed the steam rising from the greasy paper-wrapped sandwich in his hand. Eira gave him a gentle push against the wall as she looked up and down between the buildings.

"Will you relax already? Eat your 'mutton-slider' thing before it turns into an icicle." Callum took a bite. "This is lamb? It tastes like lamb."

"I think we're being followed," she said. "Two men with the same style of boots have been behind us for the past several blocks."

"Relax." Callum took another bite. "No one on Crann Bethadh knows who we are. We're just off-worlders getting a bit of a snack of maybe-chicken-maybe-lamb from a stand. When was the last time you had something that didn't come out of the ship's kitchen or that slop in the barracks galley?"

Eira took a cautious nibble at her own food. Then her eyes widened and she chowed down enthusiastically. It had disappeared well before Callum finished his.

"So," he said. "Snacks out of the way. What's next? There's a holo theater with years-old movies, although the locals don't know how out of date they are. Better clothes? That seems a little more pressing, actually, because what you're in doesn't fit. I'm surprised ship's stores couldn't do better than that."

"They aren't from ship's stores, Sir."

"No? Then where did you get them?"

"Left behind by the last governor's staff," she said. "I found them . . . in the trash."

"We can't have that," Callum said.

"I'm sorry. Will I get in trouble for stealing?" Eira pocketed her sandwich wrapper. "On Inverness, the magistrates would—"

"No, you're not going to get into trouble. What *we* are going to do is get you into the nearest boutique and have you scanned for a wardrobe. Maybe some evening wear while we're at it. Crann Bethadh has a number of formal functions Dad has to attend, and there's no such thing as a uniform that looks flattering on a lady. Some may disagree, but they're wrong. I would've left this to Faeran, but if I asked her to get you clothes, she'd take you hunting and send you back covered in pelts and woad." Callum glanced at his slate. "There's a place just a few blocks from here. Lots of good customer ratings. Come on."

Eira stepped out of the alleyway. Despite the cold air, her ill-fitting jacket was unsealed and she walked ahead of Callum until he pulled her back and had her match pace to his right, with him between her and the street. The sidewalk was lightly dusted with snow and lined with kiosks selling onetime slates with magazines or street food and more than one souvenir stand.

"Sir, I need to be either ahead or behind you. If I'm not, Smaj Logan will be—"

"Knock off the 'sir' stuff when we're out of uniform. Let's blend in as just two people out shopping, and not a lost little lamb with his cyber ninja protector. Isn't that how Logan wants you to be? Blended?"

"I think I saw one of the men trailing us." She craned her neck, sweeping the passersby with her eyes. "Stepped into a store selling men's skirts."

"Kilts, I think they call those kilts," Callum said. "And no one is trailing us. Hey, those look neat."

He stopped at a stand that displayed small trees in glass display cases with heavy wooden bases, about the right size to fit into the palm of his hand. The trees were all silver, carved with bark that wound up from the roots and twisted like twine in a rope.

They stepped inside the open-air kiosk and found a woman with welding goggles holding strands of metal up to a small blue flame.

"Just a moment," she said, and they watched as she carefully wound the heated part around a small frame, then removed the eye protection.

"Welcome," she said. "How can I help you?"

"I was just admiring your work," Callum told her. "I don't think I've ever seen anything quite like it."

"Well, we don't call them 'silver trees' for nothing. They only grow near veins of silver ore and they incorporate the metal into their leaves and bark. Some people think it's to help fight off the cold, but I think it's mostly to discourage dire moose."

"Dire moose?" Callum repeated.

"Three meters at the shoulder and antlers with razor tips. Best leave them alone if you see one." She smiled. "But are you two interested in something to take home? All handmade."

"They do look nice, don't they, Eira?"

Eira didn't reply, and Callum looked down at her. She had her eyes on a bigger piece, at least fourteen or fifteen centimeters tall, within a slowly rotating glass globe. Light winked off intricate leaves and cast yellow reflections off the glass.

"Eira?" he repeated and she shook herself.

"Wow," she said. Then she looked at the price tag. She winced, and the artist smiled.

"Pricey, I know, but that one took me six weeks to make," she said. "Modeled off the great tree of the Corrán Tuathail Range, Craeb Uisnig—Silver Tree—itself."

"I'll take it." Callum pulled off his glove and pressed his thumb to a reader. "I'll have my drone pick it up. It's coded to my pay chip."

"Oh, my." The artist beamed as the transaction went through. "Can I interest you in anything else?"

"I don't know. Eira, do you think—?"

Eira's face had gone from wonder to concern as she caught movement reflected off another of the glass globes. She stepped to one side, her hand sliding inside her unsealed jacket.

"You're not going anywhere, right?" Callum said to the artist. She shook her head, and he nodded. "We'll come back."

He put a hand to the small of Eira's back and gave her a push to move along with him as he headed back outside.

"Sorry, Sir. I swear—"

"Then let's get into that boutique, where you can watch the doorway and we can at least be warm and paranoid instead of freezing and paranoid."

"Yes, Sir."

They started back along the sidewalk, Eira's eyes sweeping the pedestrians once more.

"I didn't realize you liked that statue so much," she said as they reached the boutique.

"It's not for me."

"Your sister? Mother? Someone...else?"

"For you, Eira," he said, and she stopped dead, staring at him.

"You act like no one's ever bought you anything before," he said lightly, and her mouth pressed into a thin line. "Wait, I didn't mean it like that." They stood in front of show windows filled with mannequins, spinning slowly as the holo projection of their clothes changed every few seconds. "I meant—I'm... I'm trying to take care of you, Eira. And maybe I'm trying to make up for some of the shit that's come down on your life. You deserve that much."

"No," she said. "Not for me! You don't owe—"

"'Loyalty down the chain of command is just as important as loyalty up.' I've heard O'Hanraghty say that a bunch, although I'm pretty sure he didn't come up with it. So let's get you a wardrobe and then go looking for something a little more substantial than those sandwiches. We deserve a break and a little treat now that we've settled in for the long haul."

She looked rebellious for a moment, then closed her eyes and nodded.

"If you want. I just need you to secure my weapon while I change."

"It's all scans and digital projections, Eira, and carrying a gun seems pretty normal on Crann Bethadh. I'm starting to feel silly without one. Now let's get inside where it's warm."

"Here you are." A waitress set two white ceramic plates between Callum and Eira. Steam rose off mashed potatoes and peas, and he sniffed appreciatively.

"Great, thanks." The waitress departed, and he stuck a spoon into one edge and lifted out a bit of ground meat with the potatoes. "See? It doesn't look so bad." He stuck it into his mouth and chewed. "It doesn't taste bad, either."

"I'm not sure." Eira sniffed at her food. "Are you sure about the ingredients?"

"It's not made from shepherds; the shepherds are the ones that make it." Callum took a sip of beer. "Tastes legit to me. Doesn't have the oh-so-yummy chemical tang that the galley's combiners have. I always wondered if that was some sort of spice popular with the ranks and that's why everything has that plastic aftertaste."

"We've got a problem," Eira said, looking over his shoulder.

"How can you tell? You haven't had a bite yet."

Someone bumped into Callum's chair and a drink poured onto his food. Beer suds soaked through the potatoes.

"Oh, did I do that?" a drunk with a scar-cracked face asked. He was tall, in workman's clothes, and smelled of long hours at the bar.

Eira slid a hand inside her jacket.

"I'm pretty sure you did," Callum said. "I've got my own drink, and I don't think this recipe called for it to be beer battered."

"Off-worlders?" The drunk swayed on his feet. "Couldn't tell until I heard ya. Say, the other ones got the brand. She for rent, or have you got her booked through dinner?"

Callum tried to get up, but the drunk put a heavy hand on his shoulder and forced him back down.

"Who says all imports are worthless, eh?" he said.

He shifted off balance and bent over Callum with a beer-laden sneer.

Eira popped to her feet, and her pistol had materialized in her grip. She held it two-handed, the muzzle out of arm's reach, and leveled it right between the man's eyes.

"Up," she said flatly.

"Who gave the slave a piece?" The drunk burped and straightened up slowly. "Thought the pimp would have the weapon."

"Sir, you're clear of the line of fire," she told Callum, never looking away from the drunk. "But you'd better duck so I don't get blood on your clothes."

"Now just—" Callum began.

An arm snapped around the drunk's neck from behind and he stumbled backward into a choke hold. Cormag Dewar dragged him back another step as his face went red.

Eira raised her weapon's muzzle to point at the ceiling, her finger laid along the frame to clear the trigger, but she didn't holster it.

"Let's all take a moment." Dewar tightened his grip, and a rasping sound escaped the drunk. "Mr. Thomas here's had a bit too much, haven't you? 'Course you have. You know it. I know it. Anyone with a nose can make an informed decision about it. But Thomas is sorry for what he's done. Aren't you, Thomas?" Dewar used his chokehold to move Thomas's head up and down.

"So now, Agents Gaughran and MacMannis will take Thomas out of here and make sure that he's really sorry for bothering our guests."

Dewar twisted to one side and dumped the drunk to the floor. A pair of men in civilian clothing rose from nearby dining tables and dragged the offender out by the arms.

"General," Callum said, using a napkin to brush beer spatter off his clothes. "I don't think we've been formally introduced."

"Holster your steel, lass," Dewar said to Eira. "We're all friends here."

She looked at him for a ten-count, her eyes cool and measuring. Then she set the manual safety and slid the pistol back into its holster.

"Better," Dewar said with a comfortable smile. "Don't see too many situations like that here on Crann Bethadh. An armed society really is a polite one...usually. Won't you two join me at another table? My treat. That's not how we want you to think of Crann Bethadh or Tara City."

He motioned to a round table overlooking the lower dining area of the restaurant.

"Don't see why not," Callum said, and the three shifted over.

"What will your men do to him?" Eira asked as they sat down.

"Well, if he's contrite, then I'd rather not burden him with an arrest that he has to explain to employers for a long while. A good kicking in the alley and he can be on his way. Lesson learned."

"Bit brutal." Callum frowned.

"Welcome to Crann Bethadh, young Mr. Murphy." Dewar chuckled. "Thomas can be a bit thick, and he's a logging foreman out on the southern range. Robots handle most of the work, but they can't manage it all, and the ice sabers go for more warm-blooded targets. Drone sentries can scare them off most of the time. Most. And people that make mistakes out there end up in a bad way, so best we teach him the error of his ways in a way that'll stick. And I've found that lessons that come with a bit of pain tend to stick more than a firm talking to and a ticket to see the magistrate."

The same waitress who'd taken Callum's and Eira's orders appeared, and Dewar glanced back over his shoulder at the table they'd left.

"Shepherds and Lough Neagh Draft, was it?" he asked. Callum nodded, and Dewar looked at the waitress. "Make it three, lassie," he said.

"You had us followed," Eira said as the waitress headed off. "Two men. A hundred sixty-two centimeters and a hundred eighty-two. Black slacks. Charcoal coats—"

"What gave them away?" Dewar asked in a disappointed tone.

"Identical shoes," she said. "Very new looking."

Dewar looked at her speculatively, one eyebrow raised, then grimaced.

"I'll have a word with them. Unprofessional to get spotted like that on their home turf. At least you only saw two."

"How many were there?" Eira's eyes narrowed.

"A toast?" Dewar said as dark beers with firm heads appeared. "Welcome to Crann Bethadh."

He lifted a stein and Callum joined in with a clink of glass. Eira sat very still.

Callum glanced to one side and at the patrons below. Most of them seemed to be watching the general's table.

"This your normal table?" he asked.

"How could you tell?"

"Good place to be seen." Callum relaxed and drank.

"I'm a known quantity most everywhere," Dewar said. He was gazing at Eira. "That mark's a bit unfortunate," he said to her. "A gene burn?"

"That's right," she said.

"Gene burn?" Callum repeated.

"Old tenet of slavery," Dewar said. "You keep the slaves from ever blending in with the masters. Sometimes those with a different skin color could be marked out easy enough for what they were. Marks and brands are options—used to be, anyway—but medicine's improved to the point that most any maiming can be fixed with a trip to the auto surgeon. But a gene burn . . . it changes the underlying DNA so that the mark always returns to the same spot, even if it's removed. I'm sorry to bring up something painful, my dear."

"A mark doesn't make me who I am," she said.

"That's the spirit." Dewar raised his stein to her.

"Nonsense. It has to be treatable," Callum said.

"It is. All it costs is an artist's touch to fix what a brute wrecked," Dewar said. "Too expensive for the Federation to pay."

"I was never sold, just marked for the pens," she said.

"The surgeon on *Ishtar* can have this taken care of easily enough," Callum said.

"No." Eira shook her head. "He said as much. No resequencer aboard."

"Not surprising," Dewar said. "Gene burns are one thing the service isn't generally geared to fix. Freed men and women rarely enlist, so it's not cost effective. There *is* one doctor here in Tara City who might have the equipment. But it's not cheap."

"Send me his contact information." Callum put his stein down a bit harder than usual. "How is it the Federation can afford a new class of FTLCs but something like healing her is out of the question?"

"New to the Fringe, lad?"

"What gave me away?"

"That air of optimism. Veteran care isn't a spending priority. You saw that shithead's scars? Noticed a few men and women with cheap cybernetics for legs and arms? The Federation will pay the bare minimum to get a wounded soldier back into the workforce. You can walk? Good enough. Hand with a bad nerve shunt that can't quite pick up an egg? No issue. It's not in the Federation's interest to send us through a proper biosculpt after our time's up."

"You seem all right," Callum said.

"An enlistment in the Marines and not a scratch on me, not that the Leaguies didn't try. I'm luckier than most." Dewar shrugged. "Let's set aside the macabre. Here comes our order."

CHAPTER TWENTY

"COMMODORE GRANGER, SIR," CALLUM SAID, AND MURPHY STOOD as a small, trim woman stepped into his office.

Harriet Granger reminded him a bit of Simron. She had much the same coloring and was only a centimeter or two taller. She was considerably older, however, with a look of hard-won competence. He reminded himself not to leap to any conclusions, but her record did seem to back up that first impression.

"Commodore," he said, extending his hand across the desk.

"Admiral," she replied.

There was a certain reserve in her tone, Murphy observed. It might have something to do with the fact that she was fourteen years older than he was and she'd been a Battle Fleet commodore when he'd still been a Survey captain. Yet here he was, a shiny new rear admiral with an entire task force under his command, while she had a single understrength task group.

"I understand *Tiamat*'s harmonic is giving the local yard a hard time," he said out loud, gesturing for her to seat herself, then looked over her shoulder at his son.

"Could you organize coffee, Callum? Unless," he glanced back at Granger, "you've decided you like the local teas as much as I do, Commodore?"

"If you're referring to General Dewar's confiscated tea, I probably do," Granger replied with just a hint of a smile.

"Make it tea, then," Murphy said, and Callum nodded and withdrew.

"About *Tiamat*?" Murphy said then, parking himself on the corner of his desk and crossing his arms rather than resuming his comfortable chair.

"We might've been able to make it back to the Heart," Granger said, "but Engineering projected a fifteen percent chance of fan failure and we'd have had to hold the entire task group down to no more than three hundred lights." She shrugged. "Under the circumstances, with New Dublin right off our shortest route home, it made sense to stop off here for repairs."

"And their current status?"

"Apparently, they just hit another glitch." Granger grimaced. "They've been fabricating replacements for the defective nodes, but when they began replacement they carried out a routine test of the Zadroga generators. We hadn't asked them to; they were just being thorough, and it looks like it's a good thing they were."

"Ah?"

"Yes, Sir. They turned up a possible catastrophic fault in the beta conduit generator. Didn't show up on our internal sensors, but the yard tells me the damned thing looks like the primary inhibitor must have arced across. With only the secondary, there's a twenty percent chance of complete failure. Which I guess most people would consider a bad thing."

Murphy snorted at her understatement. If the beta Zadroga conduit failed, there was nothing to stop a starship short of a disastrous encounter with its own black hole. It was one of those failures that never got reported...because, if it ever happened, no one could possibly survive it.

"I think we could agree to consider it that," he said dryly after a moment. "So what does that do to your schedule?"

"I'm not sure yet, Sir," she admitted. "When it was just the Fasset nodes, we were looking at another three weeks. Now, though, they'll have to tear a third of the fan down just to get the bad initiator out. The yard tells me they don't have a mil-spec replacement for a *Marduk*-class Zadroga inhibitor in stock, so they either have to adapt one from a *Horus*-class, which would be...suboptimal, or else they have to fabricate a new one, and that could take up to a couple of months."

"Ouch." Murphy grimaced sympathetically. "On the other

hand, it sounds to me like it's a damn good thing you did stop off here at New Dublin. Fasset resonance *and* a skitzy Zadroga conduit?" He shook his head. "It's been a while since we've lost an FTLC to 'hazards of navigation.' Just between you and me, I'd like to keep it that way."

"I agree entirely," Granger said. "It is a pain in the ass, though. The Oval already told us they can't spare a carrier to replace *Tiamat*, so we're stuck here until we complete repairs."

"I see." Murphy rubbed his chin thoughtfully for a second.

"I see," he repeated again, more forcefully, "and I'm sure it is a pain in the ass for you, but there's that old saying about an ill wind."

"In what way, Sir?" She looked at him narrowly.

"You've read my report on Scotia and Inverness?"

"I have." Her mouth tightened. "An ugly, ugly business. If you'll pardon me saying it, the people on Inverness are damned lucky you were willing to divert. A lot luckier than they were in their 'Governor.'" She shook her head, eyes dark. "I've known Yance Drebin for a long time. I can't say anything in your report surprised me where *he* was concerned!"

"Really?" Murphy cocked his head. That was a response he hadn't hoped for.

"Not a bit. It's not the first time he's cut and run on a responsibility. Just like it's not the first time—" she met Murphy's eyes levelly "—the *Navy's* cut and run. Leaves a bad taste, Sir. Thank you for at least picking up the survivors."

"'Least' is probably a good word for it," he said quietly. "It was the least I could do . . . and it didn't matter a lot to too many people."

"Do what we can, Sir."

Granger looked up as Callum returned with the tea service. Callum poured for both his father and his guest, then withdrew again, and Murphy sipped from his cup.

"Well, I know you need to get back to the Heart as quickly as you can, Commodore," he said then, "but in the meantime, as the governor and senior officer here in-system, I'd like to combine your task group with my task force units and the elements of BatRon Seven-Oh-Two for maneuvers. I'm sure the yards will get that conduit repaired as quickly as they can, but I'd be lying if I said your task group wouldn't be a reinforcement godsend if the League decides to follow up on its success at Scotia."

"And Drebin's piss-poor performance is likely to encourage them to do just that, isn't it?" Granger murmured.

"I wasn't going to put it that way, but since you obviously share my own high regard for Captain Drebin, I'll just say that it seems...possible," Murphy said, and the commodore snorted in bitter amusement.

"Makes sense to me, Sir," she said after a moment. "I'll have my chief of staff get in touch with yours—Captain O'Hanraghty, isn't it?"

"It is. You know him?"

"Not well. I know him by reputation, and our paths have crossed. That was a long time ago, but my husband was from New York, too."

"I didn't realize that," Murphy said, and it was true. That information hadn't been in his available records on her.

"Marrying a Fringer's not exactly a career-enhancer, Sir." The reserve was back in her tone, and Murphy realized that in that moment she was seeing a member of the Five Hundred, not the flag officer who'd diverted to Scotia. "He was a civilian, of course, so it wasn't quite as bad as it could have been. But—"

She broke off with a shrug, and Murphy nodded.

"I understand exactly what you're saying," he told her. "Not from firsthand experience, but Captain O'Hanraghty's one of the finest officers I know."

"But he's not just a Fringer; he's a Rish-conspiracy nut, too," Granger said with a crooked smile. "Don't worry. I won't hold it against him."

"I'm glad to hear it!"

Murphy smiled again, then stood, signaling the end of the interview. Granger finished her tea and rose as well.

"I'm having dinner tonight with General Dewar," Murphy said, extending his hand once more. "Captain O'Hanraghty and Captain Lowe, my flag captain, will be there as well. Would you care to join us? Nineteen hundred hours at the governor's mansion."

"I'll be there, Sir," she said, reaching out to take the proffered hand. She gripped it firmly. "You know, it's probably a good thing they checked that conduit in a couple of ways, if you think about it. Having it fail would have been a really unpleasant experience for *Tiamat*, but it's handy how it seems to have provided an unanticipated reinforcement for New Dublin, isn't it? Especially so close after Inverness, I mean."

"Fate works in mysterious ways sometimes, Commodore," Murphy said with a serene smile. "Obviously, it would have been better if you hadn't had serviceability issues, but I'm not about to look any gift horses in the teeth."

"No, I don't imagine you are, Sir." She smiled and released his hand. "I'll look forward to dinner tonight, Admiral."

CHAPTER TWENTY-ONE

"I DON'T LIKE IT," ALAN TOLMACH GROWLED.

"I misremember the last thing you *did* like," Cormag Dewar retorted with an edge of genuine exasperation. "Damn it, this is a win-win!"

"Says you," Tolmach retorted.

"What's the *down*side?" Dewar demanded, throwing both hands in the air. "We get a huge upgrade in our defenses, and every penny of it's paid by the federal government. How could that possibly be a bad thing?"

"And when was the last time the Feds paid an 'unauthorized expenditure' this damned big?" Tolmach shot back. "*I'll* tell you when it was—*never*! You do remember how they charged us for the missiles we used defending ourselves ten years ago, I presume."

"But those missiles were expropriated by the New Dublin System Government," Dewar pointed out. "They could argue that we lacked the legal authority to do that. It was a bean-counter, dipshit argument, but it *was* legally valid, damn their eyes. Murphy, as Governor, is signing off on everything he's planning on spending, though. He's got the legal authority to authorize emergency expenditures, and we're not the ones stepping out of line like bad little peasants to do it in defiance of our system governor. They can take it up with *him* if they want, when he gets home, but *we're* covered."

"Assuming they pay any damned attention to their own damned laws," Tolmach grumbled. "They're not so very good about *that*, either, you know, unless it suits their purposes."

"No, but we *are* on very solid legal ground, and if they're too blatant about it—especially when we can point out that one of their own precious Five Hundred signed off on the order—it's going to cost them big time in the Fringe. I know they're not so very worried about Fringe opinion, most times. But this close after what happened to Inverness?" He shook his head. "Not now."

"Then they'll just bide their time. They've the memory of an elephant and the disposition of a shark—Old Earth or Crann Bethadh, take your choice! They'll wait a few years, and then they'll find some way to screw all this money—hell, we're talking about an entire year or two of our system budget!—back out of us."

"First, we have to survive long enough for them to do that. I don't know about you, but I'm thinking that's my first priority at the moment. Second—" Dewar's tone dropped and he looked at Tolmach very levelly "—I'm not so very sure they'll have years to wait. Of course, you'll probably know about that even better than me."

The office was silent for several seconds, then Tolmach snorted.

"I'll not know until I've had the chance to discuss it with the other sector chiefs, but it might be you're not so very wrong about that. Whippersnapper."

"Well then?" Dewar sat back, raising cupped palms in front of him.

"If I'm honest, part of me is worried the damned Hearts will be more likely to think of themselves as a hammer and us a nail—or a walnut—if we build what he's asking for. There's a reason we're not authorized that kind of capacity."

"Still covered," Dewar said. "I hadn't really thought about it until Murphy pointed it out, but those new-gen printers they installed in the yards are perfectly capable of printing out missiles and drones. So if he's willing to authorize the man-hours, and he's willing to sign off on the raw materials we'll need, there's no reason we can't build what he wants us to build. Not in the numbers he'd *like* to have, mind you. Not enough printers and not enough time for that, most likely. But one hell of a lot more of them than the Leaguies are going to expect."

"And the fact that we've done it will suggest to the Hearts

that we can go on doing it," Tolmach said. "That's what I'm worried about, truth be told."

"We can't control what they decide to do, Alan," Dewar said seriously. "We know that. We can nudge things, push things, and hope like hell. But if the damned Heart Worlds have proved one thing, it's that they'll do whatever the hell they want to do and screw the rest of us." He shrugged. "First, I want my family—including *you*, you curmudgeonly old bastard—to survive. Secondly, I know I can't control the Hearts, so I'm not even going to try. And, third," he bared his teeth, "if they do decide to come the ugly, I want all the missiles I can find to fire at the bastards before we go down."

"You don't think Murphy hasn't thought the same thoughts?" Tolmach asked cynically. "He has to be making his own plans to keep us from being naughty boys and girls."

"Oh, I'm sure he is." Dewar showed his teeth again. "And damn all good it will do him in the end."

Murphy clasped his hands behind his back as he stood on an observation deck in Goibniu Alpha's spin section and gazed down through the vast expanse of its thick, tough crystoplast floor across the processing station's drone farm. The spin section was eight hundred meters in diameter and completed a slow, majestic rotation every ninety seconds or so, producing a comfortable one gravity.

Someone who'd never experienced it before probably would have felt a few qualms about standing on a perfectly clear floor, looking "down" into the endless depths of space while the centripetal acceleration made them feel as if they were plunging into it. Most people could adapt to it—eventually—but some, like Simron, never did. That was one reason floors like this were normally made of smart crystoplast that could be turned opaque with the touch of a screen.

Unlike his wife, however, it had never been a problem for Murphy. In that respect, at least, he and his father-in-law were very much alike...which irritated his wife immensely. At the moment, he and O'Hanraghty wore reinforced vac suits—industrial models, not Navy combat gear. Ian Markel stood with them in a suit which was pitted and considerably older.

"Anything new on our arrival?" the admiral asked his chief of staff.

"No, Sir. Just the one Fasset signature, though, so I doubt it's the League. Be another—" O'Hanraghty checked his chrono "—sixteen minutes before we get any light-speed info to confirm that one way or the other." He shrugged. "Lowe and Mirwani are on it, and whoever it is, he's still at least seven hours out. Plenty of time for Mr. Markel's demonstration."

"Good enough." Murphy nodded and turned to their host. "The view's already impressive, Mr. Markel. I'm looking forward to being even more impressed."

"We strive to please, Governor," Markel assured him.

Goibniu Alpha held geostationary orbit above New Dublin Extraction's Goibniu Three base on the planet's scorching surface, and an outsized hologram to one side showed an overhead of the mining station's protective domes and automated ore extraction platforms. As Murphy watched the holo, four hatches on the dust-caked carapace of one of the platforms—a massive sealed disk a good seven hundred meters in diameter and designed to be deployed to new locations by counter-grav tenders—opened. A quartet of counter-grav drones, each about half the size of a standard cargo shuttle, arced upward. Once they'd risen far enough to clear the platform, fusion thrusters lit off in a blinding bubble of hell-bright brilliance and they streaked toward Goibniu Alpha.

"Spectacular," Murphy said, watching the drones speed higher. "Don't often see active fusion drives in atmosphere."

"The counter-grav simplifies things within the planetary gravity well, but once you hit the hard ceiling where it can't provide any more lift, you need something... more energetic. And since nobody lives on Goibniu—outside the domes, that is—the System High Court ruled that the usual regulations don't apply. I can show you—"

"That was an observation, not an accusation," Murphy said soothingly. "Please continue with your description of your operation here."

He waved a hand at the holo of the extraction platform which had spawned the drones.

"That platform's named *Sheila*," Markel said. "Not the oldest. Not the newest. But she can extract three hundred thousand tons of ore a month. Right now, she's working four shafts at between seventy-five and a hundred meters. Goibniu Three's particularly high in platiniridium and the orebody measures four kilometers by three-point-seven kilometers—you can see two more platforms working it, there and . . . there." He used a handheld unit to high-light Sheila's sisters. "It's also three hundred sixty meters deep, and survey says it's about three hundred fifty million tons of ore, graded at almost twenty-two grams per ton of platinum group metals. We've mapped out seven additional orebodies, some of them even larger but none quite as rich as Three, so we've con-centrated half our platforms here. The three of them, combined, are capable of processing just over nine hundred thousand tons a month, so that comes to—"

"Just under two hundred and forty tons of platinum group a year," O'Hanraghty said.

"Theoretically," Markel said with a grimace. "That's why I want to put smelting plants here in Goibniu orbit. By the time we ship the ore all the way back to Crann Bethadh and it gets run through those antiquated platforms, the production queue's so long and so complicated that Goibniu Three's running at only about sixty percent of capability. If we could cut the transport time, and increase efficiency in—"

"Why aren't there already smelters here?" O'Hanraghty asked innocently, and Markel turned away to glower at the drone farm as the planetary drones decelerated toward the space station.

"FARP," he growled, and Murphy nodded.

The Fringe Assisted Revenue Program, passed during the third year of the war, had been intended to bolster the production of strategic resources in the Fringe. It had become a casualty of direct military wartime spending—in other words, Heart World corporations had succeeded in diverting its funding to more "criti-cal" needs—decades ago, but before it had been . . . redirected, it had actually generated quite a bit of the Fringe-based industry it had been designed to foster. Especially in extractive industries, like New Dublin's mines and Inverness's gas refineries.

One of FARP's provisions, however, had been that FARP-financed facilities must, as far as possible, be co-located with any given star system's inhabited world. The intention was to place all of the system's critical targets in the same volume of space in order to reduce the volume which must be defended and facilitate their protection. Exceptions to the provision could be made, but rarely were. Or, rather, rarely *had* been when FARP had still been a viable program.

"So the administrators were willing to help finance Goibniu-based extraction facilities, but not *refining* facilities," the admiral murmured.

"Exactly." Markel shook his head in disgust. "We pointed out to them at the time that transporting un-smelted ore seven light-minutes—at opposition!—would be a huge bottleneck, but they weren't interested. Typical Heart stup—"

He broke off abruptly, flushing, and Murphy chuckled.

"I'm quite familiar with how Heart Worlders are regarded in the Fringe, Mr. Markel. And just between the two of us, we probably deserve it more often than not. Actually, I'm impressed you're managing to operate at sixty percent efficiency down there."

"We couldn't without the deep-space drones," Markel told him, obviously both surprised and relieved by his reaction.

"I realize that." Murphy nodded again. "I don't think I've seen the same approach anywhere else."

"No, you haven't, I'm pretty sure," Markel said with a slightly complacent smile. "My Uncle Liam served his compulsory hitch in the Navy and got out about the time the Hauptman-drive drones came online. He's the one who pointed out that all the old Mark Thirty-Seven launchers had just become completely obsolete."

Murphy glanced at O'Hanraghty's profile. The chief of staff's lips were pursed as he gazed out through the crystoplast, and his expression gave no indication of how intently he was actually listening to the conversation.

Anti-ship missiles and counter-missiles were both powered by Hauptman coils, which no one had yet figured out how to apply to manned vehicles. The Hauptman drive could produce over three thousand gravities, but mere protoplasm couldn't survive a fraction of that acceleration. Then there was the minor fact that an active coil poured out a flood of lethal radiation. Missiles didn't really *care* about that, though, which made it ideal for them. It had taken quite some time to produce a Hauptman coil that could (a) be turned on and off again once it was initially activated and (b) didn't burn itself out after a maximum of no more than fifteen or twenty minutes. As a result, shipboard reconnaissance, electronic warfare, and missile-defense drones had been forced to rely on the same sorts of fusion drives manned ships did. They'd been slow, compared to missiles and Fasset drives, and relatively short ranged, but their acceleration rates had still dwarfed that of any manned sublight craft and they'd had the endurance and flexibility to make themselves useful.

Getting them deployed far enough out quickly under emergency conditions had loomed large in the tactical analysts' thinking, however, and the answer had been the Mark 37 drone launcher—an unusually large-bore mag driver capable of ejecting a drone with an initial velocity of 40,000 meters per second, which was actually ten percent higher than that of a broadside K-gun. But fusion-powered drones had been enormous, far bigger than manned fighters and over three times the size of an antiship missile. The energy costs of launching something that size at that velocity had been high and the recoil forces had been brutal. That was why the Mark 37s had been installed aboard FTLCs, not sublight units. The big carriers had sufficient volume to accommodate the launchers, enough mass to absorb the recoil, the power budget to feed their voracious appetite, and the effectively unlimited acceleration to maintain vector despite the recoil, although even something Ishtar's size had heaved like an old wet-navy battleship firing a full broadside with each launch. The newer Hauptman-drive drones, on the other hand, required no mag drivers. They were fitted to almost every class of ship, and even the FTLCs had happily used the volume the Mark 37s had consumed for other purposes.

And all of those unneeded launchers had had to go somewhere.

"We had to redesign the deep-space drones, but they're local-build here in the yards," Markel continued. "They've only got about two-thirds the capacity of a standard deep-space ore pod, but operating expenses are barely a quarter of the conventional pod's. Took just over a month for the first-generation to make the trip to Crann Bethadh, even at opposition, but put enough of them into the pipeline, and you had a continuous flow. Then one of my techs had another brilliant idea. He—"

Markel broke off and nodded out through the crystoplast as warning lights flashed.

"Coming up on a launch, Governor," he said.

Murphy couldn't see anyone out in the drone farm, but he was very much in favor of those lights. Getting in the way of something like this would be a . . . career-ending event.

A digital timer ticked downward in one corner of the hologram, and then even the massive bulk of Goibniu Alpha, at least five times the mass of Ishtar, quivered underfoot as a trio of cargo drones erupted from the converted Mark 37s far too quickly for the human eye to follow. Alpha was fitted with a relatively low-powered civilian-grade Fasset drive at the end of an extraordinarily long central spindle to adjust and maintain its orbit in the wake of such launches, although it could—theoretically, at least—have been used to move the entire station across the star system, if there'd been any reason to.

"Don't really need the full initial velocity anymore," Markel said as the warning lights blinked out. "The Hauptman coils we've fitted to the drones—that was my tech's bright idea—could make the entire trip without it, but it reduces 'burn time' on the coils at least a bit. Fifteen minutes' acceleration, and they're up to point-two cee. Make the entire trip to Crann Bethadh at our current range in less than an hour, even allowing for deceleration at the other end. Each trip only puts half an hour on the coils, so they're good for twenty round trips before we have to take them down for maintenance."

He beamed with what Murphy recognized was justifiable pride.

"And you built all this from reclaimed military equipment?" O'Hanraghty asked.

"Surplussed." Markel's smile of pride disappeared. "Picking up cheap components from the breakers is the economic thing to do. Is there an issue?"

"I wasn't aware that there was a significant market for surplus drone coils," O'Hanraghty said thoughtfully, and Markel shifted his weight from side to side. "On the other hand, I did notice that the New Dublin yards seem to have quite a bit more capability to manufacture Hauptman coils than I anticipated."

He looked away from the crystoplast and raised an eyebrow, and Markel swallowed hard. Federal law restricted the possession of current-generation drone drive coils to the military and a relative handful of major Heart World transstellars with the right connections.

"I..." Markel looked back and forth between Murphy and the chief of staff. "Um. Some years ago—seven or eight, I think—when they started upgrading the yards here. I...think the extra coil tooling was installed then. Is...is that going to be an...issue?"

"All Federation military hardware is standardized for integration," Murphy mused, "so there's likely no issue with our current-generation systems getting spliced into your operation, is there?"

"What...what do you have in mind? I'm operating at pretty much full capacity, so I'm not sure I'd have the margin—"

"Nervous?" O'Hanraghty asked. "There's something you'd like to tell us?"

"I just—"

"We need to rent some launch time," Murphy said, and Markel blinked.

"Sorry...You said *rent*?"

O'Hanraghty handed him a slate and double-tapped an icon. Markel's eyes darted back and forth.

"This is insane," he said. "I don't even think it's possible. And even if it were, it...it'll void my insurance!"

"All three of your space stations are logical targets for the League," O'Hanraghty said. "If they arrive in force, the chance of your stations surviving is pretty low, wouldn't you say?"

"That's why I carry so much insurance." Markel offered the slate back, but O'Hanraghty didn't take it. "If the League takes them out—God forbid—I get a percentage back to rebuild. Only about a third of their actual replacement cost, but better than nothing. Enough to put one of them back online, in fact. I can rebuild from there. But if I do what you're asking, I get zero. Nothing."

"You're with Del Webb for your coverage," Murphy said. "You know what their local adjusters at Jalal ruled for Inverness? Complete write-off. System not eligible for reconstruction; no claims honored."

"Those bastards." Markel dropped the slate. "Those absolute bastards. How can they do that? Do you have any idea what my premiums are?"

"You're operating perilously close to the League," O'Hanraghty said. "A Supreme Court case a couple of years back ruled insurers weren't responsible for damages resulting from acts of war in 'economically unviable' systems."

"A ruling that would never apply to a Heart World!" Markel snarled. "I'm going to fire my attorney. Wait. You think the League can hit New Dublin as hard as Scotia? We've got more warships in orbit than they had, and Crann Bethadh—"

"We're concerned with Goibniu right now, not Crann Bethadh," Murphy said. "Think of it as an opportunity to squeeze blood from this stone, if you will. We stockpile the missiles aboard your stations, and all of a sudden your old Mark Thirty-Sevens provide a significant upgrade in our firepower."

"And 'militarizing' the stations *absolutely* voids my insurance under that 'act of war' clause," Markel replied.

"Inverness," O'Hanraghty murmured. "Inverness."

Markel glared at him.

"If I give up space for these missiles of yours—and how *much* space are we talking about here, by the way?—I sacrifice room for my own deep-space drones, and that'll cut into my overhead," he said.

"You can lose a little now," O'Hanraghty said, "or you can lose everything if the League arrives and we can't stop them."

"What are the chances of that?" Markel licked his lips. "Really, I mean?"

"If I could answer that question, I would," Murphy told him frankly. "The problem is we don't know. But no one expected Inverness, and the fact that they got in and out completely unchallenged can only increase their confidence if they decide to up the ante and keep pushing out here. Whether it's for propaganda victories or simply to distract us from Beta Cygni doesn't really matter as far as New Dublin's concerned, now does it?"

"And we stand a lot better chance of stopping them with your cooperation," O'Hanraghty said.

"Well..."

Markel bent and picked the slate back off the deck. He studied it for a few seconds, then shrugged.

"Okay, there's a method to this madness...sort of. Theoretically. But if my insurance finds out—"

"We'll keep your involvement a state secret," Murphy said. "And we'll see that the payments to you are...fungible. Just don't get too creative when it comes tax time."

"That's reassuring, but there is one...smaller detail that might be an issue."

Markel, Murphy noticed, had begun to sweat.

"Go on," O'Hanraghty invited, crossing his arms.

"During construction, I used a number of subcontractors for some of the minor systems," Markel said. "And, over the years, we've found some League parts here and there. Never an issue! Just had to patch some code, jerry-rig a few power splices... maybe source some replacement components...that sort of thing."

"Subcontractors. How unfortunate," Murphy deadpanned.

"Fly-by-night types! Fired them all as soon as I found out what they were doing!" Markel said.

"As one does," O'Hanraghty said with a sober, understanding nod.

"We can overlook this...minor treason on your subcontractors' part," Murphy said thoughtfully. "If it becomes a hardware issue, we'll subtract the cost of any necessary replacement components from your rent. Fair enough?"

"My guys aren't as up on current-generation military tech as I might like for something like this," Markel said. "I mean, they're mostly ex-Navy and they could probably handle it, but most of them have been back in civilian life for years. I'd feel better if you brought in some of your own people to ride herd."

"Uniformed personnel onboard civilian stations could make that whole state-secret thing a bit harder to maintain," Murphy said.

"You could send them in civvies," Markel suggested. "Have them cross-training as miners for concealment purposes."

"That can work, Admiral," O'Hanraghty said.

"Then let's drive on." Murphy nodded decisively. "The sooner the better."

The slate in Markel's hand buzzed with a new message. He handed it to O'Hanraghty, who tapped to accept. One eyebrow twitched ever so slightly.

"We have a guest who needs attending to, Sir," he said, looking at Murphy. "Word from the *Ishtar*."

"I don't like your tone," Murphy said. "Hostile?"

"Not as clear-cut as a League task force dropping sublight, but could be about as bad," O'Hanraghty said. "We just got a transponder code on that Fasset signature. It's *Papsukkal*."

He paused, and Murphy nodded. *Papsukkal* was one of the *Hermes*-class FTL courier-transports. Far too small to carry any worthwhile parasite complement—the *Hermes*-class was barely two kilometers long—they were configured to carry passengers and high-priority cargoes, instead. Their Fasset drive fans were almost as big and powerful as a *Marduk*'s, however, which gave them an awesome acceleration rate and made them some of the fastest starships in the galaxy once they wormholed.

"Apparently, she's come straight from Sol. With dispatches," O'Hanraghty told him.

CHAPTER TWENTY-TWO

MURPHY STRODE INTO HIS OFFICE ABOARD *ISHTAR*.

Callum was there, leaning back against his desk with a tea service next to him. Callum looked up and smiled, and the man he was speaking to—Murphy could see the back of his head and a prominent bald spot—tipped a cup to finish his tea.

"Admiral," Callum said. "Just chatting. You know our new arrival? Captain Lipshen?"

"Terrence."

Lipshen stood and straightened his uniform. He and Murphy were of similar age, although the newcomer was several centimeters shorter than the admiral, and his chest bore a slightly modified eye of Horus branch insignia. It also showed a distinct lack of combat ribbons. Patrician features smiled as the two shook hands, but Murphy detected no warmth or sincerity in Lipshen's face.

"Been too long," the captain said.

"I prefer not to make formal inquests a regular event," Murphy replied.

"He was telling me about Steelman's Star," Callum said. "Lots of details you never mentioned before."

"It was a long day, one I prefer not to dwell on." Murphy walked around behind his desk and sat. "What brings you here, Andy?"

"Orders from the Oval." Lipshen removed a data rod from a

215

sheath on his sleeve and plugged it into the desk. "Intelligence updates. Encrypted letters. Not quite the usual."

"A visitor from the Inspector General rarely is 'usual.'" Murphy touched his desk and a screen illuminated beneath the veneer. "Callum. If you'll excuse us?"

"Any news from home?" Callum leaned over, but Murphy raised a finger from the desk and his son backed away with the tea set. "Guess it can wait," he said, and withdrew from the office.

"The usual rigmarole of administrative tasks, something to keep O'Hanraghty busy," Lipshen said. "How well's he working out for you? I was surprised to hear you picked him as your chief of staff."

"Eminently competent and a key part of my command staff." Murphy glanced up. "You expected me to pick who, exactly, as my XO?"

"I would've guessed someone a bit more... mainstream. But such is commander's prerogative. Shall I get down to brass tacks? There's a highlighted intelligence file—an update on the attack on Scotia."

Murphy swiped up and down next to his screen and a holo bust of a dark-haired woman in the uniform of an RLH admiral appeared over his desk.

"Xing Xuefeng," he said softly, and Lipshen nodded.

"Herself," he said. "She's been all over the League's Infonet as the 'Hero of Inverness.'" He grimaced. "There wasn't time to get many details from their coverage before I shipped out—just the initial announcement and heroic fanfare. But we have some additional info on her, because she was on Intelligence's radar as an up-and-coming commander. She was on the usual career progression—smaller vessels, then a squadron command on the Beta Cygni front to see if she was lucky enough to survive and get promoted via attrition. Apparently she was, so they pulled her back home and gave her her very own carrier strike group. Turns out she became something of a black swan event when she led the raid on Inverness."

"The League hasn't held us to a stalemate for the last four or five decades because they choose their commanders through battlefield luck," Murphy said, scanning the dossier displayed on his screen. "She was at Gargant and Theseus IV, both decisive League tactical victories. Didn't you lead the inquest on those battles?"

"No, I was back at the schoolhouse as an instructor, though I did read the final IG reports." Lipshen half smiled. "Perhaps you've had some time to reflect on what you learned when you picked up the pieces from Inverness? Because her tactics—as I understand it—were nothing particularly brilliant there."

"They didn't have to be," Murphy said. "She arrived in-system and Drebin tucked tail and ran. She was smart enough to know how to inflict damage with no casualties in return...especially when there was no one in her way."

"Let's not put any motives on Governor Drebin." Lipshen raised his hands. "That's the IG's final call to make."

"And when *is* the inquest for the massacre at Inverness?" Murphy asked.

"It was under consideration when I left Sol."

"I don't see anything here on Xing after Scotia. Any idea where she is now?"

"There hasn't been time for that," Lipshen pointed out. "What we know so far about the League's take on Scotia is only from the public boards. Our human intelligence sources take a lot longer than that to get info to us, so any real intelligence is months old."

He cocked an eyebrow, and Murphy nodded. The slow flow of information was a given in an interstellar war that had raged for over fifty years.

"That said, Admirals Yuan and Quyền are still in command in Beta Cygni, as far as we know."

"I'm aware. What about Than? Where's he been?"

"What does it matter?" Lipshen shrugged. "Than's been a propaganda device for years. They won't risk him at the front. But the Oval has made collection on Xing a priority going forward. She seems ambitious, and she could shake things up for their Eternal Forward and get them to one-party rule by the next election season."

"Which is...soon?"

"Which is soon," Lipshen confirmed. "And which is why I'm here with an additional order. Magenta file. Code Victor Charlie Delta Six-One-Nine. I'm required to be present when you read it to confirm receipt." The captain slipped a small disc from where he'd had it palmed and onto the front of his uniform. "Recording."

Murphy read aloud from the memo that had replaced Xing's dossier.

"Order hash Everest Crown Ninety-Nine. To: Admiral Terrence Murphy, commanding officer, Task Force Seventeen-Oh-Five. From: Fleet Admiral Fokaides, CNO." He paused as he digested the sender, then continued. "New Dublin System new designation tier Delta. Any significant threat to TF Seventeen-Oh-Five FTLCs hereby requires local system displacement to nearest tier Gamma system. Signed...orders received. Rear Admiral Terrence Murphy, Commanding."

Lipshen removed the disc from his uniform.

"This can't be right," Murphy said. "There are a hundred million people on Crann Bethadh, and the Oval wants me to *give ground* if the League show up in force?"

"Orders seemed quite clear to me," Lipshen said. "And it's to protect your carrier squadron. FTLCs are vital strategic assets, but I don't think I have to tell you that."

Murphy brought up a star chart, and his jaw tightened as one of the icons on it changed.

"I see the nearest Gamma system is Endymion. It's a mining system. Says here—" he raised his eyes to Lipshen "—that total system population is under *twelve* million."

"The Chaegul Conglomerate's sunk considerable resources into developing the mines there as a strategic resource," Lipshen said. "We've got to keep the long term in mind, Admiral."

"Which is why this chart just updated from your data rod," Murphy observed in a flat tone. "Endymion was a Theta tier system up until now, ranked well below New Dublin. Or even Scotia, for that matter. Now you're telling me that Chaegul's 'strategic capital investments' are worth more to the Federation than every life on Crann Bethadh? And a mining colony is more strategically important than the repair yards here?"

"*I'm* not telling you anything. I'm just the messenger." Lipshen shrugged. "We're all cogs in the machine, Murphy. The IG does what it can to make sure everything runs correctly."

Murphy's face darkened.

"Let's not pretend about the reasons this decision was made," he said.

"And just what are you suggesting?"

Lipshen raised an eyebrow, and Murphy's nostrils flared. He swiped the star chart aside and looked down at the list of document headers which replaced it. He had to guess whether or not Lipshen's recorder was still on, and he reminded himself that the IG officer was probably as trustworthy as any other officer in his branch.

"Clearly... the war will continue for the foreseeable future and our long-term material interests are critical to that effort," he said without looking up.

"Again, I'm not one to speculate," Lipshen replied.

Murphy leaned back in his chair, then tapped one of the files.

"You're assigned to New Dublin?"

"That was my next order of business, yes," Lipshen said. "With domestic tensions—I hesitate to call it discontent, although it seems to be headed in that direction—rising throughout the Fringe sectors, Admiral Fokaides wants more eyes on the ground so the Oval can send any... appropriate response to local developments."

He eyed Murphy speculatively, and the admiral shrugged.

"New Dublin's been most welcoming," he said.

"I've heard! Your son was telling me about the drills, cultural outreach efforts... I'm pleasantly surprised, Murphy. Most commanders would take their time before rocking the boat in a new system. You're doing much more than I'd expect."

"Walking through the massacre on Inverness set my priorities straight."

Murphy stood, signaling that he was done with Lipshen.

"Then I'll speak with the adjutant and have my things delivered to the governor's mansion," the captain said. "My role as Inspector General's representative is rather passive, as you know."

"I'm well aware of your role," Murphy said, as they shook hands.

He smiled and leaned both hands on his desk as the other man left. He waited another moment, then reached under the desktop to press a button.

O'Hanraghty arrived through a side door a moment later, scanner in hand. He waved it, and the device beeped more and more rapidly as he approached a set of cabinets built into the bulkhead. He reached underneath and removed a bit of plastic film, which he slotted into the side of his scanner.

There was a small flash, the beeping ceased, and the scent of ozone filled the room.

"That fucking snake," O'Hanraghty said.

"I'll assume you got all the bugs he planted, if you're going to say that out loud." Murphy sank back into his chair and loosened his collar. "Zapping that device won't be an issue?"

"You think he's going to admit it was his?" O'Hanraghty pocketed the scanner. "I had the room swept by my people before Callum brought him in. It was clean then. It wasn't when he left." He shrugged.

"I'd almost be insulted if he *hadn't* bugged my office," Murphy said. "His arrival is a bit of a wrinkle, though."

"My guess is that our trip to Scotia raised some eyebrows. They thought you'd be nothing more than a wide-eyed tourist marking time on the frontier."

O'Hanraghty sniffed at the seat Lipshen had occupied and sat in another.

"And then Callum told him everything we're doing in-system— everything he knows, at any rate." Murphy laced his fingers behind his head and leaned back. "We're going to have to bring him into the fold, Harrison. We just need to give him a bit more time to catch on."

"Not so bad, really, if the Oval's spy thinks Callum has loose lips," O'Hanraghty pointed out. "We could feed him disinformation that way."

"Not my son." Murphy shook his head. "Callum's a bit naïve, but he's no fool. And he may not be ready for the whole truth yet, but he'd figure it out quick enough if we started lying to him just so he can pass it on to Lipshen. We use him that way, and he'll lose trust in me. In us. Speaking of which, trust will be in short supply if Tolmach finds out about the system redesignation. Gamma. I can't believe it."

"Not the first time the Heart Worlds have sacrificed a Fringe World for something more... economically viable. Keep that quiet or have it leaked?"

"Quiet. Tolmach is warming to me, but he hasn't made his mind up yet. If he hears that his planet is suddenly worth less than a mining operation in a star system with fewer minerals and metals than New Dublin Extractions has already proved on Goibniu, alone, he'll lump me in with all the other Heart Worlders he doesn't trust."

"As you like, Sir. And if I can't isolate one IG snake, then I don't deserve to be on the inside. But, much as I agree with you about Tolmach, we're not really here to make friends with the Fringe. We're here for evidence... and speaking of that, we have another visitor."

"He's here?" Murphy sat up straight and tapped a fingertip on his desk.

"Silas is here." O'Hanraghty nodded. "Came in on *Papsukkal* along with the snake. Different passenger pods, but he decided to keep a really low profile when he realized Lipshen was aboard. I've got the details for the meeting. This is the hard part, Sir. Hope you're ready for it."

Murphy took an unsteady step off the curb.

The lifts in his boots made walking through the fresh snow-fall in Tara City more difficult than usual. They also made him preposterously tall, in his considered opinion, given his natural height, but O'Hanraghty had insisted that people on the lookout for skulduggery expected those bent upon nefarious deeds to try to blend. Which meant that *not* blending in was often the most effective way *of* blending in.

There were times he found wrapping his mind around his chief of staff's logic more difficult than others.

He glanced at the window of an architectural firm and almost paused when he didn't recognize his reflection.

The beard was the oddest part of his new features, but scarcely the only one. The thicker forehead and wider jaw would've been out of place with his lean frame had his broad shoulders and back not looked like they belonged to a laborer.

He shouldered open a hotel door and tugged his gloves off as he entered the warmth. The carpet was worn near the door, and the lobby had a musty smell of old coffee and too-full garbage cans. The robot at the counter tried to turn toward him, but its servos malfunctioned and snapped it back forward with each attempt.

Murphy removed his hat, and overly long hair fell into his eyes. There was a coffee station in a corner of the lobby, with two white streaks of what looked like spilled creamer dribbled down the cabinet beneath the coffeemaker.

"Complimentary caffeinated beverage," the robot clerk said with a hiss of static. "Courtesy of the Hibernian Arms Lodge."

Murphy poured himself a cup and, in the process, brushed against the two streaks, erasing them with a pass of his coat. He affixed a snap-on lid to his cup and went to the lifts. A bit of graffiti near the UP button caught his eye as he hit it. A crude hat with an arrow to a hallway to one side. He looked up and spotted a bathroom sign, then ambled toward it, ignoring the lift's open doors.

He rounded the corner and saw a man in an overcoat leaning against the wall with a slate in his hand.

"You here for the consulting job?" the man asked.

"Aff, fluvial spectrographs. Old models," Murphy replied. His accent was very different from his usual one.

"Go on in."

The man nodded to a set of double doors, and Murphy pushed through them. Beyond them, several round tables were dressed for a wedding reception. Two men sat near the entrance to a kitchen. One was dark-skinned, with a dome of short-cropped hair, and a golden hoop in one ear. The other wore an overcoat very like Murphy's and looked like a Viking raider lost in time, with unkempt blond hair, a bladelike nose, and a long, droopy mustache.

"Amateurs," the dark-skinned man said. "The both of you."

"Good to see you, too, Silas." Murphy pressed a thumb beneath his chin and his false face split down the middle and retracted beneath his jacket collar. "You didn't even bother with a sheen?"

"That's what I said." O'Hanraghty squeezed an earlobe, and the Viking raider façade came down.

"You've got your double in place?" Silas asked.

"My son's in my office at the mansion engaged in very serious paperwork that I didn't give him enough time to finish." Murphy sniffed at his coffee cup, made a face, and set it aside as he joined the others. "O'Hanraghty's got the baffles on the windows and floor sensors. Anyone watching my office will see me in there, and I made it clear I'm not to be disturbed. Calls are on hold."

"And what did you to do about the snake?" Silas reached across the table for Murphy's discarded coffee cup. His arm stretched from his shirt and Murphy saw jagged scars on his skin, left by a bite from some massive and toothy animal.

"His shuttle down from *Ishtar* experienced an emergency maintenance issue in the launch bay," O'Hanraghty said. "He's still stuck in his seat for, oh, a couple of more hours until the new part is installed. Can't be too careful with radiation leaks, even if the readers are showing a false positive."

"Then maybe you two aren't as amateur as I feared."

Silas shook Murphy's hand.

"We can't all be Federation Intelligence out beyond the blue line," O'Hanraghty said. "How's life out there? Must be something interesting, if you've come in from the cold."

"Crann Bethadh is just balmy." Silas drank coffee and smacked his lips. "Free space is free space. Every last criminal, scumbag, and deviant that can't function in the League or the Federation ends up out there. You carry the law in your holster and hope someone with an ounce of respect tends to your body." He flicked the hoop earring. "Operating just outside Rishathan borders is a bit risky, but there's opportunity for the ruthless and those that won't ask too many questions."

"And you've come across just such an opportunity," Murphy said.

"One of my long-term sources has." Silas leaned forward slightly. "We've got something this time, Murphy. Proof the Rish are supplying the League. Not with tchotchkes and victuals, but lethal aid."

"And why bring it to us?" O'Hanraghty asked. "Every time you come up for air, you put yourself at risk. It's not just Federation Intelligence operating out beyond the blue line. The League's there. So are the Rish's proxies."

"There are a couple of Leaguies working for me . . . not that they know I'm Federation." Silas snorted. "Which is how I came by this bit of information; there's a ship transiting the Alramal System in twenty-three days. A merchantman registered as the *Holy Oak*. She's a regular in the area, and her skipper has contacts in Alramal. He's about due for one of his normal cargo drops, but my information is that this time he'll be making another drop, 'losing' an entire nine-hundred-meter cargo pod on his way back out."

"Really?" O'Hanraghty leaned back. "That would be very careless of him, Silas."

"And also pretty nearly traceless," Silas replied. "Which would be a good thing, for him at least, since the pod in question is carrying Rishathan-made parts for the League."

"You're confident of that?" Murphy asked.

"About as confident as it gets in this business. The shipment originated in Hardasik." Murphy raised an eyebrow, and Silas shrugged. "Hardasik's one of the Outer Sphere's systems, but the cargo's moving through Fringe space."

"Why?" O'Hanraghty asked, cocking his head. "Why not just load it onto a Rishathan FTL bulk carrier and take it straight through wormhole space to its destination?"

"Because the Rish don't think like us?" Silas shook his own head with an expression of mild disgust for O'Hanraghty's obtuseness. "Aliens, remember? Hell, the worst mistake humans ever made was mirror-imaging Rishathan thinking! They don't think like us, and we don't think like them, and sometimes they do things that don't make a hell of a lot of sense to a human. But there's usually a reason for it if you look long enough and think far enough out of the box."

"And have you found this one?" Murphy asked.

"Not really, but two possibilities do come to mind." Silas sipped more coffee. "One is that the Sphere's a hell of a long ways away from Alramal. They've got to cross an entire lobe of human-occupied space to get there from Hardasik in the first place, and if they've got to drop the cargo there for some reason, they don't exactly want a Rishathan bulk carrier being spotted that far from home, now do they?"

He looked back and forth between Murphy and O'Hanraghty until O'Hanraghty shrugged to concede the point.

"The second possibility that comes to mind," he continued then, "is cut outs. The one thing I can tell you about how Rish think is that they're...devious. They really like this clandestine shit, and the better xeno-anthropologists I've talked to about it tell me it's a sort of ritual substitute for open warfare between the clans." He shook his head. "They've done a pretty damn good job of hiding a lot of their history from us, but we do know that up until a couple of centuries ago, they spent a hell of a lot of time shooting at each other. *Eating* each other, for that matter. They stopped a while before we ran into them, but they didn't stop competing for power and resources. They just do it a different way now, and there are honor considerations—what you might call prestige points—involved in how slick they are in that competition. I think this may be at least partly a reflection of said cultural...idiosyncrasy.

"And there's just 'medium confidence' of that, if you want to go by secret squirrel speak." He shrugged. "That's part of the problem. But I think this information is solid or I wouldn't have brought it to you."

"I already knew that, Silas." Murphy reached across the table to pat the other man's shoulder. "It's just that there's a lot riding on this. Harry and I had to pull a lot of strings and cash in a lot of debts to get me out here, and I don't think we're going to get very many bites at this apple."

"Well, in addition to the fact that my agent in Cranston— that's the system where *Holy Oak* picked up the cargo pod—saw her collect it from a 'free trader' with Rishathan smuggling connections shortly after one of the Rishathan smugglers in question arrived on a back-vector into the Sphere, someone's taking unusual pains to grease the skids this time around. Free-traders always pay a fair amount of bribes—or transit tax, if you're into weasel semantics—to the feral system 'authorities' as they go through the unregulated lanes. It's the price of doing business. But a known League agent's been clearing the path for *Holy Oak*, paying a little extra to keep pirate bands and local despots off of her. And not just any League agent. This one's a true believer, the sort they tap for sensitive cut-your-own-throat-after-reading security-level operations."

"Um." Murphy frowned, rubbing his upper lip, and glanced at O'Hanraghty. The chief of staff looked back, then shrugged.

"Tempting," Murphy said.

"'Tempting,'" Silas repeated. "Admiral, there's enough smoke here. Let's go snuff out the fire."

"Like I said, tempting. *Very* tempting, actually, even if it is circumstantial."

"Circumstantial? Do you want a Rishathan-language confession along with a mountain of physical evidence? I'm not law enforcement where 'beyond reasonable doubt' is the standard. This is intelligence work, where a reasonable *suspicion* is enough for me to arrange an accident or a visit from a homicidal associate. The smoking gun we need is on that ship. This is the best lead we've had since the Montclaire disaster."

"No leads in the twenty years since that," O'Hanraghty said. "The Rish and the League have been too careful. So why are we picking up on something so juicy now?"

"Because something's going on in the League." Silas stood up and began pacing. "Something's changed. It's not about them just hanging on by their fingernails in Beta Cygni. Not anymore. There's rumors of a call-up of retirees and reserves. The next two draft classes are conscripted early. Experienced shipwrights and engineers are just vanishing off the grid. They're up to something big. And then there's this shipment..." He shook his head. "I don't care how good you are, if what you're trying to pull off is big enough, managing the endgame and keeping the details out of sight always gets tricky. Always. That's one of the things that bothers me. If they've been that careful for so long, and now their security's starting to spring a leak, that suggests they may be moving *into* the endgame, whatever the hell it is."

"We need cover," O'Hanraghty said. "Some plausible deniability for why we'd cross the blue line and intercept this ship."

"Well, you *could* do it because another Federation agent will show up in-system tomorrow or the next day with actionable intelligence of a slave ship moving survivors from Inverness through Alramal." Silas stopped pacing and grinned. "You leave right after that, and you'll be in Alramal when the *Holy Oak* shows up."

"This other agent is on the team?" O'Hanraghty asked.

"No, he's a complete imbecile I've been feeding middling information to since he was assigned to free space. Now he's got his first big break, so expect him to be very certain when he arrives."

"That'll pass the smell test," O'Hanraghty said with a nod of approval.

"Except that we know there were no slavers on Inverness," Murphy said.

"We're talented enough to play dumb." O'Hanraghty donned his very best, earnest, wide-eyed credulous expression. "You know the nav buoys and recon satellites were all taken out in the initial attack, Sir, so there's no sensor record to tell us whether or not someone else visited the system immediately after Xing hit it. It's entirely possible that some loathsome slaver—some bottom-feeding scavenger—following in the Leaguies' wake—or maybe even in cahoots with them!—took the opportunity to scoop up a personnel pod full of prey before we could get there."

"I see." Murphy's lips twitched. "Of course, none of the survivors we rescued said anything about it."

"Sir, I hate to admit this, because I'm your chief of staff and I'm the one who's supposed to be in charge of your intelligence briefs, but I never *asked* anyone about slavers. An oversight on my part, I know, and I apologize. None of them volunteered anything about that, either, but, you know, those people were all in a state of shock. It's certainly possible that it just never occurred to anyone who actually saw these people to mention them to us. And we've sent all of them except Callum's little friend off to be resettled, so we can't ask them now. And Eira wouldn't know, anyway—she was trapped in a bunker the entire time and never saw anything. So, that brings us back to my original question. Do we want to risk not accepting this information as possibly accurate just because we don't have positive confirmation?"

"That would be ... unfortunate, wouldn't it?" Murphy murmured. "If it was accurate and we didn't act on it, I mean."

"Not just unfortunate, Sir," O'Hanraghty said somberly. "It would be *tragic*."

Murphy nodded, then glanced back at Silas.

"Tomorrow?" he asked.

"Or the day after. I came ahead by way of Jalal because I had to get here before he did so I could brief you on what to expect. I planned to be here over two weeks ago to give you more time to prep for his arrival. But somebody—" he looked hard at Murphy "—had purloined *Calcutta* and diverted her from her normal run from Scotia through New Dublin, so I was stuck in Jalal until *Papsukkal* came through from Sol. Our patsy—excuse me, I mean my fearless fellow agent, the imbecile—is coming on one of the independent free traders who maintains a regular run from the blue line through New Dublin and back. I hear he does a fair amount of quiet trade here in the system. Not that I know anything for sure about that, you understand. Wouldn't want you to think I did and feel compelled to mention anything about smuggling to the local authorities, after all."

"Oh, of course." Murphy nodded, and Silas rubbed his hands together.

"The fallout will be fun to watch," he said. "An intelligence coup like this tends to shake things up, gives me a chance to look behind the veil and see what else the League is up to. Just imagine what this will mean, gentlemen. Proof the Rish are propping up the League. If they lose that support, the entire war could come to an end."

"Ending the war ... You know, despite everything, it's hard to even imagine that," Murphy said. "Fifty-six years and billions of lives lost on both sides. Generations that have never known anything but conflict." He shook his head. "How do you even wrap your mind around *ending* something like that?"

"And we can expose the Rish for keeping it going, prolonging the bloodshed," O'Hanraghty said. "It'll be a whole new galaxy."

"We can't take the entire task force," Murphy said thoughtfully. "We can't uncover New Dublin for this. But we don't need to, anyway. One carrier—*Ishtar*—and her parasites. That's all the hammer we could possibly need."

"It would be a good thing to not have any . . . unfortunate observers along," O'Hanraghty pointed out. "Like a certain recently arrived snake."

"Well, clearly time is going to be of the essence," Murphy mused. "I'm assuming you know the heading your fearless agent will arrive on, Silas?"

"I do."

"Good. So if we just happened to have an FTLC already out beyond the Powell Limit, underway in the right spot when the information arrived, there clearly wouldn't be time to waste hours accelerating back inside the limit to pick anybody up from Crann Bethadh, would there?"

"I wouldn't think so, Sir. As you say, time will be of the essence."

"Surprise drill?" Murphy suggested.

"Surprise drill." O'Hanraghty nodded. "Won't be popular with the rank and file, but I'm not here to make friends."

CHAPTER TWENTY-THREE

"I'M TELLING YOU, IT'S ALL TRUE!" THE RED-FACED MAN'S HOLO-gram shouted. "There's a ship, loaded with survivors, in transit to the Viktrix System by way of Alramal. If you can get there in time—"

"I understand your urgency, Agent Kortnev," Murphy interrupted. "I do. But this isn't a decision I can make lightly."

"—you can prevent a horrible miscarriage of justice!" Trent Kortnev continued.

At the moment, he and the free trader *MacMillan* were 3,800,000 kilometers from *Ishtar*, which imposed a one-way communications delay of almost fourteen seconds, but he seemed unaware of the protocol which required one end of the conversation to pause and give the other end an opportunity to respond.

"All of those people are Federation citizens," he went on, "and the only one who could possibly prevent this from happening to them is you, Admiral. They don't have any idea that rescue's even possible, but surely they've already been through enough! It's not as if—"

"I'm *speaking*, Agent Kortnev," Murphy said sharply, and cut the incoming audio. Then he stood back, arms folded, watching the other man's mouth move for twenty-eight seconds until Kortnev stopped talking and closed it abruptly.

"Thank you," he said then, and exhaled a long, slow sigh.

229

He and the rest of his key staff were on *Ishtar*'s flag bridge. The big FTLC was forty-three light-minutes from the system primary, en route to Brigit, New Dublin's ringed gas giant, as part of O'Hanraghty's surprise exercise. She was slated to play the Aggressor role, coming in from the outer system at a high velocity, and her current position put her *fifty-one* light-minutes from Crann Bethadh and the rest of TF 1705.

MacMillan, a bit smaller even than *Papsukkal*, was inbound, decelerating at just under eleven hundred gravities out beyond the stellar Powell Limit. Her current velocity relative to the primary was down to about ten percent of light-speed whereas *Ishtar* was moving almost twice that fast, but the two starships were on widely diverging vectors which slowed their closing velocity considerably. *MacMillan* would reach her closest approach at roughly nine light-seconds in another seven minutes. After that, the range would begin to open once more.

It had taken *MacMillan* a long time to identify *Ishtar*—or for the free trader's skipper to be willing to allow his passenger to communicate with a capital ship of the Terran Federation Navy, at least—but Kortnev had contacted the FTLC twenty minutes earlier.

Murphy glanced at the bulkhead time display. *Ishtar* had sent a flash priority message to Tara City as soon as Kortnev delivered his initial report, but it wouldn't reach Crann Bethadh for another thirty-one minutes. He considered that for a moment, then turned back to the holo display.

"This is very unsettling news, Agent," he said. "You're asking me to leave this system for unregulated space and expose New Dublin to a League assault in my absence."

He paused, waiting. The range had fallen to only twelve light-seconds, and twenty-four seconds later, Kortnev raised a pleading hand into the field of his visual pickups.

"But think of the lives, Admiral." He wiped his mouth. "The people of Inverness suffered enough from the League attack, and now they're being carted off to slavery by savages from beyond the blue line. You can't just sit here and let them slip away into a nightmare future like that! I—"

He cut himself off and shook his head, staring imploringly from the holo.

Murphy leaned against the command ring beneath the holo projection and looked over his shoulder.

"O'Hanraghty, thoughts?" he said.

"Kortnev did bring a fair amount of supporting intelligence with him, Sir," the XO said. "I've been examining the material he burst-transmitted to us, and there's more substance to it than I really expected. It's not like we're just taking his word for it." He shook his head. "Imagine that. I'm actually suggesting it might make sense to leave the system based on trust in the word of Federation Intelligence."

"I'll try not to have a heart attack," Murphy said dryly. He looked back at the display. "Do you have any additional intelligence, beyond what you've already sent us, Agent?"

"It's all in my report," Kortnev said twenty seconds later. "But I've been beyond the line for almost two years. My network is well developed, and—"

Murphy muted the sound again with the swipe of a finger and looked at the display tied into *Ishtar*'s command deck.

"Captain Lowe, assuming I decide to buy into this wild-goose chase, how long until we could wormhole out on a heading to Alramal?"

"Commander Creuzburg's been working the numbers, Sir," the flag captain replied. "It's fortunate that we're already well beyond the Powell Limit. At eighteen hundred gravities, we'd hit the supralight threshold in about three-point-eight hours. We'd have to bend our vector, but that's a more than sufficient window. And it's a bit less than twelve and a half light-years to Alramal. We could be there in five days, if we push it a bit in wormhole space."

"I see."

Murphy nodded and glanced at O'Hanraghty. Silas's numbers had been spot on for *MacMillan*'s arrival vector, although the free trader had arrived several hours after his most pessimistic ETA. It didn't matter. In fact, it helped, because it meant *Ishtar* was farther into the "surprise exercise"... and even farther from Crann Bethadh, with a commensurately longer communications lag.

"We have *Romania*, *Kenya*, and *Russia* on the racks," O'Hanraghty said. "With Commodore Granger added to the system defenses and *Foch* and *Patton* back in service, we wouldn't make that big a hole in the heavy hitters, Admiral."

"Which will be cold comfort if they hit New Dublin while we're gone and we didn't leave enough," Murphy pointed out.

"No, Sir, but he does have a point about what'll happen to those people—assuming his info's good—if somebody doesn't do something about it. And at least the exercise plan put *Fury* on the Number Six rack. She and her fighters will be a lot more useful than another battleship would be if we have to cover any appreciable volume."

"That's true," Murphy acknowledged. "But if the League's present in Alramal in strength—"

"I don't think that's very likely, Sir," Captain Lowe offered from the display. "Alramal's a freehold system. Doesn't belong to either side. Might be a carrier passing through from time to time, but not 'in strength.' And if we delay to pull in any more of the battleships, we'll be cutting the window Agent Kortnev gave us really close. If we leave now—*right* now—we should arrive about twelve hours before his earliest ETA for the slaver. By the time we decelerate, build a vector back to Crann Bethadh, and redistribute, then accelerate back out on the right vector to Alramal, we'll lose that entire margin plus some."

"He's right about that, Sir," O'Hanraghty said.

"I don't like being rushed this way," Murphy muttered, then inhaled deeply. "But you're both right, of course."

He glanced at the time display again with an intent, frowning expression that hid a bubble of internal glee. It was the middle of the night in Tara City. In twenty-three more minutes, *Ishtar's* first transmission would reach Crann Bethadh and Andy Lipshen would find himself dragged out of bed to view it. At which point, he would undoubtedly begin feverishly planning to either abort any venture beyond the blue line or at least make sure he came along to keep an eye on things. But any message from him, would take almost an hour to reach *Ishtar*, and any response from Murphy would take another fifty minutes to get back to him. Which meant *Ishtar* would wormhole out for Alramal ten minutes before Lipshen got it.

At which point, he thought blissfully, the true frothing would begin.

He looked back at Kortnev's image. The man's mouth was moving again—or, really, moving *still*—and Murphy unmuted him.

"—on my honor as an agent of the Federation," the man was saying. "I swear that the intelligence comes with the highest level of confidence. And, of course, I'll personally accompany you.

That's only right, since it's my information which would be taking you into possible danger." He paused and raised his chin slightly.

"That's quite an endorsement," Murphy said. "I've looked at the math, however, and I'm afraid your ship can't rendezvous with *Ishtar* before we wormhole. Not if we're going to make Alramal in the window you've given us."

The inevitable transmission lag intervened. Then—

"But...but this is my operation!"

"It's your *information*." Murphy rapped a knuckle against the command ring. "It'll be *our* operation. And just in case we arrive at Alramal and discover it's a trap, I think you'd better surrender yourself to the local system authorities. They'll make you comfortable until we return."

"Am I...am I under *arrest*?"

"Just consider it...an indefinite hold until we sort out everything you've told us." Murphy smiled. "If it will make you feel better, you'll be my honored guest in the governor's mansion, and I'll personally ask my good friend Captain Lipshen to look after you until we get back. Does that sound so terrible?"

"Well. No, but I—"

Murphy cut the agent's holo.

"Well, that's one less headache," O'Hanraghty observed.

"Captain, take us to Alramal," Murphy told Lowe.

"The decision's made, Sir?"

"It's made. Now I've got to explain it. XO, with me."

"Aye, aye, Sir," Lowe said as Murphy and O'Hanraghty headed for a door flanked by two of Logan's Hoplons.

Murphy crossed the ready room on the far side and stood gazing into a visual display, watching Brigit and its spectacular rings slide across the screen as *Ishtar* altered heading. The door locked behind O'Hanraghty.

"A concern, Sir?" the chief of staff asked.

"Every point I raised against following Kortnev's information applies to Silas." Murphy turned to face him and crossed his arms. "If Silas is compromised, he could have baited us into an ambush at Alramal. He doesn't have to have turned; if he's been identified, he could have been fed the information to do that. Or just to draw us away from New Dublin to weaken its defenses. This Admiral Xing doesn't seem to be anybody's fool."

"No, Sir, but Silas got his info well before the attack on Scotia;

he just used the 'slavers' as a pretext to prime Kortnev. So if the information was planted on him to suck us away from New Dublin, they must have already been planning on a follow-up attack here. That's certainly possible, but my read—like yours—is that Scotia was more a case of testing the waters. I don't see them having set up something this elaborate to uncover New Dublin before they even hit Scotia."

"There *is* that," Murphy acknowledged. "But it could still be a counterintelligence op using him to suck us—or whoever he handed the information to—into a trap."

"You're right. It *could* be, unlikely as I think that is. But if it is, it's because they did ID him and fed him false info. It's not because they turned him."

Murphy raised an eyebrow at the grim certainty in O'Hanraghty's voice, and the chief of staff crossed to a bulkhead cabinet to remove a bottle of whiskey and two glasses.

"Don't forget that Silas...has a history, Terrence. Good agent, long list of successful ops until Montclaire went to shit. You've read the report." He poured whiskey. "A full operational detachment, best trained individuals the Federation could manage, and they were massacred by the Rish out beyond the blue line. All except Silas, and he survived by the skin of his teeth."

"And because it was a covert operation, the Federation had plausible deniability and could officially...not notice it had happened." Murphy nodded. "Which was convenient for the official line, wasn't it?"

"It was." O'Hanraghty finished pouring into the glasses and squeezed their bases to activate the cooling pads inside them. "And don't think The Powers That Be didn't sweep him under the rug with indecent haste. You're not an intelligence weenie, so you may not realize just how quickly and completely they drop-kicked him into the intelligence shitcan."

"After he claimed he and his team witnessed a Rishathan arms trade to the League?" Murphy laughed harshly. "I don't have to be 'an intelligence weenie' to know how quickly they deep-sixed *that* one, Harry. Especially since the evidence was conveniently lost when the Rish destroyed his team's ship. But that's one of the things that's bothering me. Everything the xeno-anthropologists tell us about the Rish emphasizes how much they love the long game. Could that be what's happening here? A long con? Could they have played Silas, set out to use him as a catspaw, from the moment he came back from Montclaire?"

"Now that's a tinfoil-hat conspiracy." O'Hanraghty sipped whiskey. "Coming from someone who's believed in tinfoil-hat wild ideas for so long...maybe I'm not the best judge."

"If we're right to believe Silas, this could bring the war to an end. If we're wrong, we die in an ambush. Or they hit New Dublin in overwhelming strength while we're gone, and we come back to another smashed planet."

Murphy clinked his glass against his XO's.

"It's Silas," O'Hanraghty said. "If it was only that nincompoop Kortnev, we could just nod our heads, say how interesting the information was, and then send a report back to the Oval and wait for orders. But it's Silas, and he's no fool."

"Agreed." Murphy swallowed whiskey, then squared his shoulders. "And now for the fun part. Explaining all this to Tolmach."

"It won't be that bad, Sir," O'Hanraghty said in an encouraging sort of tone. "I think he's starting to warm to you. Besides, it's a recorded message, not a live two-way."

"And I'm about to lie to him," Murphy said unhappily. "I hate that. The man deserves better."

"And we can't tell him the truth without involving him in something certain parties might decide to call treason," O'Hanraghty pointed out.

"I know that. Doesn't make me feel any better."

"Well, the good news is that everything you're about to record is based on official record of what we got from Kortnev. With any luck, he may never figure out that we just gamed the situation."

"And just what about that bloody-minded, sneaky old man makes you think that?" Murphy snorted. "For that matter, anything *he* doesn't figure out, Dewar sure as hell will. Especially if we come home with proof to back up Silas's story."

"If we come home with proof to back up Silas's story, do you really think Tolmach or Dewar is going to have any qualms about how we got it? After the price the Fringe has paid for so long?"

"No, but if this goes wrong, all bets are off."

Murphy drew a deep breath, sank into a chair, and activated the comm station built into the table in front of it. He glanced back up at O'Hanraghty.

"Let's hope we're not fools," he said.

"We'll get an answer one way or the other when we reach Alramal."

O'Hanraghty raised his glass in ironic salute.

"Thanks ever so much," Murphy said. Then cleared his throat. "Record," he said, and the display before him blinked to life.

"Hello, Mr. President," he said. "By the time you see this, I'm sure Captain Lipshen will already have been bending your ear about how important it is that he gets aboard *Ishtar*. Unfortunately, the math won't work, so I'm afraid I'm going to have to leave him behind. Trust me, I am deeply and sincerely sorry for burdening you with him."

Murphy allowed himself a smile, picturing Alan Tolmach's... colorful response to that. Then his expression sobered.

"As it happens, we've just come into possession of intelligence that requires us to act very quickly if we're going to act at all," he continued. "You've probably already seen the initial burst data packet. I'm appending a more complete version of the information to this message, just to be sure, however, and I'm also sending you the agent who delivered it. At present, we have no reason to doubt his veracity, and I'm sure Captain Lipshen will be keeping a close eye on him in our absence, but frankly, I'll feel better with you and General Dewar in the loop.

"Basically, it all goes back to Inverness. It seems that between Captain Drebin's departure and our arrival in Scotia—"

CHAPTER TWENTY-FOUR

"WELL, IT'S IN ROUGHLY THE RIGHT PLACE AND COMING IN ON the right heading, Sir," Commander Mirwani said.

"And about fifteen hours late squawking the wrong transponder," Murphy observed dryly.

"Well, yes. There is that," his ops officer acknowledged.

Murphy puffed his cheeks, clasped his hands behind him, and began pacing slowly around the flag bridge command ring. *Ishtar* and her embarked parasites had reached Alramal twenty-nine hours earlier. She'd dropped sublight just under three light-hours from the system's sole inhabited planet—which also happened to be named Alramal—and decelerated to her current position, 98 LM from the system primary and 90 LM from the planet. No one in what passed for Alramal System Traffic Control had challenged them—probably because Alramal was accustomed to visitors who sometimes chose to exchange cargoes away from any prying eyes. For that matter, it was also possible no one had challenged them because someone on Alramal who anticipated the arrival of a commerce-raider was looking the other way for a cut of the proceeds.

One of the realities of interstellar commerce was that it was just as impossible for pirates or commerce-raiders to locate prey in wormhole space as it was for FTLCs to find one another there. That meant all pirates or their at least putatively more respectable regular navy colleagues were forced to do their hunting in normal space in proximity to shipping nodes. And if their sublight parasites were going to run down any prey, they could really only operate inside a Powell Limit and, hopefully, inside a *planetary* limit, since any FTL freighter could run away from any fusion drive ship with ludicrous ease anywhere *outside* that limit.

That wasn't an issue for *Ishtar*, but even she had to wait for the fly to walk far enough into her web before she could pounce.

"Like Raleigh says, in the right place on the right heading, Sir," O'Hanraghty said. "Two out of three ain't bad. And its emissions fit the configuration of a bulk carrier, too."

"Oh, I don't doubt that it's *a* freighter," Murphy replied. "The question is whether or not it's the *right* freighter. Because if it isn't, and we're accelerating hell for leather to intercept it when the right freighter does come along, things get really, really problematical." He grimaced. "I don't suppose there's anything on that transponder in our database?"

"You don't suppose correctly," O'Hanraghty told him. "Not surprising, though, is it? Only Federation-flagged ships are in the database, and the one thing this yahoo isn't is a Federation ship."

Murphy nodded, watching the icon whose transponder code tagged it as *Val Idrak* decelerate toward the inner system at eight hundred gravities. The ship had gone sublight two and a half light-hours from the planet...and 177.6 LM from *Ishtar*. At its current deceleration rate, it had been almost ten hours from Alramal planetary orbit. Now, ninety minutes later, it had traveled just under 1.38 billion kilometers, its velocity was down to 233,480 KPS, and the range to *Ishtar* had fallen to 101.2 LM. It would take it another three hours and twenty minutes to reach *Ishtar*'s position. Well, to pass within roughly 900,000 kilometers of it, at any rate. That was less than three times the distance between Old Earth and Luna—a mere nothing when it came to deep-space navigation.

"We can't let it get past us if it is the ship we're looking for," the admiral said. "Once it makes planetary orbit, things get a lot stickier where boarding actions are concerned."

"That's true," O'Hanraghty agreed. "Force majeure is a pretty convincing argument out here, though."

"I'd just as soon not go that route if we don't have to. And I want to be sure nothing disappears planetside before we can get people on board. We don't have anywhere near enough Marines to conduct any snipe hunts on a feral planet."

O'Hanraghty nodded, and Murphy completed one more circuit around the command ring. Then he stopped and inhaled deeply.

✧ ✧ ✧

"So how come I've gotta go squishy?" Steiner complained.

"'Cause we can only fit three suits into the Moray if we take along more than *one* squishy, and we've got two. Not counting you," Faeran replied as she shuffled the cards.

"Yeah, but how come *I'm* the one who isn't in armor?"

"Because you botched the last breach-and-clear drill," Logan said, gathering up his cards as Faeran dealt. "Remember firing sabots instead of hollow points and puncturing the hull? The simulated rapid depressurization? My entirely earnest string of expletives to describe your cockup?"

"If he keeps cocking up, can I have his armor?" Eira asked.

"No," the Hoplons said in unison.

"That doesn't seem very fair," she muttered. Pinochle wasn't her game, so she was earnestly honing a combat knife as she watched them play.

"I don't think 'fair' plays a really large role in the Sergeant Major's thinking," Callum said dryly. He was tipped back in a chair in the strikecarrier *Fury*'s ready room, rereading the procedural manual on boarding actions.

"Damn straight it doesn't ... Sir," Logan agreed. "Steiner's a cockup, Eira, but at least he knows enough about the suits *to* cock up."

"Bids?" Chavez interrupted, looking at his hand.

"Ohhhhh! Somebody's got a double run or double aces!" Faeran said, grinning at him across the table.

"Yeah, some people's poker face isn't worth shit, is it?" Steiner smirked.

"Hey," Chavez said. "I've got a *great* poker face. And—"

Ooooh-GAAAH! *Ooooh-GAAAH!*

The ancient klaxon cut him off in mid-sentence and cards went flying.

"Suit up!" Logan barked, and looked at Callum. "Means you, too, Sir."

✧ ✧ ✧

"And about . . . now, I think," Murphy said, watching the plot.

"Yes, Sir," Lieutenant Mastroianni said from *Ishtar's* command deck. She touched her boom mic, moving it in front of her lips, and spoke crisply. "*Val Idrak*, this is TFNS *Ishtar*. We are a Federation Navy warship, and you are instructed to decelerate and rendezvous with us for boarding inspection. Respond."

Val Idrak had been sublight for just over four hours. Her velocity was down to 15,934 KPS, and the range had fallen to under five light-seconds as she streaked past *Ishtar's* deep space hiding place.

"Show him our fan, Captain," Murphy said, and Captain Lowe nodded to Commander Creuzburg.

"Fire it up, Augustus," he said.

Creuzburg tapped his controls, *Ishtar's* Fasset drive came online, and she began to accelerate in pursuit.

"God, I hate this 'hurry-up-and-wait' shit," Steiner groused.

"You're just full of sunshine today, aren't you?" Logan inquired sardonically.

The three armored Hoplons were anchored to the deck in the forward section of the boarding pod while Steiner, Callum, and Eira—all in armored vac suits—occupied heavy duty acceleration couches in its configurable after section.

At the moment, all of them were in microgravity as the strikecarrier *Fury* rode *Ishtar's* racks, but that was going to change, sooner or later, because their pod had been mated to one of *Fury's* Orca-class fighters. The *Orca* was a flexible design, capable of accepting a number of different weapons modules or, as in this case, a single Moray boarding pod. In combat mode, an *Orca* pilot was capable of functioning effectively at accelerations as high as fifteen or even sixteen gravities, sustaining twenty gravities before blacking out, and actually surviving under that massive acceleration for as much as thirty minutes at a time. That was possible only because he was supported in a dense, high-pressure fluorocarbon mist to support his hollow organs. It also filled his lungs . . . and every other body cavity, which led to a predictable series of flatulence jokes when his acceleration chamber depressurized. Strikefighter pilots were also equipped to plug into external blood support systems which both oxygenated their blood (which their fluorocarbon-filled lungs could not) and insured its circulation at accelerations when the human heart simply couldn't.

The Morays were intended for an acceleration of no more than ten gravities, however. Which would be quite nasty enough for their passengers.

"I'm just saying we could still be playing pinochle instead of sitting here in this tin can, Smaj," Steiner replied. "That's all."

"Well, I'll bet the Admiral's just heartbroken—*heartbroken*— about interrupting your pinochle game."

"But—"

"Oh, shut it down," Logan commanded. "Better to load up early and wait than leave it too late and find out then your pod's been downchecked! You want to go tell Captain Bisgaard how to do her job?"

"No..."

"Or the Admiral? No? Didn't think so," Logan said.

"No problem, Sergeant Major. I'll just sit here and build character."

"Smart choice."

Callum leaned against his restraints and raised a hand, then tapped the side of his head.

"Uh-oh. Zero's figured out we turned off his comms," Steiner said.

Eira reached across and flipped the switch on the side of Callum's helmet.

"Did I miss something?" he asked. "The way Steiner's wiggling around, I thought maybe we got an alert notice."

"Maybe he's just got sand in his...suit," Chavez said.

Steiner kicked his armor in the back.

"Squat and hold, Sir," Logan said. "Welcome to the Corps."

"Yeah, I didn't expect to sit here this long when I volunteered," Callum agreed. "Still, it's not so bad."

"So far, at least," Logan agreed. "Acceleration's gonna be a bitch, though, Sir."

"My tolerance is in the top twenty percent." Callum shrugged. "I don't expect it to be *fun*, but I imagine I'll survive."

"You just hold that thought," Logan told him.

"Sir, if you don't mind my asking, why *did* you volunteer?" Chavez said. "For that matter, why didn't you stay back on Crann Bethadh? You weren't on shipboard rotation."

"Heard the Admiral and Captain O'Hanraghty talking about the exercises and figured I should tag along, see how it all works in real life, not in a scenario like *Federation Commander.*" Callum shrugged again. "Not that I don't like our duty station, but every so often I have to at least pretend to take all this Navy stuff seriously. Besides, where would the Admiral be without me to screen his message traffic? Then I found out about this interception, and, well—"

He shrugged minimally, all his harness would allow, and very carefully did not look in Eira's direction.

"Since you're so close to the flagpole," Chavez said, "maybe you know a bit more about our target than what was in the mission briefing? Unlicensed merchantman carrying slaves from Inverness and...? Any particular pirate outfit associated with it? Because if they're ex-League that went AWOL, that means a different fight than your normal feral in sixty-year-old gear."

"Not much," Callum said. "According to the report that got us headed out here, it's a slave consignment being shipped to some feral world despot."

"Eira, are you going to keep your cool if we do find a hold full of your people?" Logan asked.

"I don't...I don't know if I even believe it's possible," Eira said. "I spoke to a few other survivors when I was in the hospital. No one said anything about raiders. But in all the confusion after the attack...it's possible. Just know...know that if there are prisoners, they're in cages. They'll have no protection if there's a hull breach. At least...that's how it was for me. It was a long time ago."

An uncomfortable moment passed.

"Slavers get their due," Logan said then. "Any crew on a ship carrying slaves gets an express ticket out an airlock. That's Federation law. So don't take the law into your own hands, understand me?"

"Yes, Smaj."

"Sometimes it's a lottery for who pushes the button. Sometimes it's volunteers. Either way, I'll see to it that you're the last thing any slaver sees," Logan told her.

"That's...real? I thought the airlock was just something in the vids," Callum said.

"Why waste time and effort prosecuting a slaver? In the field, the commander gets supreme judicial authority out past the blue line," Logan said. "Slavers going for a float keeps others from getting similar ideas."

"I—"

"All hands, this is the Captain," a contralto voice said over their comms. "The Admiral has required our intercept to stop and be boarded, but it's continuing to accelerate. We are in pursuit. Estimate velocity match in approximately thirty minutes."

"Thirty minutes," Faeran said. "See, Steiner? Not that much longer."

"Yeah, sure. *You're* not going squishy," Steiner retorted.

"Oh, hell, Steiner," Chavez said, turning in his turretlike helmet to glower over his shoulder. "All right, look. How about the movie game to shut you up? I'll go first. Ellen Orochi."

"*Moon over a Supernova,*" Steiner said. "Man, that one sucked. Who else was in that...Tracy Thrace."

"You always go Thrace," Logan said. "*Assignment: Void.* Your turn, Lieutenant."

"I don't know what's going on," Callum said.

"Movie game. You name another actor from *Assignment: Void* or another Tracy Thrace movie."

"Oh...Reg Parland. How long does this go on?" Callum asked.

"Hours sometimes. Greenie, your turn."

Eira shook her head, her expression baffled.

"Don't think she's seen many movies," Faeran said. "Not fair to us from the Fringe."

"I'm from Bremen-on-Sagittarius, and you don't hear me complaining," Steiner said. "*Titanium Souls.* Faeran, your turn."

❖   ❖   ❖

"Target's gone to a thousand gravities, Admiral," Commander Mirwani announced.

"So he did have some acceleration in reserve," O'Hanraghty said. "And not a peep back from him yet. You'd almost think he had a guilty conscience."

"No, really?" Murphy looked at him, then back at the plot.

Merchant ships, by and large, were slower than warships, although transports specially built for the passenger trade were often an exception to that rule. Like *Papsukkal*—but usually without her missile launchers and point defense—they were built for speed, with enormously outsized Fasset drives for their size.

Their fans also used mil-spec nodes, which were more powerful but more maintenance intensive. Cargo, on the other hand, didn't really care how quickly it reached its destination, so freighters normally opted for commercial nodes. They produced lower peak accelerations, had a slower top speed in wormhole space, and had a higher failure rate if they were pushed to the limit, but they also cost about half as much, required far less maintenance, and were much harder to break if they *weren't* pushed to the limit.

The *Val Idrak*, or whatever its real name was, had just increased its acceleration by twenty-five percent, which pushed it into the upper brackets for merchant vessels. *Ishtar*, on the other hand, could generate eighteen hundred gravities of acceleration without redlining her drive out here, beyond the stellar Powell Limit. That was far more than she would require, however, and she was maintaining a leisurely (for her) *sixteen* hundred gravities.

"The idiot should be capable of doing the math," O'Hanraghty said. "There's no way he can stay away from us."

"He may just be spinning it out," Captain Lowe put in from the command deck. "It's always possible we could blow a fan quadrant. Not *likely*, but possible."

"He still hasn't said anything to us," O'Hanraghty pointed out.

"He will," Murphy said confidently.

Val Idrak had sliced past *Ishtar* at 15,934 KPS, and the interval between the two vessels was continuing to increase as the freighter stopped decelerating and started accelerating. Unfortunately for *Val Idrak*, *Ishtar*'s stupendous acceleration was sixty percent greater than her prey's, which meant that, despite the freighter's best efforts, the velocity differential was shrinking by 5.8 KPS every second.

✧   ✧   ✧

"...Marcus Hammer," Faeran said. "*Red Sky over Mars*."

"Damn, you guys see a lot more movies than I do!" Callum said. He drummed his fingers on his thigh for a moment. "I think...Margje Katers was in that one?"

"Good one, Sir," Logan said. "One of her first roles, in fact, I think. Let's see...so was Jonas Atlan."

"*Atlan?*" Steiner repeated. "*He* was in *Red Sky*?"

"You wanna challenge?" Logan asked.

"Well...yeah," Steiner replied, and Chavez gave an excellent imitation of a game show buzzer.

"Wrong answer, but thanks for playing," he said. "Atlan was that jerk Timmons."

"Timmons? But he was only in the movie for, like, fifteen seconds before he got blown up!" Steiner protested.

"It's called a 'cameo,' you uncultured moron," Logan said scathingly.

"And now that Steiner's sidelined, maybe we can do some complicated ones," Faeran said. "Wha'cha got, Lieutenant?"

"Okay," Callum said after thinking for a moment. "*Casablanca.*"

"Casa what?" Faeran asked blankly, and Callum smiled.

"Oh, come on, guys! This one's a true classic of the genre!"

"Never heard of it," Chavez said suspiciously.

"Feel free to discuss it among yourselves while you think about it," Callum said expansively. "I'm not going anywhere."

"Velocity equalizing...now," O'Hanraghty announced.

Ishtar had been in pursuit for thirty-nine minutes, during which her velocity had risen to 35,851 KPS. The range between her and *Val Idrak* had increased to fifty-four light-seconds, but from this moment, it would shrink remorselessly.

"I wonder what he's going to do now?" the chief of staff continued. "You'd think—"

"Communications request," Lieutenant Mastroianni announced.

"Put it through, Lieutenant," Murphy said, and a dark-faced, whippet-thin man appeared on the holo display.

"Federation vessel, this is Captain Buckley of the *Val Idrak.*" He had a peculiar accent, one Murphy couldn't place. "Please state your business."

Murphy glanced at O'Hanraghty, one eyebrow arched, then looked back at Buckley.

"I am Rear Admiral Terrence Murphy of the Terran Federation Navy. I think we've made that amply clear already," he said. "If we haven't, however, allow me to reiterate. You will decelerate to rendezvous with us and stand by to be boarded for inspection."

He sat back to wait out the communications delay.

"I don't believe you have any legal authority here, Admiral," Buckley replied two minutes later. "This isn't Federation territory."

"It's Federation territory if I'm in it." Murphy smiled and shook his head. "Care to argue with me and the carrier that has ten times the Alramal System's total firepower on her racks? We can do this the easy way...or we can do a forcible hull breach, followed by handing you an invoice for our operating expenses and impounding your ship until you pay it. Either works for me." He shrugged. "Which would *you* prefer?"

"What?" Buckley asked after another couple of minutes. "I mean, why do you want to inspect me? All I'm carrying is terraforming equipment." His face sank to half size on the display as a shipping manifest appeared beside him. "If you want to make me an offer on it, I might just accept it. I got stiffed in my last port of call." He shrugged. "Fly-by-night developer went belly-up while his equipment was in transit."

A mute icon came up, and Lowe appeared on the command bridge holo link. A wire diagram of *Val Idrak* appeared beside him. The freighter was a typical ship of her type, with four seven-hundred-meter racks. At the moment, there were pods on three of them.

"Admiral, we're not seeing any personnel pods," the flag captain said. "They all look like standard bulk carriers."

"Slavers don't usually worry about things like state rooms," O'Hanraghty pointed out from behind Murphy.

"A valid point," Murphy acknowledged. "Can we tell from here if they're pressurized, Captain?"

"Not with any certainty, Sir. Heat signature suggests they are, but we can't prove that. *Val Idrak*'s spin section is a lot smaller than ours, too—just enough for the ship's crew—so they're in microgravity. And there's no sign of a life-support section on any of them, so they'd have to be tied into the ship's mains. That's not going to support a whole lot of additional sets of lungs." Lowe's hologram shrugged. "On balance, I don't think they could have a lot of people packed into them, but it's not impossible."

"Noted."

Murphy stood in thought for a moment, then shrugged.

"We've come this far," he said, and un-muted the link to *Val Idrak*.

"Thank you for sharing your manifest with us, Captain," he said. "However, I'm afraid I'm going to have to insist on at least a cursory examination to confirm its accuracy. If everything is as you say, then I'm sorry to inconvenience you. However, we're in-system searching for a suspected shipment of illicit human cargo. I'd be derelict in my duty if I weren't to make certain you're who you say you are." He showed his teeth in a brief smile. "Wouldn't look good in my report at all, you know."

"That's . . . that's patently ridiculous," Buckley said. "I've already sent you my manifest: atmosphere converters and ocean seeders!"

"Indeed you have, and we appreciate it. We're still going to take a quick look to confirm it. I'm afraid we need your full compliance . . . bearing in mind that if we're forced to fire on your vessel, you'll be liable for all costs associated with conducting the search. And, just to be forthright with you, our munitions are rather expensive. I was dead serious about that."

Buckley's expression tightened as the transmission reached him a minute later. A tic appeared at the corner of his mouth, and he started to say something quickly. Then he visibly stopped himself and inhaled sharply.

"'Cursory examination,' is it? Fine!" He leaned to one side and spoke rapidly in a language no one on *Ishtar*'s flag bridge recognized, then straightened again. "I'm going to eight hundred gravities' deceleration," he announced.

"Thank you, Captain." Murphy glanced at the plot as it updated. "At that rate, I believe we will rendezvous in approximately ninety-six minutes."

✧　　✧　　✧

"What did you say?" Captain Cho Su demanded sharply.

"I said it looks like that freighter you were so worried about has a visitor, Irene," the bearded man on her comm display replied.

He wore the uniform of Alramal System Traffic Control, and he had no idea what Cho Su's real name was. She was pretty sure that he knew damned well the one she'd given him was a fake, but he didn't care about that. All he cared about, she thought with carefully concealed contempt, was money. He didn't have a clue what commitment to a *cause* was.

"What do you mean?" she asked now.

"We just picked it up," he replied. "From the plot, though, looks like we've had a Fed FTLC in-system and didn't know it. Our data's running behind, of course, but about two minutes ago, we picked them up going in pursuit of what sure as hell looks like the ship you've been concerned about. They were ninety light-minutes out, so that means they've already been chasing it for an hour and a half by now." He shrugged. Light-speed limitations were a fact of life. "Your boy—assuming, of course, that this is your boy—is at least six hundred gees slower than they are, too. Crunching the numbers, they're probably still eighty-five light-minutes out or so, and I imagine he's about to recognize the virtues of discretion. Sorry about that."

"You're sure it's a Federation carrier?"

"Hell, no, I'm not *sure!*" The Alramalian snorted. "Whoever the hell it is and whatever they may be saying to your boy, they aren't bothering to talk to us. They're cranking right on sixteen hundred gravities, though, so they're *somebody's* FTLC!"

"Couldn't be one of the freelance raiders?"

"I doubt that very much. Drive's way too powerful, and most of the raiders who might have a ship that big don't poach here in Alramal. We're too valuable as a cargo transfer point."

As a place to fence plunder, he meant, she thought. But that didn't make him wrong.

"Thank you," she said after a moment. "Please keep me informed."

"Sure."

The display blanked, and Cho Su pushed up out of her chair and began to pace. Things had gone so well—for so long! And now, *this*. She didn't know all the details. In fact, she knew practically *none* of the details; that was known as operational security. But she did know two things. First, the cargo aboard *Val Idrak* was essential to the war effort, the golden key to final victory over those murderous Federation bastards. And, second, because it was, it could not, under any circumstances, be allowed to fall into Federation hands.

Her job had been to ensure its safe passage to this point. It was the fifth shipment she'd overseen, and her unbroken record of previous successes only made the looming probability of failure hurt even worse.

Nonetheless, her instructions for a case like this were clear, concise, and nondiscretionary.

She wrestled with herself for another sixty seconds or so, trying to find an alternative to her orders. But there wasn't one. And so, in the end, she squared her shoulders, leaned over the keypad beside her comm, and began entering a long, complicated code.

✧　　✧　　✧

Red warning lights flashed as the *Orca* came almost to a halt relative to *Val Idrak* and released the Moray.

The boarding pod accelerated fiercely across the remaining gulf between its transporting fighter and the freighter, then decelerated with equal ferocity. The twenty-five-minute trip from *Fury* to their target had been just as bad as Logan had suggested, under six gravities of acceleration, and *de*celeration, the entire way. The Morays were designed to hit *fifteen* gravities on final approach, however, and the sudden jolt of deceleration drove Callum deep into his couch, then sent his stomach whirling sideways as the pod spun fiercely on its attitude thrusters to reach its target nose-first. One arm shot out, and his face went warm as a last burst from the nose thrusters threw him forward against his restraints and blood pooled in the front of his body.

Then the Moray hit hull plating at a "mere" 1.5 meters-per-second in a perfectly coordinated maneuver. The shock-absorbing collar functioned exactly as it was supposed to...and the impact slammed him back in his seat and rattled his teeth, anyway.

"Damn, that never gets old!" Chavez shouted over the Alpha Team's channel.

"Hot mic!" Logan snarled. "Bravo Team's securing the target's bridge now. Compliant boarding so far, but stay frosty."

"Why aren't *we* securing the bridge?" Steiner slapped the center of his restraints and they snapped off and retracted into his seat. "Thought we'd be the main effort on this."

"Main effort is the cargo." Logan's armor rose. "Faeran, left flank. Chavez, center. Squishies...stay behind us."

"Oh, good." Callum unstrapped and drifted upward from his couch. "Thought we'd be going first."

"Sir," Eira tapped him on the arm then pointed to his carbine, still locked to his acceleration couch.

"Right...almost forgot." He nodded. "You think I'll need this? A trio of Hoplons should take the fight out of anyone, I'd think."

"You know what's waiting for us in there, Sir?" Steiner asked.

"Not exactly, no."

"Then you need your weapon. Sir."

Callum wrapped his right suit gauntlet around the pistol grip and a sighting optic appeared on the inside of his visor, along with an ammunition readout.

Doors at the front of the boarding pod snapped open. There was no sound in vacuum, but Callum felt the impact through his feet as they slammed back into their housings. The Moray was almost, but not quite, perfectly located. Thrusters fired, moving it sideways, adjusting its position until the bay doors of the cargo pod were properly centered. Then the umbilicals locked to the hull, the docking collar inflated to prevent catastrophic pressure loss in the event of an airlock malfunction, and Logan reached one armored hand toward the locking bar. A green light blinked above it, indicating that the freighter's command deck had disconnected the interlocks.

"Weapons hot," he said. "Bravo's got the bridge and they're playing nice so far, but I'd rather not lose any of you idiots."

"You say the nicest things, Smaj," Faeran said.

"Yeah, sure."

He yanked the bar and the outer doors slid apart to reveal a standard airlock.

"You okay, Eira?" Callum asked on their personal channel. "You seem…more focused than usual."

The young woman had her carbine at the shoulder ready, eyes locked forward.

"Inverness was never a home," she said. "But no one deserves to be a slave. The Smaj promised me blood." She nodded. "I'll take it."

"Then I'll just…stay behind you," he said.

"Don't need to convince anyone to let the Hoplons do the work," Steiner said. He was looking at the bulkhead telltales. "Definitely pressure on the other side. Everyone's got hollow points loaded, right? Navy has a pretty good track record of picking up anyone that gets sucked out during an explosive decompression, but it's not a hundred percent."

Alpha Team moved forward into the airlock. It was a tight squeeze with the three massive Hoplons, but they made it, and the outer doors slid shut behind them.

"Open it up, Steiner," Logan commanded, and Steiner tapped the controls beside the telltales. It would have been far more difficult for a Hoplon to activate them without breaking something.

The inner doors slid open, the right panel moving at an uneven pace, to reveal a cavern of crates fitted into stacks. They appeared to all be identical, each about the size of a small ground car, and none bore any markings. A pair of deckhands floated to one side in the hold's microgravity. They wore raggedy vac suits and simple helmets and held their hands high.

"Clear," Logan said. "Heads on swivels, people."

Gas jets pushed him forward into the cargo pod's central hold. Chavez and Faeran followed, each of them sweeping the interior and overhead as they moved forward to flank him.

"So far so good," Callum said.

"Sir, *please* don't say that," Steiner said, his voice going an octave higher. "Now Faeran's gonna have to sacrifice a duck or something to un-jinx us."

"Inspection element forward," Logan said.

Callum hefted his carbine and pushed himself forward. He lifted his visor forward and shifted it onto the top of his helmet. The air was unusually warm for a cargo pod and smelled of static and ozone.

"Hello," he said. "Federation military. I'm here to help."

The two deckhands, diminutive even in comparison to Callum, far less the towering Hoplons, smiled and nodded.

"Both scan clean for weapons or augmentation." Logan turned toward the forward end of the hold.

"Bill of lading," Callum said. He held out a hand. The deckhands glanced at each other, then looked back at him and kept smiling.

"Bill?" Callum mag-locked his carbine across his back and tapped the side of his right hand against the inside of his left forearm. "*Ishteema. Houyon. Naubhara.* Um...*lulan?*"

The deckhands started chattering. None of it meant a thing to Callum.

"Dialect drift out beyond the blue line," Logan said. "Not that uncommon."

"Damn right. I had to relearn your heathen standards, and you all *still* sound strange as hell," Faeran said. "Sir. Suggest you get your point across, or I'll start breaking shit."

"Charades it is." Callum used a toe against the deck to push himself toward the nearest stack and gestured at the bottom crate, then mimed a box opening.

"*Illata. Illata!*" One of the merchant spacers ducked behind Logan to put the Hoplon's bulk between him and the crates. The Sergeant Major swiped him aside with a forearm sweep that sent him pinwheeling across the hold into his companion. The Marine swung the massive barrel of his rifle around and drew down on the deckhands.

"Guess they don't want you to open it," Steiner said.

"I'm close enough." Callum popped a scanner off his belt and toggled the display. He looked down at it, then frowned. "Huh. There's a scrambler field built into each crate. Guess that explains the ozone smell."

"There people inside or not?" Logan asked.

"Not alive." Callum adjusted a dial on the scanner. "Fields like this cause severe neurologic damage after prolonged exposure."

"Now ain't that interesting?" Logan observed. "Patching you through to the Beta Team."

"—swear I don't know what we're carrying." Captain Buckley's voice came through Callum's helmet speaker. "I was hired to collect the pod and drop it in the system for someone else to collect. That's all I know!"

"And who would that 'someone else' be?" Callum asked.

"Oh, this is a new voice. Who? Sure as hell wasn't the Federation! All I know is a contact here in-system would identify himself by asking me if *Val Idrak* was named *Holy Oak*, and I'd get paid when I said she was."

"And where were you supposed to drop it?" Callum asked.

"On my way out," Buckley said reluctantly. "I've done the same run once before and I've got the release vector, but I don't know—"

"Lieutenant Murphy," O'Hanraghty cut in. "*Ishtar*'s close enough for real-time discussions with the Captain. Continue your inspection and leave him to us."

"Aye, aye, Sir."

Callum pushed himself closer to the rack and ran his scanner up and down the metal frame.

"The scramblers are connected to external power," he said. "Makes sense—batteries wouldn't last that long. Let's see."

He looked around, then pointed at a panel on a bulkhead.

"You two," he said to the merchant spacers, then switched his scanner on and off rapidly and motioned them toward the panel.

They shook their heads.

"At least we're communicating," Callum said dryly. "Oh well. Shouldn't be too hard to figure out on my own."

He started toward the panel, but Eira stopped him with a hand to the chest.

"Don't take the risk, Sir," she said.

Logan snapped his middle fingers together, opening them just wide enough to fit over a skull, and loomed over the recalcitrant deckhands.

"I'll crush your heads," he said.

"And I'll pinch your face," Faeran said, miming the same gesture.

The deckhands looked nervously at one another, but they still didn't budge.

"Look," Callum said, "I'll just open the panel. I promise I won't touch any buttons until you've had a chance to make sure they're not wired to a bomb or something, Eira. But if we don't—"

"Callum!" Murphy shouted over the comm. "What's going on in there? What did you do?"

"We haven't touched anything, I swear." Callum slammed his visor down. "Why? What's—"

The hum of scrambler fields died, and a crate at the forward end of the hold exploded. The thunderous blast and wall of overpressure was stunning in the cargo pod's confines, even from within the protection of a vac suit, and a wall of flame washed against the bulkhead.

"Collapse!" Logan shouted.

Another explosion, closer to the team and high up on one of the stacks. More explosions rippled down the crates, and an even more violent blast ruptured the pod's thick skin. The howling hurricane of escaping atmosphere sent Callum tumbling toward the hull rent, but a dark shadow hurtled toward him. It slammed into him, something grabbed his right arm with a jerk that almost dislocated his shoulder, and he whirled sideways, instead. His visor slammed into the bulkhead—hard—but at least he wasn't moving anymore. Darkness enveloped him as the entire ship shook and rattled with more explosions.

He covered the back of his helmet with his hands, mind racing as he tried to remember what he was supposed to do aboard a ship during a cascading failure. Life pods?

"Eira? Eira!" he called.

There was no answer, and an icy calm descended upon him as the shaking died away. He tried to push away from the bulkhead, but a huge hand on his back prevented it.

"Not yet, squish," Chavez said over the comm.

"Thunder! What the hell happened?" Faeran asked.

"Extraction's en route," Logan said. "Keep a perimeter."

The shadows shifted, and Callum turned. There was still a tiny bit of atmosphere—enough left to send him drifting toward the rent once more as it bled past him—but Eira grabbed him by the ankle. She gripped a tiedown on the deck with her other hand, and at least he could see what the dark shadow had been. Two of the Hoplons—Faeran and Chavez—had formed a blast wall between him, Eira, and Steiner as the explosions rolled around them. Both of them looked somewhat the worse for wear, and one of Chavez's armored arms hung motionless at his side, the shoulder joint dented by some heavy impact.

The cargo hold was a blackened ruin, the remnants of the stacks twisted like fallen branches. Red-hot bits of crates and whatever they'd contained floated in the microgravity, drifting toward the hull breach on those last eddies of atmosphere.

"Fuck my life," Steiner said.

"Get it together," Logan said, although Callum couldn't see the Sergeant Major. "Count off."

"One," Chavez responded. "Integrity holding, left arm inop."

"Two," Faeran announced. "Systems up."

"Three," Steiner said. "All good, but I'm gonna need a really good internal clean."

Callum got his magnetic boot soles onto the deck and stabilized himself. The instant he did, Eira was beside him, her expression fierce, running her hands along the seals of his suit. He saw his own expression mirrored in her visor and couldn't find the same level of confidence in the reflection.

"I'm fine." Callum pushed one of her hands away. Then he noticed a crack across one edge of his visor. He crossed his eyes to look at it and swallowed. Was it *growing* ever so slightly?

"Wait," he said. "That's not—"

Steiner yanked him into a headlock and pressed a nozzle against his visor. A mist shot out and covered half Callum's vision before hardening into a lattice.

"He's sealed," Steiner said. "Not to—Eira! What the hell?"

Eira was in front of Callum, her hands poised beneath the ring of her helmet. The emergency latch was already cocked open.

"Give him mine!" she said.

"He's. *Sealed,*" Steiner said. "He's fine. Now button up before you spill your air."

"Where's Logan?" Callum twisted around, keeping one mag-locked foot on the deck and using the other to push himself in a circle. The Sergeant Major was at the edge of the hull breach, pushing one of the ground car-sized crates in front of him. One section of it had been ripped away, and Callum glimpsed bent metal bars that glittered with inlaid golden flecks through the opening.

"Got a scan when the scramblers fell," Logan said. "The explosives in each case were easy to spot, so I managed to get hold of this one and do a field expedient bomb disposal before it went up. Contents don't look that banged up, do they?"

"You risked your life for that," Callum said, reaching up to touch the spray on his visor. Steiner slapped his hand away.

"Shame for us to go through all this trouble and have nothing to show for it," Logan said.

"Hey," Faeran said. "Where'd the deckhands go?"

"Not positive, but there's a couple of smears on the deck," Chavez said.

"All hands alert," Captain Bisgaard's voice came crisply over the comm. "All boarders, evacuate the ship immediately. I repeat, evacuate immediately!"

"You heard the lady," Logan said. "Chavez, take lead. Faeran, you and me on the crate." He patted it with a massive, armored paw. "Not leaving this baby behind now."

"What's the rush?" Callum asked as he turned toward the hull breach. "Oh, wonderful!" What was left of their Moray was definitely not going to get them home.

"Central, Alpha Team," he said over his comm "Our ride's sort of broken. We've got one crate, more or less intact, so we'll hold here until you can pick us up."

"Negative, Callum," O'Hanraghty said sharply. "Get off that ship *now*. And if you have a crate in one piece, it's even more vital that you do."

"But—"

"There's no time for discussion. *Do* it. Activate your beacons. Search and Rescue will pick you up."

Both of Callum's eyebrows rose, and he opened his mouth and turned his head toward Logan. Which was why he was looking in the right direction to see the Sergeant Major's enormous hand hit him in the small of the back and send him spinning out the breach.

The rest of the team followed rather more gracefully. Logan and Faeran brought up the rear with the crate between them, and the three suited Hoplons used their thruster packs to send the entire team scudding away from the *Val Idrak*.

Callum looked back at the ship, receding rapidly behind them, as the Beta Team Moray detached from the forward hull and started in their direction. Aside from the long, jagged rent down one flank of the cargo pod, the freighter didn't seem especially damaged to him, and he frowned.

"I wonder what that was all about?" he said.

"Mostly about somebody not wanting us to find out what was inside the damned crates, Sir," Logan said. "Duh."

"I wasn't talking about that. Why the rush to send us floating around out here?" Callum shook his head, still staring back at the freighter. "I hate going EVA! Especially when there's a more or less intact ship I could wait aboard, instead. I mean—"

The explosion was blindingly bright but silent in the vacuum about them.

CHAPTER TWENTY-FIVE

TERRENCE MURPHY AND HIS STAFF SAT AROUND THE BRIEFING room table. Callum and Eira stood against the compartment's outside bulkhead, still in their vac suits, while a true-scale wire diagram of a thick diamond rotated slowly in a holo above the table.

"It's League tech," O'Hanraghty said. "A singularity manifold for a mil-spec Fasset drive. Ours are designed a bit differently, but there's no mistaking it. Besides—" He highlighted a flat pane of readouts at the front of the diamond. "All the maintenance LEDs and system connectors are standard RLH format."

"Callum." Murphy leaned forward in his seat and stroked his chin. "You're fresh from your engineering program. What's the cost of one of these?"

Callum had been examining his cracked helmet with a thoughtful frown that was far away from the ready room. Now he looked up suddenly and squinted in thought.

"I'm not really as up on mil-spec components as I am on the civilian-grade side," he said, "but I'm damn sure they're more expensive, not less, and the singularity manifold is the most expensive part of any Fasset-drive ship. They have to be manufactured to insanely careful tolerances, but the real bottleneck's the exotic matter incorporated into one of them. Producing that much exotic matter is a royal pain in the ass. Like I say, I'm better read in on the civilian side, but my understanding is that the military version uses even more exotic matter. I'd be surprised if building one of these things didn't eat up thousands of hours per unit."

"And how many manifolds were destroyed on that ship?" Murphy asked.

"From the Hoplons' video," O'Hanraghty glanced at a slate, "two thousand four hundred and ninety-nine. That's assuming each crate had a manifold. The scan pulse from Logan's team detected just that in the first third of the hold his armor was able to get through, so I think it's reasonable to assume that they all did."

"That's enough manifolds for... forty FTLCs," Captain Lowe said. "That's almost thirty percent of the Federation's total fleet."

"Why?" O'Hanraghty asked. "We know the League's shipbuilding capability, and they can't build that many ships. So why do they need so many manifolds?"

"Manifolds are one of the great bottlenecks in ship construction," Callum said. "Laying keel and hull's not difficult—that's mostly automated in the yards. It's the Fasset drives that matter, and building them is what really takes the time. Especially fabricating the manifolds. When an FTL is decommissioned, everything but the Fasset drive goes to the breakers. Not the drive fan, though. Instead, they build a new ship around it. They may upgrade by replacing the *nodes*, but the core of the drive is almost always recycled. My brother's... He's big into that. Family business."

"Then if building these things is so hard, where were these manufactured?" Lowe asked. "And where were they *going*?"

"Unfortunately, Captain Buckley and his crew died when their ship blew up," Murphy said. "The Beta Team that seized the bridge didn't have time to un-encrypt Buckley's ship's logs before they had to abandon. I don't know if they had time to download a copy." He shook his head sadly. "None of them made it home to tell us."

"Speaking of which, Sir," Callum said, "how did you know *Val Idrak* was going to blow?"

"I didn't 'know' anything of the sort," his father said. "But whoever shipped those manifolds obviously didn't want anybody else finding out about them. The scramblers and the demolition charges in each crate proved that. So it seemed reasonable to assume that they'd like the entire ship—and those encrypted logs, for example—to become... unavailable to us, as well." He shrugged. "I figured there might be a scuttling charge on a timer, so it seemed like a good idea to get all of our people off. If the ship hadn't blown in the next hour or so, I could always have put you back aboard."

"Well, all I can say, is *I'm* glad you played your hunch," Callum said.

"Actually, I don't think that's exactly what happened," O'Hanraghty said. He switched the holo to a system view and a thin line of light traced itself across the plot from the inner system to *Ishtar*'s position. "Oh, the hunch was good, but that's a data spike. It originated on Alramal, and at this range, even a tight beam had plenty enough scatter for us to catch it. It reached *Val Idrak* just about the time it blew."

"Which presents an interesting question," Murphy observed. "The timing is about right for that detonation command—and does anyone here really think that isn't what it was?—to reach *Val Idrak* if it was sent as soon as the system sensor net could pick up our Fasset drive in pursuit of *Val Idrak* and transmit that information to the planet. So, who sent it, and why?"

"I doubt we'll ever know," O'Hanraghty replied, "but I don't think there's any doubt that whoever it was is working for the League. And the fact that they sent the destruct command that quickly, without even waiting to see if Buckley would be able to fob us off or if the scramblers would fool us, is an indication of just how determined they are to keep all this a secret. Callum's just told us how expensive, in terms of both time and industrial capital, these damned things are. And they just blew up forty FTLCs worth of them on the *probability* that we might find them. That's ruthless as hell, and it indicates just how much they're willing to write off to maintain security."

"Is that why they wanted *Val Idrak* to drop them off here, instead of in a League system?" Murphy mused.

"Probably." O'Hanraghty nodded. "It gives another layer of separation from whoever built the manifolds for them."

Callum deposited his damaged helmet on the table and opened a screen.

"But why would the League subcontract this work at all?" Tanaka asked. "Finding a manufacturer out past the blue line has to be expensive. There's damn all for heavy industry out here, outside someplace like Hell Hearth, and they've been aggressively neutral from the get-go. And quality control would have to be a major issue on most feral worlds. Then there's the risk during transport, as we just saw. Or are we going to suggest that the Leaguies built an entire secret manufacturing facility all the hell and gone way out *here*? Please! It's not like they're hurting for space closer to home to get this work done, assuming they've got the manpower to build it and the cash to pay for it at all!"

"I don't think they did find a feral world to build them," Callum murmured.

"Excuse me?" Tanaka said. "*Somebody* built them."

"Sure, but I don't think it was the League. For that matter, I don't think it was anybody out this way. Look at this." He pressed fingertips to a reader, then flicked them up at the holo. The wire diagram of the captured manifold reappeared, and the view zoomed in on a ring linked to the bent edges.

"You see the quantum filament readers? They're . . . the string elongation buffers don't match the Greene Theorems."

"Not everyone here is an engineer, son," Murphy said.

"They're weird!" Callum raised a hand and smacked his helmet. "They shouldn't work! But I've been doing the math, and it *does* work. And I don't understand that. It's an approach that sure as hell wouldn't occur to any engineer *I* know. In fact, it hurts my head to even try to think through these equations—more than quantum mechanics normally do, I mean. But weird as it is, I think it's actually more efficient than our own designs, at least marginally."

O'Hanraghty pulled up a screen of his own and began tapping a virtual keyboard. He looked at the results for several seconds, then raised his eyes to Murphy.

"I think it's bothering Callum because this isn't how a human mind would solve these equations," he said.

"Wait." Tanaka held up her hand. "Wait. Just what are you suggesting?"

"That Callum's right. These manifolds weren't built by the League or to a League design by a feral planet full of humans. They were built *for* the League, yes. But if we have a xeno-anthropologist examine the problem-solving that went into the design, I think they'd come to the same conclusion I have. These manifolds were built by the Rishathan Sphere."

Tanaka wasn't the only officer present who groaned.

"Not that old conspiracy theory," she said. "That idea's been floating around the dark feeds since the war started. No rational person believes it."

"Then how do you explain that?" O'Hanraghty waved a hand at the holo. "The Rish have never let anyone examine their Fasset drives. And League FTLCs—"

"Scuttle," Lowe said. He frowned thoughtfully. "Not all of them, but a damned high percentage."

"How high a percentage?" Callum asked, still gazing at his own data screen.

"Maybe a third?" Lowe looked at O'Hanraghty and it was the chief of staff's turn to frown.

"Not that high, I don't think," he said. "More like a quarter. But you're right, a hell of a lot of them do if they're boarded. Or if they're disabled with no way out of the system. And when they do, the command and engineering teams go up with the ship."

"Exactly." Lowe nodded. "The Federation isn't so...committed. I'd just overload and fry the manifolds if the *Ishtar* was in too much trouble, and I'd always thought the Leaguies who didn't were just plain bloody-minded. But if there's anything to this theory, then..."

"They couldn't let us get hold of their hardware...or of engineering people who might let something slip," Mirwani said. "And," his eyes narrowed, "if there's anything to it, that might give us a rough meter stick for how many of these Rish-built manifolds—what percentage of their total FTLC force—they've got."

"That's not evidence," Tanaka scoffed. "It's conjecture. Is this what we're going to do, Sir?" she asked Murphy. "Send this back to the Oval with our scientific and not-so-scientific wild-ass guesses that the Rish built a fortune's worth of manifolds for the League? Based off a number of increasingly coincidental discoveries while we were out past the blue line?"

"There's a lot to process here." Murphy stood and made his way slowly around the conference table. "But this is a significant discovery. Does anyone disagree?"

He paused beside Callum to put a hand on his shoulder and squeeze, then resumed his pacing.

"I'd caution against even mentioning the Rish in your report, Sir," Tanaka said. "It will only rile up the crazies. A hint of evidence—"

"So you agree there's evidence of Rishathan involvement?" O'Hanraghty asked.

"Yes. I mean, no. I mean...none of us are qualified to make that judgment," she said. "But just because a Rish was involved in the design doesn't mean the Sphere is responsible for its manufacture."

"No Rish ever leaves the Sphere," Murphy said. "They haven't since this war began. We come to them at their designated trade worlds; they don't come to us. So let's draw the idea out for the sake of argument. What if this is—hypothetically—proof that the Rish are giving significant military aid to the League?"

"Fuck trading with those lizard bastards ever again, for one thing," Captain Bisgaard said.

Fury's CO glared at the holo. The Alpha Team had gotten home battered but intact; a sizable chunk of *Val Idrak*'s hull had struck the Beta Team's Moray. None of its passengers—or the *Orca* which had been maneuvering to pick it up—had survived.

"One thing, if I may," Ortiz, the fleet adjutant said from the far end of the table. "Does anyone doubt those manifolds were going to League warships? No? Then *where* were they going? Where are the ships waiting for them? The main League yards are at Dongguan and Urumchi. Even Urumchi is five months from here for a military drive, closer to six and a half for a merchie. Dongguan's still farther away. And for that matter, we've got a fair grasp of the Leaguies' building capabilities from prisoners and our own intelligence operations. They don't have the hulls in production for this many drives, not even at Dongguan and Urumchi combined."

"And they degrade," Callum said, looking up from his data screen.

"Degrade?" his father repeated, eyebrow arched.

"Manifolds need to be installed and linked together in their final configuration or the quantum—"

"How long?" Murphy asked.

"Five months—six, max—from construction, or they become worthless." Callum shook his head. "Which is why seeing so many manifolds in one place is just plain insane."

Ortiz tossed his hands up in frustration. Then he paused.

"So the League must have a bunch of hulls—probably within five or six months of completion—sitting around waiting for them...somewhere." His brows furrowed and he looked off to one side.

"This rabbit hole has some potential after all, doesn't it?" O'Hanraghty said.

Murphy continued his slow walk around the conference table, deep in thought.

"If the League has a hidden shipyard..." he said thoughtfully. "Buckley said this was his second delivery here in Alramal. Assuming he delivered the same cargo both times, then the League has an enormous fleet out here that we don't know about. Thoughts?"

"The League's manpower's under a lot of strain, but they aren't exactly desperate yet," Commander Mirwani said. "If their reserve pools are on par with ours—proportionately; their base population's a lot smaller—they could probably crew another fleet the size of what's fighting in Beta Cygni, by last count. I don't know that they could crew any more than that, though."

"I think doubling what they already have fighting in Beta Cygni would be quite enough," Murphy said dryly.

"So what was on that ship?" O'Hanraghty scratched his beard. "Say forty FTLCs' worth of manifolds. That's—what? A third of the strength they have deployed around Beta Cygni?"

"We may have poked a bear, people." Murphy stopped pacing and his expression was somber. "Worst case: that was the final shipment this ghost fleet needed to reach full strength. Best case: we caught them earlier in the process and they're a lot farther from ready than that. But either way, whoever sent the self-destruct signal is going to be leaving shortly for that hidden shipyard with very bad news."

"You're worried the League will attack," Lowe said. "Attack with whatever they've got, because if the Federation connects enough dots we can find out where their hidden yards are."

"Those manifolds had already been in transit, probably for weeks," Callum said, "and the clock on their degradation was already ticking. Wherever they were going...can't be too far."

"O'Hanraghty, do an analysis of all League systems in range. We can send a number of possibilities back to the Oval," Murphy said.

"Aye, aye." O'Hanraghty nodded quickly.

"We'll hit the wormhole threshold in about seven hours," Murphy said to the ready room in general. "Attend to your duties. We'll reconvene after we go supralight. Dismissed."

The assembled officers stood and clicked their heels together, then filed out. Murphy stopped Callum from leaving. Only the two of them and O'Hanraghty remained.

"Well done out there, Son," Murphy said. "You gave me a scare."

"I'd rather not make a habit out of being aboard exploding starships." Callum picked up his helmet and turned it over in his hands, then looked his father in the eye. "We weren't here for slaves, were we?"

"No." Murphy shook his head. "That was the cover story."

"So Federation Intelligence knows about this? They sent us out here?" Callum asked.

"That take is mostly correct," O'Hanraghty said. "We have a different intelligence source that led us to this system. He was right about every detail except for the target vessel's actual name."

"The *Holy Oak*?" Callum asked. "Buckley mentioned that before he died."

"The *Holy Oak*," Murphy agreed. "Our source didn't realize it was an identity challenge, not the ship's actual name."

"And he told *you* about it, Dad." It was not a question. "Not his superiors in Intelligence."

"Not his superiors. Callum, O'Hanraghty and I are part of an effort to bring Rishathan involvement in the war out into the open."

"Wait. You two are part of those conspiracy theories?" Callum looked back and forth between them. "The nut jobs with the scrambled feed casts and the tinfoil hats?"

"You put it like that and it sounds a lot worse than it really is," O'Hanraghty said. "But is it really so far-fetched? Look at what you just went through. What you recovered from that ship. And you found the Rishathan design in that manifold all on your own without a single 'paranoid' suggestion from your father or me."

"Oh God, I'm going to get dragged into it." Callum sat down hard. "My name in the feeds with it. Even *Grandpa* won't hire me. I'll have to marry some girl who thinks fluoride is in the water so the Five Hundred can mind-control the rest of the population!"

"Look at this objectively," Murphy said. "What if the xeno-anthropologists confirm your suspicion? That no human mind would've designed that manifold the same way. What then?"

"Then the Rish would have some explaining to do," Callum said.

"Damn betcha," O'Hanraghty said. "And we'll make sure this doesn't get swept under the rug. The Five Hundred's trade deals with the Sphere are lucrative, but not worth the groundswell against the Rish that will rise up from the people."

"That's a distant problem," Murphy said, "and we've got a more pressing concern. There's been a terrible mistake. And I made it."

"How do you figure, Terrence?" O'Hanraghty sounded surprised. "This isn't a *mistake*. For the first time in decades, we've got evidence of what the Rish have been doing. Proof!"

"What did we find? Key components to a League fleet. Given the time constraints on installing them, they're probably the *final* components for at least thirty or forty FTLCs. We don't know where the fleet in question is, how much of it's crewed and ready, or what their operational planning looks like. But they're going to know what we've done soon...and then they'll come for us. For New Dublin. They'll strike before the Federation can muster a defense."

"If they're anywhere closer than their base in Zohar, they could be in New Dublin before we even get word back from Earth," Callum said. "The math just doesn't work for us. How long, Dad? How long were you part of this tinfoil-hat brigade?"

"Wow, he figured out our club's name," O'Hanraghty said. "We should've read him in sooner."

"I've been a member for a long, long time, Son. Since before the Academy." Callum's eyes widened, and his father smiled crookedly. "The more I studied the battle your grandfather died in, the more I came to believe that the League might be using Rishathan tech. I kept going down the proverbial rabbit hole and came across others who suspected the same."

"Like me," O'Hanraghty said. Callum looked at him, and he shrugged. "I told you I was at Brin Gap. What I didn't tell you is that my uncle was your grandfather's chief of staff. They died together. And the bastard who ordered your grandfather—over his protests—to launch that Alpha strike doctored his report to make it all your grandfather's idea. His and my uncle's."

O'Hanraghty's expression was grimmer than Callum had ever seen it.

"I was a snotty on my midshipman's cruise," he said. "I didn't have much of a clue, yet, but Uncle Seamus had friends on the flagship's staff. One of them told me what really happened. It took a while, but once I had my commission, I went back and dug until I found confirmation. Couldn't do much with it, and digging for it is one of the blots in my copybook, but I came to very much the same conclusion your father did—that you did, really, in a way—about where the Leaguie carriers' acceleration came from."

"And the fact that my father and his uncle were friends was how the two of us made connections and embraced our tinhat-tedness," Murphy said.

"We don't advertise for membership," O'Hanraghty said. "That tends to bring in the real crazies. But we're out there, and there are more of us than people like Tanaka would ever believe."

"Is there a handshake or something?" Callum asked.

"Goat sacrifice," O'Hanraghty said solemnly. "We'll do it proper once we're back on Crann Bethadh."

"Harrison!" Murphy snapped.

"But the look on his face is priceless! No, Callum. No goat sacrifices. No secret handshakes. We don't need them, because once you've gotten a peek behind the veil, you really can't ever go back. So until and unless this goes public—*fully* public—you keep everything about the Rish to yourself."

"What about Mom? Or Vyom?" Callum asked. "Grandpa?"

"Absolutely not." Murphy shook his head, his expression sad. "I'm afraid they'll be some of the last ones convinced. They've been part of the Heart World system for so long that they literally don't know anything else. They're about the farthest thing from idiots, all of them, but their entire worldview says this is impossible. It'll be up to us to show them what we've learned, prove it to them and give them time to accept it. One can never force belief."

"If I hadn't been on that ship, *I* wouldn't believe it," Callum said. He looked back and forth between his father and O'Hanraghty for a moment, then inhaled deeply. "I need to go fix my gear. Maybe get cleaned up. And the whole Hoplon team saved my ass in there. I'll write up award recommendations."

"Protecting you is their duty," Murphy said, "and in a lot of ways, medals are cheap. Give them your thanks instead... and maybe chop off on a few extra days of shore leave when we're back on Crann Bethadh. If we can afford the time."

"And in the meantime?" O'Hanraghty said.

"And in the meantime, we need to figure out how to defend New Dublin from an overwhelming force." Murphy put his hands on his hips and turned to gaze at the holo of the manifold. "We need that plan before we get back."

CHAPTER TWENTY-SIX

"YOU CAN'T FIRE ALL OF THEM, MA'AM," THAN SAID. HE STOOD before Xing's desk aboard *Nüwa* with his vac helmet in the crook of his arm.

Xing cracked open the shoulder of her own combat-rated vac suit and sat down.

"You're telling me what I can and can't do, Than? Is there some confusion as to who's in charge here?"

"This was our first full-scale exercise with the ready ships," Than replied. "A degree of friction was to be expected."

"Sunwar had squadron command before they let him resign his commission for 'compassionate cause,' but he still fouled up his missile salvo." Xing laid her palms on her desk and looked at Than. "Unacceptable."

The older admiral frowned.

"Sunwar lost two daughters and a brother to a munitions malfunction. That's what he resigned his commission to deal with, and he's still working through issues. I understand why the Office of Personnel sent him here . . . but that doesn't mean he really is the best choice for his command."

"Then why are we still talking? Shitcan him and put Jin in the captain's seat." Xing raised her hands, palms uppermost.

"It's the other four you want me to shitcan along with him," Than said. "There're no replacements for them, and I believe their issues can be corrected with training. Our officer cadre are older men and women—they're rusty, but experienced—and Personnel won't send us more people, even for the parasites, until more of the carriers are ready to commission. Even when they do, the next tranche won't be any better. Which means we need to deal with that rust problem here, in Diyu."

"This is why you were in charge of Project Astra for so long..." Xing muttered.

She drummed her fingers on her desktop for a moment.

"All right. Sunwar, gone. We'll kill that chicken to send a message to the rest of the monkeys."

"I'll see that it's done," Than said.

Xing leaned back and tapped her chair arm's keypad. A holo of the just-completed exercise in which her forces had closed with and overwhelmed the ersatz Federation fleet commanded by Than came up.

"You managed a one-to-ten tonnage loss against me," she said with a frown. "I expected better performance from my fleet."

"With respect, your approach was too aggressive, Ma'am," Than said. "You attacked assuming I'd try to make it supralight and escape rather than stand and fight, but not every system will fold as easily as Scotia did. When the Dragon Fleet appears in-system, some Federation commanders will know the battle's hopeless but still try to inflict as much attritional damage as they can."

"The Feds are cowards." Xing wave a dismissive hand. "They'll run if I give them a route out. Sun Tzu knew what he was talking about."

Than bit his lip. Xing was fond of citing Sun Tzu; she was less careful about citing in context.

"The only fleet engagement we'll have," she continued, "will come when they scrape together enough ships to manage a fight they think they can win. That's the fight I need to win."

"This is why we have exercises," Than said. "To be prepared for what we don't expect."

"Five hours for crew rest, then we reset. And I want you to turn and run, this time. Let me see which of my squadron commanders are hungry for glory."

Than drew breath to protest, then saluted. He was almost to the door when a message chimed on Xing's desk. She glanced down at it, then raised a hand.

"Hold on," she said. "Naytash wants to see us. She says it's urgent."

✧   ✧   ✧

Naytash paced furiously around the control room, tracing a circle with Xing and Than at its center. Her cranial frills were erect and engorged, and a thick musk wafted from her as she spoke to herself in her own language. A small pack of males huddled against the wall.

"*All* of the manifolds were lost?"

The hovering sphere translated Than's question into the twittering snarls of Rishathan.

"*All!*" The translator reproduced Naytash's rage perfectly as she stamped a claw into the flexible deck sole hard enough to leave a puncture. "The human agent in the system reports the Federation commander claimed they were searching for slaves taken from Scotia. Lies! There was a containment failure somewhere. Now I must destroy the entire network we had established through the feral worlds."

"When can the Sphere deliver more manifolds?" Xing asked.

Naytash swung toward the second admiral. Her massive head shot forward and her jaws clashed the air ten centimeters from the human's face.

Xing didn't flinch.

"You think that producing that equipment is *simple*?" the alien snarled. "That the Sphere is your own personal foundry? We deliver you this gift, and you complain it isn't enough?"

"No, High War Mother," Xing said. "It is enough. But we must consider the effects of this... incident. Did the Federation discover the manifolds?"

"The cargo was programmed to self-destruct if anyone without the proper codes inspected it," Naytash growled. "They found nothing but blasted metal."

"Are you positive?" Xing pressed.

"Do you question my word?" Naytash demanded.

"No, High War Mother. But if the Feds recovered anything, even the ship's logs, they *will* piece things together."

"They recovered nothing," Naytash said. "The human agent is competent. She used the override code to destroy the entire ship."

"What conclusions could they draw, Second Admiral?" Than asked. "A single smuggler. As the High War Mother says, the consignment was scan shielded and equipped to self-destruct, and if—"

"There weren't any slavers in Scotia," Xing said flatly. "So there's no reason they should have been looking for slaves from Inverness *anywhere*, far less someplace like Alramal. It's an obvious false flag, a cover. And if they were there to intercept the shipment, then they must know about Project Astra—must know it was en route to us. They may not know its full extent, and they can't know where our anchorage is, because they would have attacked sooner—and here—if they did. But *something* led them to that shipment."

"Too many variables," Naytash said. "This was not the plan."

"Indeed," Xing said. "And it means we must accelerate our timetable."

Naytash stopped pacing and canted her head to one side.

"Replacing those manifolds will take...time, Fleet Mother," she said.

"I realize that." Xing rubbed her chin. "Do we know who the Fed commander was?"

"*Val Idrak*'s comm traffic was repeated to the human agent. She reports that the FTLC was the *Ishtar* and that the senior officer identified himself as Admiral Murphy."

"Never heard of him." Xing frowned and raised an eyebrow at Than.

"Terrence Murphy, probably, Ma'am," Than said. "He's part of the Murphy dynasty and he married into the very top tier of the Five Hundred, but until recently he was detailed to Survey. He's the one who won that skirmish at Steelman's Star. They announced they were going to promote him to flag rank and send him out as New Dublin's governor."

All of which he very carefully did not say out loud. Xing would have known for herself if she'd been paying proper attention to her intelligence briefs.

"New Dublin?" Xing pounced on the information. "Then that's our target. It's their only real yard facility this side of Jalal, so we can be sure it'll get their damned attention! And we have eight carriers and their strike groups ready to hit it with. Twelve, counting *Cai Shen*, *Li Shiji*, *Sun Bin*, and *Chen Qingzhi*. I'm launching my punitive expedition now."

"We've only just begun integration training, Second Admiral." Than raised a hand level with his shoulder. "If we launch now—"

"—we have a chance of success!" Xing snapped. "Who the hell is this Murphy, anyway? He may have a famous family name, but he was a *survey* officer, Than! He stumbled into a victory at Steelman's Star, and they gave him a governorship to play with as a reward, but he's nobody to the Oval, name or not, or they wouldn't waste him out here."

Her expression was eloquently scornful.

"He's a second-stringer, and he hasn't even had time to return to New Dublin yet. But he will. And whatever led him to Alramal, he has to know *something* about Project Astra, or he wouldn't have been there. He's going to pass that on to the Oval, but New Dublin's two hundred light-years from Sol, so it'll take eleven weeks for his report to get there. That's how long we have until the Oval will know whatever *he* knows. If we wait for a new shipment of manifolds, make sure every button's polished aboard the fleet, the Feds will have months—*months*—to get ready for us!"

"That's assuming they believe Murphy and react immediately, and that's far from a given unless he did find evidence—conclusive evidence," Than said. "The Federation is ponderous, fractious. There's too much we don't know, and if we—"

"Why are you so scared, Than?" Xing asked. "The reason we have the fleet is to punish the Feds, isn't it? Well, we can eviscerate the entire Concordia Sector, even cut as deep as Gouden, before they manage a response!"

Her eyes blazed at the thought of reaching a Heart World sector like Gouden.

"We probably can," Than agreed. "But will it be enough? Astra—the Dragon Fleet—is supposed to be our final blow. Building it, manning it, has taken everything we have, and it has to be *decisive*. Anything less is a waste."

Naytash grasped at the air and a local map of the galaxy appeared.

"The timetable is disrupted," she said. "The Great Council will need time to reassess, recalibrate—"

"There *is* no time," Xing said. "We'll depart for New Dublin as soon as my ships can take on munitions and supplies. We'll visit this Murphy first and teach him a lesson." She flashed her teeth. "The death of a name so important to the Federation Navy will play well with Dragon Fleet's first appearance, don't you agree, Than?"

"This is a mistake, Second Admiral," he said. "We're not ready yet."

"We'll hit New Dublin with overwhelming force. Against a Fed single-system defense force?" Xing snorted contemptuously. "It will be a lightning bolt. We'll crush this Murphy and push as deep as we can before they finally come up with something hard enough to give us a *real* fight, then cycle back to Diyu. That'll burn up *months*, and by the time we get back here, the rest of the fleet will be ready for the final blow. Won't it, High War Mother?"

Naytash hissed, then swiped her claws through the holo.

"Five of your months," she said. "At least that long, and the technology installed on the remaining fleet may be...less human. We may have to put engineers of the People aboard and the delivery will be more overt."

"Which will be acceptable." Xing smiled. "It will be the end of the war, so what will secrets matter then? Come, Than. It's time to make the Federation suffer."

✧　　✧　　✧

"But we're leaving eighty percent of the fleet behind."

Su Zhihao reached into a holo display to touch the space yards around the gas giant's moon.

"Thank you, XO," Than said as he signed off on a batch of orders. "This is the third time you've made that point."

"Sir, I don't—" Su glanced over his shoulder at the bridge crew making final preparations, then lowered his voice. "I don't get this. No one outside the system knows about Project Astra."

Than raised an eyebrow at him.

"High-level members of the Accord, fine," Su said quickly. "But what's the rush to wormhole out now? Has the Federation broken through Beta Cygni?"

"Not to my knowledge," Than said.

"Have they launched a new offensive somewhere else? Put a fleet over Anyang? Because the only explanation short of that I can imagine for why we're leaving with a quarter-full quiver is that Xing wants an easy victory before the next election. Am I wrong, Sir?"

"The election..." Than pursed his lips. "You know, that slipped my mind."

"That wasn't your first idea?" Su pulled back in surprise. "I know you're a spacer's admiral, Sir, but even I—"

"Second Admiral Xing has issued her orders. Focus on getting our magazines topped off instead of her motivations, XO."

Than set his slate aside.

"Yes, Sir. My apologies. We're really going to hit the Feds that hard?"

"Zhihao, if Xing's plan goes through, it will be worse than Baiknor."

"Baiknor? That was almost three hundred million dead." Su tugged at his goatee. "She's going for the Heart Worlds, isn't she?"

"It's *we*, XO. We. The good admiral has opted for mass civilian casualties to bring this war to an end. Let's pray the Federation chooses peace before Xing gets her fill."

"Sir, direct targeting of cities is . . . I don't know if our people will do it. *Cai Shen* is your flagship, and you've handpicked your squadron commanders over the years. None of them are butchers."

"If we refuse . . . then Xing has others who won't even hesitate. This war's gone on too long. There's too much blood between us and the Federation."

"And that's the answer? More bloodshed? It's one thing to destroy their warships, kill their spacers. Hell, we're damn good at that. Maybe a bit of mercy would—"

"Xing left Inverness to die a slow, cold death. You're expecting *mercy* from her? Here we are, Zhihao. This is our war, and there's no escaping it. All we can do is to do what we can to finish the fight with their heads held high."

"Better to be alive with a dirty conscience than dead with peace of mind? That's how most of this fleet thinks, isn't it?" Su said with a curled lip.

"Speculation is useless. But I don't have to guess about the number of missiles in Magazine Seven, do I?"

"That was supposed to be loaded hours ago." The chief of staff brought up a directory. "One moment, Sir. This conversation won't be for delicate ears."

"I'll leave you to it."

Than gave him a slap on the shoulder and crossed to the flag bridge control ring, gazing up at the displayed plot. He watched as more and more FTLCs moved into formation around *Nüwa*. Twelve of them, he thought. There were empty racks, here and there among them, because they simply had too few people to man that many sublight parasites. But they still had well over a hundred of them, and those empty racks provided redundant hardpoints in the event of battle damage. Even without Dragon's other forty carriers, he hadn't seen a fleet of such size and power in one place for over ten years... and what should have been his command had been given to another. One who would wield it far differently from the way he'd intended.

His face was stern, calm, but behind the mask of command, his soul was in turmoil.

CHAPTER TWENTY-SEVEN

"QUIT FUTZING WITH IT."

Alan Tolmach pulled back as his daughter adjusted a medal-laden sash over his dress uniform.

"If you'd stand still a moment, I wouldn't have to keep futzing, Pa," she said. "Same kit every year—we barely have to clean it."

"I'll be buried in it, so you'd best run it through the refresher for me." He gave her a mock snarl and looked out the window to a gray sky. "Bless me, I hate this day."

"Then stop standing for reelection," Moira said. "Let someone else do it."

"I'll not let another take this pain," he said. "Not when I still have the strength for it."

Moira's eyes misted, and she put the back of one hand to her mouth.

"What?" He looked at her. "That's always been my reason."

"But this year's...just a wee bit different," she said.

"Mr. President?" The door opened and a militiaman held it against the wall as frigid air poured in. "It's time."

"'Sides, sometimes the job has its perks." Tolmach pinched Moira's chin. "No one can start without me, so I'm never late!"

He cackled at his own joke as he exited the entry hall to a wave of applause.

The steps to the capital building were lined with rows of

275

young men and women, all in the unadorned black overcoats of the Crann Bethadh Militia. A priest in white vestments stood next to a metal arch, and a Federation Marines officer—it should have been Army, but no one could recall the last time the Army had been seen in New Dublin—stood on the other side with a holo logbook floating in front of her.

The applause came from parents arrayed around the formation of young adults, and it was polite, perfunctory, not celebratory. This was no day to celebrate.

Tolmach stepped around the arch, its thin bars adorned with medallions, each with a year stamped into it. At this very moment, he knew, this same ceremony was being repeated in every county capital across the face of Crann Bethadh. He looked over the formation of young men and women. Every year, they got younger and younger, he thought.

A microphone drone hovered just in front of him.

"Crann Bethadh, as your President, I welcome the top class of 2551." His voice echoed from the speakers spotted around Capital Plaza. "Let the Declarations begin."

He rapped his cane against the pavement twice, and the drone flitted away.

"O'Brallaghan, Michael J."

The Marine's voice came from the same speakers, clear through the windy cold, and a fresh-faced young man walked up the stairs to Tolmach. He removed a medallion from his pocket and snapped it onto the arch.

"Your mother know you're here, son?" Tolmach asked.

"Yes, Mr. President. She's right over there."

O'Brallaghan pointed to the crowd behind him.

"Congratulations on being top of your class," Tolmach said. "I can't say there's much luck to it." He looked the youngster in the eye. "You know what to do?"

"Of course, Sir. For God and New Dublin." O'Brallaghan turned and raised his right hand. "Preference!"

A smattering of applause answered.

"Preference recorded," the Marine said.

O'Brallaghan turned and stepped through the arch as the priest began a prayer. He dipped a silver tree branch in a bowl of blessed water and sprinkled some on the new recruit as the young man emerged from the far side of the arch.

Tolmach shook O'Brallaghan's hand as he passed.

"Well done, lad. Welcome to the profession of arms."

"Ansell, Erin!" the Marine called, shifting to alphabetical order for the remainder of the class, and the next recruit mounted the stairs. She announced for the needs of the service, and Tolmach shook hands again, concentrating on the young woman's face. He'd kept memories of this day for so many years, and none of those he'd received had ever come back with the same light in their eyes.

A third recruit bounded up the stairs with a spring in her step. She reached the top and gave Tolmach a smile... and his heart stopped.

"Dewar, Christina D.," the Marine said.

"Preference!" she shouted, and took a long step through the arch.

"Krissy." Tolmach stared at his granddaughter. "But you're not—"

"Eighteen on Monday," she said. "The Federation accepted the age waiver. I'll be a strike pilot. Sorry I won't be infantry, like you and my uncles, but that's not for me, *Daideó*."

"No... you can't..."

"Sir, if you please," the Marine said quietly, her microphone muted.

Tolmach's entire body was an icy, empty void. A voice somewhere deep inside that void wailed in protest, telling him he *could not* let this happen. But he had no choice, and so he held out a numb hand and his granddaughter shook it. Then she gave him a quick kiss on the cheek and hurried back into the capital building to continue the induction paperwork.

"She can't," the President of New Dublin whispered, his single eye burning as the wind blustered about him. "She can't..."

"Fargig, Adrian R.," the Marine continued.

❖   ❖   ❖

Tolmach made his way down the dimly lit steps, one hand on the railing while the other used his cane to poke at the next lower step.

"Aren't I just the finest example of strength in leadership?" He chuckled to himself as he felt the pain in his knees. The stairs ended at a basement door set into moisture-slick bricks. That basement was part of New Dublin's first-wave construction, it had never been connected to the newer underground infrastructure—or its dehumidifiers—and it was one of the few places they could be *certain* contained no listening devices that might report to the wrong set of ears.

A pair of Cormag Dewar's men stood on either side of the door.

"Mr. President," one of them said, nodding respectfully. "All invitees are here."

"Hope I didn't keep them waiting too long." Tolmach shuffled forward. "Else they'll be drunk and nothing'll get done. Men and women away from home, eh?"

"Wouldn't know anything about that," the other guard said with a slight smile.

"I know your father," Tolmach told him. "Best watch yourself."

He banged the door with his prosthetic fist and it opened to a smell of mustiness and sweat. A dozen men and women sat in leather padded chairs, all facing a single antique chair with a stool and glass of water. Most wore the plain, serviceable garments of typical Fringe Worlders, but one bear of a man wore fur-lined robes and one woman, her face covered by a porcelain mask, wore a silver and white kimono. Dewar stood at the back of the room, behind them, and a single seat amongst their number was empty.

They rose as one as Tolmach entered the room.

"Sit. Sit, all of you!" Tolmach wagged his cane at them. "We'll have time for the formalities tomorrow. For now, I hereby call this unofficial and off-the-record meeting of the Concordia Sector leaders to order. Not that we're keeping minutes, now are we?"

"We only get to see you every four years," the man in the robes said. "And these off-the-records are the only reason many of us even bother to come. No harm being polite when you finally show up."

"Thank you, Saul." Tolmach sat down and twisted his artificial hand out of the socket, then hung it by the cane handle off the small table. "But we're not all here, are we? Ms. Genovese of Scotia won't be joining us. Shame to lose her to the League like that."

"It wasn't the League that killed her," another man said. "It was the Federation's cowardice."

"Where's your new overlord, Alan?" the woman in the mask asked. Her voice carried perfectly from the speaker beneath her painted lips. "Mine got called back on 'urgent family business' as soon as we got news of the massacre."

"Tomiko, that you under there?" Tolmach squinted.

"Aiko." The woman inclined her head. "My mother is ill. I wear her authority."

"Such are Ryukyu's ways," Tolmach said. "In answer to your question, Murphy's hunting slavers out past the blue line. You all may have noticed that we've got a few extra carriers in-system, but his isn't one of them at the moment."

"Slavers? A Heart who worries about *slavers*?" someone else said, and Tolmach shrugged.

"He's a Murphy," the President said. "Those of you old enough should remember his grandfather, the Murphy that got the Federation Navy's act together barely in time before it turned out we needed it, and his father died in uniform. This one's won a battle for the Federation, and now he's doing his level best to piss me off by turning New Dublin upside down with new system defenses. You should hear the business owners squealing, but soon as I mention Inverness, all of a sudden they get a lot more cooperative."

"Don't care what his last name is," a rail-thin man with a long white goatee said. "He's a Heart, through and through. You know what family he married into."

"We can gossip about him later." Tolmach tapped his stump against the stool. "What's more important is Inverness. The loss. What it means for us going forward. You've all had four years to think on our last proposal. Johns? You were the most opposed to secession last time. How have you and Gregor II fared since?"

A young-looking man with a ponytail stood.

"There are nine million people in Gregor," he said. "The Federation has a small service and support yard there, but with barely more ships on station than it had in Scotia. If that butcher Xing came calling, we wouldn't do any better." He motioned to the empty seat. "I've demanded more from the Heart Worlds, year after year, and every year it's 'in committee' or they tell me about 'budgetary constraints.' Yet, somehow, the Federation always has the funds to send their black ships to collect taxes and collect my sons and daughters for their war. They take blood and treasure and give back platitudes."

A murmur of agreement flowed through the room.

"The Federation chooses its ships over its people!" Saul roared, then visibly pulled his emotions back under control. "Inverness is dead because they did exactly that," he said flatly. "And they'll make the same decision for our planets, too."

The goateed man rose.

"If we leave the Federation, then what?" he asked. "We'll never join those bastards in the League, but we all know what the Federation did when Gobelins rebelled."

"But Gobelins was a single system," Tolmach said. "One governor gone mad with power. We're a *sector*, and a sector that's been on the front lines of this war for years. And we're not the only ones in this. The Siobhan Stars and Theseus Sector are taxed and drafted at even higher rates than we are. If we show backbone to the Heart—"

"Treason," the goateed man said. "Let's be honest."

"Treason?" Tolmach rubbed a knuckle against his dead eye. "I remember the first Harvest Day, not that it had the name back then. A freshman in college, I was, and every last man of my class, and a fair number of the women—fifty of us, there were—we mobbed the recruiting stations the minute word of the war against the League reached New Dublin. What a time it was. We were the *Federation*, and those bastards in the League had dared to attack us? Had K-struck Minotaur and then lied through their teeth and laughed about it? War sounded like such a great adventure. Had to join up quick," he moved a fist across his chest in a lazy cheer, "or it'd all be over before we got a chance to be part of it. Then there was Isonzo and all those days beneath the sun. Then the Battle of the Bloody Moon. Then Changsha.

"I came back home at the end of my five years. Came back with fewer parts than I left with, but I was luckier than most, it turns out. Came back and learned that of all my class that enlisted to fight the League... only eleven of us had survived, and just two of 'em not missing bits and pieces of their own. Then the black ships came for the next crop of our young men and women and took the other two along with them. Rian and Corey, their names were. They'd managed to score high enough on the exams to rate tech training, and 'needs of the service' got them back in uniform after they'd thought their obligation to the Federation was fulfilled. Never saw them again. Me, I was too broken to be of any more use.

"Then, ten years later, the annual tithes began. Every year we send the Federation our future, and every year they send back burned-out, scarred veterans. Three sons. I sent three sons to the war, all of them given to the Federation. All I got back was a certificate of service to pass on to my daughters-in-law. And I just recorded my eldest granddaughter's oath of service."

"We know your pain," Saul said. "Every world in the Fringe knows that pain. But the Heart Worlds? Their *poor* may know the pain, pay the butcher's bill, but the Five Hundred and anyone they decide is vital to their profits? They barely know there's a war going on."

"After fifty-six years. I don't believe that pain's going to end," Tolmach said. "I can't, because the Heart Worlds don't care if it ends. They don't *need* it to. I was loyal to the Federation, gave all I could to the Federation, and how did it repay me? Repay any of us? The Federation's betrayed all of us. So are we going to just sit here and bleed, or are we going to stand up and take our future back?"

Cheers broke out from everyone but Johns and Dewar.

"It's not that simple!" Johns shouted over the other voices. "We can't just flip a switch and declare ourselves a new nation. The Federation can't afford to lose us, if only because we'd be an example too many other sectors might choose to follow. And even if Olympia was willing to let us go, we'd be easy prey for the League, or for pirates beyond the blue line. Don't act like this will be easy."

"There's a garrison force in every system," Saul said, "and our people know how to fight. God knows the Federation's taken enough of us away and taught us how! We can take the ships, consider it part restitution from the Federation for taxes, and be just as secure as the Federation ever made us!"

"The 'garrison force' here in New Dublin's just a bit bigger mouthful than most," Dewar said, "and with Murphy at the helm. What will the Federation do when we buck someone with that name?"

"He's not his grandfather," Aiko said. "But his family has money...Ransom?"

"It's not even official, and you're already thinking like a barbarian," Tolmach said. "But what if Murphy comes back with a hull full of rescued slaves? We rebel against *that*? What will our people think? 'Thank ye for saving all those women and children. Now kindly put these cuffs on and get in the nice cell.' Bollocks."

"*If* he comes back with something better than a snipe hunt," Dewar said. "We'd need the Federation to remove him, in that case. That...would play well to the feeds. Icing on the cake against the Heart Worlds."

"Now, just why would the Federation do that?" Tolmach asked.

"They've got a snake in our grass—Captain Lipshen. Don't know exactly why someone might have knives out for Murphy back home, but if Lipshen gets the right words whispered in his ear, he'll pass them on to the right people back at the Oval. And then Bob's your uncle."

"I don't know," Johns said. "Murphy sounds like a good man. He deserves that?"

"His reputation might take a hit," Tolmach said. "Might even get him retired. I suppose he'd just have to make do with being filthy rich back on Earth. Oh, he'll suffer, no doubt."

"Can this be done without shedding blood?" Johns asked. "With no martyrs for the Federation to rally behind?"

The room went quiet.

"Let's make the decision first," Tolmach said. "Then we'll decide the best way to do it. Let's make this official. Roll call vote in favor of secession from the Federation."

CHAPTER TWENTY-EIGHT

EACH BREATH STABBED AN ICY BLADE INTO CORMAG DEWAR'S lungs. Wind sighed through the empty branches above him, and he slapped his gloved hands together as that same wind shredded the steamy plume of his breath. A faint silver light reflected down upon him, creeping into the darkness, and he looked up as a sliver of dawn broke over the distant mountains to the east.

A massive tree, its trunk thicker than his house, stood sentinel behind him. It was so tall its majestic crown had caught the dawn light well before the sun ever cleared the mountains from Dewar's position there at its foot. Coils of silver bark wound high, braiding through each other, and the light of New Dublin scaled the uppermost branches' shimmering surface with a brilliance that was almost painful to the eye against the still-dark heavens above them. Beyond the tree, night-wrapped mountain slopes fell away to the west.

Formations of militia made two lines behind long, tight-stretched ropes that marked off a wide corridor leading to a mound at the base of the tree. The ropes were whiter than snow, strung with red poppies, dark as fresh blood in the frail light, and Dewar stood atop the mound.

"Procession on time," his earbud told him.

"Confirm. Cut radio traffic unless there's a civil defense emergency," he said, and there was a click in his ear.

"Say again?" Captain Lipshen asked. The IG officer wore considerably more cold-weather gear than the senior members of the New Dublin Militia gathered behind them, despite which his teeth still chattered.

"Hush." Dewar put a finger to his lips. "You don't want to miss this."

In the distance, still deep in the mountains' shadows, a river of light flowed slowly through a pass.

Dewar closed his eyes, listening as faint cheers carried on the wind.

"Bit pagan, isn't it?" Lipshen asked. "Dawn torchlight parade to a sacred...oak tree? Will there be a druid? Always so interesting to be part of an outlying system's customs."

"This is Craeb Uisnig." Dewar kept his tone level, conversational, despite an even stronger than usual temptation to strangle the Heart World cretin. "It's so big the original settlers identified it from orbit. In fact, they made First Landfall not far away so they could come and see it for themselves. Once they did, they moved the main landing site to Tara City and created a permanent nature preserve around Craeb Uisnig. Access is forbidden except on Graduation Day."

Lipshen looked up as a single silver leaf, smaller than a child's hand, fluttered down, sparkling in the dawn. It slipped from light into the shadows nearer the ground, and Dewar sidestepped as it fell. It landed on the grassy mound, dull side up, and he looked down at it, then extended his right arm to the side and turned his hand thumb-down.

A worried murmur spread through the militia's ranks.

"I miss something?" Lipshen asked, and Dewar sucked in a sharp breath. Then he clenched his jaw and exhaled slowly.

"Bad omen," he said, not looking at the Heart Worlder. He picked up the leaf, kissed it, and slipped it into a pocket. "If it lands silver side up, the recruits will fare well during their service. Down, and the future's not as bright."

"Again, this is all a bit pagan." Lipshen looked out at the approaching procession of torches. "Still, allowing systems...a bit farther from the Core to conduct their own basic training courses was an excellent idea from the Oval, don't you agree? Less cost to the federal budget, more incentive on the recruits' part, and they're ready to be assigned to advanced training before they ever muster in. All they need is to be sorted and aptitude-tested for virtual instruction during their transit to the replacement depot. It really was a great initiative."

"It was the Fringe Worlds' idea," Dewar said flatly. "Our draftees breezed through the Heart Worlds' training and embarrassed too many drill instructors. And our casualty rates were too high if we relied on the Heart World systems to get them ready. So we decided to do it right. Do it ourselves. And this is the capstone exercise: movement to daylight. They'll all transfer to the black sh—personnel transports later this evening. Last day with hearth and home."

"More dramatic than some outlying systems," Lipshen said.

"We consider it more *solemn*," Dewar snapped. "Now be so kind as to keep future observations to yourself. President Tolmach's conducted the ceremony for the last many decades, but he's ... taken ill. So this falls on me."

Lipshen shrugged, and Dewar climbed three steps to a poppy-draped podium on a raised platform and checked a slate already in place. He tapped a gloved knuckle against the screen and his speech came up on a holo-prompter. He'd cribbed from many of Tolmach's previous speeches, but there hadn't been much variation in recent years. What could be said to young men and women about to leave their homeworld—most for the first time—and join a war that had already killed six billion? Over the years, Tolmach had learned to say what could be said far better than most, and it was not a subject that lent itself to improvisation.

The fact that Dewar was the one to give this speech would be a surprise to the recruits once they arrived at the end of the path. Fair enough—it had surprised Dewar, too.

Tolmach had been in a particularly foul mood since the sector leaders' private meeting had adopted the draft Declaration of Secession. It was still completely "unofficial"—its very existence was a deeply held secret until the moment of its announcement came—but Dewar suspected the only reason it had passed was that Tolmach had stopped trying to prevent it and thrown his weight behind it, instead. Inverness, he knew, was part of the reason he had, but there were ... other factors, as well. Factors that drove Dewar, as well. Yet his father-in-law's vehemence against the Federation had been more overt in recent weeks, and that was a source of tension for Dewar, both as a family member and as the CO of the system's defenses. And now, on exactly zero notice, he'd announced that he was too ill to preside over this year's ceremony.

Actually, Dewar was fairly certain Tolmach felt just fine. Or as close to it as the old man ever came these days, at any rate. He suspected the sudden illness was mostly a ruse to put Dewar in his place for this ceremony, and there was only one reason for that: his daughter, Christina.

Most of Dewar was grateful for Tolmach's gift, but a part of him...

Bad enough to send a child to war, but to be the last Crann Bethadh officer to oversee the process that sent *his* child to the death mills before secession ended it forever?

That stung. Dewar had gone through the ceremony himself, deployed off-world several times, and been here year after year, since his own service, to say goodbye to the recruits and welcome the remains—the few times they were recovered—and see them delivered to grieving families. Being part of that process for children not his own was difficult enough, but to send Christina into the same grinder...

Glittering leaves continued to fall, filling the air with the flicker of close stars before they dropped into the shadow at the mighty tree's base. Craeb Uisnig itself wept for its children, he thought.

The procession's lead ranks drew nearer, marching out of the darkness, and Dewar leaned forward over his podium to squint in disbelief as the fuming torchlight let him pick out details. There was a man in a black overcoat at the head of the procession, flanked by two torchbearers in combat fatigues whose pattern differed from the recruits' plain field utilities.

"What the hell is *he* doing here?" Dewar muttered.

"Is that...Murphy?" Lipshen asked from behind him.

"Appears so." Dewar gripped the sides of his podium.

"This is irregular, isn't it? I knew *Ishtar* was back in-system, but I didn't expect him to make planetfall so soon," the captain said.

"Nor did I. I'm more interested to find out how he managed to get planetside, join the procession, and march all the way here without my hearing about it."

Dewar glanced sideways at Patrick MacDowell, and his aide flushed and looked away in embarrassment.

The waiting lines of militiamen came to attention as Murphy and his two flankers—Dewar recognized Callum Murphy and the former slave girl—passed down the corridor between the poppy-laden ropes. They continued steadily to the base of the mound leading up to Craeb Uisnig and the podium. The three of them set their torches into metal cylinders in the ground, and then Murphy made his way up. The river of light flowed down the same passageway, then halted behind him. The column of recruits raised their torches higher, held them there in the silver-spangled dawn light flowing from Craeb Uisnig to greet them.

"Welcome back, Governor," Dewar said as Murphy reached the platform. The admiral's face was red and covered in sweat, and he winced as he covered the last few paces to the podium, but his breathing was remarkably steady. "Bit of a surprise to see you here."

"I thought I'd join in," Murphy said. "Everyone I need to speak with just happens to be here, and flights are restricted so close to—"

He looked up at the tree.

"'It's magnificent,'" he said softly. "Even more than I expected. I wouldn't dare endanger it with a close landing, even if the air-space had been clear. And we do have a bit of time; O'Hanraghty's getting some parts moving."

"Time? What parts?" Dewar leaned to one side to be sure the rear of the procession had closed up with its leaders. "This ceremony has a process to it that I—"

Murphy gripped his shoulder and leaned over to speak into his ear. Dewar went pale and looked at him with wide eyes. Murphy nodded slowly, and the general swallowed. Then he nodded back, and Murphy looked down at that sea of raised torches. He beckoned with the fingers of his right hand, and Callum took the torch his father had borne from its holder and ran it up the mound to him. The admiral raised it aloft, held it for a long, slow thirty count, then twisted its base.

The flame went out... and in the same instant every torch snuffed out down that long, long column, and the river of light disappeared into the dawn.

Dewar looked at the holo-prompter. Then he tapped his slate with an oddly decisive gesture. His waiting speech disappeared, and he tapped the slate again to activate the mic drone floating

before him. He cleared his throat, drew a deep breath, and began
to sing.

> In Flanders fields the poppies blow
> Between the crosses, row on row,
> That mark our place; and in the sky
> The larks, still bravely singing, fly
> Scarce heard amid the guns below.

The lines of militia joined their massed voices to his with
the third line. Crann Bethadhans were singers, and the *a cap-
pella* harmony rose like slow, solemn thunder. At the end of the
verse, the column of recruits joined their voices to their elders',
as well, until the entire valley rang with the stately majesty of
the ancient, ancient words.

> We are the Dead. Short days ago
> We lived, felt dawn, saw sunset glow,
> Loved and were loved, and now we lie,
> In Flanders fields.

> Take up our quarrel with the foe:
> To you from failing hands we throw
> The torch; be yours to hold it high.
> If ye break faith with us who die
> We shall not sleep, though poppies grow
> In Flanders fields.

Silence fell once more, broken only by the sighing Crann
Bethadh wind in Craeb Uisnig's mighty boughs, and Dewar wiped
a palm across his eyes, then crossed himself. He looked out across
those young, expectant faces, felt them waiting for his words, but
he didn't speak. Instead, he stepped back and motioned Murphy
closer to the mic drone.

"Soldiers of Crann Bethadh, this is a unique time," the governor
said somberly, speakers carrying his words across the valley. "I
thank the Class of 2551 for allowing me to join in your capstone
exercise. Craeb Uisnig is even more than I'd imagined, and I am
honored to be part of this ceremony. Of this tradition. Because
tradition matters. It is what makes us what we are—*who* we are.

Yet solemn as this tradition is, we must make some changes in what the graduates expect next."

"What's he going on about?" Lipshen hissed in Dewar's ear.

"Just wait."

The general tapped a code on his wrist comm and opened a live feed to Tolmach's number.

"The League is coming," Murphy said, "and it is my belief that they will attack New Dublin with a fleet much larger than the force that destroyed Inverness."

He paused for a moment and looked across those young faces, and the silence was deeper than the sea as the glittering dawn light crept steadily farther down the massive tree behind him, wrapping that mighty trunk in braided fire.

"I hereby announce that a Declaration of Emergency is in effect," he said then. "As Governor General of New Dublin, I now cancel follow-on training for the Class of 2551. Your service is required here, and we will assign you where you are most needed across the system. In addition, all Federation Navy vessels in-system are transferred to my command, effective immediately."

"Now just a sec—" Lipshen started forward, but Dewar's hand to his chest stopped him.

"I have not made these decisions lightly," Murphy continued, "and responsibility for the consequences—good or ill—will be mine alone. But I've walked one dying world. I will *not* see that fate befall another if I have the power to prevent it. Every life in the Federation is worth fighting for. Every home under threat is a call to arms. Today, it's time for you to defend yours, and I will be with you at every step. We will stop this attack... or we will die together trying. Long, long ago, another ancient Earth poet said, 'a man can die but once; we owe God a death and let it go which way it will, he that dies this year is quit for the next.' I do not intend to die here, but if it comes, I will die knowing that I did my duty before God and my own conscience, and what man can ask better than that?"

He looked out over those faces, Craeb Uisnig a mighty column of silver fire at his back, and every eye looked back at him.

"That is all," he said quietly. "May God bless us all, and may God bless New Dublin."

He stepped back from the podium. For a moment, only the sighing wind broke the silence, and then the cheers erupted, rising like thunder as the dawn light reached Craeb Uisnig's base and those assembled men and women realized what he'd just said.

The cheering faded at last, and a very confused looking militia colonel crossed to Dewar. They spoke briefly, and the colonel nodded—slowly at first, then more rapidly. Dewar patted him on the shoulder, and then he, Murphy, and Lipshen moved to the rear of the platform as the mic drone floated to the colonel and he began giving instructions to the recruits.

"Admiral," Lipshen had gone pale, and Dewar wondered if it was from the cold or from shock at Murphy's announcement, "you can't do this. These recruits and anything in the yards belong to the Federation. They're expected in other systems. There's a *process* for all of this, and this isn't it."

"The Governor General's the chief executive," Dewar said. "Seems to me he can do whatever he damn well pleases. So long as it's legal."

"Emergency powers," Murphy said. "All authorized under Section Four of my Governor's commission. And quite necessary in light of the current threat. General, can we head back to your headquarters? More planning's needed, and I'm guessing you didn't march out here."

"I've a ground car," Dewar said. "Let's walk and talk."

"Wait. Wait! I'm the IG here in New Dublin, and any declaration of emergency powers mandates an immediate report back to the Oval. In fact—"

Dewar straight-armed him in the chest, and the smaller man staggered.

"Sorry, Captain." The general gave him a polite smile. "Murphy's taking your spot in my vehicle. Maybe there's room in another car? If not, feel free to join the graduates on the next leg of their march. You did want to experience the ceremony."

Lipshen stood dumbstruck as the other two left him behind.

"I don't believe it."

Alan Tolmach hobbled over to his office window and looked out over the city as snow whipped across the sky.

"The tech readouts on the Fasset manifold fit his theory." Dewar, his uniform jacket off, warmed himself by a fireplace. "I'm not sure I could swear the design's Rishathan, but it's sure as hell not anything any of our people here in the yards have ever seen. And I saw the video taken by the boarding parties." He shrugged. "Serendipitous that they just so happened to be in the system looking for slavers when they came across the smuggler, instead."

"'Serendipitous,' you say?" Tolmach looked at him darkly. "Didn't know you knew what that word meant. Not sure you do, truth to tell, from the way you just used it!"

"We can go with it, unless you've a better one." Dewar opened and closed his hands slowly before the flames as warmth crept back into his joints. "This aging thing is miserable. I don't know how you deal with it."

"Don't change the subject," Tolmach growled. He glowered at his son-in-law for a moment, then shrugged. "I take it the snake's not happy about any of this?"

"He wasn't when we left him at Craeb Uisnig, and I doubt he's gotten any happier since." It was Dewar's turn to shrug. "On the other hand, I don't think Murphy gives a rat's ass about the snake's opinion."

"Which means Murphy's gone rogue," the President growled.

"Are you playing devil's advocate again, or do you really doubt the man? His theory passes the smell test. The league has a secret yard complex; it's somewhere in striking distance; and the manifolds were the last piece of their construction. If they have a combat-ready task force, they'll deploy it before the Federation can react, and New Dublin's the most likely target. So Murphy's declared our recruits stay here, and his task force—and every other ship he's managed to hang onto since he got here—is going to be our defense. We've been turning out those drone bodies of his for over three months, and the production rate is about to skyrocket now that he's put the pedal down. If the Leaguies base their planning on what we had the *last* time they came to call, he's about to kick their asses up one side and down the other. Like he said himself, it may not be enough, but it's a whole damned sight better than what'd happen *without* him! You have a problem with any of that?"

"What if he's wrong?" Tolmach asked. "He gets New Dublin all spun up, and then the Leaguies don't show?"

"Then we've got our system defenses improved and we get to keep our kids home for a change. No harm."

"Until the Federation yanks him for crying wolf and stepping on too many military toes. They'll haul him home and install a complete stooge with orders to undo everything he's done. Including holding the boys and girls here in-system."

"And if he's right and the League does come for us with this ghost fleet of theirs?"

"And if he's right, God help us all." The old man used a couch arm to steady himself as he limped back to his desk. "Sit," he commanded, pointing at a chair in front of the desk, and Dewar settled into it.

"How far have you gone on that poison pill of yours?" the President asked.

Dewar's mouth scrunched to one side of his face.

"Um. Forgot about that." He frowned in thought. "The forgeries haven't been delivered to the snake yet, but he's got some documents. You don't want to pull the trigger now, do you?"

"No. In fact, let's cancel all that. The Federation doesn't need a planted suspicion to panic over Murphy; he's just given them plenty of reasons of his own. Damn it! Every time I expect him to act like the incompetent, selfish Heart Worlder I need him to be, he goes and delivers like an actual leader, instead." Tolmach sat down heavily behind the desk and kicked his bad leg out to one side. "Why can't he be incompetent?"

"If he were, we'd have no idea about the League's ghost fleet." Dewar leaned back and crossed his ankles. "If it's real, that is."

"If," Tolmach sighed.

"How are the streets and alleys taking to his appearance at Craeb Uisnig?"

"They love him," Tolmach said. "And the rank and file?"

"Love him, too. No one enjoys the movement to daylight march for the capstone—you know that. It's designed to be tougher than hell, and the fact that Murphy joined in, with his son and that…girl of theirs, and marched the whole damned way with them…" Dewar shook his head. "Man's got a way with words, too. Heart or no, he *thinks* like a New Dubliner. The system crews and militia are about as motivated to get with his plans as they could be."

"No one's mentioned that we might get wrecked because Murphy poked the League beehive?"

"Unintended consequences from the good deed of trying to

rescue slaves." Dewar crossed his hands over his sternum and began twiddling his thumbs. "Like the League needs a reason to kill us. Every man and woman on this planet knows they just need the means and the opportunity, and I think Murphy's right about why they've been assembling this force out here in our neck of the galaxy. They see us as the Federation's 'soft underbelly'—compared to Beta Cygni, at least—and that means they were coming through New Dublin no matter what, Alan. All he's done there is to maybe start the clock ticking a little early...and with, oh, forty less carriers or so."

Tolmach grunted sourly, and Dewar raised an eyebrow.

"So where does all this leave us with our independence announcement?"

Tolmach propped his elbows on his desk and rested his face in his hands.

"On hold," he said. "The sector conference has another five days yet, and I can hold 'em over indefinitely, given Murphy's emergency decree. We'll see if people can keep their mouths shut. But, frankly, the only way I see it happening now is for the attack to never materialize and then for the Federation to yank Murphy out. Otherwise, we become the elites having to explain a revolt against a Governor who's finally doing all the right things, and I'll let you guess how that'll turn out."

"If I'm going to be hung in Court Square, I'd rather it be by the Federation than by my own people," Dewar said.

"I'll be just as dead beside you, but if that happens, let's have history view the event as tragic instead of righteous. I'm all for Murphy's plan, and you're in as well. Just need you to take care of that snake."

"Allegations can't be taken back, but I'll see that everything's fixed as well as it can be."

"Good." Tolmach puffed his lips and shook his head. "We live in interesting times, son. I still don't know if Murphy's a blessing or a curse."

"I imagine we're about to find out," Dewar said.

✧   ✧   ✧

Eira dropped her space bag at the foot of her bed. The tiny apartment was immaculate, with perfect hospital corners on the bed's sheets and not a speck of dust to be seen. The lingering scent of disinfectant hung in the air. In fact, the only hint that anyone actually lived there was the Craeb Uisnig statue perched on one corner of her desk. The light in the glass globe's base shone up from below, gilding the tiny leaves with a textured silver sparkle.

She opened the bag and took out a uniform top. She smoothed it out and refolded it.

"This is how you spend your first little bit of time off in like weeks?" Callum asked from the open doorway.

"Sergeant Major gave us six hours to repack and handle personal needs before we report back for duty," she said. "We've been assigned to the *Kolyma*. You saw the notice?"

"Ship's assistant engineer." Callum puffed out his chest. "Guess the Admiral doesn't need his best coffee boy on standby if the League shows up. Rather not be on one of Drebin's ships, in some ways, but O'Hanraghty says they've come a long way since Scotia. And it's nice to be considered marginally relevant for once. May I?" He motioned to one of the two seats at the small round table. "My feet are killing me."

"You don't have to ask, Sir." She lifted a vac helmet out of the bag and did a quick function check on the seals.

"I should've listened to you about my socks." He sat and bent an ankle over his thigh so he could squeeze the heel of his boot. "Marching. Ugh. I joined the Navy to avoid all that."

"Sergeant Major had us hump the entire length of *Ishtar*'s core hull—back and forth, four times, in full kit—several times while we were in transit. Worked out at fourteen and a half kilometers each time, and that doesn't count the hatches, the ladders—no lifts, Sir." She smiled slightly. "We didn't even have a ruck on the capstone march."

"Are you calling me weak?" Callum asked.

"I'm calling you untrained, Sir. You'll develop calluses. They don't feel pain."

She set down her helmet and went into the kitchen.

"I see you've got that statue out," Callum said. "I still think it's gorgeous, but it doesn't really do the real thing justice, does it?" He flexed his foot back and forth. "It's different on Crann Bethadh. People here are more...aware than back in the Heart Worlds. I went through the recruit depot at Olympia, and you'd think those people were reporting for a jail sentence. We joined that slog, and the recruits in it were brimming with excitement.

Strange, if you think about it. They're going to the same fight, but they were actually motivated."

"It was the end of their basic training," Eira said from the kitchen. Then she returned with two steaming cups of instant noodles and extended one to him. "I don't have anything else, Sir."

"You're too kind." He lifted his cup in ironic salute.

"And part of their 'motivation' is that it's New Dublin custom to give graduates a two-day pass after the ceremony," she continued. "Family, friends—"

"—and booze!" Callum wagged an eyebrow. But then he frowned thoughtfully. "They didn't seem too upset when the Admiral canceled the pass, though."

"The League's coming. Better to be prepared and in place than sleeping off a hangover when the fleet drops sublight."

Eira sat down and stirred a spoon through her ramen.

"You think they're coming?" Callum asked.

"It doesn't matter what I think. We're assigned to *Kolyma*."

"It matters to me, Eira."

She stopped eating, then brushed her hair back behind one ear, exposing her slave mark, and looked at him steadily.

"At least we'll be ready—as ready as we can be," she said. "Inverness never had a chance. Everything was as normal and awful as ever one moment; the next...it was worse. The League's known to K-strike planets, and sometimes the Federation does the same thing. The only reason anything survives in the dead zone between them is that sometimes the commanders think it's better to launch a ground attack and seize resources. The people on less valuable worlds?" She grimaced. "Just targets, Sir. Just targets. That's all I was on Inverness. Now I can fight back. So if we get steamrollered...at least we'll go down fighting, like your father says. He gave me that...and I'm okay with it. I really am." She shrugged. "Your noodles are getting cold, Sir."

"Yeah." Callum stirred his own cup, watching the little bits of carrots and peas floating in the chicken-flavored broth. "Dad and O'Hanraghty, at least they have a plan," he said. "But plans and the enemy...you know how those work out."

"How?"

"I don't have a clue who first said it, but it was a long, long time ago," Callum told her. "'No plan survives contact with the enemy.'" He shrugged. "Makes you wonder why we even bother, but it works both ways. If the League shows up, they'll have a plan with them, all neat and ready to smash us nasty Feds. And Dad and O'Hanraghty are putting together some surprises of our own for them—take that, Leaguies! But nobody's got a clue how it'll really work when the shooting starts. Should be interesting."

Eira's face fell.

"If it'll be that bad, maybe I should have Steiner take my place as your security detachment," she said.

"Nonsense. I don't want anyone but you watching my back. For that matter, if it was Steiner, he'd have his passive aggression turned all the way up because he can't fit his Hoplon suit into *Kolyma*'s engineering section with me. Besides, what would Logan have you doing back on *Ishtar*?"

"Cleaning things, probably."

"There. Much better to have you along with me. Who knows? Maybe we'll actually like *Kolyma*."

✧   ✧   ✧

"Lieutenant Callum Murphy and party of one reporting, Ma'am!"

Callum came to attention rather more snappily than usual before Lieutenant Commander Kunigunde Seydel's desk. He told himself that was because he represented his father in front of an officer who'd become one of Admiral Murphy's ship commanders under... irregular circumstances. He suspected, however, that at least part of it was that he knew that however well he executed the courtesy, Eira would do it better.

He watched from the corner of one eye and found he had not been mistaken in that expectation. Eira's stiffly erect posture, squared shoulders, and level, straight-ahead eyes could have served as a recruiting poster. Or as an illustration in a training manual.

The blond-haired officer behind the desk sat back, blue eyes gazing steadily at them for a moment, then waved her right hand.

"Stand easy, Lieutenant. Corporal."

For a moment, Callum wondered if Eira would remember that "Corporal" meant her. The single chevron on each sleeve of her perfectly pressed fatigues had been there for less than thirty minutes, after all.

She did remember, he saw, although rather than "stand easy," she went to a rigid parade rest, hands at the small of her back, eyes still fixed steadily ahead at a point on the bulkhead two centimeters above the lieutenant commander's head. Seydel looked at her for a moment, then shook her head minutely, and turned back to Callum.

"I wish I could say I was happy to see you, Lieutenant Murphy," she said. She paused, as if inviting a response, but he simply stood there, waiting, and something like amusement flickered in those blue eyes. "Note that I didn't say I wasn't *pleased* to see you," she continued after a moment. "To be honest, I'm rather desperately in need of another engineering officer at the moment, which is why I *am* pleased to see you. There are downsides to your assignment, however.

"From a purely selfish perspective, letting someone with your family connections get killed under my command would not be what they call a 'career enhancing' move. On the other hand, if you get killed, the odds are pretty good I'll be killed right along with you, so I can live with that one. A more immediate concern is the fact that, for reasons I'm sure you'll understand, not every man and woman aboard *Kolyma* holds a favorable opinion of your father. This is less because they were exceptionally fond of Commodore Drebin than because of the circumstances under which we came under the Admiral's command." Her mouth tightened and the eyes which had been amused turned cold. "The New Dubliners haven't hesitated to draw comparisons between his behavior—and, by extension, our own—and your father's, however. Three of my people spent several days in sick bay getting patched up after one of those comparisons—one of *several*, actually—turned physical. I'm sure you can understand why some of them might feel rather...ill-used."

Callum decided that continued silence was undoubtedly the best course of action.

"I have made it plain to them that, first, your father's actions were completely justified and resulted in the rescue of almost forty-five thousand Federation citizens *our* commanding officer had left to die. Any consequences of those actions for us are completely acceptable in my eyes.

"Second, that you are not he, and so are not responsible for those actions in the first place. And, third, that neither I nor the XO had better hear any reports of insubordination or slackness. Having said that, *you* had better understand that you are not he, as well. You are a very junior lieutenant, with limited experience, and it would behoove you to keep that in mind while interacting with people who have served together aboard this ship for upwards of four years, in many cases. Is there any need for me to expand upon that?"

This time, she clearly expected a response when she paused, and Callum shook his head once.

"No, Ma'am. I believe I understand you."

"Good."

Seydel's body language eased a bit, and she let her chair come back upright.

"To be honest, Lieutenant, I was more than a little surprised when your father made you available to *Kolyma*. In light of what I understand about his ops plan, I would have expected him to want to keep you aboard *Ishtar*."

"He didn't explain his reasoning to me, Ma'am." That wasn't quite the truth, the whole truth, and nothing but the truth, but Murphy *hadn't* explained his reasoning fully. "What he did say to me, rather forcefully, was that my engineering training would probably be more useful to *Kolyma* than 'one more green-as-grass, underutilized, under*qualified* lieutenant could be on a carrier flag bridge in the middle of a fight.'"

Callum allowed himself a fleeting smile, and Seydel actually chuckled.

"More seriously, Ma'am, I finished a course on ship propulsion systems—I specialized in the Fasset drive—at Harriman just before we deployed. I realize *Kolyma* doesn't *have* a Fasset drive, but we did do a two-semester on Fleet fusion drives, as well. And probably more to the point, my mother's family is a major player in ship construction back home." From Seydel's slight eye roll, she considered "major player" a gross understatement. "My grandfather believes in hands-on experience. I spent the better part of two years in power systems, yard-based and shipboard, for Venus Futures between high school and Harriman. We built most of this class, and I'm thoroughly familiar with both her layout and her systems." He shrugged ever so slightly. "I guess Dad figured it was time to make use of some of the experience I *do* have."

Seydel cocked her head thoughtfully for a couple of seconds, then nodded.

"I'd wondered about that," she said. "That power systems experience of yours isn't in your service jacket."

Callum nodded in understanding, and she leaned forward and rested her hands on her desk.

"I'm going to get Lieutenant Pêşrew in here shortly. He's my senior engineer, and I think he's going to be delighted to see you. He's been pulling watch-and-watch for two months now, ever since the power surge that sent your predecessor off to the base hospital. Before I do that, however, I want to share a thought *I* had about why the Admiral may have assigned you to this ship."

"Ma'am?" Callum said cautiously.

"You may not be aware of this, Lieutenant, but I'm a Fringer—from Neues Bremen, in fact. I won't go into how that may or may not have affected my feelings about your father's actions in Scotia. I will say, however, that I understand the Fringer mindset, I know my people here aboard *Kolyma,* and from his record, your father understands the Fringer mindset better than most Heart Worlders would. And that, Lieutenant, is why I suspect that the Admiral sent you to us as a promise."

"A promise, Ma'am?"

"A promise that he will stand by all of us in exactly the same way he would stand by his own son," Seydel said, and her voice was very, very soft. "A promise that whatever Commodore Drebin might have done in Scotia, neither New Dublin nor the crews of the ships in the system are casually expendable in his eyes."

It was very quiet in Seydel's cabin as she held Callum's eyes for a ten-count. Then she reached across and tapped the slate lying on her desk.

"Yes, Ma'am?" a voice responded.

"Please tell Lieutenant Pêşrew that it's time for him to meet his new assistant engineering officer, Chief," Seydel said, then sat back in her chair again with a smile.

❖   ❖   ❖

"I thought it went a lot better that time," Murphy said, rubbing his eyes wearily.

He and O'Hanraghty sat in the ready room off *Ishtar*'s flag bridge, cups of coffee on the table between them, and the collars of their uniform tunics were unbuttoned. It would be hard to decide which of them looked more exhausted, Murphy thought.

"It did go a lot better," O'Hanraghty acknowledged. "Of course, most of it's simulations, not actual ship movement, but they really are starting to operate as a unit. Carson and Cerminaro have done more with BatRon Seven-Oh-Two than I would have believed anyone could, to be honest."

Murphy nodded. He'd pulled Commander Carson from *Burgoyne* when Drebin headed off to explain himself to the Oval. He'd suspected things might have gone...poorly during the lengthy voyage. Besides, he'd needed competent officers, so he'd brevetted her to the rank of captain and given her the battleship *Foch* as soon as he could get the ship back out of the yard.

Aurika Kuosaite, *Foch*'s assigned captain, had been Yance Drebin's senior ship commander. She'd also been one of his cronies, and she'd taken advantage of the battleship's scheduled deep-maintenance overhaul to make a "quick trip" back home to the Sol System long before the attack on Scotia. As nearly as Murphy could tell, no one aboard *Foch* had missed her, and Carson had done wonders to kick the dispirited ship's company's morale in the ass and get her people up and running.

Pryce Cerminaro, *MacMahon*'s CO, was next in seniority to—and a very different proposition from—the absent Kuosaite. He and Carson got along like a house on fire, probably because of how much they'd both despised Drebin, and their enthusiasm was spreading through the short task group Murphy had "borrowed" from its commodore.

"I think the truth is that, whether they wanted to admit it or not, every one of them was ashamed when Drebin cut and ran in Scotia," the admiral said, tipping back in his chair and cradling a cup of coffee in both hands. "I think there are a lot of people in uniform—those who have actually 'seen the elephant,' anyway—who are ashamed, Harrison. More than I realized."

"You think?" O'Hanraghty smiled crookedly. "Terrence, there's only two kinds of officers who can spend much time at the front without being ashamed—the ones who are busy playing the game for their own profit and advancement, and the ones too stupid to pour piss out of a boot. Of course they're ashamed. Drebin's not the first system governor to cut and run instead of defending the people he's supposed to protect. I wish to hell he were, but that's the way things work out here, and he knew damned well when he ran that there'd be those back in the Heart—hell, in the Oval—who'd think he did the right thing. The smart thing. After all, why throw away ships just to protect *Fringers*? It's not like they *matter*, is it?"

His crooked smile had turned bitter, and he shook his head.

"Too many of our officers are Heart Worlders, and somehow they're the ones that always gravitate to higher command. The Fringe perspective's not represented at the top. Hasn't been for at least the last twenty, thirty years, and the Fringers—who, I remind you, make up a good fifty or sixty percent of our ships' companies—know it. For that matter, *I* knew it when I headed off to the Academy from New York, full of piss and vinegar. But the people out here—they're still *people*, Terrence. They're *our* people. I know you know that, you *understand* that, but sometimes I think that despite everything, you don't really grasp how extraordinary that is coming from a member of the Five Hundred."

Murphy gazed at him. Maybe O'Hanraghty was right. Maybe that was because it *was* so clear to him. He knew what lengths he'd had to go to, the hoops through which he'd had to jump, to get this command, and he'd resented hell out of the corruption and the inertia and the plain blind arrogance he'd had to circumvent along the way. But in an odd sort of way, he'd never really considered his own motives for doing it in the first place. Clearing his father's reputation, proving what he'd come to suspect, doing something to protect the people of the Fringe, the possibility of actual hastening the end of the dreary, unrelenting slaughter . . .

All of that had been wrapped up in it, but he'd never thought of that as anything that made him special. It was what a man of honor did if he was in a position to do it. Did believing that truly make him *that* different from other Navy officers?

Surely not. The man sitting across the table from him believed in those same things, didn't he? Of course he did!

"I had an interesting conversation with Commodore Granger," O'Hanraghty said after a moment, in a rather lighter tone.

"Really?" Murphy smiled.

He liked Granger. She'd buckled down to integrate BatRon 912 into his task force command, and BatRon 912 had increased his battleship strength by fifty-five percent. Actually, it had doubled TF 1705's assigned battleship strength, although he'd come to think of Drebin's ships as "his," as well, over the last few months.

"Yeah." O'Hanraghty sipped his own coffee. "I don't think that 'damage survey' on *Tiamat* fooled her for a second, Terrence."

"Really?" Murphy repeated. O'Hanraghty lowered his coffee

cup and gave him The Look, and the admiral chuckled. "Actually, I sort of suspected she'd figured out what had really happened when I first spoke to her about that Zadroga conduit," he admitted.

"Not much doubt about that, now," O'Hanraghty said dryly.

"No?"

"Let's just put it this way, she seemed mighty calm when the yard suddenly started throwing *Tiamat*'s drive fan back together around that 'damaged' inhibitor of hers. In fact, she's asked to be part of the Hammer. I don't think she'd have done that if she thought there was really anything wrong with *Tiamat*'s Zadroga conduits."

"She's a smart lady," Murphy said mildly, and O'Hanraghty snorted.

"She's smart enough she hasn't questioned the yard's downcheck because it covers her—and you, I suppose—for her...extended stay here in New Dublin. She's also smart enough to make it clear in her official correspondence that she's willing to risk operating with only the secondary inhibitor solely because of the nature of the emergency. But there's no way she'd be willing to stress it as part of the Hammer if she really thought the primary was bad."

"And smart enough to be a real asset when the shit flies." Murphy nodded. "Her and Carson both. We've got some good people out here, Harrison. I hope we don't get too many of them killed."

"Best we can do is the best we can do, Sir."

"I know." Murphy stretched, feeling the fatigue tugging at the back of his brain. He glanced down into his coffee cup. He didn't remember finishing it, but it was empty, and he ran a hand through his hair.

"Six hours until the next simulation?" he asked.

"Yes, Sir. I've got a few fires to put out, but nothing that requires your attention. Could I suggest you see about getting a little shut-eye in the interim?"

"I think that's a very good idea," Murphy said wryly. "Alert criteria in effect if you need to disturb me, though!"

"Understood," O'Hanraghty said with a nod.

Murphy nodded back, then stood and headed for the side door to the sleeping cabin set aside for his use. There were times when an admiral didn't need to be wasting any time getting to the flag bridge, and the cot waiting for him looked more inviting than usual at the moment.

The armor layer for his vac suit was laid out next to the cot, and he sat, removed his boots, and felt the weariness spread from the back of his neck through his entire body. He was sure he'd been more tired sometime in his life; he just couldn't remember when.

The slate in the thigh pocket of his shipboard utilities pinched his leg, and he slipped it out. A slew of inbox messages pulsed on the screen, but if there'd been anything truly vital, O'Hanraghty would already have brought it to his attention. He started to toss it onto the bedside table, then paused as his eye caught a message heading.

It was from Vyom. From the timestamps, it must have been delivered on *Calcutta*'s most recent run from Jalal—the old FTLC was back on her regular route after delivering the refugees to safety—and he wondered why he hadn't already seen it. He frowned thoughtfully, then sighed. He'd been running every second since the return from Alramal and this one was marked personal, not for the "System Governor's" attention, so it had probably just gotten shoved to the back of the message queue by more pressing, official messages.

"Maybe it's good news," he sighed as he lay back on the cot. He swiped the message open, and the screen changed to Vyom. The background was someplace tropical, with palm trees and blue ocean waves, and his oldest son looked happy, with his hair waving in the breeze.

Murphy smiled slightly and tapped the PLAY icon.

"Dad!" Vyom said. "I hope you're doing great things out there in the Fringe. Don't know if you've heard, but the ship trials for the *Cormoran*-class went smoothly. None of that's classified—Grandpa made sure the feeds carried the news far and wide. Something about an appropriations meeting. So, yeah…that's going well.

"Mom's neck-deep in work, of course, and planning for another event. She's—"

"Just tell him already," a woman said from off-screen, and Murphy's brow furrowed as he heard the unfamiliar voice.

"And Reagan's getting the same middling grades as always," Vyom said quickly, then flashed a grin. "Enough suspense? Right. Well, you remember Ingrid. Tall. Blond. Gorgeous. So much fun to be around?"

"Stop it!" The woman laughed.

Vyom grinned again, wider even than before, and turned the camera to the tall, blond—and, yes, gorgeous—young woman standing beside him. She held up her left hand and an oversized engagement ring flashed in the tropical sunlight.

Murphy almost dropped the slate.

"She said yes!" Vyom hugged her and gave her a quick kiss. "No real rush on the wedding, though. Mom and Greta—my future mother-in-law; she's great, too—are having high-level talks to plan the big day. Looks like it'll be after your tour, so don't think you have to go AWOL or something to make it back."

"I can't wait to meet you!" Ingrid said.

"What's happening?" Murphy asked the empty cabin. "Wait... when did...?"

"So that's the big news back on Earth," Vyom said. "Can't wait to see you again. Reagan's already itching to come out there for a visit, but I don't think Mom or I could pull ourselves away from work commitments for the trip. You understand. How's Callum? Tell him to stay away from those farmers' daughters!"

Ingrid rolled her eyes.

"That's all I've got, Dad. Love you," Vyom said.

"Bye, Dad!" Ingrid waved at the camera and the video ended.

"'Dad'?" Murphy glared wearily at the blank slate and tossed it onto the table.

He pinched the bridge of his nose, his tired brain sliding in a tractionless spiral as he tried to grapple with his eldest offspring's latest escapade. He reached for the slate again, to fire back a message, then closed his eyes.

No, a tiny voice told him. Better to deal with that later, when he didn't have little things like potential League invasions to distract him. And when his mind was actually working again. He shook his head and slumped back onto the cot.

"Give him a good talking-to later," he mumbled. "Yeah. That's the ticket. Later..."

He drifted off to sleep.

CHAPTER TWENTY-NINE

THE TENSION ON TFNS *ISHTAR'S* FLAG BRIDGE COULD HAVE BEEN sawed up and used for armor plate.

A ship traveling supralight couldn't see into normal space, but it pushed a "bow wave" of distortion ahead of it along the boundary between its private pocket of wormhole space and the rest of the universe. That boundary distortion could be detected from normal space at a range of several light-months. Although, given that a Fasset-drive ship, especially one with a mil-spec drive fan, could travel at up to nine hundred and fifty times the speed of light, that wasn't a lot of warning.

This particular Fasset signature had been picked up at twenty-six light-weeks, and Murphy's defense plans had sprung into action. Two hundred and ninety-one minutes later, the drive signatures had vanished as the ships they belonged to went sublight, approximately six light-hours from Crann Bethadh.

It was one of the most frustrating things about system defense, Murphy thought, glowering at the plot. As long as an intruder was in wormhole space, he could be seen at a range of light-months in real time. Once he dropped sublight, however, the defender was reliant upon light-speed sensors, which meant he knew *approximately* where his visitors had arrived, as well as their initial sublight vector, but that was all he knew for literally hours.

"It's not big enough to be the Leaguies," a voice said behind him. Commander Mirwani and Commander Ortiz had been rehashing the same argument ever since the incoming Fasset signatures disappeared. "It can't be more than two or three FTLCs!"

"Maybe not," Ortiz replied stubbornly. "That doesn't mean it's not a scouting expedition. They could stooge around out there and send drones into the inner system for weeks—get a lot better read on our dispositions than we want them to have! So if they're *smart*, that's exactly what this is."

"They probably already think they know pretty much what we have," Mirwani shot back. As Murphy's operations officer, he'd been integral in evolving the plan for New Dublin's defense. "New Dublin's normally a task group station. It doesn't have a full task *force* assigned to it, and the only one of our FTLCs they've actually seen is *Ishtar*. So they're probably going to avoid tipping us off with recon missions and come in fast and dirty and count on overwhelming firepower, not finesse."

"I'll grant you, if someone like this Xing is in command, 'finesse' is probably not going to be prominently displayed. But if they have somebody on the other side with half a brain, then—"

"Incoming Fasset drives," the tactical section announced. "Two signatures at six light-hours. Consistent with FTLCs."

"So it's either Ortiz's scouts, or else Mirwani's right and it's not the League at all," O'Hanraghty murmured, and Murphy nodded.

The sensor data Tactical was seeing was actually six hours old, but that was something naval officers learned to factor into their thinking. At such an extreme range, they could see little more than the Fasset drives themselves, but more data would be available soon, and—

"Excuse me, Admiral."

Murphy wheeled toward the master holo display as Lieutenant Mastroianni appeared on it.

"Yes, Lieutenant?" Murphy's tone sounded calm and courteous—preposterously so, to his own ears, given the rock-hard lump of tension in his gut.

"We've just received a burst transmission addressed to you."

"Indeed?" Murphy arched an eyebrow. "Put it up, please."

"Aye, Sir."

Mastroianni's face disappeared, replaced by that of a dark-skinned man with intense brown eyes. He wore the Terran Federation Navy's uniform with a commodore's single star on each side of his collar.

"Admiral Murphy," he said, "I'm Commodore Esteban Tremblay, Task Group One-Seventy-Five. I anticipate entering Crann Bethadh orbit in approximately ten hours. I have dispatches relayed from Sol on board. I look forward to seeing you. Tremblay, clear."

"Oh, shit."

O'Hanraghty's voice was low enough only Murphy could hear it, and the chief of staff had his best poker face on, but the disgust in his tone was profound.

"A problem, Harry?"

"I thought this was supposed to be Admiral Fitzgerald's command, Sir."

"That's what the movement alert said." Murphy nodded, not trying to hide his own vast relief that the newcomers weren't a League attack force. "But things change. You know that."

O'Hanraghty nodded. Snaillike interstellar communications were a fact of life, and it wasn't at all unusual to learn about command structure changes only long after the fact.

"Should I take it that you aren't exactly enthralled to see the good commodore?" Murphy asked dryly.

"Let's just say that Stevie Tremblay and I...don't see eye-to-eye. He's a Heart World son of a bitch with a broom handle up his ass and no use for uppity Fringers, especially those in uniform."

"I see." Murphy turned to face him fully and his lip twitched. "But aside from those sterling qualities, how do you *really* feel about him?"

"How about 'not my favorite person'? More to the point just now, he was junior to me some time ago when he pulled a tour with Intelligence."

"One of the Rish-denier crowd?"

"The way he'd put it—in fact, he did—is that anybody who buys into that 'lunatic conspiracy theory' should be retired before they hurt themselves or somebody else."

"Charming."

Murphy puffed his lips for a moment, then shrugged.

"Well, maybe this time we've got the evidence to change his mind."

O'Hanraghty's expression said volumes about his opinion where that possibility was concerned, and Murphy grinned. But then his expression sobered.

"And, even if we don't change his mind," he said in a much

more serious tone, "it adds two more FTLCs *and* their parasites to our order of battle. Another task group is a godsend under the circumstances, Harry."

"If we can hang onto it, Sir," O'Hanraghty said grimly, and Murphy's eyes narrowed.

"Oh, I feel confident we can," he said softly.

⬧   ⬧   ⬧

Callum Murphy lay on his back in the engineering crawlway with the control slate on his chest. The imagery coming back from the multi-legged remote as it crawled nimbly along the cable runs on the other side of the inspection panel was less than perfect, but it was enough for a visual exam of the junction box. The box's cover slid back as the remote physically accessed the override button, and Callum sighed.

"I'm in, Sir," he said.

"And?" Lieutenant Dadyar Pêşrew's voice said in his earbud.

"And every one of them is back in standby mode. Resetting now."

The remote shinnied down into the box and began resetting the open switches. Red LEDs blinked to green, one by one, around the rim of Callum's slate as the circuits came back online, and he waited as patiently as possible—which wasn't very—until all of them had been reset. Then he ordered the remote to close the box and waited until it had made its way back to him and crawled back into the waiting recharge niche in his kit.

"All green here, Sir," he said. "Your end?"

"Green . . . for now." Pêşrew's disgust was obvious. "I guess you'd better come on back out. Although we're going to have to send somebody else in sometime in the next three hours, mark my words!"

"Headed back," Callum said with a tiny smile. He'd decided he liked Pêşrew, but the thin, shaven-headed lieutenant wasn't what anyone would have called excessively optimistic. In fact, he was decidedly on the lugubrious side.

Callum moved rapidly along the crawlway. His height and shoulders made it more cramped than it would have been for others, and he would have preferred to send the remote from the air-conditioned comfort of Reactor Two. But reception sucked this deep into *Kolyma*'s gizzards, and at least, unlike some people—his brother Vyom came to mind—claustrophobia had never bothered him.

He arrived at the final bend, reached up for the handhold in the crawlway overhead, and curled around to come feet-first out into the reactor room. Eira was waiting for him, arms crossed, her expression as un-delighted as it usually was when he wandered out of her sight, but she knew better than to say anything. He gave her a crooked grin and turned to Pêşrew.

"Everything tested out fine locally, Sir," he said. "As long as I had—well, the remote had—access to the *physical* switches, no problem."

"I know," Pêşrew grunted, scowling at a diagnostic panel. "This is the seventh . . . no, the *eighth* time it's happened, and I don't have a *clue* what's causing it." He shook his head. "It's driving Chief Pallares crazy!"

Chief Petty Officer Moreno Pallares was the senior noncom of *Kolyma*'s engineering department, and he took anything remotely like a malfunction as a personal affront. Although from Pêşrew's tone, Callum suspected Pallares wasn't the only member of *Kolyma*'s engineering personnel the maddening, intermittent fault was driving crazy.

"It's just the one box, Sir?" Callum mused, right arm folded across his chest while he rubbed his chin with his left index finger.

"No," Pêşrew said, turning to lift an eyebrow at him. "The Gamma-Three box is doing the same thing. That's one reason it worries me as much as it does. We can get along fine without either one of them, but if they both go down, we're cut off from almost a third of our damage control remotes. And given what's likely to be happening around here Sometime Real Soon Now . . ."

He shrugged, and Callum nodded, frowning intently. Then he stepped up beside Pêşrew.

"May I, Sir?" he asked, waving at the diagnostics, and Pêşrew snorted.

"Be my guest."

Callum started tapping in commands, and the diagnostic flickered and changed. Blocks of alphanumeric data crawled up its right side as he scrolled rapidly through it. Clearly, he was looking for something, and Pêşrew cocked his head. He'd just opened his mouth when Callum stabbed the screen and the display froze.

"What *do* we have here?" he murmured. He read carefully for a moment, then entered another query. Then another.

"Are you looking for something in *particular*, Lieutenant?" Pêşrew asked just a bit testily.

"Um?" Callum blinked, then gave himself a shake. "Sorry, Sir. I was checking the maintenance history."

"Why?" Pêşrew shrugged. "The Chief and I have torn the Beta box completely down and rebuilt it twice now. Somehow, I don't think it's a maintenance issue."

"Oh, I think it is, Sir," Callum told him. Pêşrew gave him a less than happy look, and Callum shook his head quickly. "Not at *our* end, Sir. Or not directly, at least."

"What are you talking about?"

"It says here—" Callum waved at the maintenance history "—that *Kolyma* spent three weeks in the yards here in New Dublin."

"Yeah." Pêşrew frowned at him. "The power surge that sent Lieutenant Simmons to the hospital fried half a dozen connections before we got it shut down. The yardies jumped right on it—guess they didn't want us deadlined any longer than they could help after what happened to Inverness."

Like most of *Kolyma*'s ship's company, Pêşrew's mouth tightened ever so briefly at his own mention of Inverness, but he continued steadily.

"Didn't try to fob us off with rewiring or rebuilding, either. We weren't sure what caused the surge, so they tore out that entire portion of the net and replaced it from scratch. All new components."

"Yep." Callum nodded. "And it just so happens that they took Beta-Three and Gamma-Three out of the same lot of stores. Which is where our problem comes from."

"How are brand-new, base-certified relay nodes a 'problem'?" Pêşrew asked skeptically.

"Because what we're looking at here isn't a hardware fault, it's in the software," Callum told him. The engineer looked even more skeptical.

"There's some reason you think the Chief and I didn't go through that code line-by-line?" he said.

"Oh, I'm sure you did, Sir. And I'm sure it all checked out. But the problem's not in the control software, it's in the boxes' internal processors."

"Oh?" One of Pêşrew's eyebrows rose, and Callum nodded.

"It just happens that these boxes were manufactured by Venus Futures, Sir. And there was a controller problem with them when they first came into service ten, fifteen years ago. So Venus introduced an internal software patch as a temporary fix while we tracked down the gremlins. Turned out it was a problem with the nanoprinters. This is one of the first components we turned out with genuine mollycircs, and there were still a few...bugs in the process. Only about two percent of the units were affected, but that was enough to create the problems the Fleet was reporting. We fixed it in the manufacturing process, and there haven't been any problems with it since."

"That's all very fascinating, Lieutenant, but what does it have to do with *our* problem?"

"The New Dublin yardies wanted you back online as quickly as possible, Sir. So they hauled these boxes—*certified* boxes, as you pointed out—out of stores. The yards here are licensed to fabricate new ones, but these aren't local build. According to the manifest, they've been in stores for twelve years."

"Twelve—?"

"Not like they've got a use-by date, Sir. And they were certified, and they passed all the circuit tests after they were installed. *But—*" he held up his right hand, index finger extended "—I will bet you that when we take a look, we'll find out that they have the 'temporary' patch tucked away in their processors. And if they do, what's happening is that every few days, maybe every couple of weeks, the boxes are getting an input that the patch's code flags as a potential fault. Then the *patch* is sending a query to the Damage Control computers to be sure it isn't a fault. If everything were working properly, the computers would tell them to shut the hell up and just do what they were told. But the computers don't know about the patch, so they don't respond, and—"

"And the damned patch shuts the boxes down until somebody resets them physically!"

"And sends *another* code the computers don't know to look for telling them what they've done." Callum nodded. "If I'm right, that's exactly what's happening. And it shouldn't be too hard to find out."

Callum thought for a moment, then tapped in an authorization code from memory. Nothing happened for a second or two, but then a crimson code began to flash on the diagnostics panel.

"There it is." He stood back with a headshake and folded his arms. "I guess maybe Grandpa wasn't as unreasonable with that whole 'hands-on' stuff as I thought he was."

"What do you mean?" Pêşrew asked.

"He insisted that I serve a regular apprenticeship in power systems back home. And a lot of the classroom work included 'real-life' problems from the archives." Callum chuckled. "Man, talk about *boring*! I'd've cheerfully slept through at least two-thirds of it, if I hadn't known old Rantala would rat me out to Grandpa in a heartbeat. That would've been...bad. A short way with slackers when it comes to yardwork, my grandpa. His father put him through exactly the same program back in the Dark Ages, and I think he figures it's his karmic duty to inflict it on every generation that comes after him!"

Pêşrew's eyes had widened as he realized—*really* realized, for the first time—that "Grandpa" was *Kanada Thakore*, CEO, chairman of the board, and majority stockholder in Venus Futures.

"Anyway," Callum went on, still looking at the diagnostic panel and not his superior's expression, "one of the study problems from the archives was about this. Not this box, in particular, but the problems from faulty fabrication and the various fixes for it, which *included* the patch in our rebellious relays here. And it just so happens that I have a sort of mental glitch. I remember codes and commands way better than anybody should. That's why I remembered this one."

He jutted his chin at the flashing code.

"And what do we do about it now that you've found it?" Pêşrew asked slowly, his eyes intent, and Callum shrugged.

"Well, we could just scrub the processors, but I wouldn't recommend it. It's unlikely our boxes are faulty, but it's not impossible, and I'd rather not find out they are only after we start taking damage. So I'd suggest that I get into Damage Control and tell the computers what they need to be looking for to tell the boxes that everything's okay, so *please* don't reset to factory default standby!"

"I think that sounds like an excellent idea," Pêşrew said. "As a matter of fact, I think we should probably go take care of that immediately. Assuming you know how to tell them what to look for, that is?"

"Oh, no problem there, Sir." Callum unfolded his right arm to wave an airy hand. "Easy peasy."

"Well, take the Chief with you. I think he deserves to be in on the kill where this little problem is concerned."

"Aye, aye, Sir," Callum said with a smile, and Pêşrew shook his head.

"Don't take this the wrong way, Lieutenant Murphy, but from looking at your service jacket, I had my doubts about how useful you'd be. It would appear I was wrong about that. So in case I forgot to say this earlier—" he held out his hand "—welcome aboard."

✧　　✧　　✧

"Welcome to Crann Bethadh, Commodore," Murphy said, rising behind his governor's desk to extend his right hand. "I admit, you aren't who we were expecting, but we're still glad to see you."

"Thank you, Governor."

Tremblay gave Murphy's hand a somewhat perfunctory squeeze and looked past the governor's right shoulder to Harrison O'Hanraghty. His eyes were cold, and the nod he gave the chief of staff was curt.

"Please, have a seat," Murphy invited, waving at the comfortable chair in front of his desk, and Tremblay settled into it.

"Can I offer you a hot drink?" Murphy asked, and chuckled. "Crann Bethadh's winters take some getting used to!"

"Thank you, Sir. Perhaps later."

"Fine."

Murphy sat back down in his own chair, propped his elbows on the arms, and steepled his fingers under his chin.

"May I ask what became of Admiral Fitzgerald?" he asked.

"The Admiral's father died unexpectedly back in Olympia, Sir. He was granted compassionate leave to deal with the situation."

"And they gave you his task group?"

"They did. And since I was bound for New Dublin to collect CruRon Four-Sixty-Nine, they tasked me to deliver dispatches from the Oval as I passed through." He reached into a tunic pocket and extracted a data rod. "I'm afraid I'm in a bit of a hurry to reach my station, so I'd like to drop this off and have it receipted so I can be on my way. No offense, Sir, but—" his eyes strayed to O'Hanraghty again "—it's important that I get to Acanthus as promptly as possible. I'm already going to be several days late."

"I see."

Murphy un-steepled his fingers and extended one hand to take the data rod. Then he tipped back in his chair, turning it in both hands, and crossed his legs.

"I understand the importance of your orders, Commodore," he said, "but I'm afraid there have been a few developments since they were written that may require a modification."

"With all due respect, Sir, no one out here has the authority to 'modify' my orders," Tremblay said.

"That isn't quite true, Esteban," O'Hanraghty said with what might have been described as a smile. "Section Four."

"'Section Four'?" Tremblay repeated.

"Section Four of the Governor's commission. The section that enumerates his Emergency Powers. Specifically, paragraph three: 'Shall have authority to take control and command of all military and naval forces of the Federation in the system of his jurisdiction for the duration of the declared emergency.'"

"That's preposterous!" Tremblay said. "I'm not *stationed* in this system; I'm only in transit!"

"It doesn't say 'all military and naval forces of the Federation stationed in the system,' Esteban. It says '*in* the system,' and unless I'm mistaken, you're sitting in a chair right smack in the middle of Tara City."

Tremblay glared at him, jaw muscles tight, then whipped his eyes to Murphy.

"Governor, I think you'd better read those dispatches before you go any further with this," he said.

"Oh?" Murphy held the data rod up between his thumb and index finger. "You know what's in them, Commodore?"

"I—" Tremblay began, then stopped short. "I was given some idea of their content when they were delivered to me in Jalal," he said carefully.

"I would hate to think you'd been improperly made privy to any of the confidential sections of my official dispatches," Murphy said.

"I'm sure that any confidentiality issues were respected when they were handed to me for delivery, Sir."

"But you haven't viewed them yourself?"

"Of course not, Sir!"

"Ah." Murphy leaned forward, opened his desk drawer, and dropped the data rod into it. "Well, I assure you that I'll peruse them very carefully at my earliest opportunity. In the meantime, however, I'm formally informing you that, pursuant to Section Four of my commission, I'm placing you and your task group under my command."

"With all due respect, Sir," Tremblay said through gritted teeth, "I do not recognize your authority to do anything of the sort."

"I advise you not to make any rash pronouncements in that respect until you've had time to consult with your JAG," Murphy said gently. "I assure you, Captain O'Hanraghty's citation was accurate, and in the case of the Dubrovnik System in 2378, his interpretation of it was upheld by the court of inquiry...and the subsequent court-martial."

His voice was no longer remotely gentle, and his eyes bored into Tremblay's.

"And if I refuse to acknowledge your authority?" Tremblay asked.

"Why, in that case, Commodore, I would have no alternative but to place you under arrest and confine you to quarters here on the planet. I would hate to do that, for several reasons, including—whether you believe this or not—the consequences for your career and this system's loss of a fine commanding officer."

Tremblay looked at him incredulously, and Murphy let his chair come back upright.

"I'm now speaking completely off-the-record, Commodore," he said. "Having said that, it may be that the dispatches you've delivered to me contain instructions requiring me to do something other than what I fully intend to do. Legally, I have the authority to amend—or ignore—instructions that have been outdated by information I possess that the drafter of those instructions did not. I am in possession of precisely that sort of information. I anticipate an attack on New Dublin in force within the next two to three weeks, maximum. I'm prepared to share with you the evidence which leads me to that conclusion. You may not draw the same conclusion from it that Captain O'Hanraghty and I have drawn. If, however, there's the smallest possibility that we're correct, there won't be a hole deep enough for the Oval to bury you in if you don't cooperate with me now."

Tremblay's eyes had widened, and Murphy tapped his desktop with an index finger as he continued.

"We're both Heart Worlders, Commodore. For that matter, we're both part of the Five Hundred. You know how it works. The Heart may be prepared to write off any number of Fringe systems rather than 'risk critical strategic assets,' but both the Oval and the Government have been very careful to never officially tell their

Heart World citizens anything of the sort. If I'm correct—if *we're* correct—in our suspicions, this system will shortly be attacked by a force which might very well contain as many as eight or nine FTLCs—possibly even more. I realize that that sounds preposterous, especially here in Concordia, but it's *going* to happen. And when it does, I'm going to defend the system."

The admiral's eyes were gray, hammered iron.

"There are a hundred million citizens of the Federation in New Dublin. I will *not* place the value of my ships and their personnel above the lives of those civilians, no matter what the Oval's standing orders may say. So whether you choose to cooperate with me or not, there *will* be a Battle of New Dublin, and we'll either win it or find ourselves with a dead planet and the shredded remnants of its defenses...and defenders. *That's* the story that will hit the newsfeeds, and it will hit them before the Oval can spin it, before the Five Hundred can clean up the messy details. And if that happens, and there's an officer who refused to assist in New Dublin's defense, someone whose refusal can *possibly* be construed as the reason that defense failed, they will nail that officer to the cross to cover the Oval's ass and keep anyone from looking closely at the policy which has abandoned one Fringe System after another. I'll be dead, so it won't matter to me, but if you're not, I guarantee you they'll make you wish you were."

Silence hovered tautly for a long, still moment. Then O'Hanraghty cleared his throat.

"Esteban, you don't like me much, and I don't like you much. You think I'm a lunatic conspiracy theorist, and I think you've willfully refused to look at the evidence. I think the evidence the Governor is talking about now might actually change your mind—a bit, at least—if you're willing to consider it at all openly. But whether you agree with us or not, he's absolutely right about what your friends in the Heart Worlds will do to you if they need a living scapegoat for the sort of unmitigated disaster this could turn into. You know that as well as I do."

Tremblay glared at him, and the chief of staff smiled crookedly.

"All that's true, but much as I've disliked you over the years, I never once thought you were a coward. And I don't think you'll be able to live with *yourself*, whatever anyone else says or does, if the Governor and I are right about what's headed toward New

Dublin and you're not here to try to stop it with us. I can think of a lot of people I'd rather die with, and I'm sure you could to, but—" the smile vanished "—I'd rather do that than let what happened to Inverness happen here on Crann Bethadh, where there are a hundred times as many civilians in the line of fire."

Tremblay frowned. Then he looked back at Murphy.

"Two to three weeks, you said, Governor?"

"That's our projected window." Murphy nodded. "Obviously, we may be a little off on either end. So let's say I'm pretty sure the hammer's coming down within the next month. I've already sent a dispatch directly to Earth, by the way, with that same information."

"So you'd be talking about holding my task group here in New Dublin for no more than a month?"

"No," Murphy said. "Honesty requires me to say that I'll be holding your task group here until the anticipated attack comes in or I hear back from the Oval. I sent my dispatch off five weeks ago, so it will reach Sol in another six weeks. Then we have at least eleven more weeks before any response can reach us here."

Tremblay scowled, and Murphy shrugged.

"Everything I told you the Five Hundred and the Oval would do to you will most certainly happen to *me* if I'm wrong about this, Commodore. You, on the other hand, will be covered by my orders as Governor in a declared state of emergency." He smiled suddenly. "Trust me, they'll be so busy turning me into dog meat, they won't have any time or attention left for you!"

"And think about the upside, Esteban," O'Hanraghty said. "If we're wrong, you'll get to be a star witness at the inquiry that finally nails me as the paranoiac I've always been. There has to be a certain satisfaction in *that* thought!"

Tremblay glared at him, but, manifestly despite himself, his lips twitched.

"Commodore," Murphy said, "I don't believe you could be as privy to our operational stance as I know you are and not realize what's been happening to the Fringe for far too long. It has to stop. Even if that weren't true simply on the basis of common decency—and the moral responsibility we bear—the Fringe is near the end of its endurance. The last thing the Federation needs is to have the Fringe go up in flames, and if we let Crann Bethadh be destroyed the same way Inverness was—especially when we had a substantial force here to defend it—that's precisely what will happen. Don't think for a moment it won't. And when we're already pressed to the limit on the Beta Cygni front, and the League is opening another offensive here in Concordia, do we really need to be fighting a *civil war* at the same time?"

"You honestly think that could happen, Sir?"

"I don't think it could happen; I think it *will* happen, if we abandon New Dublin," Murphy said flatly. "And I think it would be totally justified from the Fringe's viewpoint. And I think it would be the most disastrous thing that could happen, not simply to the Federation but to the human race."

"I have to believe you're wrong about that," Tremblay said after a moment. "But I'm aware that it's what I *have* to believe, because if the situation's really that far gone, then ..."

His voice trailed off, and Murphy nodded.

"I'm afraid it is. But I don't think it's gone so far we can't still do something about it, and that's why I'm here. That's why this system *has* to be defended."

He held Tremblay's eyes for several seconds, then leaned back in his chair again.

"So, Commodore. Do I call in Sergeant Major Logan and have him march you off to durance vile, or would you like me to brief you in on what we've discovered and show you our ops plan, first?"

✧   ✧   ✧

Commander Whitten held up the empty bottle.

The human bartender glanced his way, then picked up a fresh bottle of *Craigmore Nua*. He peeled the foil, drew the cork, and crossed the pub to Whitten's table. Then he refilled the commander's glass and set the bottle on the table, and Whitten nodded his thanks.

"*Tá fáilte romhat*," the bartender replied with a broad smile, and headed back to his post.

"Bit different from when we arrived," Elaina Iglesias observed, reaching for the single malt to refill her own glass. They had four more hours before they had to report aboard ship, and there'd be no more shore time until whatever was going to happen had happened.

"It is that," Commander Gao agreed. "Different, I mean." He looked across the table at Commander Stanley. "You still pissed at Murphy for pulling us out of Jalal early, Joe?"

"I still say the crews had a right to bitch about it," Stanley said stubbornly. Then shrugged. "On the other hand, Inverness was...more of a wake-up than I really wanted. And maybe—*maybe*—I was a tad...hasty in my initial evaluation of the Admiral."

"*Hasty?*" Iglesias repeated with a hoot of laughter.

"Tell me *you* would've expected something like this out of a Heart from the damned Five Hundred," Stanley challenged. "Go on—tell me!"

"Okay, you've got me," she acknowledged. "I'm willing to admit I was wrong—that we were all wrong—about Murphy. About whether or not he was just another ticket-puncher. Or O'Hanraghty's sock puppet, for that matter! It's sort of refreshing to find out just how wrong we were, actually."

"You mean it's scary as shit," Whitten said with a crooked smile. "If the intelligence briefings're anywhere near right, we're most likely about to get reamed, you know. The kind of reaming that gets a whole bunch of 'regret to inform you' letters texted to next of kin."

"Yeah, I know," Gao said. He raised his own glass, looking through its honey-smooth amber depths at the overhead light, then lowered his eyes to his fellow cruiser commanders. "But, you know, that doesn't bother me as much as it should. Wonder why?"

"Maybe because it's the first time in years we aren't just being ticket-punchers ourselves," Adriana Lawson said quietly.

She and Iglesias were CruRon 1102's only female skippers, and despite very different backgrounds, they were close friends. Physically, they were a study in contrasts. Iglesias was red-haired, muscular, green-eyed, and 173 centimeters tall. Lawson was slightly built, almost bird-boned, with dark hair and brown eyes, and stood barely 160 centimeters. Her lack of body mass didn't noticeably impair her ability to handle alcohol, however, and she took a sip of the whiskey, savoring its liquid heat and hint of peat. Then she looked at the others.

"Admit it," she told them. "*I* certainly will. What was the point in getting our asses killed? The frigging war's lasted almost sixty damned years—*sixty*—and six billion dead. A *hundred million* a year. And what've we got to show for it? Huh?" Those dark eyes challenged the other officers around the table. "Fuck-all," she told them. "That's what we've got to show for it. Abso-fucking-lutley nothing. The front hasn't really moved in Beta Cygni for almost ten damned years, and it's not going to. So what was the point? Take our commissions, serve our time, and try to get the hell out alive. Tell me that wasn't *exactly* what you were thinking, too."

The pub's background voice-murmur and clinking glass seemed louder, somehow, in the silence that enveloped the table.

"I'm a Heart," she said after a moment. "You and me, Vinnie— we're both Hearts. And, sure, we've got 'friends' who're Fringers, like the rest of you guys. Well, maybe not you, Joe. You're such a dick I've always thought of you more as an 'associate.'"

Stanley raised his right hand, middle finger extended.

"But my point," Lawson went on more seriously, "is that aside from the Fringers I came into direct contact with, I didn't think much of them. Bunch of ignorant rubes, who keep whining about how the Navy isn't doing its job back home. How much they resent being sent to Beta Cygni, where the important fighting is, because nobody's looking after their mommies and daddies back in the Fringe. That's how I thought of them."

Her voice was low as she made the admission, and she inhaled deeply.

"But you know what? The reason I thought of them that way? It's because I knew they were right. I knew the Fringe always gets the shit-end of the stick. *Any* stick. They're taxed to death, we take their kids off to get killed, the Five Hundred stomps all over any industrial investment out here that could challenge its bottom line, and those assholes—those unmitigated *assholes*—in Olympia and the Oval, they just write off their star systems, because they're not 'important enough' for us to defend. And I've known it, just like you guys have known it, for my entire career. So every time one of those whiny Fringers started going on and on, bending my ear about how the Fringe always gets shafted, I told myself they were idiot yokels who didn't understand what really had to be done. Because if I didn't, then I had to face all the things we *haven't* done."

The others looked at one another, then back at her, and Sergey Tsimmerman, *La Cateau*'s skipper and the flag captain of CruRon 1102, a bearded bear of a man, nodded.

"Cuts both ways, Addie," he rumbled. "Me, I understood exactly why Crann Bethadh wasn't all that fond of us when we got here. Like you say, I'm Fringe, and I've always thought most Hearts are assholes. After all, it's clear as hell they don't give a rat's ass about the Fringe, except for what they can squeeze out of us for places like Beta Cygni, or to fill the frigging Five Hundred's pockets! So if they aren't going to risk their precious asses for my people, why should we risk ours for them? Why should *I*? So, yeah, I'm a ticket-puncher, too. Do my service, go home with my hide in one piece, and let the damned Federation burn."

They looked at one another again, their eyes dark, wondering how much of this conversation had come out of the bottle of *Craigmore Nua*. Wondering how the Terran Federation Navy had come to this. To this cynicism—almost apathy—where the oaths they'd sworn, the responsibility they'd pledged to discharge, were concerned, and derision for anyone who thought they'd actually meant those oaths, that pledge.

To the point of being ashamed of how they and their fellows had failed the uniform they wore.

Until Terrence Murphy rubbed their noses in it. Until Inverness. Until Alramal, and the discoveries there. And until he'd stretched every regulation to the breaking point and beyond to defend New Dublin. All of them had a shrewd suspicion what the Heart World elite were going to do to him when this was all over, assuming he survived, and he didn't care. He didn't care at all.

"Look," Stanley said after a moment, "don't think you and Addie are gonna get *me* to stand up and start singing the Navy Hymn, Seryozha! I mean, I still plan to get my ass home alive and intact, thank you very much. But..." He pursed his lips, then shrugged. "But maybe you're not all completely full of shit. And maybe Murphy's right. I don't know about that, and the truth is, I'd really rather not be in a position to find out."

His companions chuckled, and Stanley picked up the bottle and topped off their glasses. Then he raised his own.

"But I'll say this. Here's to us—damn few like us, and most of 'em already dead! I expect some of us to be along shortly, but I will follow that Heart World bastard wherever the hell he takes us." His eyes swept the others' faces. "Stout ships, hot drives, and *fuck the Leaguies!*"

Six glasses clinked as one.

CHAPTER THIRTY

"ALL OF THIS WILL BE IN MY REPORT, ADMIRAL," CAPTAIN LIP-shen's tight-lipped holo said at Murphy's command station.

"Yes, you've mentioned that several times." Murphy smiled ever so slightly. "Of course, my latitude as system governor goes a long way during a declared state of emergency. That will go into your report, as well. No doubt."

"Your authority doesn't extend to military equipment and personnel not assigned to New Dublin." Lipshen's voice was icy. "You may—*may*—be covered where BatRon Seven-Oh-Two is concerned, given that they haven't been formally reassigned to another station since Scotia was abandoned. But neither Commodore Granger nor Commodore Tremblay can be remotely construed as falling under your orders!"

"I don't think we're too likely to agree on that one," Murphy replied. "And Commodore Tremblay accepts my authority." And it had been nice to get at least *one* set of dispatches that contained nothing but routine shipping movement information, too, he thought. "He doesn't seem to have any problem with it."

"Whether or not *he* does is beside the point!" Lipshen snapped. "His opinion doesn't change the law. Nor does it change the fact that you have *zero* authority over Commodore Granger or the draftees! They—"

"Bit of a gray area, there, Andy," O'Hanraghty said in a chatty tone. He stood beside the seated Murphy and smiled broadly when the IG captain glared at him. "See, the recruits were under the command of the New Dublin Militia at the time of their training. Once they're deemed fit for federal service, then they're officially transferred to a separate command. They haven't been yet, so they aren't a federal asset at the moment. And while Commodore Tremblay protested the Governor's orders, as Admiral Murphy says, he had to concede that Section Four gives us the authority to take his ships under command for the duration of the emergency. As for the other ships you're worried about, if you read the repair yard's standing orders, any units which are docked here for overhaul or repair, *are* assigned to New Dublin. That means any ship detailed to New Dublin for repairs is officially part of our command until such time as she's completed her trials and the dockmaster certifies her repairs. Um, that would include Commodore Granger's ships," he added helpfully.

"You're grasping at straws!" Lipshen snarled.

"Have you contacted the dockmaster?" Murphy asked. "I don't believe there's been time for the Commodore to run trials on her Fasset drive."

"Oh, yes. I spoke with him at some length." Lipshen's jaw clenched. "He was most liberal with his expletives at my inquiry, and Commodore Granger declined to overrule him and 'endanger her command' with uncertified repairs. Which, I observe, hasn't prevented her from participating in your 'system defense' exercises. That, too, will be in my report." The captain raised his chin slightly. "The Federation has systems in place to prevent governors from seizing too much power for themselves, Admiral. There's a reason for that. And what you're doing sets a dangerous precedent."

"Perhaps. But at the moment, the League poses an unprecedented *threat*," Murphy said. "Better safe than sorry, don't you agree?"

"My personal opinions are not relevant. Only the Federation's law matters here." Lipshen looked to one side, then tapped at a screen in front of him. "My shuttle will be departing for *Ishtar* in two hours. Some other matters which have come to my attention require a personal conver—"

An alarm howled, and Murphy jerked upright in his command chair and killed Lipshen's holo with a swipe of his hand.

"Talk to me, Harry!"

"Fasset signature at twenty-seven light-weeks, Sir," the chief of staff replied tautly. "It's a big one, and coming fast. *Really* fast. Whoever it is, he's running his fans *mighty* hot. ETA... four-point-seven hours."

"Any estimate on point sources?"

"No, Sir. Not possible yet," O'Hanraghty said, his expression grim. "Looks like this force is at least twice Tremblay's size, though. And—" he turned his head to look over his shoulder at Murphy "—they're coming in on almost exactly the projected heading. So I don't think they're more Federation ships we can 'borrow.'"

"It *does* seem unlikely," Murphy agreed dryly.

The admiral stood and crossed the flag bridge to stand beside O'Hanraghty in front of the master plot. The glaring red icon of an unidentified Fasset signature blinked at him from its depths, moving swiftly closer, and he felt as if he'd just swallowed a frozen bowling ball. This wasn't Steelman's Star. Then he'd had so little time to think, to anticipate... to feel afraid. Battle had been joined long before command fell to him. But not this time, he thought.

Oh, no. Not *this* time.

"I'm glad we had a couple of weeks to get Tremblay worked into the ops plan," he said. He put every gram of confidence he could muster into his tone and wondered if it was enough. "And they do seem to be coming in where we'd anticipated."

"Should I notify Goibniu to begin launching?" Commander Mirwani asked.

That question was a sign of the ops officer's own nerves, Murphy thought, because Mirwani already knew the answer.

"Not yet, Raleigh," he replied. "We don't have an unlimited ammunition supply, and until we actually see these people, we don't know for certain what they're doing, do we?"

"No, Sir," Mirwani acknowledged in a chastened tone. "Sorry. I—"

"You were just checking," Murphy interrupted. "That's what good subordinates do. They make sure their lordly superiors aren't about to drop a ball because they just didn't happen to think about it."

He patted the commander on the shoulder, and Mirwani smiled.

"Sir," Lieutenant Commander Tanaka said in a reminding sort of tone, "Captain Lipshen is still on the comm."

"Ah, yes! Captain Lipshen."

Murphy strolled back to his command station and un-muted the holo.

"—and another thing," Lipshen was saying. "I've been hearing some disturbing reports about certain of your...administrative and procurement policies here in New Dublin. We need to discuss those, as well. The expenditures you've authorized are, frankly, beyond merely 'excessive.' They're well into the realm of astronomically unsanctioned, and—"

"I'm afraid that's going to have to wait," Murphy interrupted.

"I'm the Inspector General's representative here in this system, Admiral," Lipshen said coldly. "When and where we discuss my concerns is *my* decision."

"Under normal circumstances, perhaps," Murphy conceded. "At the moment, however, we've just detected a Fasset signature headed our way in wormhole space. Sublight ETA is about—" he glanced at the time display "—two-hundred-eighty minutes, now. I think it would be best if you stayed safely on the planet until we sort out exactly what's happening up here."

"*What?!*" Lipshen snapped bolt upright in his chair. "The League is attacking *now*?!"

"That would be a worst-case assumption, yes," Murphy agreed. "But it could also very well be a simple merchantman. Or another force like Commodore Tremblay's, just passing through. I can't say anything more definite until they've gone sublight and I have light-speed confirmation."

Murphy heard something surprisingly like a chuckle run around the flag bridge despite his staff's tension, but Lipshen looked like a man whose brain was about to explode.

"Your orders in the event of an overwhelming attack are very clear, Governor!" he said.

"I don't know that this *is* an attack at all yet, Captain," Murphy pointed out. "Far less one in 'overwhelming' strength. I won't know *what* it is until I have that light-speed confirmation. At which point, I will, of course, bear my standing orders in mind."

Lipshen's face went a most unbecoming shade of red, and his eyes bulged.

"Admiral—!"

"I'll be back in contact as soon as we know more," Murphy said soothingly. "Don't worry. We'll keep you fully informed. Murphy, clear."

He killed the link and tipped back in his chair with a smile.

"My, that was fun," he said. "The opportunity almost makes a desperate battle to the death seem worthwhile, doesn't it?"

It wasn't a chuckle this time.

"That was better," Xing Xuefeng said.

She stood on RLHS *Nüwa*'s flag bridge, her expression fierce as she glared into the visual at the tiny pinprick of the star she'd come so far to find. Dragon Fleet's other eleven FTLCs had gone sublight in almost perfect formation with her flagship, and readiness reports murmured and flowed in the background.

"Well, they know we're here now, Ma'am," Captain Rang said.

"Within five or six light-minutes, at best," she said impatiently. "Not that it matters at this range."

"No, of course not, Ma'am."

Xing spared her chief of staff a brief grin, then turned to the displays showing the faces of her carrier division commanders.

And Than, of course.

"Very well," she said. "We'll proceed as planned. Captain Ding," she looked at her flag captain, "begin deceleration in two hours and ten minutes."

"I'm pretty sure Captain Ding already knew what 'proceed as planned' meant, Sir," Su Zhihao said very quietly in Admiral Than's ear.

"It never hurts to be certain." Than's tone was rather more serene than he felt.

"Want to place a tiny wager on whether or not her flag bridge video gets leaked to the feeds?" Su asked. "Steely-eyed warrior, fiery with impatience for battle against the ungodly?"

"Wars are also won through propaganda," Than pointed out a bit severely. "Although," his expression relented, "I certainly wouldn't bet against it."

Su snorted, but he also let it drop and moved away toward the comm tied into *Cai Shen*'s bridge. Than listened as he spoke to Captain Sun Luoyang, the FTLC's CO, but his mind was on the display as the massive RLH force bore down upon New Dublin.

He knew he'd irritated Xing immensely by arguing against her initial attack plan, but FTLCs were valuable units, especially with the destruction of the rest of Dragon Fleet's singularity manifolds. And, unlike Xing, he'd reviewed the last attack on the star system. He'd pointed out that they couldn't afford to expose her carriers to a similar ambush, especially not given that *Ishtar* and Murphy had to have gotten back to New Dublin weeks ago, at the very latest. Xing was obviously right that Murphy was hopelessly outgunned, but Than was less confident that this Federation governor planned to cut and run like the last one Xing had faced. If he didn't, then he'd had ample time, weeks of it, to make—and implement—whatever plans he could. And if he had, the one thing they *weren't* going to be facing was the rushed, desperately improvised defense the last attack had encountered.

Its losses had hardly been crippling, but they'd been nothing to sneer at, either. He had no desire to give New Dublin the opportunity to improve its score and, as he'd pointed out to the Second Admiral, every FTLC down for damage repair was twelve fewer battleships for the next system on her list.

Xing had been livid when he brought up the last attack. He was pretty sure she hadn't bothered to research it herself. Why should she, when she had such an overwhelming force advantage? But at least he'd gotten her to back off her original plan to take the carriers into bombardment range of Crann Bethadh.

He wasn't sure why she'd wanted to do that in the first place. The *Fúxīs* were big, powerful ships, a full thirteen hundred meters longer than his own *Cai Shen*—and *Cai Shen* was bigger than anything the Feds had, except their *Titans*—but they still mounted only twenty-four missile launchers in each broadside. They weren't going to be needed to turn Crann Bethadh into a blasted, lifeless wasteland, and adding their limited firepower to the holocaust certainly wasn't worth risking them in the inner system. Maybe Su was right. Maybe she'd just wanted to *personally* drive missiles into her prey and watch the fireballs spawn.

Than Qiang would have been delighted to leave that pleasure to her. The thought that his people's hands were about to be stained with so much blood filled him with both shame and despair. But they couldn't risk the carriers in that close. Not until they were certain New Dublin hadn't come up with another unexpected clutch of missiles.

And so the carriers would decelerate to a zero velocity relative to New Dublin ten light-minutes from Crann Bethadh. That would be more than close enough to bombard the planet with missiles—even K-guns. It wasn't like it could dodge, after all.

And if slowing the approach gave the people of Crann Bethadh longer to retreat into their shelters and their bunkers and seal the doors behind them, Than Qiang was just fine with that.

✧   ✧   ✧

Sirens wailed throughout Tara City and every other city and town of Crann Bethadh. This wasn't Inverness, where there'd been virtually no warning. From three hundred light-minutes, an enemy could reach attack range of the planet in little more than five hours, if they didn't decelerate at all and settled for a single, devastating firing pass. But this was a disaster for which New Dubliners had prepared—and rehearsed—for decades. The target time for complete evacuation to shelters was only *three* hours, and militiamen and designated Civil Defense wardens activated their comm nets, marshaled their volunteers, and sprang into action with the smoothness all those years of rehearsal made possible. Yet the fact that they were as prepared as was humanly possible was the coldest of comfort, and the citizens of Crann Bethadh waited for more information while fear and uncertainty gnawed at their nerves.

✧   ✧   ✧

"We should have signal in fifteen seconds, Admiral," Mirwani said, and Murphy turned from a low-voiced conversation with O'Hanraghty and Captain Lowe to face the master plot once more.

The red icon in its depths strobed to indicate uncertainty. The wormhole Fasset signature had disappeared almost five hours ago as the intruders dropped sublight. Assuming the emergence point plotted from their supralight signature was accurate, that had been approximately five light-hours from New Dublin, which placed them 282.7 light-minutes from Crann Bethadh and *Ishtar*. So, if they'd been right, they should be seeing something just about—

"Jesus Christ," someone muttered, and Murphy's jaw tightened as the strobing icon abruptly stopped blinking and an alphanumeric data block appeared beside it.

"Sir," O'Hanraghty said carefully, "CIC makes it twelve bogeys. We don't have any deceleration yet, but they're inbound at 297,000 KPS, and the outer surveillance platforms say they're all FTLCs."

"Thank you, XO," Murphy said. He gazed at the plot for a minute or so, then inhaled deeply and shrugged. "Well, this should certainly make Bug Out convincing."

"You might say that, Sir," O'Hanraghty acknowledged.

His eyes met Murphy's, and the admiral knew what he was thinking. Deep inside, neither of them had anticipated an attack in this much strength. They'd known it was a possibility, they'd said as much in their planning sessions, but they hadn't really believed it. They'd taken out the components for *forty* FTLCs, by their estimate. Had the RLH been building a *fifty*-carrier fleet? Planning on unleashing something that size on *Concordia*? Ridiculous!

But there it was, and even with Granger and Tremblay added to the defenders, they had only *seven* FTLCs, little more than half of what was coming at them.

Twelve carriers, he thought. Each with six parasite racks. Assume there were a battleship and a battlecruiser on each of them. That gave the League a hundred and forty-four sublight capital ships, and he had twenty-seven.

Twenty-seven.

"We know where they are now," he said. "Instruct Goibniu to prep for Fire Plan Agincourt."

"What about the cargo pods, Sir?" O'Hanraghty asked quietly. "We could drop one—"

"No." Murphy shook his head. "If Bug Out works, we'll need all the pods to handle them."

"And if Bug Out *doesn't* work?" the chief of staff asked even more quietly.

"In that case, they wouldn't make much of a difference to Umbrella anyway," Murphy said grimly, and O'Hanraghty knew he wasn't thinking about just the people of New Dublin. "Not that I'll be able to sleep too soundly of nights if the bastards get through to the planet. And assuming we survive this thing, of course."

He glanced at the time display.

"I think we've dithered about long enough to be convincing, so I guess it's time we get started. Captain Lowe, bring up the Fasset drive. Communications, get me—"

"Excuse me, Admiral," Lieutenant Mastroianni interrupted, "but I have an incoming priority signal. It's Captain Lipshen."

"Damn, that was fast—even for Andy with his panties in a wad!" O'Hanraghty said. He and Murphy looked at each other.

"Should we bother?" the admiral asked.

"Make it official," O'Hanraghty said. "He's gutless enough to add just the right element to it for us."

"True," Murphy said, and nodded for Mastroianni to put the signal through.

Lipshen appeared above the command ring. His face was pale, beaded with sweat, and he seemed on the verge of hyperventilating.

"You...you see them?" he asked.

"I'm well aware of the hostiles, yes."

"Admiral, you have your orders from Fleet Admiral Fokaides. You're far overmatched. Pull our mobile units out and retreat while we still have time!"

"And what about the people of Crann Bethadh? This may very well be the same monster that wiped out Inverness."

"To hell with them! We have our orders, Murphy."

"That we do," Murphy agreed, and looked at O'Hanraghty. "Twelve FTLCs. Our current strength and deployment put us at a distinct disadvantage. You agree, XO?"

"I'm afraid I do, Sir," O'Hanraghty said.

"Then Captain Lipshen is correct and we have no choice. Captain Lowe, take us out of orbit. I'm issuing Fall Back Plan Bravo."

"Yes, Sir. Breaking orbit now."

Ishtar and *Gilgamesh*, the only two FTLCs in Crann Bethadh orbit, turned and began to accelerate away from the planet toward the stellar Powell Limit. A least-time course to the limit that didn't take them directly into the League attack force's teeth put them on a heading perpendicular to the attack force's approach vector, and this far inside the limit, their maximum acceleration was only about nine hundred gravities. They could almost certainly be intercepted by an alert attacker, but it would generate the shortest possible engagement before they could escape into wormhole space. And while their acceleration might be vastly reduced this far in-system, it remained enormously higher than any reaction drive craft—like a passenger shuttle, for example—could possibly match.

"Murphy!" Lipshen shouted from the comm. "Murphy, where the hell are you *going*?"

"I'm executing Fleet Admiral Fokaides's instructions to give ground and preserve my carriers at all costs," Murphy said.

"You get me—I mean, you get our personnel off this damned planet, first!"

"I'm sorry, Captain, but I can't do that, given that they'll probably be picking up our Fasset drives in another forty minutes or so. If you work the math, I'll need every minute of that. And you're right that my orders are nondiscretionary. So I'm afraid you're just going to have to take refuge in the governor's mansion bunker and ride it out. Good luck."

He cut the circuit and flashed a quick, evil smile at O'Hanraghty. Then he nodded to Mastroianni.

"All-system override, please, Lieutenant."

"Aye, aye," she replied. "And...you're...live."

The master display flashed to indicate that the communications officer had just patched Murphy through to New Dublin's system-wide communications net.

"People of New Dublin, this system is under attack by an overwhelming enemy force. Under nondiscretionary Admiralty orders, I am executing a strategic withdrawal of all forces under my command. May the Lord bless thee and keep thee. Brighter mornings bring rising fortunes."

He nodded to Mastroianni again. She cut the channel, and he stepped back beside O'Hanraghty.

"Here goes nothing," his chief of staff said.

"Indeed. Drive on, Mr. O'Hanraghty. Drive on."

"How goddamned *dare* you!?" Tolmach shouted into the microphone. The command bunker beneath the capital was full of militiamen and women, huddled around workstations. "You coward! You absolute *coward*, Murphy! You're the same useless, dickless, spineless Heart World bag of shit I knew you were the moment you showed up in-system! I just hope the League kills me quick enough my ghost can latch onto your ship and haunt you for the rest of your useless fucking days! *Bastard!*"

He glanced up at Dewar, who gave him a thumbs-up.

Tolmach nodded back, flipped a switch, and leaned back against his desk.

"He's really leaving?" the President asked.

"*Ishtar* and *Gilgamesh* are underway," Dewar said. "'Leaving' might be putting it a tad strongly. Doesn't seem to be a very good astrogator, either. No way he can outrun 'em, and they'll catch him way outside what little support the system defenses might give him. Foolish of him. Must've panicked."

"All a trick." Tolmach sank into a chair and kicked his bad leg out. "Murphy's played it oh so well, hasn't he? But, you know, even now there's a part of me that wonders. Is the trick on the League...or on us?"

"I expect we'll find out in a few hours," Dewar replied with a shrug. "Against what's coming at us, we'd've been dead meat without him, anyway. So the way I see it, at least we're not any *worse* off."

"And aren't *you* just a little ray of sunshine." Tolmach glared at him. Then his expression sobered.

"Evacuation status?"

"Fifty percent of shelters reporting sealed already," Dewar said. "Bit ahead of projections—we'll hit a hundred percent in plenty of time, for whatever it's worth. Murphy's canceling the recruits' deployment gave everyone a hint something was up, I guess."

"Bring in Chaplain Gibson. A prayer's in order," Tolmach said. "And maybe a drink to go with it."

CHAPTER THIRTY-ONE

"TWO FASSET DRIVE SIGNATURES LEAVING CRANN BETHADH ORBIT, Sir!" Su Zhihao announced tensely.

"Two?" Third Admiral Than's eyebrows arched.

"Yes, Sir. Pulling nine hundred gravities. No way to tell yet what class ships, but they almost have to—"

The chief of staff broke off, cupping one hand over his earbud as if to help himself hear better, then looked at his CO.

"We're picking up something from the New Dublin comm net, Sir," he said.

"A challenge?" Than asked.

It seemed unlikely. New Dublin had to know approximately where Dragon Fleet had gone sublight, and if it had wanted to challenge them, it could have transmitted the challenge even before Dragon Fleet dropped out of wormhole space. Assuming they'd been detected thirty minutes before they returned to normal space, a challenge sent the instant they were spotted would have reached their arrival coordinates roughly four hours after they went sublight. Four hours by the standards of the rest of the universe, at least; at ninety-nine percent of the speed of light, it would have taken barely twenty-five minutes as far as the RLH was concerned.

Dragon Fleet had coasted ballistically at 297,000 KPS for just over two hours—eighteen minutes, by its clocks—during which it

335

had traveled 124.27 light-minutes toward New Dublin, which had shortened the transmission time for any challenge by two hours. Since then, its ships had decelerated at 1,800 gravities for another three hours and nine minutes, which had reduced its velocity to a mere 91,130 KPS, where time dilation was a negligible factor. In the process, they had traveled another 125.8 LM, just 3.5 LM short of the stellar Powell Limit, 49.9 LM from New Dublin, 32.7 LMs from Crann Bethadh, and still over two hours' flight from their planned attack point.

"No, Sir. Not a challenge," Su said. "In fact, it wasn't transmitted to us, at all. It was omnidirectional, broadcast thirty-nine minutes ago, about the time those Fasset drives broke orbit. Murphy is withdrawing, Sir! He just confirmed it to everyone in the star system."

Than frowned. Thirty-nine minutes would be about right, he thought. It would mean the defenders had spent perhaps ten minutes dithering between receiving their first light-speed sensor data on Dragon Fleet and the time they cut and ran for it. The departing Fasset drives certainly seemed to bear that out, and Than had always suspected Murphy had to have at least one other FTLC. He'd never believed the Federation governor would have left New Dublin completely uncovered while he ventured off to Alramal. Especially not after Inverness.

"Do we have a vector projection on his carriers?"

"Yes, Sir. They're breaking for the Powell Limit. CIC is updating the plot now."

Than turned to the display and frowned some more. The data was over half an hour old, but the broken line of the fugitives' projected vector streaked directly away from Crann Bethadh on a line perpendicular to Dragon Fleet's vector.

"Odd," Than said thoughtfully, clasping his hands behind him.

"Sir?"

"From what we've seen and heard about this Murphy I'd have expected him to play it smarter than this."

Su looked puzzled, and Than shrugged.

"This is a stupid deployment." The third admiral unclasped his hands to point at the plot. "If he was planning on running from the outset, Crann Bethadh orbit is the worst starting point he could have picked—the one spot in the entire star system he could be certain we'd be headed for. And running now, when we still have so much overtake velocity..."

Than shook his head and Su's puzzled expression turned into a thoughtful one.

By now, the fleeing FTLCs could have built their velocity to 17,000 KPS or so and traveled about 0.9 LM, but the third admiral was right. That was 73,000 KPS slower than Dragon Fleet's current velocity toward the planet, and the two forces' acceleration rates were virtually identical. Which meant—

"They can't get away, Sir." The chief of staff's eyes lit.

"No, they can't," Than agreed.

If Dragon Fleet altered course to intercept Murphy's departure inside the Powell Limit, its vector would become the longest side of a scalene triangle, but that triangle's base would be very short. The attack force would have much farther to travel than he would, but he couldn't build the velocity to avoid them before they ran him down. It was still his best shot at evading them—any other course would only have taken him deeper into the limit and given him even less time to build velocity—but "best shot" and "*good shot*" weren't the same thing at all. All he could hope for was to make it a passing engagement, because Dragon Fleet couldn't reduce its overtake velocity and still catch him in its engagement envelope. It would cut across his wake at a relative velocity of well over 120,000 KPS, which would limit it to a very short firing pass, but if it dropped its parasites as it crossed, its massed fire would tear any two FTLCs ever built into very tiny pieces.

If Murphy had been as smart about it as Than had expected him to be, none of that would be true. If he'd placed his FTLCs *outside* the Powell Limit on the same side of New Dublin as Crann Bethadh, he would have been positioned to intercept any threat short of the planet, and his ships would have had twice the acceleration rate they had now. And from that position, if he'd wanted to avoid action against a stronger enemy, all he'd really have needed to do was to lie low, go to complete EMCON and let Dragon Fleet charge past him toward the planet. Once they were past him, inside the Powell Limit and headed away from him, he could have evaded them effortlessly by simply accelerating in the opposite direction.

Conversely, he could have stayed exactly where he was, hiding under tight EMCON, until Dragon Fleet had decelerated to rest relative to Crann Bethadh and *then* run for it. His acceleration rate would have been identical to his pursuers, they both would have started at a relative velocity of zero, and he'd have had a ten light-minute head start. True, Dragon Fleet's reconnaissance drones were headed in-system. They *might* have spotted his carriers. But if he'd kept the FTLCs under tight emissions control, let Dragon Fleet see his parasites, but not their carriers, he could have used the parasites' defenses to kill the drones without giving away their motherships' presence.

But he hadn't done any of those things. Instead...

"Signal from the Second Admiral, Sir," his comm officer said, and Than shook himself.

"Thank you, Raksmei," he said, and turned to face the comm display as Second Admiral Xing's face appeared on it.

"I told you they'd run!" she said exultantly.

"Yes, Ma'am. You were right," he said. "But I think it's a bit odd that they left it this late. I'd have expected—"

"They left it this late because it took them so long to see what's actually coming at them," Xing interrupted. "Check the timing, Than. They panicked and ran for it the instant they saw how strong we are!"

"I agree about the timing, but—"

"Their own message traffic confirms it. And not just Murphy's gutless 'covered by my orders running for my ass' announcement, either," Xing said triumphantly. "We picked up the local Fed potentate's reply to it." She smiled nastily. "He wasn't very happy with his federal governor."

"I don't imagine he was, Ma'am. I wouldn't be either, in his place. It's just that I would have expected a smarter deployment than this."

"That's because you give the Feds too much credit," Xing told him. "I told you Murphy wouldn't be out here if he wasn't a second-rater."

"It would appear you were correct," Than said. "Shall we go in pursuit and show him the error of his ways?"

"I'll take Alpha and Beta to deal with him. *You* continue on profile and deal with Crann Bethadh."

Than's jaw tightened.

"May I suggest keeping the fleet concentrated until we're positive Murphy's been taken care of, Ma'am?"

"Whatever for?" Xing sounded just short of incredulous. "You've got three FTLCs and their parasites in Gamma. That's more than enough to handle Crann Bethadh."

"I wasn't thinking about the planet, Ma'am. It's not going anywhere, so we can always come back and deal with it later. I was thinking about keeping our combat strength concentrated until Murphy's carriers have been destroyed. The engagement window's going to be—"

"There are *two* of them, Than," Xing said in the tone of someone speaking to a particularly dull child. "I'll have nine carriers. I know you don't think we've had enough time to drill adequately, and you may well be right. But I feel fairly confident even our people can win at five-to-one odds. And, of course," there was more than a little contempt in her smile on the comm display, "you'll have our best trained and most experienced ships to deal with the planet."

Than started to reply, then stopped himself as her eyes mocked him. He wondered if she thought he was as shallow as she was. It was so like her to cut him out of the command net for Dragon Fleet's first ship-to-ship engagement. To ensure that the only person credited for the crushing victory she anticipated was her.

But that wasn't all, of course. Oh no, not all. Leaving him behind to carry out exactly the kind of attack he'd argued so strenuously against gratified her sick-sadistic side, as well. She'd be off commanding in a decisive fleet battle while *he* was the one the Federation—and history—would remember as the "Butcher of Crann Bethadh."

And there was absolutely no point arguing further. It would only amuse her.

"Whatever you think best, Ma'am," he said instead.

"Excellent!" On the master plot, Dragon Alpha and Dragon Beta had already begun to separate from Than's task group as they resumed acceleration at their full 1,800 gravities while Beta continued to decelerate and the velocity differential built by 35.3 KPS every second. All of them would have to reduce to 900 gravities when they hit the Powell Limit, but that gave Xing ten and a half minutes to build additional overtake on Murphy at twice his own acceleration rate. "This shouldn't take too long, and then we can move on to our next target. Xing, clear."

❖   ❖   ❖

"I sure hope to hell your dad knows what he's doing, Callum," Dadyar Pêşrew said from Reactor Two's main comm display. "It's going to get kind of lonely around here if he doesn't."

"He knows what he's doing," Callum said—just a bit more confidently than he actually felt, if the truth be known. "Of course, there *is* that old saying about plans surviving contact with the enemy."

"You just *had* to add that, didn't you?"

"Well, it seemed best to lay out what Captain O'Hanraghty calls a 'sheet anchor.' After all, if we get blown up, I wouldn't want your last thought to be that I'd been wrong."

The comm circuit was open at Callum's end, and several people laughed out loud at that.

Their response was a far cry from the guarded attitude which had greeted him when he and Eira first reported aboard, and he wondered how much of that was because they, too, had figured out what Commander Seydel had called his father's "promise." And he wondered, sometimes, how *he* felt about the fact that she was probably at least partly right.

The notion that his own father had cold-bloodedly calculated that exposing him to death would be good for morale was ... chilling. But in another way, a way Callum was pretty sure wouldn't have occurred to him a few months ago, it was even more reassuring. Reassuring both as proof that Terrence Murphy the admiral would do whatever he had to do to win this battle and protect the people of Crann Bethadh, and as proof that Terrence Murphy the *father* believed his son had experienced and learned and grown enough to understand why that was. And to understand, if Callum did realize that was indeed the reason he'd been assigned to *Kolyma*, that his father the admiral had made the right call.

The crews of Drebin's purloined ships had arrived in New Dublin sullen and resentful. Angry because everyone condemned their squadrons' actions—or *in*actions—in Scotia. Resentful because their collective noses had been robbed in their "cowardice," when the decision to run the hell away hadn't even been theirs to make. And angry and resentful, most of all, because their actions had, in fact, *been* shameful. Because whoever had given the order, their honor had been fouled beyond recovery.

And Terrence Murphy was the one who'd demonstrated that.

It was Murphy who'd done the *right* thing in Scotia. The one who'd dragooned their ships and their personnel into doing their pitiful best to mitigate at least some of the damage and forced them to face the people whose families, whose *children*, they'd left to die. And it was Murphy who'd assumed command of their ships, dragged them off to Crann Bethadh, where the New Dubliners had made their own scorn and contempt for the cowards of Scotia abundantly clear. And so it was Murphy who was the avatar of all those tangled emotions—shame, humiliation, anger, resentment...

The list went on forever, and so it was little wonder they'd had reservations about Terrence Murphy's son.

But even before Callum had reported aboard *Kolyma*, the men and women of BatRon 702 and CruRon 960 had begun to find themselves once more. They'd realized—reluctantly, almost against their will—that Terrence Murphy was everything as a system governor that Yance Drebin had never been. And, they'd realized, he was giving them the chance to be everything *they* had never been—never been *allowed* to be—under Drebin's command.

If everything went exactly according to Murphy's plan, there was a very high chance some or all of them were about to die. They didn't like that, but they'd discovered there were things they liked even less. Like running away. Like abandoning civilians they were sworn to defend.

Like living with the shame of being the crews who had done that yet again.

"What the hell is a 'sheet anchor'?" Pêşrew demanded suspiciously.

"I dunno," Callum admitted.

"Pretty clear from context, Sir," Chief Pallares said. The Chief was in Reactor One, standing in for the extra commissioned engineering officer *Kolyma* was supposed to have, and tied into the same comm channel.

"Yeah?" Pêşrew growled.

"I'm pretty sure it means an ass cover, as in covering the Lieutenant's," Pallares said, and it was Callum's turn to laugh.

"But 'sheet anchor' sounds so much more *cultured*, Chief!" he protested.

"Hey, Sir, I'm just an ignorant Fringer," Pallares replied. "I don't know from cultured."

Callum laughed again, this time with a hidden edge of gratitude. Since Scotia and Inverness, he'd learned just how bitterly Fringers in general despised Heart Worlders. What was worse, he'd learned that their contempt for Heart Worlders—Heart Worlders just like Callum Jagadis Murphy had been before his father dragged him off to the Fringe—was totally, one hundred percent justified.

It burned, that lesson. It burned deep. He only had to look at Eira to see the cold, horrible proof of the consequences of Heart World... disengagement. And he knew he would never be able to make that up to her, however hard he tried. Nobody could. All they could do was learn from it and, as his father had always said, "drive on."

He didn't want to die any more than the crews of BatRon 702 and CruRon 960 did. He didn't want to do that to his mother, or to Reagan, and there were still a hell of a lot of things he wanted to do with his own life. But in an odd sort of way, if he did have to die here, he was... okay with that. At least he'd die doing what the damned, callous, cowardly, fucking ignorant Heart Worlders like Drebin *ought* to have been doing.

And maybe, just maybe, the fact that Fringers like Pallares were willing to jab him about the differences between them said they'd come to the conclusion that there was a difference between Callum Murphy and the Heart Worlders they had so much cause to hate.

He hoped so.

"Hell, Chief," he said now, "I figured that was probably the case, but then you went and used a word like 'context.' What kind of ignorant Fringer knows what *that* means?"

More chuckles rolled around the comm link, and Callum glanced over his shoulder.

Eira was there, floating at his back, the way she always did, alert-eyed and ready, even here. Getting her into Reactor Two at Action Stations had required a little finesse, since she was totally untrained for any power room duties. But she was basically a supernumerary, as far as *Kolyma*'s watch bill was concerned, so Seydel had signed off on letting Callum's guard dog follow him around. Lieutenant Commander McGhee, Seydel's XO, had actually even issued her a master-at-arms brassard, making her an official part of *Kolyma*'s onboard police force. That let her carry her sidearm openly, which made her happy.

Not that she wouldn't have figured out some way to carry it anyway, Callum thought with a hidden smile.

She sensed his gaze and looked at him, one eyebrow raised, and he shook his head with a "don't worry about it" expression. She regarded him doubtfully for another moment, then shrugged and returned to her protective stance.

"Well," Pêşrew said, "since the Chief has brought up the fact that we have a lot of ignorant Fringers aboard the ship, I suppose it wouldn't hurt anything to conduct a few drills for their edification while we wait for the ball to open. Lieutenant Murphy?"

"Yes, Sir."

"Reactor One has just taken a direct hit from a laser head, which makes you *Kolyma*'s sole source of power. This is an awesome responsibility, and you are about to be hit by a power surge, courtesy of Reactor One's damage. What do you intend to do about it?"

"Clancy, kill the circuit breakers! Isolate us from Reactor One!" Callum snapped without even consciously considering it. "Jacobson, reroute command inputs to my station. Shapiev—"

✧   ✧   ✧

The shock of recoil rippled against the soles of Lieutenant Commander Ulf Danielsen's space boots as yet another salvo of pods streaked out of Goibniu Alpha's launchers.

"Well, there goes the last one, Sir," Chief Petty Officer Ronin said at his elbow.

"Then we can begin abandoning now, Commander Danielsen?" Ian Markel asked. The mining executive's expression was strained, and one of his eyebrows twitched ever so slightly.

"You can pull the last of your people, Mr. Markel," Danielsen replied. "Just leave us the keys to the power rooms and the launchers."

"But like Chief Ronin says, that was the last launch!" Markel protested.

"The last one under Agincourt," Danielsen corrected. "We still have the reserve pods. Anyway—" he shrugged "—all the fire control links are right here on Alpha. If we have to do any corrections, this is where they'll come from."

"But—"

To Markel's credit, Danielsen thought, his concern over the naval personnel aboard his space stations was genuine. Of course, his concern over what would happen to those same space stations if Agincourt didn't work, or if the Leaguies figured out where the drones had come from, was even more genuine. Hard to blame him for that, though. The man had worked his entire life to build his corporation, and now it might all be about to go into the crapper.

On the other hand, Markel had a much better chance of all

his hard work and sweat *not* going into the crapper with Terrence Murphy calling the shots.

Danielsen had been one of the officers of TF 1705 who'd been more than a little doubtful about serving under a Survey officer. Survey was where the incompetents or the cowards went— everybody knew that.

But "everybody" had obviously been wrong about at least one Survey officer.

"Mr. Markel, we're shutting down all of our active emissions, so there's no reason the Leaguies should be looking in our direction. But if we have to go active with fire control commands, that may change. So go ahead and get your people out of here. They've all done great. From here on, it's up to the Navy."

"If you're sure, Commander?"

"I'm sure. And—" Danielsen grinned suddenly "—I solemnly promise we won't get it dinged or dented if we can help it!"

"Gee, thanks."

Markel actually managed a smile, but he also nodded and headed for the exit at a brisk walk, and Danielsen smiled at Ronin.

"Not such a bad old bastard, really, Sir," Ronin replied. The chief petty officer was a Heart Worlder who'd stayed in after serving her compulsory time as a conscript, and she'd seen a lot. "Gotta say, I prefer him to how some of the Hearts I can think of would've reacted in his place!"

"A point, Chief. Definitely a point," Danielsen conceded.

He crossed to the fire control station which had been spliced into Goibniu Alpha's central traffic control computer net. He was as confident as he could be about their installation, but that wasn't to say *totally* confident about it. It had performed up to specs in the trial runs, though, and the odds were that they weren't going to need to adjust the pods' firing orders significantly, anyway.

He rubbed one eyebrow as he looked at the tactical plot.

The last three waves of drones were clearly visible to his own sensors, building velocity at 3.9 KPS². That was only half of their maximum acceleration, using the Hauptman coils which had been incorporated into their design, which was low enough for them to be effectively invisible to League sensors at this range. They'd be cutting acceleration very soon, however. They were only running that hot to let them catch up with the drone swarm's initial launches.

There really wasn't a technical reason the highly modified drones *had* to be launched from the space station's launchers. The initial acceleration boost was the next best thing to infinitesimal compared to the acceleration their coils could sustain for up to ten hours before power exhaustion. But the old, repurposed launchers still had the original Navy fire control circuits and data uplinks, which had formed a critical component of Admiral Murphy's planning.

If they had to send in the reserve pods, they wouldn't be using the launchers. The reserve spotted in space around Goibniu Alpha would be less accurate without the pre-launch data uplinks to its payloads, and it would undoubtedly be fired off in a single strike, using its Hauptman coils from the start, because it wouldn't be the surprise Agincourt was going to be.

The surprise it's supposed *to be, Ulf,* he reminded himself. *Supposed to be.*

It was interesting, he thought. If Murphy pulled this off, he'd probably just revolutionized the strategy of star system defense, and it was so damned simple. Not cheap, but simple. Which was another excellent reason to keep the Leaguies from figuring out where the attack had come from. No point giving them breadcrumbs to how to do the same thing to the Federation down the road!

"Well, Evie," he said now. "In the words of every bad war holo ever made—'now we wait.'"

✧   ✧   ✧

"Point Luck in thirty seconds, Sir," Commander Mirwani announced, and Murphy looked at O'Hanraghty. *Ishtar* and *Gilgamesh* had been "running" for over an hour and ten minutes now, and their velocity was up to 60,000 KPS. The League carriers, on the other hand, were back up to 113,200, remorselessly eating away the empty space between them.

"Any sign of Hammer?"

"No, Sir." The chief of staff shook his head. "Well, that's not entirely true. We're picking up a little bit of a heat signature, but it's going to be harder than hell for the Leaguies to see even if they're looking for it. Which, I have to say, I don't think they are." He smiled nastily. "They're on almost exactly the pursuit vector you predicted."

"*We* predicted, Harry. *We* predicted," Murphy corrected almost absently, looking at the plot.

There hadn't really been a lot of prescience involved in that prediction, he reflected. Not if the League commander wanted to catch *Ishtar* and *Gilgamesh*, at least. But he'd counted on a smaller attack force, and he'd hoped the League commander would be smart enough to avoid splitting his force. If New Dublin's mobile defenders could be destroyed or driven off, Crann Bethadh could always be attacked later. So why dissipate his combat power when there was no need?

He'd planned his "escape vector" to tempt the RLH FTLCs into chasing him. After all, who could pass up taking out a pair of carriers? Of course, their vectors would intersect over 13.3 LM from Crann Bethadh, and the RLH's velocity relative to the planet—it's *passing* velocity relative to the planet—would be almost 120,000 KPS. No missile had the acceleration and endurance to kill a fraction of that much velocity, so until they could decelerate to rest and get back into effective range, Crann Bethadh and its people would be safe from them.

But that other damned force . . .

I should have shown him at least one more FTLC, he thought grimly. *At least one. I hadn't counted on his having so many carriers of his own that he wasn't* worried *about "dissipating" combat power to deal with "just two" of ours.*

"What's the status on their other force, Harry?" he asked quietly.

"Still decelerating," O'Hanraghty replied. "They're shooting for a perch ten light-minutes clear of Crann Bethadh. It's not perfect from Agincourt's viewpoint, but it's pretty damned good."

"But is Agincourt enough?" Murphy's voice was too low for anyone else to hear, and O'Hanraghty looked at him.

"I don't know," he said frankly. "But I do know these murderous bastards are about to get hurt one hell of a lot more than they ever anticipated. And at least we left an insurance policy behind."

Murphy winced inwardly at the reminder. But no trace of it reached his expression. He looked at Mirwani, and his voice was calm and confident.

"Deploy as planned, Raleigh."

"We'll have them in range in another twelve minutes, Second Admiral," Captain Rang said.

"Very good. Deploy the parasites." Xing Xuefeng smiled viciously. "It's time to show the Dragon's teeth."

That would play well for the video feeds, she thought, standing at the center of *Nüwa*'s flag bridge with her arms akimbo, right hand resting on the butt of her holstered pistol.

"At once, Ma'am."

The big carriers stopped accelerating, and fifteen seconds later, forty-eight *Huang Di*-class battleships and fifty *Hou Yi*-class battlecruisers erupted from her carriers' racks and accelerated outward into battle formation while the FTLCs *reversed* acceleration to stay clear of the combat. It was unlikely anything the two Federation carriers and their parasites had could have gotten past the ninety-eight capital ships she'd just deployed, but there was no point taking chances. No doubt the hypercautious Than would approve, she thought scornfully.

"Send 'Agincourt,' Lieutenant Mastroianni," Murphy said, his eyes on the master plot as the range dropped steadily.

The gap between *Nüwa* and the parasites had grown swiftly as they continued ahead ballistically and the carrier force decelerated at 8.83 KPS^2, and Xing split her attention between the chronometer and the plot as the minutes trickled by. The Feds would be deploying their own parasites soon. They had to if they had any hope at all of surviving her own ships' torrent of missiles. Not that they would, whatever they did. It was all a matter of numbers, and the numbers were on her side. In about—

"Hauptman signature!" her tracking officer snapped suddenly. She wheeled toward the lieutenant commander, her expression incredulous.

"They can't be launching yet!" she snapped.

"No, Ma'am," Commander Jiang looked up, her eyes wide. "I just caught a flicker of it. It looks more like a drone signature than a missile."

"Drones? Out *here*?"

"Yes, Ma'am. Almost directly astern of us."

Xing frowned. That was ridiculous. The only way drones could be directly in her decelerating carriers' path was for Murphy to have launched them a good fifteen minutes earlier, and why would he have done that? Or had he simply dropped them as he ran and let her catch up to them? But that didn't make any sense, either. It wasn't—

"Missile launch!" Jiang screamed. *"Range two-hundred-fi—"*
The universe exploded.

✧   ✧   ✧

The weapons system Terrence Murphy had cobbled together was big, ugly, and ungainly. Its descent from the old Mark 37 was plain to anyone who looked, but it was twenty-five meters longer than even the Mark 37 had been. It retained the same cross-section, but New Dublin Extractions' engineers had wanted more capacity, so they'd significantly reengineered the forward hull. Murphy had proposed his own alterations to it, and the result was a self-propelled "cargo drone" loaded with three of the TFN's Bijalee shipkiller missiles.

The New Dublin yards had worked round the clock, cranking out both the modified cargo drones and the missiles to go into them. Manufacturing his own ordnance without express authorization from the Oval violated at least six regulations, two of which were theoretically punishable by death—a point Captain Lipshen had been at some pains to include in his reports to the IG. Murphy understood why the Navy might be reluctant to let Fringe systems manufacture state-of-the-art weaponry. One never knew when one of them might decide it had finally had enough and go "out of compliance." Giving it the means to shoot back when the Navy and Marines moved in to show the error of its ways would probably come under the heading of a bad thing.

That didn't mean they didn't have the *means* to *manufacture* them, however, and the upgraded yard facilities in New Dublin had torn into the task with a will once they realized he was serious. Their repurposed, reprogrammed automated production lines had also started building them well over four months ago, and *Ishtar* and *Gilgamesh* had each docked a pair of cargo pods on two of their parasite racks. Each pod contained one hundred and thirty-two of the modified drones, and Murphy had deployed all five hundred and twenty-eight of them at "Point Luck," programmed to hold their fire until the range dropped to 250,000 kilometers. If the League carriers followed doctrine, they would deploy their parasites well before that point . . . and they had.

Which meant the pods were *between* the parasites—and all of their missile defense systems—and the FTLCs of Dragon Alpha and Dragon Bravo.

✧   ✧   ✧

Fifteen hundred missiles exploded into Xing Xuefeng's face. None of them carried electronic warfare or penaid warheads. Every one of the Bijalees mounted either a laser or a kinetic warhead, and their sensors had been uncaged and tracking on passive from the moment the pods launched.

At such short range and with such a massive rate of closure—Xing's carriers would overrun the pods in little more than two seconds—a high degree of accuracy was unlikely. On the other hand, Xing had been right about its being a matter of numbers.

She'd simply been wrong about whose side they were on.

The FTLCs' missile defense crews had been given no more time to train together than the rest of Dragon Fleet's personnel. It didn't really matter, though, because even if they'd been as superbly trained as Than Qiang's crews, there was literally no time to react. If Xing had taken the precaution of bringing her missile defenses online, the computers might have had time to knock down at least some of the incoming fire, but she'd known she was safely outside the despised Feds' range. Her merely human crew people were like Commander Jiang. They had time—barely, fleetingly—to realize what had come for them, and then it was upon them.

Bijalee meant "lightning bolt" in Hindi, and Terrence Murphy's lightning bolts lived up to their name in that terrible instant.

Eight hundred and twelve laser heads detonated as one, driving their bomb-pumped lasers deep into ships' hulls and the human beings within them. Seven hundred and eighty-four nuclear warheads attacked a tiny sliver of a second later. Sixteen of them actually achieved kinetic kills; the others detonated in fusion-fueled proximity bubbles of hell, and Dragon Fleet blazed like tinder at the heart of a furnace.

There was no time for evasion, no time for active defenses—no time to even secure combat harnesses—and the massively armored, six-kilometer-long ships heaved like wind-sick galleons in the maw of a hurricane.

Hulls shattered, atmosphere spewed through gaping rents, weapons and sensors and parasite racks were swept away, splintered, turned into shrapnel and debris, and the merely mortal human beings in destruction's path were blotted away like moths in a blowtorch.

It happened so quickly that most of the dead died unknowing, but they were the lucky ones. The ones who didn't find themselves trapped in shattered compartments, bleeding out with no one to help. The ones who weren't immolated as flash fires swept through before the air could vent. Who weren't caught in depressurizing compartments without their helmets because, like their admiral, they'd known they were out of the Feds' reach. And the ones who weren't hurled from their feet, thrown out of their command chairs, to break arms and legs—or shatter spines and skulls—as the brutal concussion bled through their ships' bones.

The carriers *Ao Ch'in*, *XieZhi*, *Huánglóng*, *Shu*, and Xing's old flagship *Chen Qingzhi* died almost instantly. *Xuánwǔ* seemed undamaged for a moment, but then her entire hull disintegrated in a chain fire ripple of internal explosions. *Báilóng* coasted ballistically on into the depths of interstellar space, her Fasset drive shattered and seventy percent of her crew dead.

Only *Nüwa* and *Pangu* actually survived. More wrecks than starships, perhaps, but they survived, with their Fasset drives online.

✧   ✧   ✧

Xing Xuefeng dragged herself back to her feet, left arm hanging broken at her side, blood streaming from a gash in her scalp, and stared at the hideous plot with disbelieving eyes. Both task groups, shattered—not broken; *shattered*—in less than a heartbeat. It was impossible.

Nüwa's displays flickered as whole quadrants went dead, and the damage control schematic was a lurid sea of crimson. There were far too many damage codes for Xing to absorb, but she didn't have to. Even her surviving carriers were little more than shambling wrecks.

"Maximum deceleration," she heard her voice say. No one answered. "Rang! Damn it, I said maximum de—"

She turned furiously toward her chief of staff and stopped in mid-word. Rang Yong-Gi hadn't been strapped into his seat, either. He'd gone headfirst into his console, and his shattered skull lolled at an impossible angle.

Xing clawed her way to the command deck comm panel across a flag bridge littered with motionless bodies and others that writhed and screamed. She slammed her good hand down on the screen, and it came to life.

"Captain Ding!" she snapped.

"I'm—I'm afraid the Captain is dead, Second Admiral," a lieutenant Xing had never met said. "I think—" The young woman paused and shook her head like a fighter who'd just been punched. "I think I have the conn, Ma'am."

"Come to one-nine-zero, one-eight-zero and take us to maximum deceleration!" Xing said.

"But, Ma'am ... the parasites ..."

"The parasites are on their own," Xing grated. "We don't have the racks to recover them. And even if we did, we can't risk running into another ambush trying to! Is that *understood*, Lieutenant?"

"Yes ... yes, Ma'am."

"Then do it. And do we have a comm officer?"

"Chief Petty Officer Xun has the duty, Ma'am. I'm afraid Comman—"

"Yes! Yes, I understand," Xing interrupted. "Have him patch me through to Fourth Admiral Xie."

✧　　✧　　✧

Fourth Admiral Xie Peng stared at his tactical plot aboard the battleship *Tǔdìshén* in horror. One instant, that display had shown two full carrier squadrons. The next ... carnage. How in the names of all the gods had the Feds *done* it? First they'd intercepted and destroyed the singularity manifolds for the rest of Dragon Fleet's carriers, and now *this*! Who *was* this Murphy and what daemon had spawned him?!

He needed the answers to those questions, and he needed them badly, because *Tǔdìshén* was the flagship of BatRon 183, *Nüwa*'s senior squadron. That made Xie the parasite force's tactical commander, and now that their carriers had been smashed—

"Sir, the Second Admiral is asking for you." His communications officer sounded as numb with shock as Xie felt.

"Of course," Xie said.

He was surprised Xing was still alive, given how badly *Nüwa* had been pounded. The FTLC's acceleration was down, suggesting she'd taken Fasset damage, and she was haloed in venting atmosphere that indicated heavy hull breaching. But it would seem her flag bridge had been spared. He was a bit ambivalent about that, because he really wasn't looking forward to Xing's orders. Unfortunately, he had no choice about hearing them, and he moved to the command ring on *Tǔdìshén*'s flag bridge.

"Fourth Admiral," Xing said, the instant she saw him. "It's imperative that you continue the attack. Press it home! The Fed carriers *cannot* be allowed to escape. Is that clear?"

The range was over two light-seconds by now, and she wiped blood from her forehead while she waited out the transmission lag.

"Of course, Ma'am," Xie replied. "But how are we going to recover our sublight units?"

"We can't," Xing said harshly, five seconds later. "*Nüwa* and *Pangu* may have three operable racks between them, but I doubt it. We have to get both of them clear and back to base for repairs."

"But if you can't recover us...?" Xie's voice trailed off.

"We can't recover you *now*," Xing said. "But I have your vector. I'll send a relief force to recover your ships—or at least your personnel—as soon as I return to Diyu. You have more than enough life support and onboard endurance to carry you over until we can find you and bring you home."

Xie stared at her, wondering if she realized how insane she sounded. And wondering even more strongly if she was mad enough to expect him to believe a word of that. The only intact carriers Dragon Fleet had were Third Admiral Than's, and he didn't have a fraction of the lift capacity—or life support—to recover Xie's ships and people.

"I know this isn't what we expected," Xing went on, "but I'm depending on you, Peng. The entire *League* is depending on you. I know you won't let us down."

"Of course not, Ma'am," Xie said. It was all he *could* say.

"Good man! And now, I'm afraid I have to go. We're all a little...busy over here."

The comm display blanked.

The whoops and cheers aboard TFNS *Ishtar* pummeled Terrence Murphy with hammers of sound as the tactical displays filled with the sheer devastation of the drones' Alpha strike. He stared at the master plot while Harrison O'Hanraghty pounded him on the back.

"*Seven* of them!" the chief of staff shouted in his ear. "*Seven* of the bastards—total kills! My God, Terry! *Seven!*"

Murphy nodded, still trying to process it himself, and a part of him cringed as he thought of the nine or ten thousand men and women he'd just killed.

"And it looks like the survivors got hammered, too. Look at those accel numbers! The Leaguies haven't had their ass kicked like this in *decades!*" O'Hanraghty exulted. "This was a war-changer!

We just turned their entire grand strategy on its head! This was their Sunday punch, their decisive surprise, the knife that was going to stab us in the back, and you just ripped the *guts* right out of it! They'll *never* recover from this!"

"Maybe," Murphy said, watching the two badly damaged survivors change vector as they clawed away from New Dublin. They'd stay just outside Hammer Force's envelope, despite their damages, he saw. Pity about that. And in the meantime...

"You may be right about all that, Harry," he said. "However, we still have a minor problem."

He flicked a finger at the forest of icons still sweeping toward them across the plot. No sublight unit could match an FTLC's acceleration, but they didn't have to. They had so much overtake velocity they couldn't have *not* cut across *Ishtar*'s wake if they'd wanted to. And between them, those ninety-eight ships had enough missile launchers to do to Murphy's carriers what he'd just done to theirs. That had always been a possibility.

"Then I think you'd better speak to them," O'Hanraghty said. "And they ought to be seeing Granger and Tremblay about now."

"Yes, I imagine they are." Murphy smiled thinly. "Lieutenant Mastroianni, please raise the League senior officer for me."

❖   ❖   ❖

"Where did *they* come from?" Xie Peng's chief of staff demanded. "They can't *be* here!"

Xie looked at him sideways. Commander Ye was a good man, under most circumstances.

"I don't imagine we'd like the answer to that question if we knew what it was," the fourth admiral said after a moment. "It's hard to see how it makes our situation a lot worse, though."

He looked at the plot, where five new, undamaged *Federation* FTLCs had just lit off their Fasset drives. They were well outside any range at which they could have fired upon him, but they also had unlimited acceleration two thousand times higher than anything his crews could survive. And he very much doubted that their parasite racks were empty.

There's no way we can outrun them, but Xing *certainly can,* he thought bitterly, watching *Nüwa*'s receding icon in the plot. *And unless—*

"Excuse me, Fourth Admiral," *Tŭdìshén*'s communications officer said.

"Yes, Sun?" Xie Peng managed to not rip the man's head off.

"Sir, I have a message for you. It's . . . it's from the Fed admiral. From Admiral Murphy."

Xie looked at the lieutenant for a long, still moment. Then his nostrils flared.

"Put it on my display. Audio to my earbud only."

"Yes, Sir!"

A strong-jawed, sandy-haired *gwáilóu* appeared on Xie's display. The gray eyes were remarkably hard and steady.

"I am Admiral Terrence Murphy," the recorded message said. "I have just destroyed or crippled your entire FTLC element. You have no way home, and I doubt very much that there are sufficient carriers at your secret building facility to come and collect you even if your commanders cared enough about you to do it. I imagine that by now you're picking up the Fasset signatures of my other carriers, however. We *do* have the capacity to rescue all of your personnel. Or to hunt you down and destroy you to the last ship. And given what I'm sure you were planning to do to New Dublin, that is very tempting at the moment.

"So here's my offer. You will not fire on my ships as you pass. Instead, you will jettison every missile and drone aboard *your* ships. After that, you will decelerate, by squadrons, so that each squadron is separated by a minimum of one light-second. And then you will surrender your ships to my boarding parties without resistance, as we close with each squadron in turn.

"You don't have to do any of those things, and you can undoubtedly inflict severe damage on the two carriers in front of you, if that's what you choose to do. If you do, however, I promise you, not a man or woman under your command will survive."

Those agate-hard gray eyes bored into him, and there was no question in Xie's mind. This was the man who'd rescued the tattered survivors of Xing's butchery in Scotia. The man who'd somehow found and destroyed the last critical component of Dragon Fleet's construction. And the man who had—somehow—just orchestrated an impossible massacre of Dragon Fleet's completed carriers.

He meant every word, and his voice was chilled steel as he finished.

"The choice is yours."

❖ CHAPTER THIRTY-TWO ❖

"DEPLOY THE DRONES," THAN SAID.

The RLH was less copiously provided with reconnaissance platforms than the Federation. It was a weakness he'd raised several times with the Admiralty's operational analysts, but they preferred to concentrate on attack and missile defense platforms. A *Sun Tzu*-class FTLC like *Cai Shen* carried ten drones (Hauptman coil drones tended to be big, so no one could carry a lot of them), only one of them a Wàngyuǎnjìng "spyglass" platform, optimized for the recon mission. Sublight battleships carried two Wàngyuǎnjìngs apiece, but that was mostly because their fusion drives lacked both the acceleration and the endurance of a Fasset-drive starship. Because they were so much slower and shorter-legged, they were provided with more spies they could send out ahead, so his embarked capital ships would give him over seventy-two more of them... eventually.

At the moment, however, all of his parasites were still on their racks. They lacked the fuel to brake from the sorts of velocities Fasset-drive ships handled with ease, and he had no intention of launching them until his FTLCs had decelerated to rest relative to Crann Bethadh. Nor did he plan on sending them in until he knew exactly what they were looking at in the inner system. That was why the ops plan he'd finally gotten Xing to accept called for staying ten light-minutes out until they'd swept the area around Crann Bethadh thoroughly, which brought him back to his dearth of Wàngyuǎnjìngs. Until the parasites did launch, their drones were inoperable. which restricted him to only the three of his own *Cai Shen* and her sisters *Sun Bin* and *Li Shiji*.

The Wàngyuǎnjìng, unfortunately, had a shorter operational radius than the Heimdallar, its TFN equivalent. The big Federation drone was a more modern—and expensive—design, good for almost twelve hours of acceleration, while the Wàngyuǎnjìng could manage only seven. That made RLH commanders wary of spending any more of that endurance than they had to, but in this case Than could be as tightfisted with it as he liked, because his target wasn't going anywhere.

The drones separated from their motherships and continued ballistically toward Crann Bethadh at just over 22,850 KPS while the carriers continued to decelerate at 900 gravities. Deceleration to rest relative to their objective would cost the drones forty-nine minutes of their endurance, and Dragon Gamma was 11.56 LM from the planet, so they would coast ballistic for just over two hours before they began braking.

"The Second Admiral's caught them by now, Sir," Su Zhihao observed quietly from beside him. Than looked at him, and the chief of staff scowled. His eyes were on the time display. They wouldn't know the final results for at least another thirty or forty minutes, but Xing must have crossed Murphy's wake five minutes ago.

"It ought to've been us, Sir," Su said with low-voiced bitterness. "It should've been *you*. You're the one who created Dragon Fleet. And instead of letting you lead it in battle, she's turned you into her butcher. She'll get all the credit for the campaign, and you'll be the one who gets blamed for all the blood."

"That's enough, Zhihao." Than kept his own voice low, but his tone was sharp. The chief of staff looked at him rebelliously, and Than shrugged. "We can't change it. We can only do our duty. And after almost sixty years there's been plenty of butchery to go around, hasn't there? What's one more slaughtered planet?"

Su started to reply quickly, then clenched his jaw and nodded.

"Of course, Sir. I should know by now that justice is an abstract concept."

✧   ✧   ✧

"Signal from Admiral Murphy, Sir," PO 1/c Santolaria announced, and Lieutenant Commander Danielsen looked up from the plot the Crann Bethadh shipyard techs had installed aboard Goibniu Alpha.

"It's Agincourt!" Santolaria said.

"Well, then." Danielsen set down his coffee cup with deliberate calm. Then he looked at Ronin. "Are we queued up, Chief?"

"Yes, Sir. The geometry's not perfect, but it's gonna be pretty damned good," the CPO replied in a tone of profound satisfaction. "We're looking at a...four-point-five-minute burn on the pods, so they'll see them coming. Don't know how much *good* it'll do them, though." She flashed a sharklike smile. "They're still decelerating, and their parasites are still on the racks. Not much missile defense there!"

"Just between you and me, Chief, I'm glad we didn't have to fire before the Admiral was ready. Let's send the update and enable the birds."

"Aye, aye, Sir!" Ronin said with a huge and hungry smile.

"We've just picked up something...odd, Sir."

"Odd?" Than turned from the plot. "What do you mean, Zhihao?"

Dragon Gamma had deployed the Wàngyuǎnjìngs eight minutes earlier, and the chief of staff was frowning again. This time with a puzzled expression.

"It was a burst transmission, Sir. Murphy must've sent it eight or nine minutes before the Second Admiral engaged him, and he sent it in the clear."

"In the clear?" Something twanged deep inside Than. A signal from Murphy in the final minutes before he was attacked by an overwhelming force? What could have been so important...?

"Yes, Sir. We're not sure who it was addressed to—at that range, there's so much signal spread it could've been almost anybody—and there wasn't any header or address. In fact, it was just one word. Or, I assume it's a word, anyway."

"You *assume* it's a word?"

"Well, if it is, it's not in any language I've ever heard of."

"What is it?" Than asked a bit impatiently.

"It's nine characters, Sir—Roman alphabet: A-G-I-N-C-O-U-R-T."

Than blinked.

"That's gibberish," he said. "Could it be some sort of letter substitution code?"

"I don't know. Lieutenant Hu is running it through the computers, but so far, nothing."

Than rubbed his chin, frowning intently, then jerked upright and turned to Lieutenant Commander Yuan, Dragon Gamma's ops officer.

"Stop decelerating," he said. "I want an alpha launch on the parasites right now."

"Now, Sir?"

Yuan sounded surprised. Dragon Gamma was still almost two million kilometers short of its planned attack point, with 5,636 KPS of velocity yet to kill.

"*Now.*" Than's tone was sharper than it had been. "Murphy wasn't sending anyone love letters just before Xing blew his ships out of space! One word—or whatever the hell that was—isn't a message, anyway. It's an *execute code.*"

Yuan looked at him for a moment, then started barking orders over his comm. Status lights flashed and changed on the readiness boards as *Cai Shen*, *Sun Bin*, and *Li Shiji* abruptly killed their Fasset drives and the parasites rocketed from their racks eleven minutes earlier than planned. They exploded into space, accelerating away from the suddenly ballistic carriers at ten gravities. An alpha launch was an emergency maneuver Than's people had drilled upon exhaustively, and the plot was abruptly speckled with diamond dust as they deployed their defensive drones.

Su watched the boards, then looked at Than.

"What *kind* of an execution code, Sir?" he asked.

"I don't know." Than scowled.

"A trap of some kind?" Su rubbed his beard, eyes worried.

"I don't know," Than repeated. "And if there is one, I can't think of any sane reason for someone to try to coordinate it—tie it to an execute order—from half a light-hour away!"

"Maybe they've scraped up another clutch of missiles, like the one they used against our last attack?" Su rubbed his beard harder. "No. That doesn't make any sense. We're still way too far out—their birds would take over twenty minutes to reach us!"

Than nodded. That was exactly what New Dublin had done to the last League attack, but they'd only gotten away with it because Commodore Yao had been an idiot who'd charged straight in on a least-time course and run directly into the missile swarm's path. But Su was right about their flight time, and they'd be ballistic from the moment their Hauptman coils burned out, sixty seconds after launch, until their fusion drives cut in, three minutes from target. That would give Dragon Gamma seventeen minutes to evade at 900 gravities, which meant they could dodge any missile strike from Crann Bethadh with ludicrous ease.

"I don't know," he said a third time, "but whatever it is, I'm not letting them catch us with our trousers around our ankles." He watched the sublight ships, spreading out in a protective hemisphere between their carriers and the inner system. "Maybe I'm worrying over nothing, but we've got plenty of time and distance to work with, and I'm not rushing into anything, at least until we've heard from Admiral Xing. Which—" he looked at the time display "—ought to be in about another four minutes."

"It just seems like such a...crazy thing for Murphy to be doing at a time like this," Su said.

"I know," Than said grimly. "That's why it worries me, I—"

"Third Admiral!"

It was Yuan, and Than whirled at the raw shock—the horror—in the lieutenant commander's voice. He opened his mouth... and froze, his own eyes flaring wide as he saw the master plot.

The green icons labeled *Au Ch'in*, *XieZhi*, *Chen Qingzhi*, *Huánglóng*, *Shu*, *Xuánwǔ*, and *Báilóng* had vanished. They were simply...gone. Only *Nüwa*, *Pangu*, and the deployed parasites of Dragon Alpha and Beta remained, and the FTLCs' vectors shifted as he watched them begin accelerating desperately away from the two ships they'd pursued for the last two hours.

"What the hell did they *do*?" Than demanded.

"We...we don't know," Yuan said. "It just...happened."

"The long-range sensors didn't see *anything*?"

"We didn't see a thing on passives, Sir." Yuan sounded stunned. "Not a *thing*. Until ...this."

He tapped a replay command, and Than's blood turned to ice as a sudden, brutal, utterly cataclysmic flash of massed nuclear detonations devoured the space around Xing's carriers like a brief-lived sun. It was like an old-fashioned photographer's flashgun glaring in space—that fast, and that sudden—and then only *Nüwa* and *Pangu* remained.

Missiles. It had to have been missiles. They wouldn't have picked up Hauptman signatures at this range. But how had *Xing* missed them? For that matter, she'd had her parasites deployed. How the *hell* had the Feds gotten an alpha strike *that* devastating past the sublight ships without their killing a single missile?

Without the parasites sucking up a single one of them before the carriers got hit? That was—

It happened half an hour ago, a small voice said in the back of his brain. *Half an* hour *ago. You can't let it paralyze you* now, *Qiang!*

He was a naval officer. He'd spent his entire professional career adjusting for the delays in light-speed signals and sensor data. But it had never hit him this hard, he realized.

"I think it may be a good thing you launched the parasites," Captain Su said beside him.

"It doesn't look like it did Xing any good," Than observed harshly.

"No, but *you're* not her," the chief of staff said.

"Maybe not, but—"

Than chopped himself off and shook his head to clear his brain.

"Be sure this gets passed on to all of our sublight units," he said more crisply. "Tell them we don't know exactly how it happened, but all of them need to be on their toes."

"Yes, Sir!"

"And then you and I need to start looking at all our options," Than said in a lower tone. Su looked at him for a moment, then nodded. *Nüwa* might have survived; that didn't necessarily mean *Xing* had, and if Than was now in command of what remained of Dragon Fleet...

"Understood, Sir," he said, equally quietly.

✧   ✧   ✧

"Third Admiral, we have a transmission," Commander Vang said. "It's from Second Admiral Xing—personal to you. Your eyes only."

Than looked up from his conversation with Su. Six minutes had passed since the light-speed sensor data of Dragon Alpha and Beta's destruction had come in. He glanced at his chief of staff, then nodded to the comm officer.

"On my display," he said curtly, dropping into his command chair. Su started to turn away, but Than shook his head quickly, and the chief of staff stopped.

Xing Xuefeng appeared on the small comm display at Than's station. Her hair was thick and clotted with blood, one cheek was already bruised and swelling, and her eyes were wild.

"It was a trap!" she said without preamble. "They lured us

across some kind of deployed missile field. Our idiot captains never even saw it coming! I've ordered Xie to finish off their carriers, but *Nüwa* and *Pangu* are severely damaged. They can't recover the parasites, and I've got to get the two of them back to Diyu for repairs. I'm leaving you in command. Take out their fucking planet—burn it to the damned *ground*; I don't want anything but *slag* down there when you're done!—and then see what you can do about picking up as many of Xie's people as you can. Xing, out."

The display blanked. Than's jaw clenched, and he heard Su inhale sharply beside him.

"Sir," the chief of staff said, "there's no way we can recover all those ships. Even if we had the racks or the life support for it, we—"

"Fasset signatures!" Yuan interrupted suddenly from Tracking, and Than turned sharply. "*Five* Fasset signatures," the ops officer continued. "They just turned up."

Than looked at the plot. There weren't two Federation FTLCs on it anymore. There were *seven*.

"That's not possible, Sir," Su Zhihao said very, very softly. "*Seven* Fed carriers in a single Fringe system like New Dublin? It's got to be something else, some kind of trick. Freighters *pretending* to be carriers, maybe?"

"And where would seven *freighters* have come from in New Dublin?" Than asked while his own brain fought to process the information overload.

"But if Murphy had seven of them, why leave five of them all the way the hell and gone out there?" the captain demanded.

"I don't know where he got them, but they aren't 'all the way the hell and gone out there.' They're exactly where he ran to from the very beginning, and they're outside the Powell Limit, where they can pull their full accel. Xing was right. It *was* a trap." Than frowned intensely, watching new vectors project themselves into the plot, then nodded. "He wanted to draw us away from Crann Bethadh. And that's what he did, with Alpha and Beta, at least. They never came into attack range of the planet, so they couldn't even punch missiles past him at it ballistic. It didn't work perfectly—it looks like *Nüwa* and *Pangu* can still evade them—but it was damned well good enough. And look at the math. At eighteen hundred gees, they can get outside us and intercept *us* before we wormhole if we don't pull out within the next hour or so."

"But if we hadn't taken the bait..." Su said slowly. "He left Crann Bethadh totally undefended, if we didn't chase him!"

"*Not* chase a pair of Fed carriers?" Than snorted. "When was the last time you saw a League commander who wouldn't put catching carriers ahead of K-striking a raggedy Fringe planet he could always come back and kill later? And if *I'd* been in command, it would've worked."

His voice was flat. Su's eyes narrowed in protest and the chief of staff opened his mouth, but Than cut him off.

"Of course it would have!" he said bitterly. "I tried to talk Xing into keeping our carriers concentrated, and if she'd agreed, we'd have gotten hammered right along with her."

"So the glory-hunting bitch finally did something right," Su said.

"One way to put it, and for all the wrong reasons. But—" Than's gaze sharpened "—you're right. If we hadn't taken the bait, Crann Bethadh would be totally undefended. Unless it isn't."

"Sir?" Su's tone was game, but he was clearly falling astern of his admiral.

"The man who could put this together *wouldn't* have left Crann Bethadh undefended," Than said. "So what did he do inst—"

"Hauptman signatures!" Lieutenant Commander Yuan said suddenly. "*Many* Hauptman signatures! Zero-zero-two, zero-zero-five, range one-four-point seven million kilometers. Velocity two-two-eight thousand KPS, acceleration eight-zero-zero gravities and closing!"

✧   ✧   ✧

Than Qiang was right: Terrence Murphy's plan *hadn't* worked perfectly.

It had only worked far better than he'd truly expected it to when he put it together with O'Hanraghty.

In a perfect universe, all of Dragon Fleet's FTLCs would have pursued *Ishtar* and *Gilgamesh* and been mousetrapped. Whether the sudden, surprise attack would have been equally destructive, spread across all twelve of Xing's carriers, was another question. It would still have been devastating, though, and the hidden carriers of Hammer Force would have been there to sweep up the pieces if they kept coming.

But that wasn't the only operational alternative he'd put together. If there'd been fewer League carriers, he would have stood his ground with *Ishtar* and *Gilgamesh*, using their cargo pods of drones to thicken the fire from Goibniu. In that case, he would have tried to hit them farther out, and then brought Granger and Tremblay in from the perimeter to cut off their retreat.

He hadn't quite dared to risk that against *twelve* FTLCs. The odds were too good that at least some of them—or their parasites—would survive to launch a devastating ballistic strike against Crann Bethadh. And he'd been as confident as Than that no RLH admiral worth his stars would pass up the chance to use all his own FTLCs to run down and destroy two of the Federation's.

Second Admiral Xing's ambition—and pettiness—had prevented that, which meant the "insurance policy" Murphy had hoped never to use had become Crann Bethadh's last hope. The Goibniu space stations hadn't launched as many drones as *Ishtar* and *Gilgamesh* had dropped in Dragon Alpha and Beta's path. Partly because they didn't have all that many launchers, but also because for all of New Dublin's enthusiasm and tireless labor, Murphy simply didn't have as many of them as he would have liked.

So the space stations had deployed "only" three hundred and twenty of them, but they'd been launched in staggered waves. The leading wave had accelerated at two hundred gravities after launch; the final wave had accelerated at eight, then decelerated once they caught up with the leaders. All three hundred had matched velocity just over eight light-minutes from launch, one light-minute outside Crann Bethadh's orbit, at a final velocity of 47,533 KPS.

They'd reached that point thirty-nine minutes before Xing encountered their brothers and sisters, then continued coasting outward. If everything had gone perfectly, Danielsen would have launched on his own as the drones came into the powered range of their Bijalees just before Than had decelerated *almost* to rest and been *almost* ready to deploy his parasites, at which point his carriers would have been as exposed as Xing's had been.

But Murphy had known Than's passive sensors would detect what happened to Xing at almost the same instant Danielsen's did... and it would take at least sixteen minutes for Lieutenant

Commander Danielsen's launch order to catch up to the drones. Unless he was an idiot, the League admiral would have deployed his parasites as soon as he was alerted to the danger, and so Murphy had sent the execute code six minutes before Xing's debacle. That should have put Danielsen inside the attackers' decision loop.

Unfortunately for the Terran Federation that day, Than Qiang's instincts were too good for that.

✧ ✧ ✧

Three hundred and twenty modified drones went to eight hundred gravities as they lunged at Dragon Gamma. That acceleration rate was lower than a Fasset-drive ship's, even here, deep inside New Dublin's Powell Limit. But their base closing velocity was already almost 48,000 kilometers per second, and it climbed by 7.84 KPS every second as they streaked toward Than's ships like homicidal meteors, pregnant with destruction.

But Dragon Gamma wasn't Alpha or Beta...and Than Qiang wasn't Xing Xuefeng. Most of his personnel had served under his command for years. They knew him, they trusted him. Unlike the green units Xing had thrown into battle, he had honed their skills like a master swordsmith, and—

"This is Admiral Than." The calm voice they knew and depended upon came over the all-ships channel. "You've all seen what happened to Admiral Xing. We don't know how they did it, but these must be some sort of missile carrier. It's possible what we're seeing *are* the missiles, but they look more like drone signatures. So they're probably going to launch standard Fed antiship missiles once we're inside the missiles' powered envelope. We're calling that three hundred and seventeen thousand kilometers from this closing velocity, so expect to see the actual attack birds in one hundred and eighty seconds from...mark." Digital time displays started ticking down aboard every one of his ships. "We'll go with Missile Defense Six. I say again, Missile Defense Six. Good luck, and may the gods be with us all. Than, clear."

✧ ✧ ✧

"About three minutes, Sir," Evie Ronin said, watching the time display.

"Yeah, and we won't know what happened for *fourteen* minutes," Danielsen said sourly.

"Can't help but be better than it would've been without us," Ronin pointed out.

"You got that right, Chief." Danielsen puffed out his cheeks, then shrugged. "Start prepping the reserve drones in case we need them."

"Aye, aye, Sir."

Ronin nodded, although neither of them said what both of them feared. If the reserve drones were needed, the surviving Leaguies would have over an hour and a half to wreck Crann Bethadh before they arrived.

✧   ✧   ✧

"Here they come," Captain Su murmured.

Than very much doubted that his chief of staff even realized he'd spoken aloud. Every eye on *Cai Shen*'s flag bridge was locked to the tactical display as the Federation drones swept toward them. It was difficult to get a precise count on the Hauptman signatures, partly because drones were designed to be stealthy, but mostly because they were so damned many of them the leaders kept blocking the sensors' look at the ones behind.

"Estimate missile launch . . . *now*," Lieutenant Commander Yuan said.

He was off by less than three seconds, and the display was suddenly a solid haze of the far brighter, stronger signatures of Bijalee missiles accelerating at three thousand gravities. They came at Dragon Gamma in a solid wall, like a blizzard driving into a ground car's headlights, but every one of *these* "snowflakes" was tipped with a laserhead of thermonuclear death.

Nine hundred and sixty missiles roared in—sixty-four percent of the missile storm which had greeted Second Admiral Xing, blazing in at the sort of closing speed even missile defense crews never saw and targeted on only three FTLCs and their brood of parasites, rather than Xing's eight.

Yet that was the difference, because these ships were *Than's* ships. And unlike Xing's, his battleships and battlecruisers were between his carriers and the threat. They'd seen it coming with over five minutes to prepare, not less than two seconds, and unlike Fourth Admiral Xie's crews, they were superbly trained and battle hardened, under an admiral who'd won their iron trust. There was plenty of fear aboard the ships, but no panic, and counter-missiles raced to meet the threat.

Contact kills spalled the incoming missile wall with shattered wreckage, laserhead counter-missiles flared like bubbles of brimstone, and proximity-fused nuclear warheads flashed like chinks in the gates of hell, killing Federation missiles in dozens and scores. But they came on in their *hundreds*, and many broke past the counter-missiles. Missile defense drones leapt to meet them, stabbing hedgehogs of lasers into the swarm. Shipboard point defense lasers—more powerful, more accurate, longer-ranged, but far less numerous—stabbed at the survivors with stilettos of coherent radiation, shattering missile fuselages, burning out targeting systems. And then the League warships quivered as the last-ditch autocannon tracked and went to continuous rapid fire.

It took only a minute for the missiles to complete their flight. Only sixty seconds. But those were sixty seconds of mad, whirling destruction, burning its way through the swarm of death like some vast blowtorch, and the eye-searing brilliance flashing and flaring in the visual displays was all the more terrifying for its total silence.

And then they struck, in a cacophony of rending, tearing destruction that shattered ships' hulls—and crews—like the toys of a petulant child.

❖   ❖   ❖

Cai Shen shuddered and bucked as bomb-pumped lasers seared deep into her. Modern armor was *tough*, with photon and heat-shedding layers of ceramic sandwiched in layers of the same super-collapsed material from which K-gun slugs were forged. But even the toughest armor had its limits. Alarms wailed, hull plating splintered, lurid icons blazed on Damage Control's displays, and the brutal concussion as air-filled compartments deep inside her core hull superheated and exploded shook her to the keel.

Admiral Than clung to his command chair's armrests, his expression tight, as the damage ripped into his flagship and she surged as she shot the rapids of destruction. He'd been in battle before, aboard ships which had taken enemy fire. This was worse than anything he'd ever endured, but at least it was mercifully quick. Before he had time to feel the true terror, it was over, and he heard the crackle of the damage control teams' terse chatter on the central circuits.

"Talk to me, Zhihao!" he snapped.

"We . . . got hit hard, Sir," Su said. He'd already unstrapped from his chair and stood at Yuan's shoulder, peering intently at Tracking's detailed plot, and his tone was grim. "I think we've lost over half the parasites. Looks like at least a dozen others are total write-offs, too. And *Sun Bin's* Fasset drive is down. It looks bad. I don't think their damage control parties will be able to put it back online. But—" he looked over his shoulder at Than "—both *Cai Shen* and *Li Shiji* are still operational!"

Than felt some of the iron tension leach out of his muscles, along with a spasm of guilt. Hundreds—thousands—of his personnel had just died. He had no right to feel *relief* because his carriers had survived. Well, *two* of them anyway; if *Sun Bin's* Fasset drive was down for good, she wouldn't be coming home with her sisters. Yet he did feel grateful. Because in the end, those two surviving carriers were the only way home for any of his people who *hadn't* died.

"We've lost two racks on *Li Shiji*, and *Cai Shen's* Number Two Rack's too badly damaged to recover, as well. It looks like we've probably got enough room for everyone who's left, though. And we should have enough enviro for all our survivors. Search and rescue is underway. I don't have any estimate on how long that's going to take. Not yet."

From Su's tone, he felt exactly what Than felt, and the third admiral smiled grimly at him.

"Shall I prep for planetary bombardment in the meantime, Sir?" Yuan asked diffidently, and Than met his chief of staff's gaze across the flag bridge.

Xing's orders had been clear enough, he thought as an inner tide of despair washed through him. And this time, after what had just happened to them, not even *his* people were likely to balk at killing a world.

But I will, he thought. *Oh, yes. I will—and I'm the one who still has to give the order.*

"I think we need to sort out the damage a bit further before we get into that," he said out loud, aware of his desperate need to delay that order as long as he could. "And—"

"Excuse me, Sir," Commander Vang interrupted. His tone was diffident but determined, and the Than looked at him with a raised eyebrow.

"We've just received another transmission, Admiral."

"From Second Admiral Xing?"

"No, Sir. From the Feds. They transmitted in the clear. They say it's Admiral Murphy."

Than's jaw tightened and he glanced at Su yet again. Then he nodded to the comm officer.

"Put it through," he said.

A sandy-haired, gray-eyed man in a TFN vac suit appeared on Than's display.

"My name is Terrence Murphy," he said in a clear, calm Heart World accent's clipped final consonants. "I presume I'm speaking to the senior surviving League officer. If so, I have a message for you. By now you know what happened to your other carriers. What you don't know yet is that Fourth Admiral Xie has surrendered his entire command to me."

The face on the display gave a thin smile, and Than inhaled sharply. Surrendered? Xie had *surrendered*?

"I trust you won't think too harshly of him," Murphy continued. "He was out of good options. I don't want to speak ill of anyone's officer corps, but if pressed, I'd have to say he doesn't seem very fond of your Second Admiral Xing." The thin smile morphed into something much more like bared fangs and the gray eyes turned cold. "I see she's come up in the world since our last intelligence report on her, and I'm looking forward to the day I meet the Second Admiral in person. I have a few things to discuss with her about her heroic actions and a planet called Inverness."

The searing contempt in that cultured voice bit deep.

"At the moment, however, she appears to be running for her life. Obviously, at this range I can't yet know how badly you've been damaged by the inner system's defenses, but I'd be rather surprised if the answer isn't pretty damned bad. Given Xing's track record, I don't doubt her last order to you was to burn Crann Bethadh to the ground. Obviously, I can't stop you from doing that, if you're a sick enough bastard to emulate her. But know this before you do anything. I'm about to rescue something on the order of sixty-three thousand of your personnel, not counting whoever may still be alive aboard the hulk of the single one of your carriers which is still more or less intact, and I expect what's already happened here today to have . . . significant repercussions on the war in general. Ask yourself how you want your people treated. And how *you* want to be remembered when this is all over, because one way or another, whoever you are, you *will* be remembered. So think about that."

Those gray eyes bored into Than from the display for five more seconds. Then—

"Murphy, clear . . . for now."

CHAPTER THIRTY-THREE

"CLOSE THE HATCH," THAN SAID AS CAPTAIN SU FOLLOWED HIM into the small briefing room.

The chief of staff hit the button, then turned back to his admiral with worried eyes. Than started to speak, but Su held up a hand.

"Sir, before you say anything, I know you, and I know what you're thinking, but I've also come to know Xing. If you don't strike Crann Bethadh, she *will* demand your head."

"I know." Than folded his arms and leaned back against the bulkhead, his expression tight. "I know she will. But if I do what she wants, what happens to Xie's people? For that matter, you know we don't have time to recover all our own people from the wrecked ships. What happens to *them*? If we K-strike Crann Bethadh the way Xing wants, our people—Gamma's people—will be the 'war criminals,' not Xing, as far as the Federation is concerned. What happens to any of them we leave behind?"

Su looked at him for a moment, then shook his head.

"All that's true, Sir. But I *do* know you. You're seeing all of that as a justification—an excuse—to not do something we both know you'd hate." He waved his hand again. "I'm not saying they're not valid arguments. I'm just asking you if you're... overinvesting in them because you're not a murderer and you don't want to be one." The chief of staff's eyes bored into the admiral's. "I'm not at all confident the *Admiralty* will buy into them. This operation's turned into the worst disaster in the Navy's history. A lot of people had a lot invested in Dragon Fleet, and there's a damned good chance all of that's just been pissed right down the crapper. The people who expected it to get them credit for winning the war are going to want a scapegoat—badly—and Xing, at least, will do her damnedest to make sure the one they find is *you*."

"Maybe so. But there's such a thing as decency, Zhihao. There has to be. And if anybody wants to second-guess me, I can always point out that Xing was too busy running to save her own ass to exercise command of what's left of her fleet. I'm the flag officer on the spot, the senior officer in command, and the Admiralty didn't give me my stars just to see me shirk my responsibilities."

"But what about—?"

Than cut Su's question off with a quick shake of his head, and the chief of staff closed his mouth with an almost audible click. Of course the third admiral understood the consequences of any official displeasure wouldn't fall only on himself. Or only upon his officers. Su Zhihao was prepared to take whatever came his own way as Than's chief of staff, but his heart ached at the thought of what this could mean for Than Qiang's family.

Which was something he could never say to Than.

"So what *are* we going to do?" he asked instead.

"I'm not going to murder a planet, but I damned well *will* blow their orbital infrastructure to hell," Than said grimly. "Whatever they hit us with, it's not a standard Fed weapon, or we'd have seen it before. I think it's something Murphy cooked up on his own, and that means he was able to build so many of the damned things solely out of New Dublin's industrial base, and I'll be surprised as hell if he doesn't come looking for us—assuming what happened in Alramal doesn't mean his intel's already told him where Diyu is. The last thing I want is to give him the ability to make still *more* of them before he finds us, and it's obvious the Feds have upgraded the yard facilities here a lot more thoroughly than Intelligence suggested. So, given that our offensive power's been so reduced due to the losses we sustained following Second Admiral Xing's orders—" he showed his teeth in an almost-smile "—I'm going to task our surviving missile assets with taking out that yard capacity. The destruction of that sort of strategic asset is a legitimate act of war in anybody's book...and probably the most effective short-term measure I can take to protect Diyu and the rest of Dragon Fleet."

Su frowned, thinking hard. Anyone who actually looked at Than's reasoning about "reduced offensive power" would recognize it as the fig leaf it was. But that didn't mean he was wrong about the need to neutralize New Dublin's industrial base, especially in the wake of Dragon Fleet's devastating losses. And he was also right that it would be a legitimate act of war. Xing, no doubt, would argue that killing everyone on Crann Bethadh would also "neutralize" their industrial base, but Su didn't much care what *she* thought. Whether Than's decision to attack the orbital industry directly instead of striking the planet would be enough to keep the Fed admiral from taking out his rage on any prisoners was another question. Especially if—

"Will you tell...?" He let his voice trail off and arched an eyebrow at the admiral.

"Murphy?" Than snorted. "That would be a step too far, Zhihao! You can be damned sure somebody's going to look hard at our message logs, and I can't offer Murphy an explicit quid pro quo." He shook his head, his expression more worried than he wanted to admit. "We'll just have to hope he figures it out. And—" he looked at the time display "—whatever we do, we'd better do it fast. We're still eleven light-minutes from Crann Bethadh, but we don't have a lot of time to dance, if we don't want Murphy's ambush carriers to catch us before we can wormhole out. If we don't head back for the Powell Limit in the next thirty-five minutes, it won't matter what the Admiralty might do to us."

"That's true." Su nodded, and then he brightened. "You know, that might work for us, to some extent. If we send them in ballistic, our birds will take—what? Nine hours just to reach the planet from here?—and we're only *six* hours or so from wormholing, once we start. So we won't be around for our sensors to confirm exactly where they were targeted or what they hit."

"It's a nice thought," Than said. "I wouldn't put too much confidence in it, though."

"Confidence? Who's talking about confidence?" Su actually chuckled. "I'm talking about frail *hopes* here, Sir!"

"Well, in that case, don't let me disabuse you," Than said. "And now, I think we'd better get ourselves organized."

✧   ✧   ✧

The League SAR teams labored heroically, fighting to find and recover every RLH spacer, but all too many of them were still trapped in broken hulks coasting toward Crann Bethadh when they ran out of time thirty minutes later.

Than really ought to have blown up the surviving wrecks—especially *Sun Bin*'s hulk—but he couldn't. Not with so many of his people still aboard. He did fire the scuttling charges aboard the two battleships and three battlecruisers he couldn't fit onto his surviving parasite racks after all, but only after he'd made sure every single man and woman was off them.

And while his search-and-rescue people were doing that, his tactical officers programmed and launched their missiles.

As Su had pointed out, from this range it would take hours for something traveling at Dragon Gamma's base velocity to reach Crann Bethadh. Burning out the missiles' Hauptman coils at launch would have cut that flight time by twenty-five percent… but it would also have deprived them of their highest rate of acceleration when it came time to penetrate whatever antimissile defenses they might face.

There wouldn't be much to stop them—not in a Fringe system, when all the mobile defending units were off with Murphy. And space stations couldn't dodge any more than planets could. So they probably wouldn't need their coils, but Than was a professional and his people had paid a bitter price to get this close to Crann Bethadh. His parting shot would go in with every advantage he could give it.

He wished he could risk staying in-system long enough to evaluate the results of his strike. Unfortunately, that was out of the question. The five Federation FTLCs no one had known were there had a lot farther to go than his two surviving carriers did, but it would take over two hours for Dragon Gamma's battered starships just to accelerate back across the Powell Limit, and then another three and a half hours to reach the critical velocity threshold and break into wormhole space. They could intercept him on his least-time exit vector in less than six hours from their current relative velocities and positions. However much his heart railed against leaving any of his people behind, Dragon Gamma was out of time.

"Turn us around, Captain Sun," he said, looking at the flag captain's comm image. "It's time to go."

"Yes, Sir." Sun had been with Than a long time, and he recognized the worry in her eyes—worry for him, not for herself—but she managed a smile. "I can't say I'll be sorry to see the last of New Dublin," she said.

"Neither will I, Luoyang," Than sighed. "Neither will I."

Cai Shen and *Li Shiji* turned and accelerated away from Crann Bethadh at nine hundred gravities.

Behind them, eight hundred and seventeen antiship missiles—every attack bird they'd had left after Agincourt's devastation, although Than was unaware of the bitter irony of that number, given what Murphy had fired into Xing's teeth—hurtled toward Crann Bethadh...accompanied by 1,369 counter-missiles.

"You know, there are times I wish my dad could be wrong about something," Callum Murphy said from his acceleration couch as TFNS *Kolyma* accelerated away from the New Dublin Alpha shipyard platform.

"I'm sure he is, sometimes," Dadyar Pêşrew replied encouragingly from Callum's display.

"Oh, when I was a kid, he was wrong *all* the time!" Callum rolled his eyes. "Only problem was I usually couldn't convince Mom of that. She always took his side, no matter how unfair I told her he was being!"

"Parents are like that."

"Yours, too, huh?"

"*All* of them, Lieutenant Murphy. All of them."

Callum chuckled. That chuckle might have been just a bit strained, however, and he found himself wishing that Engineering offered tactical displays. He'd gotten used to seeing them on *Ishtar*'s flag bridge, and he hadn't counted on how...blind he'd feel without them.

Lieutenant Commander Seydel had told them what was coming, though. That was why his stomach felt so hollow at the moment.

The good news was that the Leaguies almost certainly didn't know *Kolyma* and her consorts were there. Logically, they shouldn't have been. They *should* have been with their FTLCs, chasing the League carriers. Using FTLCs for something like that without every sublight parasite they could lay hands on was...contraindicated. Callum had tried it once in *Federation Commander*, and the result had been unpleasant.

But his father had chosen to run that risk with his own command. As he'd said, *Ishtar* and *Gilgamesh* were decoys. If they needed their parasites, they were already screwed, so he'd loaded both of Commodore Granger's strikecarriers and every capital ship he had aboard the FTLCs of Hammer Force and run with empty racks . . . aside from the cargo pods of missile drones.

And he'd left every cruiser and light cruiser—and both strikecarriers—from his own task force in Crann Bethadh orbit, hiding in the sensor clutter of the shipyards and industrial platforms under strict EMCON, to provide a missile shield for the planet.

There were only thirty-seven ships, but they'd beefed up their missile defense drones, all thirty-six of the carriers' fighters had been configured for missile defense, and *Kolyma* would preposition every single one of her counter-missiles when she reached her assigned spot in the defense grid. The cruiser's launchers were mass drivers designed to get the birds out of the tubes as quickly as possible, but not to contribute to their velocity. It was to get them well clear of the ship before their Hauptman coils kicked in and irradiated everything in the vicinity. In this instance, however, *Kolyma* was defending a static target, and deploying the counter-missiles in space ahead of time would multiply the defensive fire she could throw up by a factor of eight. It wouldn't be quite as accurate as it might have been, but there would be a *lot* of it.

It remained to be seen if there would be enough.

❖　　❖　　❖

"Sir—"

"I see it, Zhihao." Than shook his head. "It would appear our friend Murphy is even more revoltingly capable than I'd thought."

Cai Shen and *Li Shiji* had been under acceleration for twenty-five minutes, during which they'd killed their remaining velocity toward Crann Bethadh and traveled just over fourteen million kilometers from their missiles' launch point toward the Powell Limit. Their velocity was back up to 7,600 KPS, and the system primary was receding—not nearly so rapidly as Than might have liked—behind them.

They were still close enough to communicate with their deployed drones, however, and those drones were still traveling ballistic with their active sensors locked down. That meant they were almost certainly invisible to the system's defenders. Than was pretty sure they were, anyway, since they were now close enough for their *passive* sensors to spot the TFN sublight units which had just fired up their fusion drives and begun accelerating out of concealment amid Crann Bethadh's orbital clutter. He very much doubted that they would have abandoned hiding so soon if they'd known he could see them.

"I should have anticipated this," he continued. "Anybody who thought far enough ahead to set up everything he did to Xing—and us—had to have considered what would happen if something got into range anyway. It looks like we may have to get used to thinking about *competent* Fed flag officers."

"I don't think they have enough platforms to stop the strike," Su said. The chief of staff leaned forward over Lieutenant Commander Yuan's shoulder, studying the tactical plot. "There are more than enough of them to take a big bite out of it, though."

"And to die trying," Than agreed grimly.

Su patted Yuan's shoulder and walked back across the flag bridge to Than.

"Sir, I don't like to say this," he said very softly, "but there's still time to retask the missiles. They might manage to save a lot of New Dublin's industry, but—"

Than shook his head. It was a tiny shake, but an emphatic one, and Su stopped mid-sentence with a vague sense of shame.

Thirty or so Federation cruisers might, indeed, "take a big bite" out of the infrastructure strike. But if the missiles were retargeted on Crann Bethadh's population centers, even a *really* "big bite" would be insufficient to save the planet. Su was certain *someone*—probably one of those scapegoat-hunting someones—would point that out. A prudent man would have ordered them retasked for exactly that reason, but he'd known, even before he asked, what Than Qiang's answer would be. He'd known. But it was a chief of staff's job to ask exactly those sorts of questions anyway...no matter how much he might loathe himself after he did.

"What do you think, Sir?" Lieutenant Commander Mendez asked quietly. "Was the Admiral's little warning enough to change the bastards' minds?"

"Your guess is as good as mine, XO," Abraham Whitten replied.

He sat on TFNS *Austerlitz*'s bridge, looking at the comm display tied into Mendez's station in Auxiliary Control. AuxCon was right off the Combat Information Center, at the center of the heavy cruiser's core hull. Hopefully, that meant Mendez would survive if something unfortunate happened to Whitten.

"I've gotta admit he's surprised the hell out of me this far," Mendez went on, dark brown eyes watching the master plot in CIC. At the moment, it showed the surviving League FTLCs accelerating hard for the Powell Limit. It did not—yet—show the missiles both of them were confident those carriers had left behind. "I didn't think he could pull it off. Not in a million years."

"I'm coming to the conclusion that everybody—yours truly, included—kind of underestimated Admiral Murphy," Whitten said. "Not by more than, oh, five or six thousand percent, you understand. No biggie." He smiled tightly, then shook his head. "Damned if that man can't think outside the box. Wouldn't have guessed that back at Jalal. But I think it's still a crapshoot whether or not the Leaguies go after Crann Bethadh anyway."

"If he's really about to take sixty-three thousand Leaguie prisoners, that's a pretty good reason for the rest of their fleet to not go around genociding any planets," Mendez pointed out.

"Granted. 'Course, the Admiral was pretty careful about not saying he'd shoot them all if whoever's in command over there K-strikes the planet. I think he got his point across, though."

Murphy's message to Admiral Than had come through in the clear to every one of his own ships, as well. It was the first time Abraham Whitten had actually heard his crew—*any* crew—cheering for a TFN flag officer.

"The problem," he continued, "is how bad we've hurt them." He shook his head. "We haven't reamed a Leaguie fleet this way—especially for pretty much zero losses of our own—in... Well, hell. I don't think we've *ever* reamed a Leaguie fleet this way! That's gotta sting. And if whoever that is hauling ass for wormhole space is as bloody minded as that bitch Xing, he may not care what happens to those prisoners. He may just say screw it all and kill the planet anyway."

"Unless we stop him, Sir," Mendez said.

"Well, there *is* that," Whitten agreed.

✧　　✧　　✧

"All right, everybody," Captain Jordan Penski announced to his COs over the all-ships net from the heavy cruiser *La Cateau*'s cramped flag bridge. "The outer drones have a count for us. They make it a little over two thousand, so things are about to get interesting."

The men and women aboard "Umbrella," the ships defending Crann Bethadh, watched him in intently listening silence. As the CO of CruRon 1102, Penski was the senior-officer-in-command. He was a well-known and thoroughly trusted quantity for the crews of his own squadron and the rest of TF 1705. He was less well-known to the other ships Murphy had begged, borrowed, and stolen.

"The good news is that we're pretty sure a lot of them have to be counter-missiles, because they didn't begin to have enough magazine space after Agincourt for that many shipkillers, But we don't know how many are. We're guessing somewhere around half, based on standard Leaguie magazine loadouts, which would mean 'only' about a thousand attack birds."

More than one of his listeners winced at that estimate.

"They're coming in ballistic," Penski continued. "That means they've got their Hauptman coils, as well as their fusion stages, for terminal maneuvers. We're tracking, and we should have solid locks on all of them by the time they get here. One thing about ballistic, it's easy to plot."

He smiled, and at least some of his ship commanders chuckled. Hitting a purely ballistic target, however small and however fast it was moving, was child's play.

"The problem—" his smile disappeared "—is those damned Hauptman coils and the counter-missiles. I'm willing to bet every single one of those frigging shipkillers is programmed to jink at an entirely different target on final. Worse, they'll be coming in hot when they cross our defensive perimeter, and they've got those frigging counter-missiles riding shotgun."

Normally, it was impossible to combine antiship missiles and counter-missiles in the same salvo, because counter-missiles simply couldn't keep up. They were smaller, cheaper, and less capable than attack missiles—they had to be, if ships wanted to carry enough of them—but they actually had fifty percent better acceleration. They needed that... liveliness to generate standoff range on intercepts against missiles coming in at thousands of kilometers per second. The problem was that the greater overload on their Hauptman coils limited them to two thirds of an attack missile's acceleration *time*. That worked out to an almost identical maximum attainable velocity from rest—1,765 KPS—but the counter-missile burned out at a range of only 35,000 kilometers, whereas the shipkiller's Hauptman coil had a powered envelope of 52,960 kilometers. In addition, its fusion thrusters provided a maximum of three minutes more powered flight time, which was nothing to sneer at when it came to defensive fire solutions, but only at an acceleration rate that was negligible compared to that of a Hauptman coil.

It was possible to adjust the counter-missile's acceleration rate to match that of a shipkiller, but not its *endurance*, and therein lay the dilemma. Under normal circumstances, even the shipkiller's Hauptman coil burned out well before the missile reached its target, and there wasn't really a problem in simply giving it a longer ballistic phase than it would normally have had. But while the shipkiller had that fusion stage for midflight correction and terminal maneuvers, the counter-missile didn't. From the instant its coil burned out, it was only an expensive, inert hunk of hardware traveling helplessly through space.

In this case, unfortunately, none of that mattered, since the entire missile cloud was traveling ballistic at Dragon Gamma's base velocity at launch. None of them had put any time on their Hauptman coils at all.

"We don't know how much good the counter-missiles will do them, but they have to take a bite out of our defensive fire. Not to mention the fact that they'll make damned good decoys until Tracking can differentiate acceleration rates. So this is going to be a hell of a shoot-out, people.

"*La Cateau* will take lead and distribute our fire, but keep an eye out for those jinks! I'm releasing your shipboard lasers and autocannon to self-defense, unless *La Cateau* overrides, but our number-one priority is the planet. After that, it's the orbital platforms. I'm afraid our own precious asses come third today."

No one felt like chuckling now.

"The thing is—and this isn't just for you folks in BatRon Seven-Oh-Two and CruRon Nine-Sixty. I know you feel like shit over Inverness. Well, all the rest of us've left enough planets to get hammered, too. The whole damn Navy has. But this is our chance to make up for that. We're not walking away this time. Not today. Not from this planet. We stop those damned missiles or we don't go home. Are we all clear on that?"

His eyes were hard as they swept the quadrants of his flag bridge comm display aboard *La Cateau*. Every one of his ship commanders looked back at him, just as they saw one another on their own displays, and—as one—they nodded.

"Good," he said then. "Now let's kick those missiles' asses."

Time dragged as the personnel of Umbrella awaited the onslaught. It was something to which spacers became resigned. Their battlefields were so vast, their sensors could see so far, and their weapons were so relatively short ranged, that they routinely got to wait hours, or even days, for the holocaust they knew was coming. In some ways, it was like a reversion to the days of sail back on Earth, when seamen got to watch the approaching sails of an oncoming enemy fleet creep closer at no more than two or three knots. And, as in the days of sail, it was hardest on the personnel who'd seen the most combat. They knew what it was like from bitter, terrifying personal experience, and all those memories of other times sat in the backs of their brains, whispering that this time *they* might be the ones whose luck ran out at last.

There were a lot of men and women like that in Umbrella.

And then there was Callum Murphy.

He felt the tension ratcheting steadily tighter and tighter in his gut. Every time he was convinced it couldn't get any worse, it surprised him by doing exactly that. He looked around the faces of his reactor room personnel, searching for signs of his own crippling fear, and saw very little of it. Were they all that much stronger than he was? Or were they simply better at hiding it?

"Don't sweat it, Sir," a voice said very, very softly from beside him.

He turned his head, and Eira smiled ever so slightly from the acceleration couch beside his. They were in microgravity at the moment, but that wasn't the reason they were strapped in, anyway.

"You'll be fine," she said. "Don't feel like it now, but you will."

"Not so sure of that," he said, equally softly. "I can't decide whether I'm about to puke or pee myself. Or—" his lips quirked "—something a bit smellier than that."

"Except for the puking, nobody else'll know," she pointed out, patting the chest of the armored vac suits all of them wore. "But it doesn't matter. What matters is doing what you have to."

"I'm afraid I'll freeze." He was a bit surprised he could admit that, even to her, but it was easier than he'd expected. "I'm afraid I'll screw up and get somebody killed. Maybe even you."

"Smaj says you're more likely to do something stupid-brave out of ignorance and get me killed *that* way." She shrugged. "I'll take my chances. You're more like your father than maybe you realize. Don't expect he'd freeze, and I don't expect you will."

Callum looked into those pale blue eyes and wondered exactly what they saw looking back at him. They were still and calm, but there was something darker and colder beneath their surface. How much of that was the memory of what she'd endured and survived on Inverness, he wondered?

"Well, I'll try not to get *either* of us killed. How's that sound?" he said in a deliberately brighter tone, and she nodded.

"I'd like that, Sir," she said with a slightly bigger smile.

❖ ❖ ❖

"Pump the air, Mr. McGhee," Kunigunde Seydel said calmly.

"Aye, aye, Ma'am!" Lieutenant Commander McGhee replied, and a buzzer sounded raucously over every intercom and earbud aboard *Kolyma*.

All over the ship, hatches and blast doors slammed shut. Helmets went on, vac suit seals were checked one last time, and any personnel who hadn't done it already strapped into acceleration couches. This time, those couches were unlikely to be needed for acceleration, but they also provided their users with semi-enclosed armored shells. And as they strapped in, the life-support blowers went into reverse at maximum speed and power. Air pressure fell rapidly as *Kolyma*'s atmosphere was evacuated into the heavily armored, high-pressure storage cells near the center of the cruiser's hull in the last step that brought a ship fully to battle stations. Partly, depressurizing was designed to conserve that atmosphere in case of hull breaching. Of more immediate importance, it also deprived shipboard fires of oxygen and removed the atmosphere that would otherwise transmit blast and concussion.

FTLCs seldom fully depressurized. They were larger than any sublight parasite, and the process would have taken far longer. There were also areas an FTLC *couldn't* depressurize, like the hydroponics sections that were their lungs. On the flip side of the equation, their size also meant they had much deeper belts of compartmentalization between their vital sections and the void. Those compartments *could* be depressurized, and FTLCs were far more heavily armored than any sublight ship. Mass literally meant nothing to a Fasset-drive ship, so the mass penalty of a meter or two of armor—even SCM armor—was perfectly acceptable to them.

As Third Admiral Than's ships had demonstrated, not even the best and thickest armor in the galaxy could fend off catastrophic damage if there was enough incoming fire, but—as they had *also* just demonstrated—it took a lot to get through to an FTLC's pressurized core sections. If damage got *that* deep, atmosphere was usually the least of the ship's problems.

The long, dragging wait dwindled slowly, and then—as also always happened—the minutes which had dragged so interminably became seconds, flying into eternity at FTL speeds.

The defenders' ability to track the incoming missiles for so long was a priceless advantage, although it would have been a much greater one if the closing velocity hadn't been so insanely high ... or if they'd had a defensive weapon capable of engaging the threat farther out. But not only were their counter-missiles shorter-legged than their potential targets, attack missiles were smart and, unlike counter-missiles, had those damned fusion drives. If the TFN had attempted to intercept farther out, the shipkillers' onboard AIs would simply have waited until the counter-missiles went ballistic, then expended however little of their fusion drives' endurance they'd needed to evade. So if the counter-missiles wanted to intercept, they had to be capable of terminal maneuvers ... which meant they couldn't be fired until the shipkillers were in range for their own terminal attack maneuvers.

At their closing velocity, the League attack missiles had a powered attack range of just over half a million kilometers. That assumed maximum burn on their fusion-powered final stages, and that none of their acceleration was used on evasive maneuvers. But it gave Umbrella's defensive planners a solid benchmark for the maximum range at which they *might* initiate their attack runs, and nerves tightened to the snapping point as they crossed that perimeter and went right on closing. They coasted onward for another thirty-four seconds, closing to 300,000 kilometers, and then—

"Hauptman activation!" *La Cateau*'s tracking officer barked, and eyes snapped to tactical displays throughout the defensive force.

Umbrella knew where every single one of those incoming missiles was. Missiles had fewer stealth features than drones, and Penski's trackers had known where these were coming from, been able to vector recon drones into their ballistic path. That path, dictated by Dragon Gamma's vector when the salvo launched, crossed "behind" Crann Bethadh's orbital position, so the fire would be coming in on an oblique angle, which simplified things a bit more. The tracking computers had analyzed the potential targeting cones for every one of the RLH birds, but that hadn't helped a lot. They were very *big* cones—large enough to envelop the entire planet—and until their coils went live, there was no way to predict which missile would go where. And from that range, they could reach their targets in only forty-seven seconds... which meant they would execute their terminal attack runs at three thousand gravities, not the six hundred maximum of their fusion thrusters.

"Fire Plan Bravo, Commander Tsimmerman," Captain Penski said formally.

"Fire Plan Bravo, aye," Sergey Tsimmerman replied, and fire distribution commands flooded outward from the cruiser.

Seven and a half more seconds fled into eternity, and then tactical displays flashed with a prairie fire of matching Hauptman signatures.

The counter-missiles lit off their coils and streaked to meet the incoming fire. Had the shipkillers gone active at the half-million-kilometer mark, there would have been a second wave, launched twenty seconds later to engage the initial intercepts' leakers after they went to their fusion drives and became much easier kills. The actual attack profile meant there was no time for that. Even at their full 4,500 gravities of acceleration, the counter-missiles would intercept only 26,260 kilometers—and three and a half seconds—before that oncoming hammer struck.

It was an awesome concentration of defensive fire power. Warship magazines had to split capacity between shipkillers and counter-missiles, and in the TFN's case, cruisers normally dedicated forty percent of their magazine space to ship defense. Penski's ships' magazines had contained 5,032 counter-missiles, and Umbrella had prespotted all of them. That worked out to just over 2.3 counter-missiles for every incoming bird, and against non-evading targets, or even targets reduced solely to their fusion thrusters, that would have been ample to stop any attack dead. Unfortunately, the targets they actually faced were not only capable of evasive maneuvering at very high gravities, but covered by penetration aids . . . and those damned counter-missiles of their own.

The League tac officers had stepped down their counter-missile acceleration rate to match that of the shipkillers, which made them effectively indistinguishable from one another. But only for a moment. Only until the Federation counter-missiles committed to launch and the League missiles' sensors could see them.

Missile sensors weren't as good as those of warships or recon drones, but they were still pretty damned good. Certainly capable of detecting and tracking incoming hostile missiles. The AI aboard a counter-missile was a bit more simpleminded than that aboard a shipkiller, and TFN AI was generally better than RLH AI. The margin of superiority was slight, however, and the League counter-missiles knew exactly what they were supposed to do when they saw that many incoming Hauptman coils.

"*Jesus!*" Lieutenant Commander Brian Denby, TFNS *La Cateau's* tactical officer, muttered.

"You think?" Sergey Tsimmerman replied as he watched the same plot. The TO had been talking to himself, Tsimmerman knew, but he had a point.

A very good one, in fact.

Over thirteen hundred of the incoming icons had abruptly increased acceleration by fifty percent, streaming to meet the defenders' counter-missiles. The range between them was still over 200,000 kilometers, but the incoming shipkillers' base velocity pared away distance like a knife, and their accompanying counter-missiles raced ahead of them with an acceleration advantage of fifteen hundred gravities.

And there were thirty percent more of them than anyone in Umbrella had estimated.

"Time to counter-missile intercept thirty-two seconds," Denby announced.

Tsimmerman nodded his helmeted head without looking away from the plot and activated his dedicated link to Jordan Penski.

"That's going to take a bigger bite out of our defensive birds, Sir," he said.

"Probably," Penski agreed. "But look at the bright side, Seryozha. If we were low on the counter-missile estimate, that means we were *high* on the shipkillers. So we've got less of *them* to deal with, right?"

"All due respect, Sir, but that's a pretty dim 'bright side.'"

"Yep. On the other hand, it's the only one we've got."

Two vast clouds of kamikazes streaked toward one another.

The defending counter-missiles had no interest in their League counterparts. Their business was with the shipkillers, and the acceleration of the League counter-missiles took them out of the shipkiller category. Unfortunately for Umbrella, Than Qiang's counter-missiles had been programmed to look for exactly that sort of acceleration to identify *their* targets. No one in Dragon Gamma had expected to actually *need* to plow the road for their attack missiles, but Third Admiral Than wasn't in the habit of leaving things to chance.

Kinetic kills—bullets-hitting-bullets—were the preferred mode for both navies, but counter-missiles were routinely fitted with proximity warheads and laserheads as backup. The Federation favored the laserhead because of its greater reach and ability to engage "off-bore" targets, whereas the League favored the simpler, more robust proximity warhead's cloud of shrapnel, but both navies used both.

Thirty-four and a half seconds after Fire Plan Bravo had launched, 6,400 missiles' vectors merged, 26,263 kilometers from Crann Bethadh.

The vacuum blazed as the counter-missiles built a wall of lightning. Their closing velocity was over 8,437 KPS. At that speed, the entire interception was over so quickly not even the computers could sort it out. It was one blinding, eye-searing cata-clysm, an instant borrowed from Armageddon, that saw 853 of the TFN counter-missiles blotted out of existence in the fireballs of kinetic impact, the stilettos of bomb-pumped lasers, and the shotgun shrapnel of blast-fragmentation warheads.

And then, as quickly as it had flashed into existence, the holocaust vanished. Clouds of debris sped onward, potentially lethal to anything that got into their path, but space was once again empty and dark.

For a fleeting moment, at any rate. Then, 3.1 seconds later, the surviving counter-missiles ripped into Dragon Gamma's shipkillers.

There were still over four thousand of them, with barely 800 targets, but those targets were far harder than the counter-missiles had been. Counter-missiles didn't come lavishly equipped with penaids; shipkillers like the RLH's Zhànchuí did.

Decoys ripple-salvoed from the lead missiles—brief-lived but powerful, mimicking the Hauptman signature of actual shipkillers. Bǎobiāo missiles, equipped with active protection systems, targeting incoming counter-missiles with hypervelocity slugs, broke trail for the Zhànchuís behind them, and Míngqín missiles—dedicated electronic warfare platforms seeded throughout the salvo—radiated massive spikes of active jamming to blind the counter-missiles' sensors.

Nothing could possibly spoof or defeat six thousand threats. Not all of them. And a second, smaller holocaust flared with equal brilliance—and brevity—as Umbrella's fire tore through the heart of Dragon Gamma's attack wave. The sheer density of the massive prespotted counter launch was impossible to stop, and despite all defenses, all countermeasures, eighty-five percent of the shipkillers died in that titanic instant of collision.

But if eighty-five percent had died, that meant just over a hundred and twenty Zhànchuís burst through the furnace intact, screaming in on their targets at seven thousand KPS.

There was no time for any additional orders from La Cateau. Umbrella had barely three and a half seconds to identify the surviving threats. Every ship in Captain Penski's force had been tracking continuously as the massive salvo came in. Probable targets had refined themselves steadily as the seconds until impact flashed downward and the targeting cone of each missile shrank. Targeting hierarchies had been established by La Cateau's tactical department, but Penski's flagship had no choice but to hand off to the individual vessels of his command as the surviving Zhànchuís came slashing in.

Human command-and-control was hopelessly inadequate to the speed and ferocity of the moment. It was all up to the computers, and the uncaring, unflustered, un-self-aware AIs aboard every ship, managing every drone, assigning targeting criteria to every manned fighter, reprioritized firing solutions as the counter-missiles ripped holes in *La Cateau*'s assigned hierarchies. None of the people aboard any of those ships, piloting any of those fighters, had time to realize precisely what targets their ships, their fighters, had been assigned. They had time only to feel the terror, to know Apocalypse was upon them, and then every defensive weapon they mounted flamed as one and the wave of fire engulfed them.

CHAPTER THIRTY-FOUR

TFNS *KOLYMA* SHUDDERED TO THE RECOIL OF HER LAST-DITCH defenses.

She and her counter-missiles, like the rest of Umbrella Force, were stationed on the threat axis. Even at a miserly single gravity of acceleration, its ships had needed barely half an hour to reach their positions, fifteen thousand kilometers from Crann Bethadh and directly between the planet and the incoming shipkillers. The two strikecarriers' *Orcas* were an advanced screen, forty thousand kilometers beyond that, configured for the missile defense role with short-range K-guns and lasers. Against any normal attack, they should have been confident of their ability to stop them, but these missiles were coming in at far higher velocities than normal, and sheer speed was its own defense in many ways. Not because higher velocity made them harder to track or made generating intercepts more difficult, but because it limited the number of interception *attempts.*

Her antimissile cannon—thirty-millimeter hypervelocity railguns—had opened fire barely seven seconds after the incoming missiles lit off their Hauptman coils, 26.5 seconds *before* Umbrella's counter-missiles went active, when the range to target was still almost 260,000 kilometers. She couldn't hope to reach a target at that range, because her cannon's muzzle velocity was only 33,500 meters per second. That was fast enough to deliver the energy equivalent of almost 130 kilograms of old-fashioned chemical explosives to a target at rest, but from the moment she started firing, she had only forty seconds before missiles traveling at twelve hundred times the velocity of a pre-space tank cannon's kinetic penetrators reached her. Given that much time, her projectiles could reach a maximum range of only 134 kilometers. That wasn't knife range against a missile attack; it was *razor* range.

The multibarreled point defense cannon had a much higher rate of fire than her antiship cannon. A cruiser's K-gun's maximum rate of fire was only about eight rounds per minute, using alternating capacitor rings; capital ships, with a third capacitor ring could manage twelve. Point defense cannon, using lighter mass drivers, multiple "barrels," and additional capacitors, could put out twenty-five rounds in a minute. Forty seconds gave *Kolyma* time for only sixteen rounds from each of the fourteen cannon systems in her engaged broadside, and there was little point conserving ammunition.

La Cateau's tactical department had assigned individual targets before Umbrella opened fire, although it was almost mathematically certain they were going to miss. But Umbrella could present a total of 174 point defense cannon, and in forty seconds they could fire over 2,780 rounds. Despite the astronomical odds, a missile that dodged one superdense slug might yet run into a slug intended for one of its fellows. SCM slugs were expensive, but not *that* expensive. If they managed to kill even *one* of the incoming birds, the cost-effectiveness would all be on the defenders' side.

Not to mention the fact that the one they stopped *might* be the one that would have taken out Tara if they hadn't killed it.

In fact, two of the attack missiles actually did walk into a slug meant for one of their fellows.

The *Orcas* opened fire seconds after the shipboard K-guns. They had less time to engage, but they were five seconds flight time closer to the shipkillers, and they were actually more effective. None of the incoming missiles had been told to look for mere fighters, and as they streamed onward toward the cruisers behind them, the *Orcas* spun, blazing away with their lasers.

There was no time for a "shoot-look-shoot" solution—for follow-up shots to engage a target that evaded the first one before it was through the intercept zone. It was a matter of assigning a single shot per target and then moving to the next in the targeting queue, and even as they fired, every single human being in Umbrella hoped like hell that the assigned target would be taken down by one of their counter-missiles, instead of their shipboard systems.

As the range fell, the probability of a kill went up, but the range to intercept went down. The Zhànchuís that survived the CMs were already outside the *Orcas'* engagement range, and there was time for only one more shot per point defense cannon before they reached their targets. The lasers aboard the deployed Bastet antimissile drones and laser defense systems in each broadside had time for three shots each, and those in the opposite broadside would each have time for a single shot at any missile that broke past the defenders before it ran out the other side of their engagement envelope. The cannon wouldn't; a projectile traveling at 3.35 KPS couldn't catch one traveling at 7,000 KPS.

The closing velocity of the League missiles increased the kinetic energy of the cannon's slugs from 130 kilograms of old-fashioned explosive to over 760 *megatons*. It was impossible for them to shed all that energy into their targets, but they drilled through any Zhànchuís they hit like hypervelocity awls, vaporizing the material in their direct paths. They were actually more like the fabled "death rays" of pre-space popular entertainment than the lasers were, in many ways, and the shock fronts generated by their passage radiated outward in all directions, shattering the missile bodies and thoroughly demolishing internal components, before they blasted out the farther side in incandescent balls of plasma.

No active defense mounted by any shipkiller ever built could stop that kind of fire. Any missile one of those slugs hit was dead...as a missile. It was not, unfortunately, dead as a *threat*. Whatever was left of it continued onward, and while the impact of the interception would impart at least some change to its vector, the change would be minimal. In fact, in terms of the time to impact, it would be nonexistent, Which meant the wreckage would continue on precisely the same vector...and something the size of a Zhànchuí traveling at 7,000 KPS packed 210 megatons of kinetic energy.

The good news was that those missiles were still accelerating to reach their targets when they entered Umbrella's engagement range, which meant that if they *stopped* accelerating, they weren't going to hit their intended target, whatever it might have been.

The bad news was that while they would miss their *intended* targets, they might still hit *something*.

In a worst-case scenario, the "something" in question might be Crann Bethadh, although atmospheric entry would tend to finish ripping the wreckage to pieces, the odds of its hitting a populated area would be slight, and the planet's citizens had all taken to their shelters. Assuming they'd been targeted on the planet to begin with, however, they were still extremely likely to hit it someplace, and if that place was a population center, casualties could be massive, despite every possible precaution.

In a next-to-worst-case scenario, the "something" might be one of the orbital platforms which had been the League's actual targets. They had no atmosphere to break up and vaporize incoming wreckage and they were far more fragile than any planet, but the defenders had been given hours to shut down their internal processes and evacuate all but the most critical personnel from them. The destruction would still be extreme if they got hit, and losing the system's orbital industry would be a severe blow, but at least the loss of life should be minimal, thanks to the evacuation.

In a next-to-best-case scenario, assuming they had to hit *something*, the "something" would be one of the defending warships. Of course, space was vast, ships were relatively small targets, and missile wreckage couldn't redirect itself to hit one of them if it hadn't been targeted on it to begin with. It could still happen, though—happen to any of them.

Like to a defending warship named TFNS *Kolyma*.

It wasn't one of the missiles *Kolyma* had engaged. In fact, it had been targeted by her sister ship, *Yukon*, and the kinetic slug which hit it tore through it at an angle, shattering the missile body into multiple fragments, the largest of which massed only about four thousand kilograms. But those four thousand kilograms were traveling at seven thousand kilometers per second, which meant they carried "only" 23.4 megatons of kinetic energy with them. Worse, there were *multiple* fragments.

Yukon had nailed the missile 92 kilometers short of Umbrella Force, a tenth of a second short of *Kolyma*. Not even the AIs had time to react to that, and it wouldn't have mattered if they had. There *was* time—barely—for the wreckage to begin to spread, but three chunks of the missile struck the cruiser, effectively simultaneously.

One hit her after section. It punched deep into her, ripping through her fusion drive and its fuel in a savage fireball that shook her like a toy in the jaws of a furious mastiff. Then it punched straight out the other side, trailing a plume of propellant, wreckage, and bodies.

The other two were worse. They hit her just forward of that, less than twelve meters apart and almost dead amidships, and splintered her five-hundred-meter hull into broken, dying halves.

✧   ✧   ✧

The end of the world came for Callum Murphy in thunder and lightning.

One instant, the taut, professional chatter of the tactical crews filled his secondary comm feed. The next, a terrible concussion tore through the ship, the feed from the bridge went suddenly and dreadfully silent, and the sound of shattering alloy came to him, not through the airless vacuum about him but through the very fabric of the ship. His armored acceleration couch bucked, leapt, seemed to twist like a pretzel. The lights in Reactor Two flickered, went down, then came back up under local power, and his hands were fumbling with his harness release before he'd even realized they were moving.

A cacophony of alarms blared in his ears and lurid red damage alerts glared across his helmet HUD. There were too many of them to sort out, and he hit the key to silence them, then shoved himself out of his couch. He pushed too hard in the microgravity—hard enough he had to grab one of the discarded harness straps to anchor himself—but it wasn't actually freefall, he realized. Not quite. The ship seemed to be spinning hard enough to exert a very faint but recognizable "downward" direction. Unfortunately, "down" was at a roughly thirty-degree angle from the compartment's designed perpendicular axis.

The rest of his six-person reactor room crew were still strapped into their couches, but not, he realized, Eira. Of course not. She was already up, toe looped into the restraining loop on her acceleration couch, as poised and alert as any thirty-year Navy veteran.

It was amazing how...reassuring he found that, a tiny corner of his brain realized. But only a tiny corner. The rest of it was too busy.

"Bridge, Power Two," he said over the comm.

Only silence answered.

"AuxCon, Power Two," he tried.

Silence.

"Damage Control Central, Power Two."

Silence.

"Sir, we've got a problem."

Callum turned himself in midair to look across the sizable compartment at Chief Petty Officer Hilar Sviontak, the senior member of his crew. Sviontak's couch back was fully upright, and his gauntleted fingers flew across his panel.

"Talk to me, Chief."

"Sir, we got what looks like a hell of a surge when whatever the hell that was hit us. It destabilized everything in sight, and we've lost half our feeds to the reactor. I can't get in to shut down the hydrogen flow, and the plant's already eight percent over max-rated output... and it's climbing."

Callum bit the inside of his lip. Not good, he thought. Not good at all.

"The bottle?"

"Holding so far, Sir," PT 1/c Sheila Clancy replied. The power tech sounded a little woozy. "Doesn't look good, though. I've got warning lights on the mag ring and the bottle's starting to fluctuate. Not too bad yet, but—"

She shook her helmeted head.

"What've we got, Green?" Callum asked.

"Nothing from Damage Control," Trejean Green said. "In fact, nothing from *anywhere*, but I've deployed our local remotes."

An image appeared on the master display, fed by a repair drone crawling along one of the conduits between Reactor Two and Reactor One. The actual conduit was only about thirty centimeters across, but the display looked like a bug's-eye view of an old-fashioned subway tunnel filled with massive power runs.

"So far, I don't see anything too bad, but—"

He broke off, and Callum swallowed hard.

"Oh, *shit*," somebody muttered over the comm.

The drone had reached the end of the conduit a little sooner than it ought to have. But that was because the conduit had been chopped off by the ragged cleaver of some enraged god. And not just the conduit. The entire front half of the ship was gone. Just... gone.

Callum could see the distant, uncaring pinpricks of stars where Power One and its entire crew was supposed to be.

At least he knew why no one had answered from the Bridge, or AuxCon...or Damage Control.

"How's that bottle, Clancy?" he asked.

"Not good. We're going to lose it. I think—"

"Shock damage to the mag ring, Sir," Green broke in. Callum looked at him, and the petty officer shrugged. "Got an eyes-on from one of the remotes and Sheila's right. There's a frigging crack clear across the primary ring. The only thing holding it's the secondary, and I don't think it's going to be with us long."

"Eject the bottle," Callum ordered.

"Ejecting the bottle, aye, Sir!" Sviontak replied.

He entered the required code, then punched the EXECUTE key, and a vibration quivered through the hull.

A fresh alarm blared.

"Negative ejection!" Sviontak snapped. "Didn't go, Sir!"

"No, but the eject *charge* went," Green said. "Blasted hell out of the reactor mount!"

"I'm losing the secondary ring!" Clancy's voice was higher-pitched.

"People, it's time to go," Callum heard someone else say with his voice. "Trejean, pass the word over any link you've got. Power Two is evacuating, and the bottle is going to blow in—?" He looked at Clancy.

"Bastard might hold another five minutes, Sir. *Maybe.*"

"The bottle's going to blow in four minutes," Callum said.

"Sending the word, Sir. God only knows if anyone's hearing it!"

"Best we can do is all we can do. Now, let's go, people!"

"You got that right, Sir!" Sviontak said. "You heard the Lieutenant! Let's *move!*"

Four of Callum's crew unbuckled, but not PT Clancy or Arnold Shapiev, Green's backup on the repair drones. Clancy tugged at her harness release, but it refused to unlock. Shapiev didn't even move.

"Crap!" Callum sent himself hurtling through the feeble gravity toward Shapiev. "Sviontak, get Clancy!"

"On it, Sir!"

Callum reached Shapiev and cursed himself when he got there. He should have required a sound-off. Maybe then he would have realized how badly Shapiev was hurt.

There was a hull breach. Not a big one. Just big enough for

whatever had torn it to punch through into the back of Shapiev's acceleration couch, and the petty officer's medical display flashed with lurid warning codes. Internal bleeding, broken bones, punctured lung... The lung must be from a bone fragment, because the only good news was that his vac suit's armor appliqué seemed to have stopped the damage short of an actual puncture.

Someone landed beside Callum. He wasn't a bit surprised that it was Eira.

"I've got this, Sir," she said. "You go. Now."

"No way." Callum shook his head and reached for the acceleration couch's medical override.

"Sir, the rest of your people need you."

"No way!" he repeated, his voice harder.

"Sir—"

"Either help me, or get the hell out of the way!" he snapped.

He punched the override, and the acceleration couch separated from the deck plating in a crackle of small explosive charges, silent in the vacuum. Shapiev's medical readout flashed brighter, then stabilized just a bit as the couch's built-in medi-kit began pumping coagulants and blood expanders through his system.

Callum grabbed the foot of the couch, and Eira took the head. The sideways thrust of the spin-induced microgravity was a bigger problem than he'd expected, but they got it moving in the right direction.

"Sir, Pod One's down," Sviontak reported. "Refuses to eject."

"Shit. Of *course* it does. Okay, you guys take Three. Eira and I will get Shapiev into Two."

"Sir, I'm headed back—"

"Not enough room for you and us in Two."

"But, Sir—"

"Get. Them. Into. Three," Callum grated.

"I—Aye, aye, Sir."

Callum could feel Eira's disapproval. Neither of the secondary escape pods could accommodate the entire power room crew. They were designed to accommodate only four evacuees apiece. Fitting Shapiev's acceleration couch into one of them would be harder than hell, and Pod Three was the nearer of the two. The odds that any of Power Two's people would make it clear before the bottle blew were no more than even, but his and Eira's odds had just gone down drastically.

If I get myself killed, she will so *never forgive me,* a lunatic corner of his mind told him. *And just my luck, there is a Heaven, and she'll spend the next million years giving me grief.*

"Pod Three separating," Sviontak said. "Luck, Sir!"

The ship quivered slightly as the pod blasted down the escape shaft and clear of the hull. Callum pictured its thrusters flaring to life, driving it away from *Kolyma*'s wreckage at fifteen gravities, as he and Eira panted down the access way with Shapiro. The hatch to Pod Three's bay was sealed, and Eira flung herself at the hatch to Pod Two. It cycled open, and she squirmed aside to shove the front end of the acceleration couch into it.

Callum heaved at the other end, shoving it farther into the pod, but it jammed. Eira skidded around beside him, putting her shoulders against the end of the couch and the soles of her boots against the opposite bulkhead. Then she straightened her spine with an explosive grunt clearly audible across the comm, and the couch shot suddenly through the hatch.

"Good girl!" Callum panted, punching her in the shoulder. "Now—"

Something flashed.

He didn't know what it was. He didn't have time to find out. There was only time to fling himself at Eira, wrap his arms about her, and bend his helmeted head forward across her.

Then Leviathan kicked him in the back, and there was only darkness.

CHAPTER THIRTY-FIVE

THE BEEPING.

It was the beeping that kept her awake as she swayed slightly on the stool next to Callum's bed. An airline was fixed over his nose, a patch of plastic covered his right eye, and the coverlet was tented over the stump of his right leg.

Stings of pain needled their way up her arm. A tiny drug pump attached to a port on her clavicle hissed, and the discomfort went away, but a fog rose in her brain, blurring her vision as the painkillers took hold.

She snapped the drug port off and tossed it onto a metal pan next to Callum's bed.

Someone squeezed her shoulder. She looked up and found Murphy standing next to her. She tried to shoot to her feet, but he pressed her gently back down on the stool.

"Thank you," he said.

"No...I was too *slow*." She shook her head, her voice bitter. "I did what I could, but if I'd just been...better, realized what was happening faster, he wouldn't have gotten hurt."

"He's alive. You saved him for me." Murphy went to Callum's side.

"He shouldn't have done it." She hung her head, tears blurring her vision. "He shouldn't have!"

Murphy put his hand gently on Callum's face and blinked back tears of his own.

"Of course he should have," he said gently. "It's what you do for people you care about, Eira."

"But—"

She bit off her sentence in mid-word as Callum shifted and his one eye open slowly.

"Huh." He blinked slowly. "Dad?" His voice was slurred, and he licked cracked lips. "Oh, no." Those cracked lips smiled ever so slightly. "I'm in hell, aren't I? No angel would be as ugly as you."

His voice was still slurred, but his father swiped at his eyes and grunted a genuine laugh.

"Never judge a book by its cover, Son," he said, his hand moving from Callum's face to squeeze his shoulder. "You might want to write that down."

"Nah, I'm too shallow to worry about things like that."

"I've noticed that." Murphy squeezed again. "How do you feel?"

"Like everything I've got hurts." Callum closed his eye again, then rolled his head on the pillow. "What the hell happened?" he asked, after a moment.

"You took a couple of good hits when *Kolyma*—"

"Christ!" Callum's eye popped back open. "*Kolyma!*" He stared at his father, then his head whipped around. "Eira—*Eira!*"

"Sir!" She popped up next to Murphy.

"Oh, good." His head fell back. "You hurt?"

"Doesn't matter," she said.

"Yeah. It does," he said, his eye closing again. "Sorry, Dad." He managed another smile. "You were saying?"

"I said you took a couple of hits," his father said.

"Is that why I can't—" Callum's hand rose to the dressing over his eye. "It's gone, isn't it?" He opened his remaining eye and looked at both hands, then lifted one leg...and the stump of the other. "Oh...oh, no..."

"It's my fault, Sir," Eira said miserably.

"No, it *isn't*," Murphy said sternly.

"The explosion." Callum's brow furrowed in memory. "What the hell was it? It couldn't have been the bottle...."

"As nearly as we can tell, it was the ejection charge for Pod One," his father said. "They left the bay hatch open when it didn't launch. There must've been a glitch in the launch circuit, and somehow it closed while you and Eira were getting Petty Officer Shapiev into Pod Two. The ejection charge went off, then the thruster kicked in, at least some of it flashed back through the hatch. You're both lucky to be alive."

"Only because you got between it and me, Sir," Eira said, her expression drawn. "That's my job, not yours! I'm supposed to be *your* security!"

"You'd look silly trying to wrap yourself around someone my size," Callum said, his eye closed again. "I know you would've done it. And don't think I thought it through. Not brave enough to do something like that on purpose. 'Course, you did say the Sergeant Major warned you about 'stupid brave.'"

"But—"

"He's right, Eira." Murphy reached out his free hand and gave her a little shake. "You'd have done it for him; he did it for you. That's what friends—and family—do."

"Friends?" Eira looked at both of them. "*Family?* But ... I'm just—"

"A very extraordinary young woman," Murphy finished for her. "One of the most extraordinary I've ever had the honor of meeting."

She stared at him in disbelief, and he looked back down at his son.

"The only reason you made it after being—what was it you called it? 'Stupid brave'?—was Eira. She did everything in the right order. She dragged you into the pod while you were still losing air through the hole in your visor. She got the hatch shut and the pod pressurized, she got you into a couch, got the pod ejected, then got a tourniquet on your leg before she put an emergency dressing on your eye. And after she did *that*, she did something about her own arm."

"You're hurt?" Callum's eye popped back open, dark with sudden concern.

"You weren't big enough to completely shield her," Murphy said. "Her left arm took a lot of the blast. Punctured her suit in three places. Put two hull splinters through her biceps. Thank God they were small and the auto-sealant worked the way it was supposed to! Oh, did I forget to mention that she did all of those right things in the right order with only one arm?"

"Well, look at you!" Callum smiled and held out a hand to her. "Talk about big things in small packages!"

She took his hand hesitantly, and he squeezed hard.

"Sounds to me like we're probably even," he said.

"No." She shook her head, but she managed a small smile of her own. "Not yet, Sir. I remember who carried me up that ladder from the bunker."

Callum made an uncomfortable waving away gesture with his other hand, then looked back at his father.

"Shapiev?"

"He's going to make it," Murphy said. "Thanks to you two—and, I don't want to start a fresh argument over which of you did more to rescue him. Let's just call it a team effort."

"Works for me," Callum said, letting his head fall back. "I don't think a noble warrior's supposed to say this, but I really feel like shit right now, Dad."

"Not surprising. You're out of the fight for a bit." Murphy shook his head. "But we'll get you back home and into rehabilitation. You can make a full recovery, Son. That's what's important."

"Mom's gonna kill me," Callum murmured, then snorted. "No, she's gonna kill *you*, Dad. You're the one who's in real trouble when she finds out. I don't think Eira and I together can rescue you from her!"

"I do anticipate a . . . testy word or two from her," his father conceded.

"You'll be lucky if it stays verbal!" Callum said. "So, I guess the next classic question—where am I? *Ishtar*?"

"Right the first time. Doc Barbeau's facilities are at least as good as anything on Crann Bethadh. I did think about sending you dirtside before we wormholed out, though."

"Damn!" Callum shook his head. "Didn't even think about Crann Bethadh! How bad was it?"

"Bad enough, but a hell of a lot better than it might have been, thanks to you and the rest of Umbrella," Murphy said. "Nothing hit the planet, at all, but we lost New Dublin Bravo completely, and two of the refinery nodes took hits, too. Fortunately, we'd gotten almost everybody off of all three platforms, so we only lost about two hundred people there." It was his turn to shake his head. "*Only* two hundred."

"Dad, there were a hundred *million* people on Crann Bethadh. Trust me, 'only' works, however much it still hurts."

Murphy looked thoughtfully at his son, recognizing the hard-won maturity behind that painkiller-slurred sentence.

"Well, maybe," he said. "But Umbrella paid cash for it. *Kolyma* and *Changsha* are total losses. *Nanga Parbat* took a heavy hit, too, but the yard says she's repairable. We lost three hundred more people in *Kolyma*, including Commander Seydel, I'm afraid. *Changsha* got off lighter—she only lost about a hundred and fifty."

Callum nodded. That was sixty-five percent of *Kolyma*'s entire crew, but it was a miracle they'd gotten any of her people out alive. *Changsha*'s loss rate was far lower—"only" (there was that word again) about thirty percent of her ship's company.

"But nothing got through to the planet?"

"Not a thing. As a matter of fact, I don't think they were shooting at the planet at all. It was missile debris that took out *Kolyma* and *Changsha*. *Nanga Parbat* took her hit from a laser-head, but I doubt she was the intended target. Looks more like a missile that got damaged on the way in, realized it wasn't going to hit anything 'worthwhile,' and settled for whatever it could get. But Crann Bethadh didn't even catch any debris, aside from some that deorbited from the Bravo platform when it broke up." Murphy shook his head. "If they'd been aiming for the planet, at least some of the missile wreckage would have hit atmosphere, and probably a lot of it."

"Well that's good, I guess." Callum smiled slightly. "I'd feel more heroic if we'd saved millions of lives, though."

"Plenty of heroism to go around, Son. And saving—I don't know, the odd trillion credits or so—of industrial infrastructure and all the people who were still aboard it probably counts for something, too."

"Maybe." Callum shrugged. Then his eye narrowed. "You said you thought about sending me dirtside before we wormholed out. We're in wormhole space?"

His father shook his head.

"Not yet. It'll be another thirty hours or so. But we *will* be leaving just as soon as we can."

"Why? Did we lose after all? Are we headed for Jalal?"

"Lose?" Murphy smiled. "No, I don't think you could put it quite that way. In fact, the problem is that we're still dealing with the POWs and captured ships."

"Captured?" It had to be more than just the drugs making him feel so confused, Callum thought.

"Yes. We took all of Xing's—prisoner interrogation's confirmed she was in command—parasites intact. Well, actually, we're still in the *process* of taking them intact. We didn't have nearly enough parasite racks to recover all of them in a single lift. Or even in a couple of lifts. And they're still headed out-system at about forty-five percent of light-speed, so each round trip's taking about twenty hours now. But I promised we'd pick them all up, and O'Hanraghty's getting good info from them. For that matter, we captured enough of their capital ships it may actually be worthwhile putting them into TFN service! Once we've got them all, though, we're wormholing out."

"But not to Jalal?" Callum rubbed the plastic over his missing eye.

"No." The word came out a bit slowly, and Callum frowned. "Then where *are* we headed?"

"Well, that's an interesting question," Murphy said. "The outer recon platforms got lucky. We got good reads on the exit vectors for both components of the League fleet. We're pretty sure the force that actually hit Crann Bethadh pulled out on a diversionary vector, because it wasn't headed into League space. It was headed deeper into Concordia. But the other one, the one we blew hell out of—*that* one was on a beeline course for the League. Now, it's possible that *that* was the diversion and that their real 'secret base' is somewhere right here in the Concordia Sector, but I doubt it."

"So you've figured out where their base *is*?"

"We've run the cone for their destinations, assuming they were on a direct vector home. It cuts across a lobe of League-claimed space, but there are only a handful of stars in it. We've already narrowed the probable destination down to about seven, and two of them are inhabited. It seems unlikely they'd put their base somewhere with eyes to see, so O'Hanraghty and I figure it's most likely one of the others. Prisoner interrogation and data from the prizes should let us narrow our five remaining candidates further—hopefully to no more than a couple. And once we have, we're going to find out if we're right."

"Did I hit my head?" Callum looked at Eira, who nodded. "Thought so. And I must've hit it really hard. You're doing... what, Dad?"

"Seizing an opportunity. One victory at New Dublin's not enough. If we take the fight to the League's ghost yards, it may well tip the balance of the entire war. It's a risk, but it was my decision."

"Maybe I can ... get a peg or something. Help out somehow."

"Doc Barbeau says you're not ready to be up and about yet," Murphy said. "Just concentrate on resting. Eira, Logan wants you with him when we reach the League system. You can fight?"

"Yes, Sir. The doctor says the nanites should be all done in another three or four days. But Callum—"

"He'll be taken care of. I want you with Logan. We'll need everyone ... if you're up to it."

"Yes, Sir. I can fight."

"Good." Murphy smiled at her, then looked back down at his son, his expression more serious. "I have to keep making the rounds. Too many injured. Too many lost for good. Don't make a habit of this, Son."

"Just a flesh wound." Callum swiped his hand over his crotch and gave an exaggerated sigh of relief. Murphy shook his head. Then he nodded to Eira and headed back out of the ward to join a group of waiting medical staff.

"How do I look?" Callum asked Eira.

"Your face is still perfect."

"Aren't you sweet?" He flopped a hand to one side of the bed and bent his fingers slightly. Eira put both hands into his, and he brought her fingers to his mouth for a kiss. "Now you tell Logan you're not allowed to get hurt anymore. One leg or not, I'll kick his ass."

"I will not tell him that." She shook her head. "He doesn't like you."

"Always looking out for me. Thanks for dragging my butt onto that pod."

"I could only do it because—"

"Eira. Shut up." He rolled his head to smile at her. "You remember what you said about my getting you killed doing something stupid brave? Well, that's exactly what I did—something stupid brave. And after I did, you got both of us—hell, all *three* of us, counting Shapiev—off that wreck alive. I owe you. I owe you, and I don't think I can ever really repay you."

"Sir ... just ... just let me stay by your side. You and the Admiral. You're all I have."

"I think we can manage that." He closed his eyes again, lying back against the pillow. "I think we can." His voice was more slurred, and she gripped his hand more tightly. "You go to Logan. Show him how to kill Leaguies. I'll stay here and...have some more of the painkillers. They're nice."

"Let me stay. Just a little longer."

"'Course you can. 'Course you can."

Callum drifted off to sleep.

She was still holding his hand.

CHAPTER THIRTY-SIX

FLEET ADMIRAL FOKAIDES SAT MOTIONLESS AS YANG NARRATED the final moments of the Battle of New Dublin playing out in a holo before the Federation's senior leaders. Most were aboard the Oval in person, including the assembled joint chiefs of staff. Several, including Prime Minister Schleibaum, attended via hologram.

"...and then, shortly after taking the final League parasite units' surrender, Rear Admiral Murphy exited the system on a course into League space," she said.

"League units' *surrender*," Schleibaum said. "You're implying he took their ships *intact*?"

"Yes, Prime Minister." For someone describing a crushing victory, Yang's voice was remarkably flat.

"How many?"

"Ninety-eight, Ma'am," Yang sighed. "Forty-eight battleships and fifty battlecruisers."

"My God," someone murmured. It was virtually unheard of for warships to be taken intact rather than scuttled before the crews attempted to surrender. No one had ever captured more than a dozen or so intact in a single instance.

"How?" Schleibaum demanded. "How did this *happen*?"

"Madame Prime Minister," Yang raised her chin slightly, "Admiral Murphy seized an unsanctioned merchant vessel out beyond the blue line. He insisted that the cargo was intended

405

for the League and that it implied the existence of a significant League force unknown to us. Evidently...the Admiral was correct."

"The League built and manned this without us knowing?" Schleibaum's holo stood up as she glared at the admiral. "Do you know what would've happened to the Federation if Murphy had lost? Fokaides! What're you even here for? Answer me."

"The League would have ripped straight through the Concordia Sector." Fokaides tapped the panel and a map of the Federation came up. "They would have taken out Jalal—" the Jalal System's icon pulsed blood red as he spoke "—then punched up the Acera Corridor." More icons turned to blood, tracing a line inward from the frontier. "Our best estimate, based on the force Murphy actually engaged, is that this Xing could have advanced through another nine Beta and Gamma tier systems before we even began deploying the strategic reserve. By the time we could actually have intercepted her, she could have been as deep as Truscott, in the Gouden Sector. Military and civilian losses would have been catastrophic. And if she was willing to risk a fleet engagement, she might have made it all the way through to Hempstead."

The trail of blood ended at HR 5209, still over 356 LY from Beta Cygni...and barely sixty-five from the Sol System.

"She could have torn out the economic center of the Heart Worlds," Amedeo Boyle's hologram said. "This would've been a disaster worse than Callao—worse than First Telemark!"

"Yet Murphy managed a victory, instead." Kanada Thakore, attending as a holo opposite Boyle, raised both hands. "Why aren't we celebrating instead of panicking?"

"A moment, please, Kanada," Schleibaum said, and looked intently at Fokaides. "What did you mean 'the force Murphy actually engaged'?"

"Admiral Murphy identified twelve League FTLCs," Fokaides replied. "Eight of them were *Fúxī*-class—six hundred meters longer than our *Titans*, and only a bit smaller than our brand-new *Cormoran*-class. We've only identified *four* of them on the entire Beta Cygni front. If Murphy's projections from the merchant cargo he intercepted are to be believed," the fleet admiral looked like a man facing amputation, "they may have been building as many as forty additional carriers."

Stunned silence enveloped the conference room.

"Forty," the Prime Minister repeated after a long, still moment.

"Forty. You mean they could have hit us with as many as *fifty* of these new monsters of theirs?"

"*If* Murphy's projections were valid," Fokaides said. "But none of my analysts believe they could be. *We* couldn't build fifty *Cormorans*—not without tripling our construction budgets and capacity—and our industrial capacity is half again that of the League. My people concede that the evidence suggests he was correct that the League has a secret construction yard somewhere near Concordia, but it's simply not possible for them to have built *that* many ships."

"The Admiral's right about that, Prime Minister," Thakore said. "I think it's obvious he overestimated the final size of the League's intended fleet. What's happened clearly suggests he was right that they've been building *a* fleet, though. So, I repeat—why are we panicking instead of celebrating?"

"Yang. Continue," Fokaides said.

"On his authority as System Governor, Admiral Murphy authorized the expenditure of federal funds—and the activation of Navy support installations in New Dublin—to construct large numbers of missiles," Yang said. A very different silence greeted that sentence. "*Very* large numbers. And he apparently mated them with some sort of modified cargo drone body to allow him to lay down extraordinarily heavy missile strikes at previously unknown ranges." The silence around her grew still deeper. "And concurrent with the report of the battle at New Dublin, we received word from several depot commanders that worlds in the Concordia Sector have not delivered their draftees for further training and assignment. Taxes have also... not arrived."

"We've got a warlord on our hands, don't we?" the Prime Minister said into the ringing silence.

"That's too far!" Thakore slammed a hand on his desktop, but there was no impact noise from his hologram. "Terrence Murphy is my son-in-law! I'll grant that he's a bit of a romantic fool sometimes. But that doesn't mean he's ambitious enough—or dumb enough—to think he could pull something like that just because his family name carries a bit of weight! Anything he did, he did because he had to if he was going to stop *that*!"

He jabbed a finger at the trail of bloody icons on Fokaides's map.

"You said he headed into League territory after the battle," Schleibaum said. "Why? And are you sure of that?"

"According to his report, he believes he may have identified the star system from which the attack originated," Yang replied. "His intention is to attack it and destroy any as yet incomplete vessels. In answer to your second question, we have no independent confirmation of his destination, but there seems no reason to doubt it."

"I think it's time we started questioning *everything* about our friend Murphy," Schleibaum said grimly. "For all we know, he could actually be headed right *here*."

Thakore made an inarticulate sound of protest, but Boyle shook his head.

"Verena has a point, Kanada," he growled. "Intercepted a League shipment beyond the blue line. Beat a league fleet that could have ripped all the way to Earth's doorstep. And now he's chasing them down to finish them off?" He shook his head again. "I say it's time to stop underestimating him."

"We cannot let this happen," Schleibaum said. "The Fringe has been on edge since word of Inverness spread. Now this. It looks like we're losing control, and we can't afford that."

"The Fringe is most of our military manpower," Boyle pointed out. "Systems start flocking to Murphy, and the entire war is at risk. And think of what this will do to our economic interests!"

"You're all worrying about the bottom line," Fokaides said. "But how did the League manage to build this fleet? Murphy's projections may be grossly exaggerated, but just the *Fúxīs* he actually identified *prove* the League's been able to build a hell of a lot more heavy metal than we even began to suspect. I hate to give oxygen to conspiracy theories, but—"

"That's enough, Admiral," Schleibaum said. "We need to regain and maintain control of the Fringe. We cannot have Terrence Murphy become a hero. He cannot become a rallying cry for the Fringe...or in the Heart Worlds."

"He's scored a victory, but he's still two hundred light-years from Sol," Boyle said. "That means we can control the message *around* that victory."

"There is a report from the Inspector General." Yang's tone was void of any expression. "Allegations of kickbacks to Murphy. Then there's his violation of the Fokaides Directive. Victory or not, his orders were clear."

"Suggestions?" Schleibaum crossed her arms.

"Change the message." Boyle raised his hands. "The size of the League fleet at New Dublin defies belief, so change it. Announce an official count in line with expectations. The actual number's bound to leak eventually, so we add a footnote that the count may change after we . . . conduct a further investigation. Then we bring Murphy in for these kickbacks and take him down a peg or two in the public's perception. War hero or not, there's no place for corruption in the Federation Navy."

"No!" Thakore slammed a fist down. "You can't railroad him like this!"

"What's the contract status on the *Cormorans*?" Schleibaum asked. "I don't believe the final purchase order's been signed yet." She stared at Thakore, eyes like ice. "Astro Engineering still has a viable bid, I understand."

"Verena." Thakore shook his head. "You can't be serious."

"You're part of the Five Hundred," Schleibaum said coldly. "That means there are four hundred and forty-nine others who can step up."

Thakore looked at her for a long, still moment. Then he forced a smile.

"The charges . . . do sound serious," he said.

"We're so worried about Murphy becoming a hero that we're willing to turn him into a martyr, instead," Fokaides said. "We're going to destroy the man who just saved the Heart Worlds, won the most one-sided victory in the Navy's history, and may well have turned the entire tide of the war in our favor. That's what you all want?"

"That a problem, Fleet Admiral?" Boyle asked. "You *are* due to retire in a few more weeks."

Fokaides exchanged glances with Yang. Boyle's message was clear. Fokaides would sign the orders against Murphy. He'd shoulder the blame for any fallout . . . and he'd have to bear that burden in the very well compensated position Boyle had already arranged for him. Yang would be blameless when she took the fleet admiral's stars. It would all be neat and tidy . . . unless Fokaides was foolish enough to upset the apple cart.

"The Federation has a chain of command," he said after a handful of seconds, his eyes circling the faces of the joint chiefs. "One that's necessary to maintain order and the stability to sustain the war effort. One that can't be upset at such a crucial moment. The Beta Cygni front is stabilizing in our favor, and the League's losses at New Dublin might actually force them to the peace table. We owe Murphy a vote of thanks for that, but his ambition and grandstanding can't be allowed to jeopardize that possibility, and these Inspector General reports are . . . disturbing. Any objections to reining him in?"

The rest of the joint chiefs shook their heads. Yang paused for a moment, her expression like stone, then shook hers.

"Then get it done," Schleibaum said. "Full censorship on New Dublin on the feeds. I want the public believing Murphy's a corrupt officer who got lucky against a League raid. Bring him back to Earth in chains."

"Sublight in twenty seconds," Commander Creuzburg announced, and Murphy turned away from his conversation with O'Hanraghty to watch the digital display click off the final seconds.

There'd been exactly nothing about their system of construction in any of the League parasites' computers, nor had any of the captured personnel ever been told so much as the name of that star system. "Diyu" appeared on no chart of the League, so it was obviously a cover name for an actual star. All they really knew about it was that it was a red dwarf—which just happened to be the most common star type in the universe—and that it was uninhabited, aside from the RLH shipyard, and had two gas giants and at least one asteroid belt.

They *had* narrowed the possible candidates—assuming that Xing's withdrawal vector really had been straight back to base—to only two, so if he was right at all, they had a fifty percent chance of coming up lucky the first time.

Or of coming up unlucky *the first time*, he reminded himself.

"Sublight," Creuzburg said, and the visual displays came up, spangled with a sudden spray of stars.

Those displays were never used in wormhole space. Only someone who'd seen the inside of a wormhole knew what true nothingness looked like, and very few people who did see it ever wanted to see it again.

Murphy spared a moment to look at that starscape, take in those distant pinpricks of light. At *Ishtar's* velocity, those ahead of the FTLC were very noticeably blue-shifted and those astern red-shifted, and the M3 star whose League discoverers had named

Hefei was a bright pinpoint as she and her consorts raced toward it at 297,000 KPS. In point of fact, of course, Hefei was *astern* of them and the red-shifted stars were *ahead* of them as *Ishtar* pointed her stern at the inner system and decelerated hard.

He absorbed the visual, then turned to the flag bridge holo display.

"I suppose," he told his subordinate commanders, "that a proper admiral ought to be demonstrating his sangfroid about now, so consider that done."

Several of the officers looking back at him from the display's windows chuckled. Commodore Tremblay wasn't one of them, but even his lips twitched. He'd undergone quite an attitude adjustment after Second Admiral Xing turned up in New Dublin exactly as predicted.

"We should see something shortly, assuming this actually is Xing's base," Murphy continued. "As soon as we know anything here in *Ishtar*, we'll pass it on to all of you."

"Preliminary scans don't look very hopeful, Sir," O'Hanraghty said, looking up from where he stood at Mirwani's shoulder, watching the data roll in. "Can't expect a lot of detail at this sort of range, of course."

Murphy nodded. He was also careful to keep his expression neutral. His augmented task force had gone sublight 2,633,400,000 kilometers from Hefei, 138.8 light-minutes outside its 7.5 LM Powell Limit. At that range, ninety-six percent of Neptune's distance from Sol, "can't expect a lot of detail" was...just a bit of an understatement. On the other hand, any construction facility capable of building the ships they'd seen at New Dublin should be radiating one hell of an energy signature. If they weren't already seeing something—

"They would've beaten us back here, Sir," Harriet Granger said from the comm. He glanced back at her, and the commodore shrugged. "They'd almost have to have gone to the tightest EMCON they possibly could. For that matter, they could be on the far side of the star."

Murphy's lips twitched ever so slightly. Granger's tone reminded him of Simron trying to encourage an adolescent on final exam day.

"Agreed," he said out loud. "There's a limit to just how tightly they *could* control their emissions, of course. But you're right that if they're on the far side of the primary, it's going to take us a while to get a look at them."

"Well, we'll be down to a low enough velocity to deploy the Heimdallars in about two hours," O'Hanraghty said, and Murphy nodded. Once the FTLCs had decelerated to 169,500 KPS they could release the recon drones and let them coast inward independently to take a look at the farther side of the system. They could decelerate from that velocity to zero relative to Hefei in six hours, which would leave them a six-hour power reserve for maneuvers, but they wouldn't even start decelerating until they'd come within sixty light-minutes or so of the star.

Ten minutes ticked past. Then fifteen.

Twenty.

Murphy sat in his command chair, forcing himself to project a calm demeanor he was far from actually feeling. More and more sensor data came in from the system ahead of them, and the more of it he saw, the less it looked like El Dorado. A worm of uncertainty gnawed deep within him, wondering if it was only hubris that had brought him here. Was he *that* convinced of his own infallibility? Had his victory at New Dublin filled him with the false confidence to fuel a wild-goose chase to nowhere?

He made himself reconsider his reasoning, testing every link in the chain yet again, and every time he did, it still came up—

"Fasset signature!" O'Hanraghty said suddenly.

Murphy twitched upright in his chair, swiveling toward the master plot as a bright, crimson icon blinked alight upon it.

"Range eleven light-minutes!" O'Hanraghty continued, then wheeled toward Murphy. "Sir, they're *outside* us!"

"Of course they are." Murphy thrust himself up out of his command chair and strode toward the command ring at the heart of the flag bridge as the icons of his task group and the squadron commanders came back to life. "It would appear Admiral Than is just as good as his press releases, Harry."

O'Hanraghty looked at him, and Murphy shrugged. Prisoner interrogation had also revealed that Than had been "Dragon Fleet's" CO, not its *second*-in-command, until Xing superseded him . . . and that his people hadn't been very happy about that. Murphy didn't blame them one bit, and he'd found himself wondering just how well his strategy would've worked against someone as wily and experienced as Than.

"If it's not Hefei, then 'Diyu' has to be Yuxi," the admiral said. "And if he really pushed his fans in wormhole space, he could have gotten back to Yuxi in time to get a picket out to Hefei before we got here. He'd have had to come pretty close to redlining them the entire way, especially with his diversionary vector to kill first, but he could've done it, given the time we spent picking up Xing's orphans."

"But why—" O'Hanraghty began, then closed his mouth and shook his head—at himself, not Murphy—as he realized where the admiral was headed.

"You're right, he *is* good," the chief of staff said.

"I haven't quite caught up with you, Sir," Granger said from the comm display, and Murphy turned to face her.

"Than couldn't know how much information we had even before their attack," he said. "I imagine the fact that we intercepted the singularity manifolds must have left them with a lot of questions about how much we know and how long we've known it. But he's probably pretty confident we didn't know where his ghost yard is, or else we'd have attacked it instead of trying to interdict its supply chain or leaving Xing the initiative to attack New Dublin.

"But he also knows Xing headed straight in this direction when she ran for it, and he obviously figured out that we'd be following her pointer. He doesn't know what we might have gotten out of prisoner interrogations or picking through computers that might not have been as thoroughly scrubbed as they were supposed to be, either, but that—" he pointed at the accelerating icon in the plot "—says he was able to predict our probable choices. So he rushed one of his surviving carriers, or possibly some other FTL-capable ship, out to sit on Hefei and warn him if we turned up."

"Why are you so sure it's Than and not Xing, Sir?" Tremblay asked. The question was genuinely curious, and Murphy shrugged.

"Everything we've seen on Xing—or gotten out of the prisoners—indicates that she's as arrogant as she is vicious," he said. "She doesn't waste time trying to put herself inside an opponent's head, because as she sees it, there's no reason she should. What matters is what she's going to do to him, not what he might plan on doing to *her*. This—" he waved at the plot again "—isn't her kind of thinking. Besides, we got a big piece of the fans on both of her surviving FTLCs. I doubt they could pull much more than four or five hundred lights in wormhole space. Even on a direct vector home, Than would've beaten her back to base. She couldn't have gotten there fast enough to get a picket to Hefei before *we* got here . . . assuming that one or both of her carriers' drives didn't simply pack it in on the way home."

Tremblay nodded slowly, and Murphy saw the shadows in the commodore's holographic eyes. A dead Fasset drive would never—*could* never—drop out of wormhole space. It was one of an interstellar spacer's darkest nightmares, because no one could possibly rescue, or even *find,* another ship inside the wormhole. And so they would drift through those nerve-crawling, simply *wrong* depths until power and air and food ran out and their ship became their coffin for all eternity.

"But why light off their drive so quickly?" Granger asked, rubbing one eyebrow with an index finger. "They must have brought their fan up almost the instant they picked us up. Why not just lie doggo until we gave up and left rather than alert us to the fact that he'd picketed the system?"

"Because he's just as good as his reputation," Murphy replied. "If we got far enough along the logic chain to be here, in Hefei, then we're obviously eliminating possibilities. And he knows what we would have been looking for: a deserted system with lots of asteroids for resources and no civilians to realize what was going on. So I'd say it's pretty clear he's operating on the assumption that we've figured out it has to be either Hefei or Yuxi. And if we have, then we'll be leaving for Yuxi just as soon as we've determined he isn't here. So his picket couldn't afford to wait until we leave, or it would get there behind us."

"But this way, it's got the lead time while we decelerate and reorient to the right exit vector," Granger said, nodding.

"Exactly." Murphy shrugged. "We can't decelerate to rest any faster than we're already decelerating, so this way they get effectively at least a six- or seven-hour jump on us. They only waited until they could get a good unit count."

Both Granger and Tremblay were nodding now, and Murphy turned to Captain Lowe's hologram.

"Get us down to zero, then lay in a course for Yuxi, Captain," he said.

CHAPTER THIRTY-SEVEN

"I STILL DON'T SEE HOW XING MANAGED TO LOSE SO MANY SHIPS," Captain Sunwar Kang's hologram said.

At least he'd managed to not say "how *even* Xing managed," Admiral Than thought. Probably only because it was an official, recorded and logged communication. Speaking of which...

"Overconfidence and a Federation commander who was more competent than our ops plan gave him credit for," Than replied.

He wasn't certain that was...sufficiently oblique, but it was the best he could manage. *And at least it sounds better than "blind stupidity and a flag officer who couldn't pour piss out of a boot,"* he reflected.

"This Murphy...thinks outside the box," he continued. "We still haven't determined how he got such missile range, or exactly what he did to the Second Admiral, but whatever he used, it wasn't a standard Fed weapon system. Nobody ever saw anything like it, so nobody took precautions against it."

And that, he thought, was nothing but the truth.

The battered remnants of Dragon Gamma had reached Diyu four weeks earlier. He'd run both of his surviving FTLCs on the ragged edge of Fasset failure to get them there that quickly, but he'd had no choice. Not after he realized that Xing—as if determined to compound her idiocy—had run directly for Diyu. She might as well have given Murphy a roadmap.

Calm down, he told himself. *It's only a* general *roadmap.*

415

Murphy can't have gotten a good enough vector analysis to nail down Diyu as her destination. All it can do is give him a general volume. But still...

He'd been a little surprised that Xing hadn't beaten him home, but only a little. It was obvious from how long she'd required to wormhole out that her Fasset drives had taken significant damage, and that sort of damage had unfortunate implications for sustainable FTL velocity, because the mass of its Fasset drive's black hole—or, rather, the ratio between its black hole's mass and the rest mass of the ship—dictated the maximum velocity it could attain and hold. Than's own ships had maintained just over nine hundred lights, but only at a very real risk of failure even on drives which had sustained little or—in *Cai Shen*'s case—no damage.

"Do you really expect him to attack here?" Sunwar asked anxiously, and Than suppressed a sigh.

He'd been able to save Sunwar's face, at least a little, by promoting him to the status of yard commander in Diyu when Xing ordered him relieved from squadron command. It was a task well suited to his experience at the Office of Shipbuilding and Office of Munitions, and he'd done well at it. But as much as Than had disagreed with Xing on an entire host of issues, the fact that Sunwar no longer belonged on a command deck in battle wasn't one of them.

As his ability to ask that question amply demonstrated.

The third admiral reminded himself that it wasn't really Sunwar's fault, not that it made the query any less irritating.

Oh, be fair, Qiang! If Murphy's half as smart as you think he is, it wouldn't matter if Sunwar was a tactical genius! We are so screwed, thanks to that idiot bitch.

"If he was able to project the Second Admiral's retreat vector with sufficient accuracy, I'm pretty sure he will," he said out loud. "It's what I'd do in his position," he added grimly.

"But he can't know what we have to defend the system," Sunwar pointed out, and Than nodded.

"That's true, and frankly, I hope that's what he's thinking, too. If he knows how many manifolds were aboard the freighter he intercepted, then he must have a pretty fair idea of the size of Dragon Fleet's intended carrier component. But he can't have any confirmation—" *unless some of our people* told *him after he rescued them* "—of how far along the carriers' sublight groups were. So it's possible he'd anticipate a much stronger defense than we could actually put up and stay home rather than risk it. But I don't think this man thinks that way." Than shook his head. "I think he'll count on the fact that without FTLCs of our own, all our parasites could do would be to defend the volume immediately around the yard facilities. He'll pop in with his own carriers and take a good look around. And—" the third admiral showed his teeth in a humorless grin "—when he sends in his recon drones and figures out we can't stop him, he'll return the favor for what we did to New Dublin's yards."

Sunwar nodded, his expression desperately unhappy, and Than didn't blame him. There were over seventy thousand men and women distributed through the building yards, outfitting docks, orbital smelters, and fabrication platforms. And, unlike the New Dublin System, there were no habitable planets in Diyu. No place to which Sunwar could evacuate those men and women.

"We can always hope I'm wrong," Than said, "but—"

"Excuse me, Third Admiral."

Than turned away from the comm as Su Zhihao knocked on the frame of his shipboard office's open door. The chief of staff's expression was almost as unhappy as Sunwar's.

"Yes, Zhihao?"

"Base Ops reports that the long-range arrays have just picked up a Fasset signature," Su replied. No ship, not even an FTLC, was big enough to mount long-range Fasset arrays. "It's coming in on a direct vector from New Dublin, but I don't think it's Murphy."

"No?" Than felt a chill.

"No, Sir. It's twenty-one light-weeks out, but it's only pulling about two hundred lights. ETA is seventeen-point-six hours."

"I see."

Than nodded. At a velocity that low, it almost had to be Xing, limping home at last. And wasn't it a hell of a note that he would almost rather it *was* Murphy.

"I'll get back to you, Kang," he said to Sunwar.

"Of course, Sir," Sunwar replied.

His holo vanished—probably with a sense of vast relief on his part, Than thought; this was likely to be one of those conversations a prudent subordinate wanted no part of—and the third admiral tipped back his chair and pointed for Su to take the one facing his desk.

"What's she going to do, Sir?" the chief of staff asked, launching into that conversation as he settled. "She's sure as hell had time to work out her next move."

"Good question." Than rubbed his cheek. "Pretend you just lost the biggest battle in decades with minimal—possibly no—losses to the other side. What would *you* do?"

"Well . . . if there's a firing squad waiting for me back at Anyang, wild space and piracy with my surviving ships would have to look very attractive. Assuming I had no sense of honor." Su shrugged. "Which probably means *she's* been thinking about exactly that . . . hard."

"Firing squad?"

"It *is* election season, Sir, and our political leadership had a lot riding on Dragon Fleet's success. What she's brought them instead—?" Su shook his head. "The best way to prove you weren't responsible for whatever's gone wrong is to shoot somebody else and convince everyone *that person* was responsible for it."

"You may have a point," Than conceded. "And the best way to be the one who doesn't get shot is to hang the responsibility on someone else. Some handy subordinate, say."

"I know," Su said. "That's why I'm so worried over how long she's had to think."

✧   ✧   ✧

"Sir?"

Su stood in Than's office door once again, and the third admiral looked up from the paperwork with which he'd been pretending to be occupied. He took in Su's expression, and glanced at the time display. Xing was still well over ten hours out, so that couldn't explain what had put that . . . odd look on his chief of staff's face.

"Yes?" he said.

"We've just picked up another inbound Fasset signature. This one's at twenty-six light weeks, and it's turning out just over nine hundred lights."

Than stiffened and brought his work chair fully upright.

"Approach vector?" he asked rather more sharply.

"It's coming in from Hefei." Su's voice was flat. "Looks like just one ship."

"*Li Shiji*." Than's voice was equally flat.

"I'd sort of hoped you were being unduly paranoid when you posted her there." Su flashed a humorless smile.

"ETA?"

"A bit under six hours. About five hours before Xing. Assuming the first bogey is her, of course. *Li Shiji* has farther to go, but she's traveling close to five times as fast."

"And she wouldn't be, unless the hounds of hell—or Murphy—were on her heels," Than said grimly.

"I suppose we should look on the bright side," Su said.

"I must be missing something. There's a *bright* side to this?"

"Well, if we have to die in hopeless battle, at least Xing should get here in time to go with us."

Than snorted, but his eyes also narrowed and he tipped back, rubbing his chin.

"You're probably right about that," he said, after a moment. "On the other hand, I'd prefer to put up at least some fight. And I can't do that from the bottom of a stellar gravity well."

"Sir?"

"Tell Captain Sun to take us out of orbit. Move us to Intercept Three."

Su's eyebrows rose. Of the four potential interception points Than had selected, Intercept Three was the one the chief of staff had least expected to use if the enemy turned up on a vector from Hefei. It was just beyond the Diyu Powell Limit, but it lay very, very close to the least-time approach vector for Hefei. He started to ask what Than was thinking, but the third admiral's expression discouraged inquiries.

"Intercept Three," he repeated. "Yes, Sir. We should be in position in about two hours."

"Good. And I want orders waiting for *Li Shiji* to join us there as soon as she arrives."

"I'll see to the transmission."

"Good," Than said once more, then sighed unhappily. "And now I suppose I should have a word with Sunwar."

"Don't envy you, Sir," Su said quietly, then nodded and withdrew.

Than swiped his desk display. A moment later, Sunwar Kang's hologram appeared above his desk once again.

"Third Admiral," Sunwar said. His expression was tight. Well, of course it was. It was *his* arrays which had picked up *Li Shiji's* footprint.

"If Murphy is as hard on Captain Pan's heels as I am afraid he is, he's probably only about seven or eight hours behind him," Than said flatly.

"You're sure he's following *Li Shiji*, Sir?"

Than successfully resisted a sudden urge to bite the man's head off. Sunwar's tone was almost desperate, and the third admiral understood exactly why he so badly wanted Than to be wrong. Unfortunately—

"Captain Pan's orders were quite specific," he said almost gently. "Only two things would have brought him back to Diyu. A recall order from me or Second Admiral Xing, or the arrival of a Fed force in Hefei, and I didn't send any recalls."

"Of course, Sir." Sunwar braced himself visibly. "What are your orders?"

"I don't have any to give you," Than said. "Not really. *Cai Shen* and *Li Shiji* are the only FTL-capable ships in-system—or about to be in-system, in *Li Shiji*'s case. And we don't begin to have the capacity to lift your people out. I wish to hell we did, but we don't."

"The *Bǐshǒu*'s still here—" Sunwar began.

"Forget it. *Bǐshǒu* won't take our people."

"The hell it won't! I can have a security team aboard within an hour and—"

"Don't," Than snapped. Sunwar stared at him, eyes filled with protest, and the admiral shook his head. "Nobody goes aboard that ship without an invitation, no matter what. You know that."

"But under the circumstances—"

"The circumstances don't matter. And you'd never see any security team you sent aboard again. Trust me."

Sunwar's face turned into a mask.

"In that case, Sir, I repeat—what are your orders?"

Than inhaled deeply, held it, then let the air out of his lungs. Sunwar had a point, he conceded. The responsibility came with Than's rank.

"Admiral Xing will be back in-system in less than eight hours. I'm about to adjust my own deployment in light of *Li Shiji*'s appearance. My orders—until and unless Admiral Xing countermands them—are to move as many of your personnel as possible, preferably all of them, from the construction and support platforms into any sublight unit that has the life support to accept them. And then, you are to move those ships at least a quarter million kilometers clear of the platforms."

"They'll be sitting ducks," Sunwar protested. "None of them

were fully operational to begin with, and then Second Admiral Xing stripped the cadres out of them for the attack on New Dublin!"

"I'm aware of that, Captain." Than's voice was icy. "But the construction facilities and the unfinished FTLCs will be the enemy's primary targets. And, frankly, the only real defense we can offer our personnel is to put them aboard ships the Feds may not waste missiles on." His mouth was a grim line as he met Sunwar's anguished gaze squarely. "If there was anything else I could do, I'd do it, Captain. Trust me."

Their locked eyes held for a moment, and then Sunwar's shoulders slumped.

"I know," he said. "I know that, Sir. It's just—"

"Just that they're your people and your responsibility. Well, they're mine, too, Kang, and I wish to hell I could do better by them. But all either of us can do is the best we can."

"Yes, Sir. Good luck."

"And to you, Kang. Than, clear."

"Ah, Sir," Su said in a delicate tone, "about *Bìshǒu*...Should we alert the envoy, as well?"

"The envoy is tied into Sunwar's systems," Than replied. "She already knows everything we do. I don't know what she's going to do about it, but that's not our problem or our responsibility. Her superiors made that perfectly clear when they sent her here."

"So we stay out of it?"

"So we stay out of it," Than confirmed grimly.

"It's Murphy, all right," Captain Pan Hanying said.

The transmission instructing *Li Shiji* to join *Cai Shen* at Intercept Three had been waiting when his FTLC went sublight. Now she was decelerating hard toward Than's flagship. The good news was that they'd make rendezvous in time for both of them to go to strict EMCON well before her pursuers came out of wormhole space. Unfortunately, that was all the good news there was.

"So you made positive ID?" Than's tone made the question a statement, and Pan nodded.

"Seven FTLCs, and two of them matched the emission signatures of the *Marduks* Xing was chasing in New Dublin. It may not be Murphy in person, I suppose, but these are definitely his *ships*."

"I wish I was surprised." Than sighed.

"The only thing that surprises *me*, Sir, is that he actually guessed wrong and went to Hefei first instead of coming straight here. The man must have his own pet demon whispering in his ear!"

"I doubt it's anything quite that arcane," Than said dryly. "I'll grant you that he seems a bit...aggressively competent, though."

"What are we going to do, Sir?"

"I'm not sure." Than shrugged slightly. "Admiral Xing should be here by the time he arrives."

"Admiral Xing?" Pan's voice was tighter than it had been. "She's here? She got back to Diyu?"

"Not exactly. But the gods appear to have a sense of humor." Than smiled tightly. "She *will* be back about...three and a half hours before Murphy arrives, according to your tracking data." Not even the base's arrays had detected Murphy yet, but given *Li Shiji*'s burst-transmitted data, that would be changing in the next forty minutes.

Or would have been, if Than hadn't ordered Sunwar to shut them down.

"With all due respect, I'd rather not be the butt of any divine humor."

"Ah, but that's why they're gods. We hapless mortals have no choice but to play our parts for them."

Pan's eyes narrowed. One thing Than Qiang had never been was fatalistic. Of course, he'd never faced a battle of annihilation against three times his own strength, either.

"As you say, Sir," the captain said after a moment.

"For right now, just concentrate on making rendezvous. Then the two of us are going to go dark, dig a hole in space, and crawl into it."

"Understood, Sir."

Xing Xuefeng prowled *Nüwa*'s flag bridge as the big, battered carrier finally dropped sublight.

The normal eight-week voyage from New Dublin to Diyu had turned into a *nineteen*-week crawling nightmare, and much of that was her own fault. *Nüwa* and *Pangu*'s best sustained velocity had been only 400 *c*, and Captain Geng, *Pangu*'s CO, had urged her to reduce even that speed in light of their damaged Fasset drives. But she'd rejected his suggestion, because it was imperative that she return to Diyu at the earliest possible moment.

And, as Geng had very carefully not pointed out after the fact, the consequence had been a dozen more blown nodes. They'd been forced to reduce to this miserable crawl, and Xing had been like a saber tooth with a toothache ever since. The only good news was that the nineteen weeks the rest of the universe had passed during the voyage had been only a little over two and a half for her.

The longest two and a half weeks of her entire life.

But they were back at last, although their astrogation had been as bad as anything else. Their best normal space acceleration rate was down to only 850 gravities, even outside the Powell Limit. At that rate, it would take them almost ten hours to decelerate to rest relative to local space, and they'd emerged from wormhole space less than three light-hours from Diyu's primary. Which meant that they were about to overshoot the star by fifteen light-minutes, then crawl *seventeen* light-minutes back to the yards.

Still, they'd made it, and her nostrils flared as *Nüwa*'s sensors began pulling in the transmissions of navigation buoys and ship transponders.

"Obviously the Feds didn't know where Diyu is," she observed to Commander Xie Kai, Rang Yong-Gi's successor as her chief of staff. Xie's darkly auburn hair hinted at *gwáipò* ancestry, but Xing had found her...adequate. So far at least.

"Given how long it took us to get back here," she continued, "they'd certainly have attacked by now if they had a clue where to find us."

"As you say, Second Admiral." Xie bobbed her head.

"I don't see *Cai Shen*'s transponder, though," Xing continued, frowning at the plot. "In fact, I don't see any of Than's ships."

"That's odd," Xie murmured. "We know at least two of them got out. Do you suppose their Fasset drives were even more badly damaged than ours?"

"Not judging by their observed acceleration rates before we lost track of them." Xing frowned. Then her nostrils flared. "Than being Than, he's probably hiding somewhere out there until he's sure we aren't the big bad Feds."

Xie started to say something, then bit her lip and simply bobbed her head respectfully again.

Xing glared at her, hearing the words the commander hadn't said. The same words all too many people were going to be saying if she didn't get a handle on the situation quickly. For all she knew Than had already dispatched his own report on the battle, and that would be...bad.

"Tell communications I want an omnidirectional transmission to *Cai Shen*. We'll find him wherever the hell he is."

"Yes, Ma'am."

✧   ✧   ✧

"My God," O'Hanraghty muttered. "I expected something big, but *this*..."

The chief of staff's voice trailed off as he and Murphy stared in disbelief at the master plot while detail after detail filled in. *Ishtar* had gone sublight a hundred and forty-five light-minutes from the M3v star labeled Yuxi on their charts, and whatever those charts may have said about "uninhabited star systems" had obviously been in error. The range was long, but the Federation's optical systems were very good, and even if they hadn't been, a solid blaze of power sources stretched around the inner system. The sheer size of the installations beggared the imagination. Venus Futures' primary yard could have been tucked into one tiny corner of the mammoth building complex.

"How the hell did the League *build* something like this?" Commander Ortiz asked, shaking his head.

"I don't know," Lieutenant Commander Tanaka said, then glanced at O'Hanraghty. "Unless they had help," she added slowly.

The chief of staff raised an eyebrow at her, and she shrugged irritably.

"I still think there's no rational explanation for why the Rish should be helping the Leaguies, but Ed's right. There's no way the League should have been able to build something like this out of their own resources. Not as tightly strapped as all our reports indicate they are. So, yes. They had to have help, and it had to be the Rish, *whatever* their reasons are." She looked squarely at Murphy. "You were right all along, Sir."

She looked less than happy as she made the admission, but her expression was unflinching.

"Well, maybe we'll have a better picture of what this is all about in the next few hours, Amari," Murphy told her, and she nodded grimly.

"I'd like that," O'Hanraghty said. "I'd like that a lot, Sir."

✧   ✧   ✧

"Than, where the hell are you?" Xing Xuefeng demanded from the comm display.

Than looked at Su and raised one eyebrow.

Xing had gone sublight much closer to Diyu than she'd probably wanted to, and *Cai Shen* was ten light-minutes from the star. There were still just over a hundred light-minutes between them, however. That equated to an hour and a half communication lag—one-way—in any conversation.

Apparently it eventually occurred to *her* that waiting the next best thing to three hours between transmissions didn't make a great deal of sense, as well.

"*Nüwa*'s taken severe damage," she continued five minutes later. "Bring up your drive wherever you are and rendezvous with me ASAP. I'm transferring my flag to *Cai Shen*, effective immediately. I have to take word back to Anyang as quickly as possible. That's our new mission priority. I'll leave you in command of Project Astra to supervise construction and repairs and as chief liaison officer until my return."

Su scowled.

"That . . . bitch," he said through gritted teeth. "She's going to leave you behind and run back to Anyang with her own version of what happened at New Dublin."

"Beat the bad news back and control the narrative." Than nodded. "It's been done before. Although I'm curious about how she thinks anyone can sugarcoat the loss of so many lives and ships."

"She won't even try," Su said bitterly. "Why should she, when she can blame it all on *you*? And use your own flagship to do it! No. This crew—our people—they won't let her throw you to the wolves!"

"I'm not particularly concerned," Than said serenely.

"You're—" Su began hotly, then stopped as a raucous buzzer snarled suddenly. The chief of staff looked at the plot, then back at Than.

"You *sneaky* son of a bitch," he said very, very softly.

"Sorry, XO—what was that?" Than said.

"Nothing." Su gave his commander a sidelong look. "Nothing, Sir. Nothing at all."

"Good, because what I *thought* I heard you say would have been grossly improper. I'm glad to discover I was mistaken."

"As you say, Sir."

"Well," Than interlaced his fingers and cracked his knuckles. "I suppose I should reply to her."

"Of course, Sir."

"Second Admiral," he said into the pickup, his expression somber, "I regret to inform you that it won't be possible for me to comply with your instructions. The base arrays detected several incoming Fasset drives several hours ago. They have just dropped sublight approximately one hundred and forty-five light-minutes from the primary. Based on reports from the *Li Shiji*, I believe this to be at least seven Fed FTLCs. Their entry vector is within forty-five degrees of your own, which, unfortunately, makes it impossible for *Cai Shen* to rendezvous with *Nüwa* from my present position without being intercepted. Standing orders in a situation such as this are clear. Accordingly, in order to preserve the strategic asset of my vessels for future service to the League, I must, regretfully, immediately depart the system. As you said, it is essential that we report back to Anyang. That is now our mission priority, and I assure you that we'll get the job done for you. Than, clear."

He managed—somehow—not to smile until he'd finished recording the message.

"*That's* why we're at the Intercept Three, isn't it?" Su said almost accusingly. "Because the math makes it impossible to match velocities with *Nüwa* on her entry vector!"

"What a nasty motive to impute to a purely tactical decision," Than replied. Then he tapped his comm display and Captain Sun appeared on it.

"Yes, Third Admiral?"

"I'm afraid there's nothing we can do here, Captain. Execute Withdrawal Alpha."

"Yes, Sir," the flag captain replied, and Than sat back as *Cai Shen* and *Li Shiji* began to accelerate away from Diyu on what was almost—*almost*—a reciprocal of Murphy's heading.

He could no more "see" Murphy yet than Murphy could see him, but unlike the Federation admiral, he had the advantage of knowing where his opponent had to be. His current course would actually close to within no more than a couple of light-minutes of Murphy's carriers, but by the time Murphy saw him, his base velocity would be well over 75,000 KPS. Moreover, their closing velocity would still be close to 297,000 KPS, because

Than's acceleration would come within a few percentage points of matching Murphy's *de*celeration on their respective headings. *Cai Shen* and *Li Shiji* would blow past the TFN force just outside their weapons envelope, and it would be impossible for Murphy to decelerate and place himself on a pursuit vector before Than wormholed out for Anyang.

"What about the people on the yard platforms, Sir?" Su asked quietly.

"There's no way I can save them," Than replied with genuine regret. "Unless..."

He looked at the plot, studying the projected vectors, then nodded. His and Murphy's ships truly were going to pass one another at what constituted a very short range on the scale of a star system. And while they would be unable to *shoot* at one another...

"Well, *those* two bastards are going to get away," O'Hanraghty growled, glaring at the two Fasset drives which had just appeared on *Ishtar*'s sensors. At the moment, those sensors were actually looking into the past as she continued to decelerate at 1,800 gravities. After just over an hour, her velocity was down to 220,740 KPS. But the light-speed emissions of the RLH carriers coming at them were also over an hour old. The computers projected their current positions as barely sixty-nine light-minutes ahead of Murphy's force.

"They knew we were coming, Sir," Mirwani said. "Their picket got back in time to tell them even before they picked us up on their system arrays."

"And they decided to show us a bit of chutzpah," Murphy acknowledged. He shook his head in unwilling admiration. "They got themselves into position with time enough to shut down and go to EMCON at least two hours before we turned up. By the time we went sublight, there was nothing to see...until they lit their fans off again."

"I'm surprised they didn't just run the other way, Sir."

"No reason to." O'Hanraghty shrugged. "We'll hit closest approach in—what? Another seventy minutes? They'll still be at least a couple of light-minutes clear when they break past us, and we'll be headed exactly the wrong direction to decelerate and go after them. So why not give us the finger as they go by?"

"Excuse me, Admiral," Lieutenant Mastroianni said.

"Yes, Lieutenant?"

"Sir, I just receipted a transmission from an Admiral Than. A message to you."

"Ah?" Murphy cocked an eyebrow at O'Hanraghty. Thirty minutes had passed since they'd first detected the League FTLCs. Their own velocity was down to 194,265 KPS, but the League ships had increased their velocity to over 102,000 KPS and the rate of closure remained unchanged. The actual range was down to little more than a light-hour, though.

"Put it on my display," Murphy said,

"Yes, Sir," she replied, and a dark-complexioned, tallish man appeared on the display.

"Admiral Murphy," he said, "I am Third Admiral Than. I'm sure it's as obvious to you as it is to me that you can't intercept me before I withdraw from the system, but I have a proposition for you. Something I think you want badly, but an offer that would require me to trust your word."

"Cheeky bastard, isn't he?" O'Hanraghty said wryly. "Confident, too."

"With reason, I'm afraid," Murphy agreed, and looked back at Mastroianni.

"All right, Lieutenant. Stand by to record a response."

"Ready now, Sir."

"Thank you." Murphy faced the pickup. "What kind of proposition, Admiral Than?" he asked, then sat back to wait.

The transmission range was almost seventy light-minutes, but that range was shrinking by just under a light-second each second. By the time the transmission reached Than, forty-eight minutes later, his ships had traveled another twenty light-minutes...and Murphy's had traveled thirty-two.

"There are seventy thousand-plus men and women aboard the yard facilities in the star system," Than replied sixty minutes after Murphy had sent his reply. "They're defenseless. Several of the sublight warships are capable of movement, and a handful are actually armed, but their magazines are empty and the FTLCs can't even maneuver. I want your word that if they surrender, you'll let them live."

"I can't take that many prisoners," Murphy replied. "This isn't New Dublin, and I don't have the capacity to lift them out of here."

"I realize that," Than said after another 3.3 minute delay, just as their opposing forces reached their closest point of approach at two light-minutes' separation. "But as I say, the ships can't go anywhere. At the moment they aren't even crewed, and even if they were, they're stuck here, in the system, without carriers. Give me your word you'll let them live—evacuate to those ships, wait for rescue—when you destroy the yard facilities, and I'll give you something in return."

Murphy's jaw tightened. He said nothing for long seconds as the two forces passed one another. The range began to open once more as Than sped off toward safety, and then Murphy squared his shoulders and tapped a command into his console. His comm image split, sharing the screen with a scrolling data file. It was a very *long* file...one that contained the name and serial number of every League POW left behind in New Dublin.

"I'm no monster, Than," he said, while that list flashed upward beside him. "And I know about your targeting decision in New Dublin. You couldn't have missed Crann Bethadh so completely by accident. You have my word...and my thanks."

"One of those two FTLCs in front of you is the *Nüwa*," Than said three minutes later. "It's the flagship of an officer I think you're probably looking for, and as of a couple of hours ago, she was still quite alive. Knowing her, I rather suspect the records will say something different from that if you permit *Nüwa* to surrender. I'd really like the other officers and spacers aboard her to have the opportunity to live, though, so please don't lump them together with that one and just blow *Nüwa* out of space."

"We have a deal," Murphy said. "Assuming *Nüwa*'s willing to surrender. However, my sensors are picking up at least one other ship in-system that appears to have an operable Fasset drive. A merchant hull."

"I'm...afraid I have no authority over that ship," Than replied with a strange expression. The two-way transmission lag was back up to four minutes. "It may well attempt to leave the system, but I assure you that no League personnel will try to escape aboard it if it does."

Murphy hid a frown as he tried to parse those two sentences. There was something...odd about them. Then he shrugged.

"If it tries to escape, then it's not covered by our agreement," he said.

"Of course not," Than agreed six minutes later. Then he grimaced. "I don't care for you, Murphy. Federation officers with a hint of competence are a problem for the League."

"I won't take it personally," Murphy said. "I assume you're bound for Anyang. Maybe this can be the last great battle of the war."

"You have enough pull in the Federation to start peace talks?"

The comm delay was back up to seven minutes and climbing as Than's acceleration started building velocity differential rather than reducing it.

"No. Not yet, at least. But I can try for it. Maybe you can, too."

"I can't promise anything. Don't assume I'll keep my rank or my influence once word gets back to the capital. Does the Federation have a habit of shooting the messenger, too?"

"I'm pretty sure I'll find out shortly," Murphy replied.

"Good luck, then," Than replied nine and a half minutes later. "And may we never cross paths again. I doubt our next meeting will be this courteous. Than, clear."

✧   ✧   ✧

Than gave Murphy a nod and cut the channel.

"Erase all record of that conversation, Zhihao."

"What conversation?" his chief of staff asked as the holo table blinked on and then off from a sudden power surge.

Than smiled, then puffed out his cheeks.

"Three hours to supralight. Maybe we'll have enough time to see if Murphy keeps his word, or if he's just another butcher."

CHAPTER THIRTY-EIGHT

"SO HOW DO WE HANDLE THIS?" O'HANRAGHTY ASKED.

The scale of the installations had grown even more incredible as they drove nearer. The range was down to barely a half light-hour, more than close enough for the optical systems to begin picking out detail, and those details were...sobering. Not only was the mammoth building complex enormously larger than they'd believed possible, it was also far more heavily automated than any of Naval Intelligence's estimates of League capability. League construction techniques had always been more labor intensive than the Federation's, but this installation appeared to rely even more heavily on robotics than most of the Federation's Heart World yards did.

Yet what truly shocked them were the number of FTLCs floating in their building areas, apparently complete but for their Fasset drives. There were *over* forty of them, surpassing their worst-case estimates based on the manifolds lost in Alramal. If they'd gotten loose in Concordia, just *appeared* in the Heart Worlds' rear...

The total carrier strength of the Federation's strategic reserve was only twenty-five, none of which were as large and powerful as a *Fúxī*-class ship. And there wasn't a single non-capital parasite in the entire system. The *lightest* unit was a battlecruiser.

"I don't really know," Murphy murmured, standing beside him at the plot. "I know I promised Than, but..."

He shook his head, then inhaled deeply.

"All right, the first thing is to see how many of those FTLCs have their environmental systems up and running. We can pack a lot of people—maybe as many as ten thousand—aboard one of those if she doesn't have any parasites on the racks."

"But those are the strategic gold standard," O'Hanraghty pointed out.

"True. But as Callum pointed out in Alramal, Fasset drives, more than hulls or armor, are the most expensive component in terms of both time and resources. We use demo charges to take out the Fasset housing and boom, and all they really are is a cylinder. Carriers don't even have fusion drives, aside from their attitude thrusters. We'll get a lot more people into each of them, and then we can blow the rest—and the sublight units—without breaking my promise to Than."

O'Hanraghty grunted, half skeptically and half in agreement. Logically, he could find no fault with Murphy's analysis. He suspected, however, that their superiors wouldn't be using a lot of logic when they complained about the "carriers" Murphy had left "intact" behind him.

"Well, we can try it," he said dubiously, "but unless—"

"New Fasset drive contacts!" Raleigh Mirwani called out. Murphy and O'Hanraghty wheeled from the visual display to the tactical plot, and two new, bright red icons flashed on it. They were 20.2 LM from the primary and 31 LM from *Ishtar*, and their original vector and *Ishtar*'s folded together at a thirty-four-degree angle.

"Ah, Second Admiral Xing!" Murphy said.

"It would appear they've spotted us, too," O'Hanraghty replied, gesturing at the icons of *Nüwa* and *Pangu*. They had stopped decelerating and begun accelerating once more, albeit at only eight hundred and fifty gravities.

"There aren't going anywhere," Murphy said with a cold smile. "We've got a closing velocity of almost twenty thousand KPS, our acceleration rate's better than twice theirs, and we know they don't have anything on the racks, because we captured all of them in New Dublin. I think we'll let Granger and Tremblay secure the primary yard complex while we have a . . . serious conversation with our friends. Just *Ishtar* and *Gilgamesh*, I think." His smile turned even colder. "Let's finish this the way we began it, shall we?"

"Works for me," O'Hanraghty agreed.

Murphy nodded and turned to the flag deck comm display.

"Commodore Granger, I'd like you and Commodore Tremblay to proceed to the construction area. I don't think we need to worry about sorting out who goes where before we blow hell out of the installations—not yet. *Ishtar* and *Gilgamesh* will sort *these* two out," he gestured at *Nüwa*'s and *Pangu*'s icons, "and then return to join you. For now, just stay alert and keep an eye on things. Let's not shoot anybody as long as they behave themselves, but your own ships and your own personnel come first."

"Understood, Admiral," Granger replied, and Tremblay nodded. The last of his reservations had clearly evaporated as he, too, saw the incredible armada lying quiescent in the building slips...and imagined what would have happened if it had been loosed upon the Heart Worlds.

"I don't imagine this will take too long," Murphy continued. "We'll check back with you shortly. If anything comes up, feel free to call!"

"I believe I have your screen combination, Sir," Granger replied with a chuckle, and the display blanked.

"I take it you heard all of that, Captain?" Murphy said, looking at his link to *Ishtar*'s command deck.

"I did, indeed, Sir. Going to eighteen hundred gravities on an intercept heading in thirty seconds."

"Excellent," Murphy said, and turned back to O'Hanraghty.

"You know," the chief of staff said, "I'm actually a little more antsy about this one than I am about any of the Leaguies."

He indicated an icon strobing a transponder labeled *Bǐshǒu*.

"Yeah, there was something...peculiar about what Than had to say about that one, wasn't there?" Murphy rubbed his chin, gazing at the icon's alphanumeric tag. "Says here she's Hell Hearth flagged, too. That could get dicey."

O'Hanraghty chuckled in mirthless agreement. Hell Hearth was the third most powerful human polity. That didn't necessarily mean a lot, since outside the Federation and the League the vast majority of human political units consisted of single-system colonies with no more than a few hundred or, at the most, a couple of million citizens. A few of the feral worlds had banded together in mutual defense associations, but even they consisted of no more than three or four systems apiece.

Hell Hearth, though, was a four-system star nation, and one of its systems possessed a pair of Earthlike worlds, both of which supported fairly substantial populations. It was a spatially compact, heavily industrialized unit—not remotely on a par with a Heart World system, perhaps, but more than big enough to provide a degree of local security that neither the Federation nor the League wanted to disturb in a region beyond the blue line. Not only that, Hell Hearth shared one of its star systems with the Quarn in a unique relationship. The heavy-grav, starfishlike Quarn weren't interested in Earthlike worlds, but Hell Hearth III boasted a supra-Earth they found quite homey...and which was orbited by an oxy-nitrogen world about seventy-five percent of Earth's mass. As a result, Hell Hearth was the only human polity which had an actual military alliance with the Quarn. And despite their well-deserved reputation as the explored galaxy's sharpest merchants and traders, Quarn warships were quite capable of looking after themselves.

That added a compelling weight to the Federation's and League's...disinclination to pick quarrels with the Hell Hearthians. Their vessels were regarded as neutrals, covered against search or seizure by either belligerent by their registry.

Of course, *Bǐshǒu*'s presence here in the middle of the League's top secret shipyard, did tend to call her "neutrality" into question.

"Odd name for a Hell Hearth-registered ship," the chief of staff observed.

"Why 'odd'?" Murphy asked, cocking an eyebrow at him.

"Because Hell Hearth's primary groups are descended from Old Earth's northern European nations, and *Bǐshǒu*'s Chinese. Means 'dagger' or maybe 'poniard.' I'd expect a Hell Hearther to be called something like '*Dolk*.' And that's a fairly...militant name for a merchant ship—even a Hell Hearthian."

"Doesn't mean a lot," Murphy replied, although his eyes were thoughtful. "There's a lot of League influences in Hell Hearth. They've got almost as many League immigrants as they do Federation."

"Granted—granted. And if not for the way Than reacted when you asked him about it, it might not seem especially odd to me, either. But we are going to have to decide what to do about her."

"So far, she's just sitting there and strobing her transponder," Murphy said. "Can't really blame her, with this many warships swarming around. But as long as she behaves herself, we can take our time about that. And it's not like she's going anywhere without our permission."

"True enough," O'Hanraghty agreed. No merchant ship could match the acceleration of an FTLC, and *Bǐshǒu* would be hopelessly disadvantaged if she tried to run from a standing start.

"So for now, let's just concentrate on our Leaguie friends," Murphy said. "In fact, I believe it's time we spoke to them. Lieutenant Mastroianni, are you ready to record for transmission?"

"I am, Sir," the comm officer said from the command deck.

"Very well." Murphy inhaled. "Second Admiral Xing, I am Admiral Terrence Murphy, Terran Federation Navy. I call upon you to decelerate to rendezvous with my ships in order to surrender...or be destroyed. And to be completely honest," he smiled thinly, "I would actually be happier if you chose not to. Murphy, clear." He paused a moment, considering that last sentence, then shrugged.

"Send it, Lieutenant."

✧   ✧   ✧

The range to *Nüwa* had fallen to fourteen light-minutes, and *Ishtar*'s and *Gilgamesh*'s vectors had bent steadily toward the League carriers' base course. At their current velocities and assuming Xing's acceleration rate held steady, Murphy's ships could have caught up to the fugitives in about forty-four minutes, although they would then have shot past at a relative velocity of 94,000 KPS. *Ishtar* was decelerating hard, in fact, to match courses and velocities in eighty-nine minutes. There was no way the League FTLCs could escape. The best they could hope to do was prolong the agony, but fourteen light-minutes was still fourteen light-minutes when it came to communication lags.

Of course, the range was falling by around a light-second every three seconds.

"I have a response from the League flagship, Admiral," Mastroianni said from Murphy's comm, twenty-six minutes later.

"Play it."

"Yes, Sir."

Mastroianni disappeared, replaced by a thin-faced woman with auburn highlights in her black hair.

"Admiral Murphy," she said in perfect, if accented, Standard English, "I am Commander Xie Kai. I have been instructed to tell you that, regretfully, Second Admiral Xing died of wounds suffered in New Dublin. Captain Ding was also killed in action. Commander Chen has assumed command as senior officer aboard. He has instructed me to tell you that he is prepared to surrender upon terms."

"There are no 'terms' except unconditional surrender," Murphy said coldly. "I am prepared to treat honorable enemies as such, but you are in no position—and neither is your Commander Chen—to demand any sort of terms from me. And, to be perfectly clear, my sole offer is that I will permit you to surrender rather than blowing you out of space. Those are the only 'terms' you will receive from me, and to be completely honest, given Second Admiral Xing's ... track record, you are more fortunate than you deserve that I'm prepared to go *that* far. I expect you to cut your acceleration immediately upon receipt of this transmission. If you do not, no further opportunity to surrender will be extended. Murphy, clear."

He cut the recording, sat back in his chair, and folded his arms, and O'Hanraghty shook his head wryly.

"Damn," he said. "That was hard *core*, Terrence. I like it!"

"Well, unless Than was lying to us—and I don't think he was—*they* are, and I don't much like that."

"I notice you didn't call them on it, though," O'Hanraghty observed.

"No, I didn't, did I?" Murphy's smile was a razor. "No point letting her know that *we* know she's still alive."

Twelve minutes later, RLHS *Nüwa* and RLHS *Pangu* cut their acceleration.

"I will take that as a sign that you've surrendered, Commander Xie," Murphy said into the visual pickup. "You will stand by to be boarded by my Marines. Be advised that any resistance to my boarding parties will be met immediately with lethal force and that it will also violate the terms under which you were allowed to surrender. Under those circumstances, I will not hesitate to destroy both of your ships and everyone aboard them. Murphy, clear."

CHAPTER THIRTY-NINE

"I SEE YOU DIDN'T NEED OUR HELP AFTER ALL, SIR," ESTEBAN Tremblay said as *Ishtar* slid smoothly into orbit around the system's second planet, accompanied by her deployed parasites. Tremblay's flagship, *Kishar*, lay in orbit four hundred kilometers ahead of *Ishtar*, and the other FTLCs were spread around the planet's circumference, each surrounded by its own spread of protective sublight parasites.

"No, they were quite cooperative...when the alternative was being blown out of space," Murphy agreed.

"Have you located Admiral Xing?" Harriet Granger asked from her quadrant of the comm display.

"No, but it's early days yet. Trust me, we aren't going to stop looking until we *do* find her," Murphy said with a thin smile, watching the visual display as *Nüwa* and *Pangu* entered orbit, as well. "I don't imagine the Oval will object to having a couple of operational *Fúxīs* to examine," he added. "Although they're going to be slower than hell on the way back to New Dublin."

"This is one highly automated yard, Sir," Tremblay said. Murphy looked at him, and the commodore shrugged. "It's several light-years closer to *us* than it is to the League, when you come down to it, too," he pointed out, "and all the evidence suggests that we've just taken out anything they might counterattack with to retake it."

437

"Tempting. Very tempting," Murphy conceded. "But let's not let hubris lead us into something we'll all regret down the road. For right now, I'll settle for just taking it away from the Leaguies."

"You're probably right." Tremblay shook his head. "It just seems like such a hell of a waste. And you might want to survey the damage on those two prizes of yours before you blow it all up, Sir. My senior engineer's been doing a virtual tour of the yard capabilities here. No manifolds, thanks to you, but unless their Fasset drives are damaged a lot more badly than it looks like they are, they could probably plug in new nodes—enough to get them up to a decent turn of speed in wormhole space, anyway—in only two or three weeks. You'd recoup all that time just on the way back to New Dublin."

"Um." Murphy rubbed his chin, then glanced at O'Hanraghty.

"It sounds like a good idea to me," the chief of staff said. "Assuming we can figure out how to push all the right buttons and that the previous owners haven't left any nasty little bits and pieces of sabotage lying around to blow us all to pieces."

"I don't think that's going to happen," Tremblay said, addressing O'Hanraghty with rather more warmth than was his wont. The commodore actually smiled. "We, ah, made it very clear to them that anything like that would tend to void Admiral Murphy's guarantee. At the moment, I think that's the last thing they want to risk."

Murphy grunted in acknowledgment. It was rare enough for a system's defeated defenders to be allowed to surrender, much less be guaranteed safety while the victors destroyed that system's industrial capacity. He was confident the League POWs had no intention of doing anything that might piss their captors off.

"We'll see," he said after a moment. "I think it probably is a good idea, assuming the damage is repairable and that we can fix it without relying on League 'slave labor.' Forcing them to do that might push some of them just a bit too far. And it wouldn't do any of them any favors when the League 'rescues' them and starts looking for examples and scapegoats."

Tremblay nodded, and Murphy switched mental gears.

"What have you heard from *Bǐshǒu*?" he asked.

"Not a peep," Granger said. "We followed your directive to let sleeping dogs lie until you got back here, but I have to say, I am a little surprised that *they* haven't said anything yet."

"No protestations of neutrality? Demands that we promise to respect the sanctity of the Hell Hearth flag?"

"No, Sir. Nothing. Nothing at all."

"And there's another thing, Sir," Tremblay said. Murphy looked at him and the commodore frowned. "We haven't had time to do much in the way of prisoner interrogation, but we've sort of skimmed the surface, if you know what I mean." He paused until Murphy nodded, then continued. "The Leaguies all seem a little . . . weird where that ship's concerned. None of them seem to know anything at all about it . . . except that it's been a permanent fixture here."

"What?" It was Murphy's turn to frown.

"According to the POWs back in New Dublin, anybody assigned to this operation—aside from Third Admiral Than's squadron, at least—was here for the duration," Tremblay said. "That's how tight security was. They weren't going anywhere until the 'Dragon Fleet' launched."

"That much makes sense. Bit rough on the personnel involved, but it makes sense," O'Hanraghty put in, and Tremblay nodded.

"Agreed. But not only has *Bǐshǒu* been here as long as anyone can remember, which seems a little peculiar for a 'neutral vessel,'" Tremblay said, "but unlike anything else that was part of the system's permanent cadre, it *has* left the system and then returned . . . to exactly the same parking orbit each time. And—this is more speculative, we only have it from a couple of sources so far—apparently each time it left and returned, a really, really big tranche of big-ticket components arrived shortly thereafter."

"Fascinating," Murphy said slowly.

"And damn *scary*," O'Hanraghty added. "If Hell Hearth is involved in this, does that mean the *Quarn* are involved? We've been figuring it had to be the Rish, but what if it wasn't?"

"That . . . seems unlikely," Murphy said. "The Quarn reserve their ferocity for trade, not something as silly as wars. That means they take treaty obligations and interstellar law really seriously. I'd be willing to bet anything I own that *they* aren't involved. In fact, I'm astonished they've allowed Hell Hearth to get mixed up in something like this. Assuming Hell Hearth *is* mixed up in it, of course."

"Beg your pardon?" Granger sounded less surprised by that last sentence than she might have, and Murphy snorted mirthlessly.

"Given the point Captain O'Hanraghty's just raised, we need to make damned sure we've IDed the right batch of alien conspirators, and right this minute *Bǐshǒu*'s behavior is popping a lot of red flags in my brain. Whatever they may be, they aren't reacting like any normal neutral face-to-face with overpowering military force. Esteban's right—they ought to have said something to us by now, and they *ought* to be demanding promises of safe treatment and eventual release. They aren't. Add that to what Esteben's just laid out, and it sounds like somebody with something to hide."

"They've got to know they'll have to talk to us eventually, Sir," Commander Mirwani said respectfully. "For that matter, they have to know we're almost certain to demand an onboard inspection. We'd certainly be within our rights, under the circumstances! So what do they gain by keeping their mouths shut? For that matter, why would they expect it to do them any good?"

"It does seem odder and odder," Murphy acknowledged. "So perhaps it's time we contacted them."

✧　　✧　　✧

"I am Captain Magnar Treschow," the tall, raw-boned blond said from Murphy's comm. His face showed virtually no expression. "I am the master of *Bǐshǒu*. To whom am I speaking?"

"Rear Admiral Terrence Murphy, Terran Federation Navy. I'm the senior officer of the task force which has just taken control of the system."

"I see."

Treschow had to be aware of just how...ticklish his situation was, but from his tone, Murphy might simply have observed that the sun was likely to rise the next morning, and his expression gave away nothing at all. He must be one hell of a poker player, the admiral reflected.

"I'm sure you can understand that I might have a few questions about your vessel's presence in a purely military League star system in the middle of a war," he said out loud.

"*Bǐshǒu* is a simple merchant vessel, Admiral. We take cargo where we are instructed to take it and deliver it to whomever we were told to deliver it to. What that cargo may be and what it may be used for is not my concern."

"On the contrary, Captain." Murphy allowed a stern edge into his own tone. "If you're transporting war materials for the League, then you're carrying contraband under interstellar law. And that means your vessel is liable to search and seizure by the warships of a belligerent power. That would be me and my ships, in this instance."

"Hell Hearth would be very...displeased if our neutrality were to be violated in that fashion," Treschow replied. "The consequences would be severe."

"But Hell Hearth isn't here just now, and *I* am. I also have my responsibilities and duties as an officer of the Terran Federation, and they supersede any obligation I might have to Hell Hearth. Your government will be free to lodge a protest and even demand reparations in an admiralty court, but that doesn't change those responsibilities of mine right here, right now."

"Then it is your intent to board and search my vessel despite my very strong protest?" Again, his tone was level, almost... disinterested, and Murphy hid a frown.

"It is," he said.

"I cannot allow that."

"Captain Treschow, you don't have any choice," Murphy said flatly.

"There are always choices, Admiral."

This time Murphy's frown made it to the surface. Surely the man didn't mean—

"Admiral, *Bǐshǒu* is bringing up her fan!" Mirwani said sharply. "Estimate activation in six minutes!"

"Captain Treschow, shut down your Fasset drive!" Murphy snapped.

"No," Treschow said simply, and cut the comm circuit.

"Shit," O'Hanraghty said. "That idiot must have SCM balls! That or no brain."

"There is something really, really off about this entire situation." Murphy shook his head hard. "And we *are* going to get to the bottom of it."

He wheeled to the command ring and tapped a screen. Captain Bisgaard's comm image appeared from the bridge of TFN *Fury*.

"Yes, Admiral?"

"Captain, that freighter is bringing up its Fasset drive. I would appreciate it if you saw to it that it can't."

"Authorized to fire, Sir?"

"Authorized," Murphy said flatly. "Try to keep your fire away from the core hull, but feel free to take out its fan and however much of the boom goes with it."

"Aye, aye, Sir!"

✧　　✧　　✧

"Foxtrot Alpha-One, Foxtrot Actual. Tasking order," the voice of Lieutenant Commander Absher, CO of Fighter Group 1020, said in Lieutenant Timmerman's earbud.

"Foxtrot Actual, Alpha-One. Proceed," Timmerman replied.

"Alpha-One, you are to disable the Fasset drive of the freighter preparing to leave planetary orbit. We want it intact for boarding and search, so don't get carried away."

"Alpha-One copies, disable the Fasset drive but don't break any eggs."

"Affirmative, Alpha-One. And you'd better get a move on."

Timmerman snorted—a snort of fluorocarbon mist, not oxygen—but Absher had a point about getting a move on. Once the freighter brought up its Fasset drive, only one of TF 1705's FTLCs could run it down. At eight or nine hundred gravities, it would pretty much simply disappear as far as any reaction-propelled spacecraft, including his *Orca*, was concerned.

Until it *did* bring up its drive fan, however...

Timmerman's *Orca* had been fitted with the close-attack module for this operation. That gave him the option of going laser or cannon, and he opted for guns. The laser was arguably longer ranged, but the SCM slugs packed a lot more kinetic energy.

He twisted his empty right fist, and his haptic glove translated that into commands through a virtual universal-movement "joystick." His *Orca*—a tiny thing, by Navy standards, little bigger than a pre-space jumbo jet with stubbed off weapon pylons instead of wings—spun around its central axis, bringing its nose to bear on the freighter.

There was something odd about the Fasset drive housing, Timmerman thought as its iris expanded. Something about the angle of the node clusters was off or ... something. His right thumb flipped a command to make certain his fighter's sensors captured detailed visual, electronic, and gravitic imagery, then flipped his *left* thumb in the glove on that hand.

Fighter-mounted railguns were lighter and even faster-firing than a regular warship's point defense systems. There were three of them in the *Orca*'s nose, and two more on belly-mounted hard points. All five of them burped out a four-second burst, and twenty-five twenty-five-millimeter slugs of super-compressed matter, which packed "only" 2.2 kilotons of energy apiece, spat from their muzzles. The fighter shuddered as its thrusters compensated for the recoil, and the SCM slugs streaked across the short gap to their target.

They hit with shattering force, drilling deep, and the power demands of a Fasset drive were...extreme. Nodes and capacitors shattered, power surges flashed through undamaged components, and the entire Fasset drive, over two hundred forty meters in diameter, ripped itself apart in cataclysmic destruction.

A third of the drive boom went with it, blowing apart into an expanding cluster of debris, but the freighter's core hull appeared undamaged, and Timmerman grunted in satisfaction.

"Foxtrot Actual, Alpha-One. How was that?" he said.

"Outstanding, Alpha-One. And now I guess it's up to the Marines."

"About time those lazy bastards earned their pay."

"Alpha-One, Alpha Actual. I didn't hear that. Because if I had, I'd have to agree with you, and that would be unfortunate."

◇　　◇　　◇

"What a waste of time," Steiner said.

Logan moved his hands within his Hoplon armor to adjust his HUD projection of the *Bĭshŏu* and the Moray landers limpeted to it. The merchant ship rotated slowly, haloed by the wreckage of its Fasset drive. The housing had blown into at least a dozen large, slagged-down fragments, and three hundred meters of the drive boom had shattered. Given how thoroughly the fan had blown itself to bits, he was actually surprised the entire ship hadn't come apart.

"Spin up," he said now. "Boarding teams aren't reporting in."

"Probably because there's nothing to report." Steiner's armor read green on Logan's display as his systems came online. "Merchie with—what? A couple of dozen crew? Thought their wonderful 'neutral' status would let them sit out the fight. Then the Old Man told 'em different. So then they panicked and thought they could run for it because they were so all 'neutral' and everything." He shrugged inside his armor. "We've seen it before."

"I mean they're not reporting at all," Logan said. "Zero comms."

"Jammed?" Chavez asked. "How's that even possible?"

"Shit. Another trap ship?" Faeran's suit came online and Logan cycled power through his own servos.

"Our people are in there. That's all that matters." Logan sent a message to the pilot of their Moray's attached *Orca* and they accelerated toward an unoccupied airlock on the freighter's spin section. "Eira. Hold the fort here. We may need you on casualty evac."

"Affirmative," she said, straining against the pressure as the thunder of the *Orca*'s main thruster vibrated through the lander.

"Maybe we'll finally get to crack some Leaguie skills," Steiner said. "Been too long without a proper knock up."

"That's true," Faeran said. "Maybe we've got time to hot-swap you and the Greenie out. Improve our chances."

"Oh, ho, ho... that stung," Steiner said.

"War faces, Hoplons," Logan said. "Unknown environment. Friendlies present. Watch your penetration."

The Moray came to its customary sudden stop. Eira's vitals spiked on Logan's HUD, but she didn't complain. The bow doors snapped open, revealing the docking collar and the beige portal of one of the *Bĭshŏu*'s freight airlocks.

"Clear!" Logan punched the hatch with his right fist, and drills bored through from housings in his gauntlet's knuckles. They bit through the outer wall of the lock and sent camera feeds to each of the suits. There was no movement inside... and no sign of the Federation's boarders.

"Breach."

Logan pulled his fist back and Chavez slapped a ring the diameter of a basketball onto the airlock's outer door. Eira crouched behind the Hoplons, pulled up a metal shell from the deck, and knelt behind it with her helmeted head down.

"Shielded," she said.

"Fire in the hole!" Chavez announced, and the ring expanded, then grew red-hot. Then *white*-hot. The center of the enormous airlock door exploded inward, littering the inner chamber with shards the size of house doors.

Logan unlocked his carbine and selected a magazine of SPLAT rounds. The first four letters of the acronym stood for "Sub-Penetrating, Lethal Ammunition;" Marines being Marines, the final letter's addition had been a foregone conclusion. He double-checked the carbine's ammo readout, then stepped aboard the ship.

He crossed to the airlock's inner door. It took him a moment to find the nonstandard opening mechanism—a heavy, mechanical bar, rather than the pushbuttons of most merchant designs. He gripped it in his suit's left gauntlet and pulled, half-expecting to find it locked down. But the door slid obediently open, and his eyebrows rose in surprise. Then they lowered in even deeper surprise. An airlock this size was clearly designed for freight, but there was no hold or storage area on the inboard side.

"We've got atmosphere," he said. "Close perimeter, and mind the corners."

He and his team moved forward into an access passageway. He reached an intersection and did a combat glance around the corner with the camera mounted in his carbine. Faeran did the same in the opposite direction. The video from both cameras fed to windows in each suit's HUD.

"The hell?" Steiner said.

The airlock through which they'd entered was obviously a sham, camouflage. It was meant to look like a freight airlock for a cargo pod, but the spaces around them were obviously for personnel, not cargo, and their design was far removed from any freight-hauler's industrial and utilitarian aesthetic. Beyond the intersection, the passageways became circular, with interlocking bulkhead plates that looked like giant dragon scales. The deck was a long mat with irregular indentations spaced along its length.

"*Fury*, you reading this?" Logan sent back to the Moray for a hop to the strikecarrier.

There was no response.

"No link to the Moray," Faeran said. "We want to set up IR relays?"

"Or pull back and get the rest of the Hoplons? That's my vote," Steiner said.

"How can you be a chickenshit in your suit?" Chavez asked. "We really should have swapped you out for the Greenie. Although she'd have to deal with the smell of you pissing yourself."

"We still got teams in here," Logan said. "I don't know what the hell this ship is . . . but the Admiral needs to know. We don't make it back, at least that'll tell him something's worth his concern. Bridge is to the fore, if this is designed like a normal merch. Move out."

Logan cut around the side, sensors scanning for any hint of movement or thermal irregularities.

"Roomy, at least," Chavez observed, and Logan grunted in agreement. The passageway was much higher than usual, which at least meant there were none of the low overhangs or constant ducking of every other boarding action he'd ever done.

The bulkheads changed from bare alloy to complex mosaics. They were abstracts, with a flow of pattern and color that clashed violently, and Chavez shook his head.

"I hate to agree with Steiner," Chavez said, "but this is getting weird, Smaj."

A scream ripped down the passageway.

"Advance!"

Logan leaned into a trot, and the slam of his team's sabatons rang out against the deck in unison. They passed oval-shaped doorways, half again the height of a Hoplon, with frames etched with alien script that pulsed with red light.

The screaming grew louder at the end of the passageway, and a blur flew around the Junction and smashed against the bulkhead. The upper half of a Marine corporal oozed down the curved wall in a wide streak of glistening red. It thudded to the deck, dead eyes staring blindly, and blood pooled around it.

Logan slid to a halt.

A Navy petty officer crawled into view. Her helmet was gone, her armored vac suit torn. Blood pulsed from one of the rips, and she looked up at Logan and reached out desperately.

A massive hand grabbed her by the ankle and snapped her back around the corner.

There was another scream...that ended in a wet gurgle.

"Ancestors preserve us," Faeran muttered.

And then the first Rish Logan had ever seen in the flesh stepped into view. The saurian alien dragged the dead spacer with its claws embedded in her flesh, straight through her vac suit. It was three meters tall, hunched at the shoulders, wearing unpowered body armor. Its helmet was shaped to enclose jaws meant for ripping and tearing, red blood was splattered across its torso and arms, and it held a belt-fed rifle—large enough to be a two-man-crewed weapon for a human—in its free hand, as easily as Logan carried his carbine.

The alien flung the corpse at the Hoplons, and Logan raised his left arm to take the impact. The body flopped across his helmet, blocking his view for a split second, and the hallway erupted with gunfire. The Hoplons and the alien poured fire at one another, and Logan went down, his feet knocked out from under him, as rounds struck his suit's ankles and shins.

The Rish charged. It loped down the passage, bounding back

and forth off the deck and bulkhead with clawed feet to throw off the Hoplons' aim. Logan, still facedown on the deck, snapped his carbine up and fired. The rounds stitched from the alien's hip to its shoulder, but the hollowpoint bullets sparked against its armor and barely slowed it down.

A bayonet snapped out from its rifle, the serrated blade glowing with energy. The Rish let out a hiss and drew back with the rifle, then swung the tip up and straight into Chavez's breastplate. The weapon punched through the battle steel alloy as easily as any human force blade and drove deep into the armored suit's chest. Electricity crackled through it, and Chavez's readings on Logan's HUD went haywire.

Logan swept his carbine to one side and hit the Rish in the knee. It stumbled into the bulkhead, and Faeran and Steiner kept firing. Their bullets spattered against the alien's helmet and ricocheted through the passageway, and Logan got to one knee. He brought his suit's left fist up in a servo-driven uppercut that caught the Rish on the chin and bounced the back of its helmeted head against the wall.

He dropped his carbine and reached for it with his right gauntlet, but the Rish was incredibly quick. It evaded his right hand, slid past him, and hit him in the side. Punch spikes on the alien's armor dented Logan's suit, and the impact actually lifted him a centimeter off the deck. Containment warnings flashed across his HUD.

He twisted hard. His left elbow rammed into the Rish, driving it back into the bulkhead, and his right fist hooked into its face. The alien's armorplast visor shattered and metal buckled beneath the impact. The alien went down, and Logan fell on top of it. He knelt on its chest, raining blows onto it, battering its helmet into a mass of violet blood and twisted alloy.

He stopped only when the alien stopped convulsing.

He knelt there a moment longer, breathing hard, and then servos whined as he picked up his carbine pushed himself back upright.

"Chavez flatlined," Faeran said from behind him. "I got his tags."

"What...what the hell *was* that?" Steiner asked.

"What do you *think* it was?" Logan snarled. "A Rish. A fucking *Rish*." He shook his head inside his turretlike helmet. "I thought the Admiral was crazy. Guess not."

Chavez lay on the deck, blood seeping from the rent the alien's bayonet had ripped into his chest.

"Load penetrators," Logan said. "SPLATs aren't working against that—"

He broke off as smoke blossomed suddenly from the seams of the Rish's armor. His suit's heat sensors spiked wildly, and he stepped back involuntarily as the incendiary blazed hot enough to melt the deck. When the blinding incandescence died, it left nothing but ash.

"Holy—Do they *all* do that?" Steiner demanded.

"Let's go kill some more and find out," Logan growled. He touched the muzzle of his carbine to his helmet in salute to Chavez. "Need to find the rest of the boarding parties while we're at it." He ejected the mostly empty magazine of SPLATs and loaded a drum from the housing on his back.

"That really *was* a Rish..." Faeran said as they went around the corner to find more bits and pieces of human bodies.

"Know any other high-tech lizards in the area?" Logan growled.

"I got this cousin," Steiner said. "Real nut job. Always said the Rish were behind everything. I mean, he's *way* out there, you know? And now I've gotta tell him he was *right*? Oh, fuck me!"

"Radar pulse shows an open area behind that door ahead." Logan motioned forward with his carbine. "Got moving radar returns in it. If it isn't human, kill it."

He broke into a run, dropped his right shoulder, and slammed into the door. His suit ripped through the thin metal as if it were paper. The chamber within—larger than he'd thought—surrounded a large sphere, at least fifteen meters across, that swelled from the deck like some high-tech fungus. Thick cables connected it to both the deck and the overhead, and there was a sealed hatch in the side facing him.

There were also three Rish between him and the hatch, two in armor and one in a thinner vac suit that left the alien's head exposed.

Logan dropped his sights onto the thick jaws and bony brow of the helmetless Rish, but then he swept his weapon to the side as the armored aliens charged. He put a three-round burst into the first Rish, and it went to one knee with a shriek.

It fired from the hip, and hammer blows struck Logan's breastplate. A single round glanced off his domed helmet, starring the two-centimeter armorplast, and he rocked backward. Steiner caught him with an elbow and kept him upright.

Faeran was firing in short, controlled bursts, but the aliens were incredibly tough. It took almost her entire magazine to put them down.

"Jesus, those things are tough," Steiner said.

"Ammo check," Logan said.

"I've got...fifty-one penetrators," Steiner said.

"I'm out," Faeran said, slapping a SPLAT magazine into her weapon. "I don't frigging *care* if it's 'just a boarding op.' Next time I'm bringing a dozen mags of penetrators!"

"I've got forty-eight," Logan said.

"Not a lot of ammo for a war, Smaj," Faeran pointed out.

"No, it's not," Logan agreed. Smoke billowed around the sphere as the dead aliens immolated. "So we'd better keep moving. Let's get in there."

"You think the other parties are in—"

"No," Logan cut Steiner off. "But they were protecting what's inside. Let's crack the shell before more of them get here."

Logan found a handle for the circular door, big enough for his armored hand. It was locked, but he twisted it to one side and mechanisms within broke apart. He kicked the door open and ducked inside.

Another Rish stood on a raised platform, surrounded by holos of the lopsided battle that had just taken place. Wire diagrams of the ship and scrolling text that Logan couldn't read floated among them. Smaller aliens crowded around the towering Matriarch, their heads barely topping its waist. They were built like human adolescents, with bulbous eyes and blunted teeth.

"You've killed my daughters, vermin," Naytash said through the translating drone. "Never have we shed blood beyond the Sphere. I would take your names back. Mark your clan for honor and death. But, alas, I will not."

"Where are the rest of my people?" Logan moved forward slowly as the smaller aliens hissed at him. Faeran and Steiner filed in behind him.

"We will all die here," Naytash said. "The League humans have failed the Sphere, and there is no way back to it." She bent and stroked the head of one of the smaller Rish, then snapped its neck with a quick twist. She killed the rest without any sign of emotion. "We've played for too long," she said. "Now is the endgame."

She lifted a glowing yellow pill to her jaws and ripped it open. Her flesh blackened and cracked around the pill, a dreadful incandescence spreading, spurting out her nostrils and through her eyes. She fell to the deck, and the holo sphere cut out. Electricity sizzled through the dais, and flames burst out of computer stacks.

"Sergeant Major...I suggest we leave," Steiner said.

"*Moray Team Alpha, status report!*" Captain Bisgaard's crackled over the comm.

"Abandon ship!" Logan shouted over the general net. He shoved Faeran through the door and pushed Steiner out. "All boarding teams—if you can hear me, get back to your landers *now!*"

They ran back the way they'd come as lighting systems shorted out and fire erupted through air vents. The ship quivered around them, concussions rattling through its alloy bones.

They got back to their entrance point, but their assault lander was gone. A hurricane of venting atmosphere poured through the breached airlock, now that the docking collar had been removed.

"Shit!" Steiner shouted.

"Smartest thing they could do!" Logan shot back. "*Jump!*"

The three Hoplons hurled themselves into the hurricane, riding it out into the vacuum as *Bĭshŏu* disintegrated behind them. They locked arms and legs, pulling into a ball for protection, with helmets down and the armored carapaces of their suits out.

And then *Bĭshŏu* blossomed into a searing fireball. Logan felt a swarm of impacts against his armor as the debris storm passed over them, and Steiner shouted something unspeakably obscene over the comm. The lower half of his suit went crimson on Logan's HUD, but at least it still showed the green of successful atmospheric containment.

The star field swooped dizzily around them as they spun and spiraled from the impact of the debris until a jet of gas from Faeran's maneuvering pack killed their motion.

"That's twice," Steiner snarled. "*Twice* the Rish have blown a ship out from under our boots!"

A Moray-*Orca* combination drifted closer to them. Logan was surprised it hadn't taken debris damage itself. If he'd been the command pilot, they would have pulled farther back, he thought grimly. But then its transponder code blinked on his HUD, and he knew why it hadn't.

Damned if he would have argued with her, either.

His HUD pinged with a text message. It was from Eira. "THREE. WHO?"

"CHAVEZ," he texted back.

"No body for his family," Faeran said. "And nothing from the other teams at all."

"He died true," Logan said. "May I follow him to heaven."

"May I," Steiner said.

"May I," Faeran completed, then began murmuring in her native tongue and shut down her comm.

Logan said nothing more while they waited in the black for retrieval. But he watched the video of the Rishathan matriarch over and over.

CHAPTER FORTY

XING XUEFENG SAT QUIETLY IN THE SHUTTLE SEAT, EYES FIXED straight in front of her while she watched the Federation Marine at the forward end of the passenger compartment. The Marine wore an armored vac suit, helmet visor raised, and carried an assault rifle on a single-point sling. Her hand curled around the rifle's pistol grip and her forefinger tapped the side of the receiver gently. Blond hair was just visible in the open-fronted helmet, clipped close to the scalp, no more than a centimeter or two in length, and her gray-green eyes were cold and hard.

The guard's position had been carefully chosen. She was between the prisoners—all commissioned officers—and the flight deck. From where she stood, she could see the entire passenger compartment. She could also kill everyone in it, if the urge struck her. She wouldn't even have needed her rifle. The button on the forward bulkhead at her back blinked a bright, ominous red, indicating that it was armed. All she had to do was flip down her helmet visor with her left hand, hit that button with the heel of her right hand, and watch every one of the sixty-four League POWs strapped into their seats try to breathe vacuum as she blew the emergency hatch seal.

The significance of that blinking button had been carefully explained to the prisoners as they boarded. Not that any of them had really needed the explanation.

Xing swallowed unobtrusively as she felt the vibration of braking thrusters and realized the shuttle was about to dock.

So far, her disguise had held up better than she'd dared to hope. Altering the surgeon's log to show that Second Admiral Xing had died of wounds on the passage back to Diyu had been simple, given her command code access. Doctoring the command log would have been much more difficult, but she'd covered that by simply deleting and shredding all operational data in *Nüwa*'s and *Pangu*'s files. Murphy hadn't specifically prohibited that when he stipulated that the ships had to be surrendered in operable condition. There might be repercussions for the command crew, but since Xing was safely "dead," they wouldn't fall on her.

She didn't see how the Feds could have accurate biometric data on her, but she couldn't exclude the possibility, and it was entirely possible that there'd been imagery of her in the wreckage left behind in New Dublin. So she'd used a rinse to change her eyes to an even darker brown, almost black. The cosmetic was guaranteed for only a couple of weeks, but hopefully that would be long enough for her to get through initial in-processing and disappear into the anonymity of just one more POW. It only had to hold long enough for her to be sent to one of the sublight ships Murphy had stupidly agreed to leave intact behind him.

The long, crownlike braid which had been her trademark for so long was a thing of the past for the same reason. Her hair was almost as short as the cold-eyed Marine's, and it had become brown instead of sable. She'd considered something more *gwáimūi*, just to get as far away from her natural appearance as possible, but she'd decided against it. Red or blond hair was so rare in the League that it would automatically draw the Feds' eyes, even if they weren't actively looking for her.

She carried her splinted left arm in a sling and wore the uniform of a lieutenant. Lieutenant Nguyễn Khánh Thủy no longer required it—she truly had died at New Dublin—and she'd been tall, almost exactly as tall as Xing's hundred-seventy-five centimeters. The second admiral was a little nervous about using the real Nguyễn's ID chip, but she didn't have a lot of choice about that. She'd substituted her own image in place of Nguyễn's in the ship's personnel files—a flag officer's command codes were a wonderful thing to have—but she couldn't do anything about the DNA code locked into the real Nguyễn's chip. It was unlikely the

Feds had a genetic sample for her or Nguyễn, but if they checked her DNA against the chip for some reason...

The braking thrusters' vibration ceased. Then the shuttle's nose thumped into a docking collar, and she felt a moment of vertigo as up and down reestablished themselves. They must have docked with one of the Fed FTLCs' spin sections. The subjective vertical axis wasn't quite perpendicular to the shuttle's. Indeed, it was off by a good fifteen degrees, and her seat shifted to accommodate it. A minute or so later, the boarding tube had run out and mated with the portside hatch.

"Everyone up," the Fed Marine commanded in truly execrable Mandarin. She gestured at the port hatch with the muzzle of her rifle. "Time to go."

Xing rose with the rest of the passengers, bracing herself against the seat in front of her with her good arm as she leaned against the angled gravity, reminding herself yet again that she was a humble lieutenant, the most junior officer on the shuttle, not an admiral. She stood in place, allowing commanders and lieutenant commanders to debark before her. So far as she could tell, none of the others had recognized her through her disguise, and she'd disappeared into *Nüwa*'s junior officers' quarters before the FTLC's command crew and her own staff had been removed from the ship. So—

It was her turn, and she drew a deep, unobtrusive breath, and stepped into the boarding tube, feeling the gravity gradient shift back into conformity with the tube deck. She followed it to its inboard end and stepped out of it into a cavernous compartment.

Two other boarding tubes, connected to airlocks on either side of the one to which Xing's shuttle had docked, disgorged their own streams of sullen-faced League officers and enlisted. *Nüwa* and *Pangu* had suffered twenty-three percent casualties in New Dublin, but they'd gone into battle with ship's companies of over a thousand apiece. That left enough still-living personnel to fill thirty of those shuttles, and she wondered if all of them were processing through the same FTLC. She doubted it. Where would they put that many additional people in any sort of secure condition? Of course, they only had to hold them until they were transferred to one of the sublight prison ships, didn't they?

A small group of senior Fed officers stood on a broad catwalk, three meters above the compartment's deck. One of them was taller than any of the others, and a pair of the Feds' heavy-armor Marines—"Hoplons," they called them—stood at his back. That had to be Murphy, she thought. Come to gloat, no doubt. Well, let her get a flag deck back under her feet again, and they'd see who gloated last! As soon as she finished nailing Than for his treasonous desertion of his post, at least. First things first, after all. But just as soon as Than was taken care of, she'd be—

A hand fell on her shoulder.

"Stop," someone said, this time in almost perfect Mandarin, and her heart spasmed.

She turned her head and found herself looking up and into the green eyes of a tall, auburn-haired *gwáilóu* TFN captain. Another Marine, this one young, female, and thirteen centimeters shorter than Xing stood beside him, right hand wrapped around the butt of the pistol holstered at her side. Her hair was as blond as that of the Marine in the shuttle, there was a mark of some sort above her right eyebrow, and her pale blue *gwáimūi* eyes were even harder than the naval officer's.

"Yes, Sir?" Xing said in Standard English. Her voice quivered a bit around the edges, but she told herself that would be a natural reaction for anyone, especially an officer as junior as "Lieutenant Nguyễn," when she was singled out in a crowd of POWs.

"English," the captain said. "Good." His lips twitched in a smile that never reached his eyes. "Come this way . . . Lieutenant Nguyễn."

"I beg your pardon?" Xing said, trying to ignore the way the Marine's hand was wrapped around the pistol grip. "I thought—" she raised her right hand and pointed along the length of the queue which had halted behind them "—in-processing was that way, Sir?"

"It is," the captain replied. "Admiral Murphy has a couple of questions for you, though."

Xing's racing heart seemed to freeze. It plummeted into the pit of her stomach, and she shook her head.

"There must be some mistake, Sir." She tried to smile back at him, and knew she'd failed. "I'm only—"

"Trust me, this won't take long," the captain said. "Unless, of course, you want to *make* it take longer," he added in a colder voice, and something seemed to flicker in the Marine's ice-blue eyes.

"No, Sir!" Xing said quickly.

"Good," he said again. "This way."

The hand on her shoulder turned her, pointing her at the latticework stairs up to the catwalk. He stood to her left, his right hand on her left shoulder, and she was acutely aware of the way that not only put him on her weak side but took him out of a direct line between her and the silent, hard-faced Marine following at their heels.

They reached the stairs. She climbed them steadily, a little surprised her knees supported her. They felt too frail, too shaky, for that, and her breathing was harder and faster than the climb could explain.

She stepped out onto the catwalk, and the captain released her shoulder and walked across to stand beside the even taller admiral who had to be Murphy.

The Marine had stopped behind her, she realized, as she came to attention and saluted Murphy sharply.

He didn't return the salute. He only looked at her.

The silence dragged out, twisting her nerves like pincers, and she felt herself beginning to sweat. She tried to wait him out, but she couldn't. She just...couldn't, and she licked her lips.

"You...wanted to speak to me, Sir?"

"Oh, I've wanted to speak to *you* for a long time." His voice was deep and very, very cold. "You might say I've been looking forward to it."

"I...I beg your pardon?" She heard the fear in her voice, and it shamed her, but she couldn't prevent it. "I don't understand?"

"Oh, I think you do...Admiral Xing."

Her pulse galloped in her own ears, and she shook her head.

"There's...there's some mistake!" she said. "I'm no admiral! I'm only a *lieutenant!*"

"Really?"

Murphy raised an eyebrow. Then he stepped to one side and Xing saw who'd been hidden behind him by his own height and the massive bulk of the Hoplons. Xie Kai and Captain Geng stood there, looking back at her expressionlessly.

"You look an awful lot like the League propaganda footage of Admiral Xing, Hero of Inverness." Murphy's voice could have frozen the heart of hell.

"What?" Xing shook her head. "No!" She tapped the name

tape on her uniform. "I'm Nguyễn—Nguyễn Khánh Thủy! Xing . . . she's dead! She died in New Dublin! I'm . . . I'm not—" She looked pleadingly at Xie and Geng. "*Tell him!*"

"You were in command in Scotia," Murphy said flatly. "Three quarter million dead of exposure and starvation and disease. Three quarters of a million *civilians* who watched their children freeze to death in front of them."

"No, never!" Xing raised her hands. "You've got the wrong person, Admiral! I'm just . . . just a prisoner of war. Nguyễn Khánh Thủy, serial number . . . serial number—" She stared at Xie. "Tell him Admiral Xing's *dead*, Commander!" she implored desperately.

Xie said nothing.

Xing's terrified gaze darted to Geng, and her soul shriveled as she saw the cold, hard contempt in the captain's eyes.

"And now, *Admiral*," Murphy said, snatching her attention back to him, "it's time."

She heard a faint sound behind her, realized it was the sound of a weapon coming out of a holster, and swayed as the blood seemed to drain into her feet.

"Turn around," the Marine said. It was the first time she'd spoken, and Xing had never before heard such frozen, distilled hate in a human voice.

Her legs obeyed that voice, not her own will, and she shuffled around to find herself staring into the muzzle of a rock-steady pistol.

"Commander Xie and Captain Geng didn't identify you for us, Admiral," Murphy said. "They're here solely as witnesses."

Xing's wide eyes rolled to the side, looking at her subordinates, then darted out over the compartment. Every person in it had paused, frozen in place, looking up at her, and Murphy stepped to the catwalk railing.

"This woman is a criminal," he told them all, raising that deep voice so that it boomed out over all the other prisoners, as well. "A monster. She fought without honor. She deserves none, and she will receive none. But those in the League who fight as *warriors* instead of butchers—openly, honorably, without befouling the uniform they wear, remembering who they are—*those* people will be treated with respect, allowed honorable surrender. I am Admiral Terrence Murphy, Terran Federation Navy. Someday, you will go home. When you do, remember my words."

He held those massed, silently watching eyes for a long, still moment, then stepped back again and turned to the Marine.

"Eira," he said. Just that, nothing more.

Xing's eyes snapped back to the Marine.

"Seven hundred and fifty thousand dead," Eira said. "But I only cared about one."

"Please," Xing whispered. *"Please!"*

"I watched the light go out of my brother's eyes," Eira told her, the muzzle six centimeters from Xing's forehead. "There in the bunker, before the lanterns died. I watched it. And now I'll see it again."

"Please!"

"This is for Sam," Eira said very, very quietly.

The pistol shot was deafening in the cavernous compartment.

CHAPTER FORTY-ONE

"AND THAT WILL CLOSE OUT THE FINAL REPORT." O'HANRAGHTY turned off the holo projector in Murphy's flag briefing room. Callum was there with his father, sitting in a wheelchair, his eye covered by a patch.

"Your report about Xing's execution is in the appendices." O'Hanraghty poured out a glass of whiskey, crossed to Murphy's desk, and offered it to him. The admiral refused with a slight shake of his head, and the chief of staff sipped it instead.

"We could leave all that out..." he said.

"No." Murphy shook his head again. "Legally, we're covered by my authority as a commander in the field." He grimaced. "People who are already inclined to piss and moan over our... shenanigans will probably add it to the fire. But when you've bent as many rules as I have..." He shrugged. "Let's just say Xing won't be the straw that breaks that camel's back."

"Xing got a better death than she deserved," O'Hanraghty huffed. "But when we make our case for the Rish's materiel aid to the League, we should have brought back an alive Second Admiral Xing in chains to testify to that. Even the most crooked fax run by the Five Hundred would've had trouble ignoring that bit of evidence."

Murphy's face darkened.

"And what makes you think that? Obviously Xing would be

461

saying whatever we wanted her to say to stave off her execution for war crimes. Obviously."

"Terry, she would've been the best witness we could have delivered. A witness that spouts a lie becomes less and less credible as scrutiny wears on. That doesn't happen when people tell the truth. Quite the opposite, actually." O'Hanraghty rapped on the desk.

"But people do lie," Murphy's shoulder slumped, "and whatever Xing would have testified to—assuming she cooperated—would come with a seed of doubt. Those that have had their head in the sand when it comes to the Rish wouldn't be moved. Physical evidence is more convincing, even if its circumstantial. Justice for Eira and the innocents killed by Xing was important. You've had your ear to the deck. What's the sentiment among our spacers about how we dealt with Xing?"

"No complaints," O'Hanraghty said. "Scuttlebutt is all for executing Xing right then and there. Not that the average spacer knows about the Rish."

"And leaving Xing alive to curry favor back home is exactly what a Heart would have done," Callum raised a finger. "That's what I overheard in sick bay. Also, a bunch of guys have been asking if Eira's got a boyfriend. But then Sergeant Major Logan made it clear that . . . no one's going to bother her. Let's just leave it at that."

"Immediate justice for Xing might have been the 'wrong' decision from a Machiavellian perspective," Murphy said. "But our fleet needs faith in me. Sparing Xing the airlock or the bullet would have been out of line with what they expect. I sow doubt and we'll reap that harvest later. Besides, this way I can sleep at night. Having that monster in my brig wouldn't have come with the same comfort."

"The Oval should give you a hero's welcome," Callum said. "You didn't just save New Dublin; you knocked the League back decades. And we found proof the Rish have been propping up our enemy. Those lizard bastards must have kept the war going for *decades* and helped kill God knows how many people without us ever suspecting."

"Without our *knowing*." O'Hanraghty raised his glass. "We suspected plenty. We just never could prove it before. Now we can."

"*Can* we?" Murphy asked. O'Hanraghty looked at him. "The Rish blew themselves up before we could drag any of them back to Earth."

"Maybe so," the chief of staff replied, "but there's still the whole damned shipyard. I don't care how good the Lizards are at hiding their tracks. There *has* to be evidence of their tech buried in something that size. All we have to do is convince the Powers That Be to come out and look for it!"

"Which would be sort of like walking from Earth to Mars without a suit...only harder," Murphy said dryly. "For that matter, it's not just a matter of convincing them to look at it. It's also a matter of whether or not they'd get the chance even if they were willing to. We left Granger to keep an eye on the POWs until the Republic can pick them up, but there's no way she can hold onto the yard if they turn up to collect them with a task group or two in their pocket. Which, if you'll recall, is why I specifically told her to not even try. She's got her finger on the trigger to slag the yards if she needs to, and she's got the early warning to skip the system and make it back to New Dublin and avoid a fight."

"Well, no," O'Hanraghty acknowledged. "But it's in an 'out of the way' spot for the League, too, Terry. Freeing up any sizable force to go take it back—and then getting it there—is going to be what you might call a nontrivial challenge. And that doesn't even consider the way you just kicked their combat power right in the balls. I'd say the odds are at least even she can hang onto it for show-and-tell if we can get the Oval to send anyone out to look in the first place."

"And if she can't?"

"In that case there's still the video from the Hoplons. And the DNA on Logan's fists from pounding that one lizard into hamburger, for that matter!"

"But nothing from the League prisoners." Murphy raised a forefinger. "They never once saw a Rish or even heard about their involvement. According to them, Project Astra was simply a long-term, carefully hidden project of the League."

"Terrence...whose side are you on here?"

"Pretend I'm Fokaides," Murphy raised both hands, "and I'm skeptical. Skeptical because I have to take it to Prime Minister Schleibaum, and *she's* going to be even more skeptical before she lays it out for the public."

"She cares about the public?" Callum asked. "She just has to speak to the Five Hundred, right?"

"Now he's starting to get it," O'Hanraghty sighed. "Oh, she does need to worry about the electoral fallout if the voters in general find out their dauntless leaders have been systematically closing their eyes to Rishathan involvement for at least thirty or forty years. That's *not* going to help her party in the next election.

"But that's the least of her problems, because the Five Hundred control the major newsfeeds, among other things. They'll shape the narrative however they want it shaped, and they generate a hell of a cash flow off luxury goods traded with the Rish. They may not care all that much about anything that splashes on the Navy and ONI, but they won't want to accept being dragged into a popular war against the Rish. It's entirely possible that's exactly what would happen if the general public can be convinced of what the Lizards have been up to, too. So, since they do control those newsfeeds—"

He shrugged.

"I doubt the average person's going to want a war against the Sphere, anyway," Murphy said, shaking his head. "Not after fifty-seven years fighting the League. Humanity's earned a peace dividend, wouldn't you say?"

"*If* we can bring the League to the table," O'Hanraghty said. "There's probably a decent chance of it after this. That Eternal Forward party of theirs will take the blame for the losses at New Dublin and Diyu, and they're the biggest plurality in the Accord. It *could* bring down their entire government, really. Or maybe Than will keep enough clout for a coup, bring this to a close." He frowned, considering it, then shrugged. "But back to you being Fokaides. Even without any captured shipyards to examine, the amount of circumstantial evidence is *enormous*, Terrence."

"But still *circumstantial*," Murphy said. "If Granger loses the yard, the only physical evidence we've got is one oddly designed Fasset drive component and the DNA on a Hoplon's knuckles. Everything else is digital. It could easily be faked. At least that's how I think Fokaides will explain it away."

"But for everyone in the Federation that suspected the Rich were involved, this *is* proof," Callum said. "And it'll convince more people, especially in the Fringe, that the Rish are dirty."

"Which should terrify the Five Hundred and the Heart Worlds," O'Hanraghty replied somberly.

"You're probably right about that," Murphy said, "but what

should terrify them—all of us—is that we don't have a clue what the Rish's endgame is."

"They've got an endgame?" Callum asked. "Aside from making a ton of money while they watch the stupid monkey boys and girls kill each other?"

"The Rish *always* have an endgame," O'Hanraghty told him.

"But they've never actually attacked anyone outside their own borders," Callum pointed out. O'Hanraghty raised an eyebrow, and he shrugged. "I've had time to do some research since I got turned into a younger version of President Tolmach," he said. "And all the sources I've found—including some almost as tinfoil as you and Dad—agree on that. So isn't it likely that what this is really about is just a way to keep us and the League bleeding each other white rather than sniffing around their borders?"

"Reasonable point," O'Hanraghty said, but Murphy shook his head.

"Really?" He leaned back behind his desk. "What about that matriarch on the *Bǐshǒu* ... Remember what she said? 'The League humans have failed the Sphere.' That sounds like a hell of a lot more than just war profiteering or keeping the Federation and the League occupied and away from the Sphere's borders."

"Like what?" O'Hanraghty sounded skeptical.

"Harry, you've been suspicious of the Rish even longer than I have. Do you really think they've been playing this deep a game for this long just to keep us and the League chasing our own tails?"

"So while we've been tearing each other down," Callum said, "the Rish have been ... what? Prepping for the moment we're weak enough?"

"Or until the League is. Or both," his father said, then snorted. "Listen to me! I've taken off my 'the Rish are helping the League' tinfoil hat and donned my 'the Rish are coming to kill us all' hat. Let's get the Heart Worlds to believe the Sphere's been backing the League for years before we go to the next ... somewhat logical conclusion."

"One impossible thing at a time," O'Hanraghty agreed. "The Fringe will believe it. The military ...? Maybe. The rank and file probably will. Maybe not the Army, but a huge percentage of the Navy's enlisted and the Marines—officers *and* enlisted—are from outside the Heart. Convincing someone like Admiral Rajenda Thakore will be a tougher sell."

"And how do we even start to convince them?" Callum asked.

"We tell the truth." Murphy let his chair come forward and rested his elbows on his desk. "What else is there to convince anyone?"

"And if they won't listen?" O'Hanraghty shook his head. "Let's not forget what we were telling Callum a minute ago. Getting the top brass and their Five Hundred masters to *admit* the truth even if we can prove it won't be easy. They'd a lot rather sweep any evidence out the airlock. And probably do the same thing for the messenger right along with it."

"I don't like your implication."

"Terrence, we've rocked the boat pretty hard. First, we win the most strategically significant naval battle in decades, maybe longer. Then we smash a League system and put our enemy back years—*decades*—in terms of production and manpower. Then we find a whole lot of smoke—maybe not from a fire, but from some pretty hot embers—of Rish involvement. And the way we did all that involved ignoring and violating command directives left and right, which puts the people who issued them in a piss-poor light. The status quo can't survive all of that. It *has* to break, when our report gets back to Earth. But something tells me the system will fight to keep it in place anyway."

"Am I supposed to be the little boy who says the Emperor has no clothes? Or am I Chicken Little pointing at an inbound dinosaur killer?"

"Tough one, Sir. Something tells me we're going to have to play this one by the seat of our pants for a while. We'll be back at New Dublin for rest and refit. I imagine we'll get a feel for the Heart Worlds' response pretty quick."

"Which is what I'm afraid of," Murphy acknowledged with a sigh.

"Dad, you remember when you said this assignment was going to be two years of just marking time?" Callum motioned to his eyepatch. "Well, I've decided excitement is actually pretty awful. Can we go back to boredom, somehow?"

"Balls are rolling, son, and they've already moved faster and farther than I ever anticipated. It's up to us to get control of the situation or get crushed by consequences of our own making." Murphy smiled crookedly. "Welcome to the Navy."

"Yeah...it's just like the posters."

CHAPTER FORTY-TWO

MURPHY GAZED INTO A MIRROR AS HE ADJUSTED HIS DRESS uniform. The sounds of stamping feet and cheers carried through the walls.

"Almost time," Dewar said as he leaned into Murphy's room. He wore the deep green dress uniform of the New Dublin Militia. "Don't worry about being perfect. Most everyone's well on their way to being drunk, so I doubt they'll notice if your ribbons are crooked."

"Is every award ceremony on Crann Bethadh like this?" the admiral asked.

"Nope—just the good ones. And the higher the award, the more boisterous. Some are just happy to have an excuse to get shitfaced after the battle, and we did have to wait months for your triumphant return to get this going. You know. Guest of honor, hero of the moment—like that?"

"Let's not go that far," Murphy said.

"I'm no dwarf, but if you like, I can whisper that you're only human along the way to the—"

Dewar broke off and turned his head to one side. He stood there, listening to his earbud, and his face tightened.

"They're here?" Murphy asked.

"They are." Dewar reached for his wrist comm. "The timing's no accident. I can have them delayed until—"

"No." Murphy shook his head. "They've done their best to

keep their presence hidden since they arrived in-system. They've chosen this moment."

"Bastards! Don't they know what this means to us?"

"Better to attribute something to stupidity than malice," Murphy said. "But here it could be a bit of both. Let's drive on. We're not unprepared for this."

Dewar looked rebellious for a moment, one hand hovering over the comm. But then he shrugged and nodded.

"If they're going to be stupid about it, they're going to be stupid about it, and stupid is the one thing no one can fix." He inhaled deeply.

"I know," Murphy said sympathetically. "Believe me, I *know*."

"In that case, right this way, Governor General."

Dewar held the door for Murphy, and they walked down a narrow passageway. It ended in a shallow flight of stairs, and heavy curtains blocked their view of a loud gathering—fueled by the clink of silverware, glasses, and laughter—just beyond.

"Bastards!" Dewar hissed, tapping his earbud again. "They're—"

"I can imagine." Murphy held up his hand. "Like I said, they chose the moment—and they didn't pick it on a whim. We'll all remember them for it."

"As you say, Sir." Dewar squared his shoulders. "It's not like you need an introduction. Just follow Tolmach's cues."

They climbed the steps and Dewar flung the curtains open. A blaze of spotlights poured down on Murphy, and he stepped forward. The crowd roared as it saw him and began chanting his name in rhythmic unison as he walked out onto a stage.

His eyes adjusted to the blinding, semi-solid torrent of light—mostly—as Tolmach made his way slowly up another set of shallow steps from the floor below. The President was more stooped than he had been. His cane struck hard at the stair treads, and the cheering grew even louder as Murphy reached forward to help him up the last few steps.

Tolmach smiled, the lines of his face deepening, as he gave Murphy a one-armed hug.

"Not what you're used to, is it, son?"

Despite the smell of alcohol hanging in the air, Murphy couldn't detect a whiff of it on the President.

"Awards ceremonies are usually a bit more somber," he said. "Combat awards, particularly."

"Well, you're on Crann Bethadh, and we do what we want. Cameras are on, broadcasting this across a system-wide feed. We'll turn them off afterwards, so don't be shy about throwing a few back later. Just don't try and go drink-for-drink with me. My liver's been through more hell than you can imagine."

"Wasn't the plan," Murphy said, looking out across the ballroom. Navy, Marine, and Militia officers, Crann Bethadh politicians, and several diplomatic contingents from across the sector sat around long tables. O'Hanraghty was at the nearest table, worry written across his face. "Speaking of plans, Dewar says—"

"Plans...they never hold up." The President looked into Murphy's eyes for a moment, then tapped his own earbud lightly and grinned the fierce, reckless grin of a far younger Alan Tolmach. "I hope you're ready, boy!"

Murphy opened his mouth again, but before he could speak, Tolmach turned to face the tables and grabbed the admiral's wrist with his flesh-and-blood hand. He raised Murphy's hand high, and camera drones flashed over the audience. He clicked a switch on his cane.

"Crann Bethadh!" His words carried through the same drones. "We've a man amongst us!"

"Hear, hear!" rose from the audience.

"Admiral Murphy saved our world from the League. Damned near gave me a heart attack in the process, but I reckon I can forgive him for that." Tolmach paused for chuckles. "But it wasn't enough that he crushed the League here. After that, he chased them back to their cave and kicked their ass again!"

Fists banged on tables.

"Craeb Uisnig is sacred to us." He touched the cutting on his jacket. "It's the final memory of home for too many of our people before they're lost to the war. So for us to take from her, for us to adorn another with her leaf...it's the highest honor we have. Which is why, Terrence Murphy, Governor General of our home—I hereby give you my *duilleog airgid*."

The room went suddenly silent as Tolmach touched the silver leaf on his lapel. He tugged, and it unsnapped.

The ballroom doors burst open, and Captain Lipshen strutted through them, flanked by two Federal Marshals and half a dozen troopers in Army-mod Hoplon armor bearing the Capital Division's flash.

They were no surprise, but Murphy's eyes hardened. The Capital Division was considered the elite of the Federation Army, but the Army never deployed to the Fringe. Its upper ranks, even more than the Navy's, were dominated by Heart Worlders, and especially by scions of the Five Hundred. It was too important to "waste" protecting mere Fringers. And that was trebly true of the Capital Division, the most prestigious, sought after posting the Army offered. If the rest of the Army never deployed to the Fringe, the Capital Division never deployed *anywhere*.

But if the Five Hundred wanted an armed force they knew they could rely on, the Capital Division was the place to find it.

The Army Hoplons were armed, their weapons held low but at the ready.

The crowd murmured in confusion.

"Terrence Murphy!" Lipshen held up a cream-colored envelope. "By my authority as representative of the Federation, as entrusted to me by Fleet Command and endorsed for the federal government by the Attorney General's office... I hereby terminate your position as Governor General of New Dublin."

He walked down the center aisle, paperwork still aloft. The marshals followed him, one of them smiling unpleasantly as he pulled a set of handcuffs from inside his tunic. The heavy footfalls of the Army Hoplons at their heels echoed off the walls in the disbelieving silence.

"And I also place you under arrest," Lipshen said. "For insubordination, graft, and misappropriation of Federation military equipment *and* personnel."

He bounded up the stairs and leveled the warrant at Tolmach like a pistol.

Murphy only looked at him and tilted his chin a bit higher.

"This comes from Fokaides?" he asked.

"And the Prime Minister." Lipshen smiled triumphantly. "Let's not make a show of this Murphy. There's a shuttle waiting outside. Cooperate, and I won't let the marshals put you in cuffs for the camera as we walk out."

"You slimy little shit." Tolmach's face twitched with anger. His voice was soft, but the drones were still live, and the words filled the silence.

"The paperwork's in order," Lipshen said. "I'd rather not have to take you in for obstruction, Mr. President."

"I'll do more than—"

Tolmach started forward, but Murphy stopped him with a gentle touch on the shoulder.

"So I surrender. Then what? You take me back to the Oval and everything that's happened here gets swept under the rug? I sent back proof the Rish are supporting the League. I crushed the League here and chased them down to finish the job. I've captured or destroyed over fifty League FTLCs. And the Heart Worlds' response is...my arrest?"

"We're about done being polite," the marshal with the handcuffs said coldly.

"Come now, Murphy. We can sort it all out back on Earth."

Lipshen reached for Murphy's arm, but the admiral grabbed a handful of the smaller man's jacket front and yanked him up on his toes.

"Yes, we *will* sort it out on Earth," Murphy said. "But not under your terms—under *mine*."

He tapped the side of his leg with his free hand and doors opened on the long sides of the ballroom. A dozen Marine Hoplons stumped into the room, carbines up and aimed at the marshals and their Army counterparts.

"If you're not dressed like me, I suggest you leave." The volume on Logan's suit's external speakers hurt the ear as it echoed off the ballroom walls.

No one left.

"Mur-*PHY!* Mur-*PHY!* Mur-*PHY!*"

The chant rose like slow-growing thunder, and Lipshen swallowed hard.

"I have my orders," he said. "We're...we're not afraid of you."

"Mur-*PHY!* Mur-*PHY!* Mur-*PHY!*"

The chant swelled louder and louder.

"Don't be a fool," Murphy said. "Go back to your shuttle. No one will stop you. I'll *go* to Earth and answer for what I've done, but I'll go in my ship, not in your brig."

Tolmach stood shoulder to shoulder with Murphy.

"Mur-*PHY!* Mur-*PHY!* Mur-*PHY!*"

The chanting voices filled the ballroom, roaring like an angry sea.

"You're bluffing." Sweat sheened Lipshen's forehead. "Don't add treason to your crimes!"

"It's only treason if we're part of the Federation, you mangy, sorry-assed excuse for a cur!" Tolmach snarled. "You've pushed us a step too far this time—you and your bastard masters! New Dublin's done with all of you after this. The rest of the sector, too!"

Lipshen's eyes went wide, and he reached for his sidearm. Two of the Army Hoplons lunged forward.

Tolmach thrust a sharp elbow into Murphy's chest, catching him off guard and pushing him back a step. The old man hammered his cane down on Lipshen's shoulder, sending the captain to one knee with a yelp of pain.

The Marine Hoplons barreled through tables toward the marshals and the charging Army Hoplons while guests scrambled out of the way.

"Stop—*stop!*"

Murphy reached for Tolmach, but the old man slipped out of his grip, snarling at Lipshen, and raised his cane again.

A single shot cracked.

Pain ripped through Murphy's left side as the bullet tore through flesh, and Tolmach stopped. A growing red spot blossomed on his back. His cane fell, and he crumpled. Murphy caught him, and blood spread thick and hot across his arms and down his hands as he lowered the System President of New Dublin gently to the stage.

More gunfire—the staccato bark of Hoplon carbines—ripped across the ballroom, drowning the sound of screams as New Dubliners dove for the floor.

"*You* did this!" Lipshen stood over them, his pistol aimed at Murphy's head. "It was all your—"

A shadow fell over the captain and he looked up as Faeran's suit loomed above him. A mechanical hand closed around his wrist and pistol. Metal digits snapped shut, crushing weapon and arm alike, and he shrieked in anguish as she tossed him away, like a rag doll hurled through the air, to crash down among the overturned tables while the rest of the Marines made quick work of the Army Hoplons.

"Son," Tolmach gasped. "Son, where's my *duilleog airgid*?"

His breathing was labored, blood bubbles frothing from his lips with every word.

"Don't say anything. We'll get you to the medics—"

"Take...take my *duilleog*," Tolmach whispered. "Light the fire...in the sky, Son. Tell...tell Cormag, he..."

Tolmach's eyelids fluttered and he looked away.

"*Medic!*" Murphy shouted, eyes burning, but the ballroom had become chaos as more wounded were dragged away and his Hoplons ripped the Army Hoplons apart.

The admiral saw a flash of silver in a pool of blood. He grabbed the leaf from Craeb Uisnig, pressed it into Tolmach's hand.

"This is *yours*." Murphy's voice cracked. "It's always been yours. I don't deserve it!"

Tolmach shook his head fiercely and thrust it against the younger man's chest.

"*Do*," he choked out through a mouth filled with blood.

He tried to say something more, but he could no longer speak. He pressed the leaf against Murphy's chest again, weakly, and the admiral cupped his fingers over that suddenly frail hand... and the leaf. He looked down into those fierce old eyes as the fire in them dimmed at last, and nodded slowly.

"All right," he whispered, touching the lined face with his other hand. "All right."

Two minutes later, Alan Caelan Tolmach, President of the New Dublin System, died.

CHAPTER FORTY-THREE

"FEELING ANY BETTER?" O'HANRAGHTY ASKED, TURNING AS MUR-phy stepped out onto the governor's mansion's balcony to join him. Dawn filled the eastern sky, illuminating the gallows erected in Court Square, and a crowd had already gathered.

"It itches." Murphy touched the dressing under his uniform. "In fact, it itches like hell. But the nanites are working on it, and I was lucky—no bone damage, and only a little muscle repair. Others weren't so fortunate."

"Five dead—New Dubliners, I mean. Only one of the Army pukes made it." O'Hanraghty shook his head. "Amazingly stupid of Lipshen. He says the order was that you were to be taken in as publicly as possible. Apparently the Heart wanted to send a message to the Fringe. So, maybe he's not the only one who was amazingly stupid. But 'following orders' is no excuse, as he's about to learn."

"Speaking of mistakes." Murphy leaned on a railing as the bitter morning cold bit his face and ears. "This is another one, Harry."

"Tolmach was murdered. That was enough for Crann Bethadh to send a lynch mob to drag Lipshen and his marshals out of their cells. At least you insisted on a trial—which proved pretty quick. There were cameras everywhere, after all."

"Executing Lipshen and the marshals—not to mention a

captain from the Capital Division with tons of connections to the Five Hundred—isn't going to help our cause," Murphy said. "The Heart Worlds will use this as more proof of treason."

"Dewar's President now," O'Hanraghty replied. "And he and the rest of the sector are no longer part of the Federation, according to them. So it's not treason—it's just the application of domestic law."

"How the hell did we miss seeing that one coming?" Murphy demanded. "We knew there was unrest, but—"

"I'm not so sure this one was on us," O'Hanraghty replied. "Oh, I don't doubt what happened here and in Diyu had a lot to do with the timing, but something like this doesn't happen spontaneously. You know as well as I do that they have to've been planning it for a long time. And it's not exactly as if either of us thinks they don't have ample justification!"

"Justified or not, the Heart's going to go berserk."

"Well, why should this be any different from everything else that's happened? You do remember the day you told me about 'Murphy's Law,' don't you? What can go wrong *will* go wrong?" O'Hanraghty shrugged.

"At what point did this entire situation slip out of our control, Harrison? We came out here to find evidence that the Rish were—"

"And find it we did. And then that snowballed into—Here we go."

O'Hanraghty broke off and pointed to a doorway at the base of the mansion where New Dublin Militia led Lipshen, two marshals, and the single surviving Army Hoplon out into the icy dawn. Lipshen's lower right arm was missing, the Hoplon limped heavily, and all four of them wore bright orange jumpsuits as they were led through a throng of armed police toward the gallows.

Boos erupted from the crowd and something flew. It hit Lipshen in the chest, and more fist-sized objects pelted the condemned.

"You want to try to stop this?" O'Hanraghty asked.

"Crann Bethadh demands blood." Murphy shook his head. "Tolmach was . . . he was the only President most of these people ever knew. They loved that old man, with *damned* good reason, and this is already racing out of control. If there's any hope of bringing the sector back into the Federation, they need to know they at least got justice for him first."

"You really think there's much chance of that?" O'Hanraghty's tone was almost sympathetic. "Of bringing them back into the Federation?"

Murphy shrugged.

"I don't know. I *truly* don't know. But I do know we can't afford for the Federation to shatter at a time like this. Not when the League's just been hammered and we don't have a single frigging idea what the Sphere's real endgame is. And I'm the only sympathetic face the Federation has out here in the Fringe. If I try to stop this…"

He shook his head.

"We're going to get a reputation," O'Hanraghty said almost whimsically. "First Xing, now Lipshen and his enforcers. The Heart Worlds will have a field day with this."

"We've got this wolf by the ear, old friend. Best we not let go."

Murphy crossed his arms as the condemned mounted the gallows. A hooded executioner fixed nooses around their necks, and Murphy touched the *duilleog airgid* on his chest and wished Tolmach could have been here to deal with this situation. But this was his fight now.

Silence fell, broken only by the voice of the wind. The hangman looked up at Murphy's balcony, and the rest of the crowd turned around to do the same.

Murphy extended his arm. If he raised his hand, the execution would stop.

He slashed it across his throat.

✧   ✧   ✧

A vase flew through a holo projection and smashed against the wall.

"He's not a traitor!"

Simron clenched her fists against her sides and stalked toward another flower arrangement.

"This is all initial press," her father said. Thakore started toward the crystal vase Simron had her eye on, but gave up. "I've got it under control."

"*Control?*"

Simron grabbed the vase by its lip and swung it through the holo image showing Terrence Murphy, his face altered to look dark and menacing, while the voice-over talked about corruption and malfeasance and warlordism. Vyom hunched forward on a couch, elbows on his knees, hands folded beneath his chin.

"Holo off," Thakore commanded, and shook his head. "This whole business could just be a misunderstanding. I'm sure that once we get him back to Earth, we'll find out it's...not as bad as it sounds. I've got my influencers in the feeds already sowing different stories that we can play up for a better...take on the situation."

"My father defeated a massive League fleet at New Dublin," Vyom said.

"There's still some doubt about how 'massive' it was," Thakore said quickly.

"Then he left to take out a League system...and probably blew up space yards we never knew existed," Vyom continued. "And no one even waited to find out what was happening! So when he gets back to New Dublin, he's going to find the Inspector General waiting to arrest him? For *graft*?"

"There were...some serious allegations." Thakore sat down. "If I—and by extension, Venus Futures, which includes both of you—pushed back against the Five Hundred or the Navy...it would ruin me. Us. Everything."

"So you just let them throw Terrence to the *wolves*?" Simron demanded.

"He's not just rocking the boat, Simmy. He's blown a hole in the bottom and he's bailing water *into* it." Thakore ran his hands over his face. "Then he sends back this ridiculous conspiracy theory about the Rish..." He shook his head. "I'm doing this to *protect* you. And my grandchildren. You're still young, Simmy. A divorce and—"

Vyom exploded to his feet and stormed out of the room.

"That's his *father* you're ruining," Simron said coldly. "My husband."

"Okay, then." Thakore tossed his arms up. "Venus Futures backs Terrence Murphy one hundred percent, publicly and privately. What happens next?"

"The Heart Worlds..." Simron went to a window overlooking Olympia. "They'll divest their Venus Futures holdings, and we'll be run out of the Five Hundred. Ruined."

"Should I throw the work of generations of Thakores away for Murphy? The man who's amassing a fleet in a sector on the edge of rebellion, and permitting the Navy yard under his control to manufacture weapons which apparently out-range anything *we* have? The man who's defying direct orders from Fleet Command? Who's about to light the fuse that sets the entire Fringe on fire? Be reasonable, Simron. We can survive this...but not if we back your husband."

Simron began to weep.

"They'll kill him," she said.

"That...I can probably stop. Just so you know, I had to put more on the line to protect our family than I wanted to. But Rajenda's been given command of Fifth Fleet. Your brother's bringing it back from Beta Cygni as fast as he can to stop Murphy from moving against the Heart."

"Rajenda always hated Terrence," Simron said, "and now you've got them going head-to-head?"

"But you and I know Terrence *isn't* a traitor, right? Not some Fringe warlord that let a title go to his head, right?"

"Of course he isn't!"

"So he'll have a stare-down with Rajenda somewhere outside the Heart Worlds, and then he can save face somehow. Trust me, Simmy. I know how the Five Hundred work. Right now, the Prime Minister is pissing herself, she's so scared, but in the end, they'd a lot rather have him publicly cooperating with the official line, pouring water on the flames, than turn him into some kind of martyr. We publicly disavow him now, and then we make sure he's got an out later. *Trust* me."

He put a hand on her shoulder and squeezed gently.

"You've told Rajenda to not fight Terrence? He's going to help end this without him—or Callum—getting hurt?"

"Of course," her father promised, and made a mental note to delete any and all trace of his last few messages to Rajenda.

"Of course, Simmy. I've got this all worked out."

TERRENCE MURPHY STOOD ON TFNS *ISHTAR*'S FLAG BRIDGE. HIS hands were folded behind him, and the *duilleog airgid* of the Order of Craeb Uisnig, cleaned of Alan Tolmach's blood, gleamed above his ribbons as he watched the main plot. The incoming Fasset signature had just strobed its ID.

"*Ningishzidu* with TG One-Sixty-Four," O'Hanraghty said, listening to the transmission which had accompanied the identifier. "Captain Yildiz in command. They say they're here to join us."

"Task Group One-Sixty-Four is out of Strammer...and wasn't under Yildiz's command, if I remember right," Murphy said.

"Correct, Sir," Ortiz said. "Yildiz is from Ryukyu, not the Heart. To get here this quickly, it sounds like he must have led a quick revolt against his commanding officer when news of the sector's secession reached Strammer."

"Not the first time we've heard that story," O'Hanraghty observed. "With all the defections coming in..."

He looked at the force organization status board and shrugged. Ships had been trickling in for weeks now, as word of events in New Dublin spread like wildfire though the Concordia Sector and its neighbors. Few of the system pickets out here were as powerful as Murphy's original force, but most of them had been built around at least one FTLC. Even with Granger still sitting on Diyu—at least, they *hoped* she was still sitting on Diyu—*Ningishzidu*'s arrival would

481

give Murphy an even dozen carriers. And he'd captured enough of Xing's parasites to leave New Dublin with a massive sublight covering force and still fill every rack his FTLCs had.

"This isn't going to play well back home," he observed now.

"What was that you said about wolves?" O'Hanraghty asked in reply, then shook his head. "And it's not just people like Yildiz. I wasn't all that surprised when Granger only smiled and nodded when you detailed her to sit on Diyu, but Tremblay?" He shook his head again. "I won't say he's happy about it, but the man's got grit, and once you rubbed his nose in it, he couldn't go on loyally spouting the party line. He's not the only one, either." He pointed at the icon in the display. "We're going to see more of this, Terrence. In fact, I won't be all that surprised if we start seeing some from *neighboring* sectors."

"Good and bad," Murphy said.

"Bad? How is there bad?" Callum limped over on a stiff prosthetic foot. He rubbed a knuckle against his temple next to his eyepatch.

"I wanted to go back to Earth with enough combat power to dissuade anyone from firing on us," his father told him. "But if we have too many warships, it'll look like I'm leading a coup."

"Dad, they're going to say it's a coup anyway. Only logical."

"We've sent Silas ahead to put out the word among his network that this *isn't* a coup," Murphy said. "I'm going to make my case to the Five Hundred and the Oval that the Rish are a genuine threat to the Federation and do my damnedest to get a survey team sent out to Diyu. And then...I'm going to resign my commission and turn myself in. Hopefully I can talk the—what's the sector calling itself?"

"The Free Worlds Alliance," O'Hanraghty said. "Just formally decided that this morning. And it's not just the Concordia Sector anymore. Three more systems in the Acera Sector have declared as well."

"Wonderful." Murphy's nostrils flared, and he shook his head, then drew a deep breath. "Hopefully I can talk Dewar and the rest off this cliff before anyone else gets killed. That's a bargaining chip that just might keep us all out of prison."

"Hooray," Callum said unenthusiastically. "Exile from the Heart Worlds is our best bet. Still sounds better than letting the Federation keep its head in the sand about the Rish, though."

"No good deed goes unpunished." Murphy sighed, then squared his shoulders. "But we can't let this—" he gestured at the incoming *Ningishzidu*'s icon "—keep building. We need to save the Federation...and not destroy it in the process."

He looked over his shoulder at the comm link to the command deck.

"Captain Lowe, has Commander Creuzburg laid out a course back to Earth?"

"Aye, Sir. With a first stop at Jalal Station."

"Good. XO, once we've gathered in *Ningishzidu* and her brood, order the fleet to dock parasites and then break orbit and take us into wormhole space," Murphy said.

✧　　✧　　✧

TFNS *Ishtar* broke Crann Bethadh orbit and turned for the Powell Limit.

Terrence Murphy had arrived with three FTLCs; he was leaving with twelve, including TFNS *Nüwa* and *Pangu*, fully repaired and operational courtesy of Diyu's automated systems.

"I've got a bad feeling about this, Ed," Tanaka Prajita said quietly. She and Ortiz stood at the rear of *Ishtar*'s flag bridge, well behind Murphy and O'Hanraghty, watching the displays. "This—" she jabbed her chin in the direction of the master plot "—is going to look an awful lot like an invading fleet to anybody in the Heart."

"Not much choice," Ortiz replied, equally quietly. "If he doesn't have a big enough stick, they won't listen to him." He smiled wryly. "You know how that works, I think?"

"Yeah." Tanaka no longer looked as if the admission gave her physical pain, but she shook her head. "Problem is, I'm afraid they won't listen, anyway. It was hard enough for me, and I was *there*. Circumstantial evidence they can explain away?" She shrugged. "The establishment view's pretty damned well dug in. I'm looking at a lot of things in a different light these days, especially after Lipshen tried to arrest him, but the Five Hundred?" She shook her head again. "*I* didn't want to accept the truth because it seemed so damned preposterous. That whole arrest thing tells me *they* won't want to accept it because of all the rice bowls it threatens. Which suggests they *won't* send anyone out to Diyu and risk finding evidence that *isn't* circumstantial."

"Of course they won't." Ortiz didn't look a lot happier than she did.

"So what happens when they don't want to admit the truth and we turn up with this much firepower?"

"If they're smart, they listen to him and they *do* send their own teams to Diyu. Or at least take a good, hard look at *Nüwa's* and *Pangu's* gizzards. Especially their Fasset drives."

"Smart?" Tanaka looked at him. "We're talking about the Five Hundred, Ed. When was the last time 'smart' trumped 'corporate profits' where the Five Hundred was concerned?"

"Then we don't do it the easy way," Ortiz said grimly. "We do it the hard way."

"Ed, he's one man—*one man*—against the entire Heart. I'll grant you he's a hell of a lot smarter, tougher, and more dangerous than I thought he was when we first shipped out. But he's still just one man."

"One man with twelve carriers at his back." Ortiz's smile was a razor. "I hadn't really looked much deeper beneath the surface than you had when we first shipped out. I have now. These people—" he moved one hand in a gesture that encompassed the entire task force; no, the entire *fleet* "—will follow that 'one man' wherever he goes. And one thing I can damned well tell you for sure about Terrence Murphy, Prajita."

"What?" Tanaka arched an eyebrow.

"Whatever it takes to get the job done, he'll do it."